The Magdeburg Relic

The Magdeburg Relic

C.M. Chadwick

Matador
9 Priory Business Park,
Wistow Road, Kibworth Beauchamp,
Leicestershire. LE8 0RX
Tel: 0116 279 2299
Email: books@troubador.co.uk
Web: www.troubador.co.uk/matador
Twitter: @matadorbooks

ISBN 978 1785899 911

British Library Cataloguing in Publication Data.
A catalogue record for this book is available from the British Library.

Printed and bound by CPI Group (UK) Ltd, Croydon, CR0 4YY
Typeset in 11pt Minion Pro by Troubador Publishing Ltd, Leicester, UK

Matador is an imprint of Troubador Publishing Ltd

I would like to dedicate this book to the memory of that great storyteller, Dennis Wheatley, who always managed to *make things happen* in his stories, and whose work has given me so much pleasure over the years.

This is a work of fiction in which names, characters, businesses, places, events and incidents are either the product of the author's imagination or are used in a fictitious manner. Any resemblance to actual persons, living or dead, or actual events is purely coincidental. Where I have made reference to real persons, they are represented in a manner in keeping with biographical details that are already recorded in the public domain.

I have drawn inspiration from the landscape of Wiltshire and its townships, but the village of Peckling is imaginary. I have, however, drawn from the folklore of that county in detail. I do not apologise for my excursions into amateur philology for I consider them to be interesting at least. I also declare that although I have spoken to people versed in the occult art during the writing of this book, I have never taken part in a magical or Satanic ceremony and would encourage any reader of this book to decline if offered a similar opportunity.

Christopher Chadwick
June 2016

Chapter One

In the Bunker

It was April 29th, 1945 and Adolf Hitler sat at a table and finished a sparse meal. He ate no meat and for many years had been adequately nourished by means of a vegetarian diet. Yet this, formerly very varied, had by the spring of 1945 become less so and on this day, resources within the Reich Chancellery afforded only a meal of clear broth into which some potato had been infused. Despite his instructions to the contrary, he knew that well-meaning staff would often add the occasional piece of animal bone marrow to his meals and he had occasionally succumbed to such delicacies as dumplings of liver. Now, so late in the war and after the encirclement of Berlin, he doubted that his servants would have the resources to make any such addition and he ate with the ease of the vegetarian conscience. Had he been pressed, he might have lacked the strength of will to reject the advice of his followers and was relieved that this choice was by now removed.

For a while, he reflected on Blondi his German shepherd dog. He liked animals and could not bear to inflict pain on them; it had been absolutely necessary, therefore, to put her beyond reach of the invading Russian army and he was compelled to instruct his Doctor to administer the poison which had done so. He had concerns too, about the quality of the cyanide capsules; were they indeed effective on an adult human? Elsewhere and at another time, he had seen the effects of supposedly humane cyanide gas on animals culled in their setts or burrows and did not wish to repeat what he had seen when the capsules were next tested, by now within a week at best.

For Adolf Hitler knew that his own time had nearly come. It was clear to all that as the Fuhrer of Nazi Germany, he must stay to the end and would, of necessity, die in Berlin. Even the most optimistic seers of Nazi fortune could not hide the fact that, by the end of April, he would be unable to evade capture for more than two or three days. Nazi defensive positions were short of ammunition and could not withstand, even for a short time, the full onslaught of Russian assaulting troops. It was, of course, quiet below ground and no machine guns or rifles could be heard, although there was the occasional detonation of a shell or bomb which shook the ground and confirmed what he already knew; yet as leader, he could not place his regret before his fellow Nazis. Only when one of them ventured above ground could the full force of war be heard, noises that he knew so well from his time in the front line during the first war. Once again, he reflected on the possibility of a breakout; some consideration had been made for a dash to the British lines, but Hitler knew that he could not do so. This world was ending and he must end with it.

Hitler wed Eva Braun on 29th April and after as little as forty hours of married life, they locked themselves away and made their final preparation for death. The next day, after 2.30pm and probably before 3.30, Eva Braun took her own life by means of one of the cyanide capsules first tested on Blondi. She suffered convulsions, a quick loss of consciousness and collapsed within seconds of biting the capsule. There had been no time for her skin to assume the pinkish colour of the taker of a marginal dose; her lips were somewhat puckered as though the orbicularis orbis muscles had suffered cyanosis: the withdrawal and blueish discolour arising from oxygen starvation.

Within that same hour and following a short period of reflection, Adolf Hitler sat on the same sofa and bit down hard on a further glass capsule of hydrogen cyanide. By means of his Walther PPK pistol, held to the temple, he shot himself in that same instant. His supporters heard the sound of the shot and after entering the room, they noted the smell of bitter almonds: that of hydrogen cyanide vapour. They removed both dead bodies and took them above, to the grounds of the Reich Chancellery. Using petrol, they burned the bodies as best they could and the blackened remains were further buried in a shell or bomb crater.

Adolf Hitler had hoped there would be little left for the victorious Russian forces to uncover. However, remains (reported to be of blackened bones) were retrieved by the KGB who expected that at first, they would prove useful for the purposes of propaganda. After only limited success, the KGB eventually reburied them at Magdeburg in February 1946, at a site within territory which later became part of East Germany.

*

One thousand, six hundred miles to the east of Berlin, Feodore Alkhimovich, a former KGB officer, remembered in 1991 his part in the removal of the Magdeburg interment from cold ground during 1970. As a young medical officer of 25 years, he and other officers of the KGB had been required to raise flagstones and dig carefully for the remains, but their task had been made easier by the existence of precise records of the site. Five wooden crates of remains were excavated and the relics they contained removed for inspection.

Shortly, the KGB had destroyed the contents of most of the crates, but not all. Skilled at the task of disinformation, they had let it be known that all the artefacts removed had been pulverised into the smallest fragments, burned and tipped into a nearby river. Now, in 1991, Feodore Alkhimovich at 46 years again handled that small proportion of the relics which had been disinterred and actually returned to the

Soviet Union. His manner was not with distaste, but was with the detachment of the trained KGB medical and science officer.

Alkhimovich knew that one crate, *Магдебург 005,* contained the remaining burial relics of Adolf Hitler. It was generally held that they had all been destroyed to prevent them from becoming a shrine to Fascism in the emerging state of East Germany. In fact most of the remains were indeed destroyed, although contrary to popular belief, not those in crate *Магдебург 005*. The latter had been preserved because Alkhimovich, a fastidious man, had himself insisted upon it. He believed that a fastidious nature was good; it was a general feature of Soviet public bodies and there were many examples in which that characteristic had been shown to be useful. It was precisely that which had led to the Russians storing their last stock of the deadly smallpox virus at Novosibirsk: although smallpox might yet pass the walls, razor glass and barbed wire designed to keep humans out, its preservation had given them an opportunity for medical research on smallpox and on bioweapons. True to character, the fastidious Alkhimovich had considered that they might one day regret the destruction of an article of such historical importance as the Magdeburg relic and so it had remained in its crate while the other crates were pulverised and thrown into the river.

So in 1991, Alkhimovich, now of the Federal Counterintelligence Service, worked alone on the relic at his office in Moscow. He also had a small laboratory equipped with a costly Zeiss microscope and camera, together with fine surgical instruments like those of a dentist, driven by compressed air. Although it was too early for the modern computer, he possessed its forerunner, an electronic word processor. Visible in green, on its steadily blinking cathode ray tube, were the following observations, to which daily additions were made:

January 12th

I have today opened the container of archive Магдебург 005 and note that it contains human relics. The purpose of this investigation is to assess their origin and general morphology.

Judging from the thickness of the remaining frontal and parietal bones, I estimate that the skull would have been heavy when intact. It therefore has a less than average likelihood of being female in origin.

The front of the skull is receding rather than upright and so is unlikely to be female.

The attachment point for the temporal muscle at the temporal line is intact and the ridge is pronounced; it is neither more nor less obvious than for the average male, but is more so than would be the case for a female skull.

I have examined the eye sockets which are also intact. The lower part of the orbit has a blunt ridge in keeping with that of a male skull and looking at the skull from the front, supercilliary arches are visible. However, it is noted that some reconstruction of the skull would be necessary by means of wire supports in order to assemble the fragments into a larger structure.

January 13th

I have now carried out a reconstruction of the skull. Although incomplete, enough of the skull is present to suppose that it would have had a cephalic index of approximately 79-81% of its length, moderately long-headed although not to the extent of the 76-78% category, a characteristic of North Germany, Scandinavia or Great Britain. However, although partly conjectural, the skull would not have been broad and to any degree brachycephalic; certainly not to the extent shown by populations of the Slavic and Magyar intrusions into eastern central Europe, nor by those of Finland or Estonia where such skull formations are prevalent. The skull is unlikely to have come from the Anatolian peninsular for similar reasons. The cephalic index is remotely in keeping with a possible Semitic origin, with moderate dolichocephaly, yet this is unlikely in view of its history.

Taken together, the evidence suggests that the skull was of a male individual from central Europe, possibly to the south of the North German plain and west of the Slavic area and if so, within the linguistic area best described as that of Hochdeutsch; it is clearly Aryan in origin, if that term can still be used without prejudice.

There is evidence of penetration of the right side of the skull by means of a hard implement. The hole is of 8mm diameter, in keeping with the entrance wound of a 7.94mm bullet as anecdotal evidence reported it to be.

January 14th.

I have today made an examination for evidence in the bones of dread disease.

- i. *There is no evidence in any of the remaining bones of the skeleton of lesions which might have been the product of tuberculosis.*
- ii. *There is no evidence in the long bones or skull of syphilis; neither of enlargement nor crumbling, nor of erosions or the formation of thickening. Further, there are no cavities in long bones that would provide evidence of spirochaetal infection.*

Taken together, I conclude that the person had probably not suffered from TB or syphilis.

January 15th

I have used the method of Meindl And Lovejoy, 1985 to assess the possible age of the skull by observing the closure of cranial sutures. Although a full analysis is not possible from the incomplete archive, I confidently estimate the age of the individual upon death as being over fifty, but less than sixty.

January 16th

Evidence from the mass and length of the surviving long bones would suggest an individual of 1.70 to 1.75 metres in height. The bones are blackened at the surface only, but there is a continuity of them for the right arm, together with a complete collection of disassembled bones of the right hand. I have reassembled the bones of the hand using wire and Araldite. The hand and limbs can be made to articulate for the following reasons:

The acromion and coracoid processes of the scapula are intact, as is the glenoid cavity. Since the greater and lesser tuberosities of the humerus are also intact, a working ball joint can be constructed despite a degree of damage to the subscapula fossa. There is, for example, a crack at the position of the scapular notch which extends to the inferior angle so that the medial border of the subscapular fossa is absent.

However, the clavicle can be made to associate correctly with this putative shoulder joint. Working surfaces of the acromioclavicular joint are in good condition and all bones can be fixed in place by means of olive wires and surgical hinges. Having done so, the limb has an almost complete degree of freedom of articulation.

The joints of the long bones and the long bones themselves show no evidence of joint-space narrowing, or of the marginal erosions characteristic of rheumatoid arthritis. However limited bone loss was observed in the knuckle joint, the union between metacarpal and phalanges, which was most pronounced in the third finger. In summary, the bones show the early onset of osteoarthritis and some pain may have been experienced or loss of freedom of movement at that position. Such pain may have been enough to cause mental distress or psychological perturbation.

Alkhimovich continued for the whole of that month and intermittently, made further entries in his file on many later occasions. Finally, he elected to remove the Magdeburg Relic in order to continue his researches. There were no questions asked during the upheavals within his department; he was fulfilling a perfectly legitimate official function. Individual small bones were removed, taken from his laboratory to his office in Moscow and later, to his home in the Arbat district of that city. He continued to study the archive and his written file grew further, with drawings, measurements and reasonable suppositions. At home, bones were numbered and where possible, were temporarily reassembled by wiring them into a hand and skull, and into complete long bones by using adhesives. Casts were prepared and plaster facsimiles produced.

After being drawn and described, some and eventually all facsimiles rather than originals were returned to the state archive. In time, all the original bones were disassembled and stored in a separate airtight metal container over sachets of silica gel. Over the years, Alkhimovich ceased to have concerns about any issues of security with his pursuit so that the original archive rather than facsimile copies, together with other objects of an increasing collection, continued to be stored by him.

*

Two thousand, five hundred kilometres to the west, it was a September morning in 2016. The days were hot for England, but it had become cold at night so that condensed water hung in the air as the sun rose, giving heavy mists which caused travellers to keep their headlights on until mid-morning. Hedgerows were heavy with the wealth of a late season of mellow fruitfulness; rosehips, sloes, blackberries and occasionally, wild hops festooned them. In gardens, the wasps were now angry and continued their work with urgency; they stripped the surface of wooden gates and fences and collected water from puddles and ponds in order to complete the paper of their nests. They damaged garden fruit, which fell to yield a sweet crystalline sugar upon which gorged ants, mice and in the large orchards of farms, the pigs also. The land was rich and fat with the wealth of nature, but the radiation of heat at night into a clear, starry sky indicated the advent of frost quite soon.

At his large house, a late-Victorian former rectory, Johan Pal observed a myriad of spiders, each at the middle of its own large web and the latter in turn covered in droplets of water. There were very many of them living in his grounds, perhaps even a surprisingly large number.

Although the snakes of pine heathland were not common nearby, he had also seen with some satisfaction, that the poisonous adder had taken station there; he could see them at times and could hear them rustle and slither. They were multiplying, for they had adequate food; a croaking of frogs and toads indicated not only the presence of water nearby, but that they were drawn to settle there.

Johan Pal was a short, swarthy man of part German extraction, with a heavy black beard growth which shaving could not hide, together with receding hair, cropped short. During the war, his grandfather Alfons von Pal, had gained experience of liquid propellants as the motive force for rocket flight while at a fairly young age. After the war, he had fled to England and like many others of his colleagues with an experience of Peenemunde, had found work in the British armaments industry. He had produced a son Dieter, an academic, and eventually Herr Doktor Dieter von Pal had wed a Welsh woman and this unusual union had produced a son Johan. The family name von Pal was a form of the name Paul, which Johan decided to keep. He maintained a circle of like-minded people of German extraction, was fluent in the languages of his forebears and had an immersion in the history and culture of both Britain and Germany. In his middle-years, Johan von Pal, now most often addressed simply as Johan Pal, had other matters to consider.

Johan Pal, scientist, advisor to the armaments industry and to Government, was also a proficient student of the occult. However unlike many others with the same pursuit, his intelligence and perseverance had enabled him to make greater progress than with the simple demonstrations of magic achieved by his peers. His abilities were now well-advanced – and very dangerous to those who crossed him. They were also very beneficial to his supporters and allies. Yet he was conscious that he had not yet found a means of advancing to the ultimate, a position for which he needed a Grand Project.

At this particular time, Pal was a fairly secretive individual and had naturally sought a secluded position for his activities. And again, quite naturally, he had chosen carefully. His choice, a country rectory in Wiltshire, was suitable by virtue of its history and position, but also because of something further. There was also a carefully-accumulated body of legend in that neighbourhood, as though people were drawn to worship there throughout history. By now, he was a man of considerable wealth; it was quite easy to foretell a favourable change in the value of a share. However approaching middle age, he was rich, but his house was neither costly nor particularly grand. And he had been thinking; he knew that he must shortly realise his grand project or must give up his pursuit altogether in order to do something else.

Many people knew him, but a surprising number were unable to say that their familiarity was more than an acquaintanceship. He had servants at home, and did occasionally mix at parties. His servants were reliable, however and had been chosen carefully. They were generally shrewd enough to be inscrutable and were supplied with a salary which facilitated that characteristic. Yet Pal was solitary but not lonely. He was not in the least temperamental, and maintained a small circle of like-minded friends. To them, he was known as 'The Master,' at first a nickname, but one which grew in significance when they grew to know him better. He then elicited respect, fear, awe, admiration and terror in equal measure.

Johan Pal noted the date. It was 30th of September, a full month until All Hallows Eve; the evening of the Christian feast of All Saints Day. Yet time was not pressing since via a series of what could only be described as academic meetings he sought, in the main, academic knowledge in the written artefacts of the middle ages. His interests therefore took him to those who dealt in rare books and ecclesiastical antiquities. As a collector, he had an interest in the esoteric religious creeds of those whom he thought enlightened.

More immediately, he was pleased with his new domestic arrangements since they had been chosen in order to facilitate his work. His property was at a confluence of ley lines: the inter-connecting lines falling between natural features in the landscape. Like Alfred Watkins, the scholar who first wrote about that subject in the 1920s, he could see the connection between local valleys, hills and ridgelines and with man-made features such as churches and forts; and wells and barrows. He had dowsed ley lines with a pendulum and confirmed their presence, just as Watkins had before him. Older civilisations from farther afield had done the same at other times; it was the dragon lines of the Chinese and the song-lines of the Aborigines which confirmed the existence of hidden or occult power more readily than any other evidence.

He had considered the merits of other places but was pleased with his final choice. More locally, he felt the energy arising from the notable St Michael's ley line. Passing through Glastonbury and Avebury, it was an extensive source of power in his present neighbourhood. Here, primitive man had felt that energy when in Neolithic times he had built temples and barrows, carved horses into the chalk, built stone circles and tumuli and had constructed Silbury Hill above notable ley lines. That ability had not been lost; enlightened modern man had erected the Lansdowne monument at Cherhill above a major ley line, of which the natural vibrations were as evident to Pal, because of his training, as the moon by night. Overall, he was quite sure that local lines would help him in his present researches and was pleased they were so powerful there.

Ley lines alone, however, were no more significant than the presence of water. That element had been important to Neolithic man who had considered it in the placement of Avebury, below which a well of natural water had been found. Elsewhere a seismic survey had revealed water in a natural well at Stonehenge and it was clearly a feature of many significant temples nearby. As ancient man had walked, so Johan Pal had followed: when at Stonehenge he felt as though converging forces were evident there and in a like manner had diverted an underground stream at his home. The natural seepage through chalk hills had made this straightforward and he had been correct in his calculations: there was now an energy confluence on his property which many creatures could feel and found attractive. In his discussions with his supporters, they had reviewed a collection of literature on the subject, including the work of Watkins and the group was competent in that interesting field. Johan Pal took an academic approach to occultism and presented to them the factual case for advancement.

Pal now addressed Barrett, his housekeeper, general servant and gardener; a local man in his fifties, 'I shall be going to Cambridge for a while and will be looking at antiquarian books from my usual sources. I shall be gone for about two to three days and will be attending an auction there on Thursday. While I am away, please keep house in the normal manner. There is an account for you to draw on, and keep all receipts as usual.'

He continued, 'I would also like you to think about our large party at the end of October, when I shall be having several guests to stay. Please arrange for an outside catering company to provide cold collations and a buffet-style meal for about twenty-five. You will have the day off, fully paid, for the duration. Twelve guests will stay here with me, but some will stay at hotels nearby. Please research rooms for them; they will stay for three days. Here is a list.'

'Yes, thank you, Sir,' said Barrett.

*

Creighton and Ivy Brakespeare opened their shop to a private viewing of books on Wednesday afternoon, which Johan Pal attended. They would both be present at the auction the following day, but many of Brakespeare's clients liked to handle and view stock beforehand. Today, there were ten potential clients present and they browsed happily among collections of classical literature and signed first editions. Brakespeare was in no hurry and was anxious not to seem so, for Pal was normally a big spender.

Brakespeare said, 'These are quite interesting. They are quite old guides to the flora of England from the point of view of cures, remedies and medicines. I don't know whether they are quite for you, but they are well-illustrated and probably of the eighteenth century. In fact, I have an interest in natural history myself, so it could be said that I bought them partly for my own pleasure.'

Pal looked through them, nodded in a positive but non-committal manner, and turned his attention to a further volume with illustrations of the orchis and other families. Leafing through, he paused briefly to read a section entitled "*Conium maculatum* and its common names: hemlock, or devil's bread". He narrowed his eyes to read a short section on the origin of the word Conium: that of the Greek for vertigo or to 'whirl around'. He noted that he was being observed but his eyes were inscrutable as he turned the page and said, 'Bit of an orchid collector. It is interesting to see the origin of the word orchis; perhaps the bulbs are an aphrodisiac? I doubt whether I shall find out! But I'll certainly look at this in the auction. Now have you anything to do with comparative religion or medieval literature, or culture and philosophy; you know, something unusual, as we discussed?'

'Yes, I've got a very nice original King James Bible. There are supposedly only about two hundred known and this one was found recently in a church in Devonshire. They agreed to sell.'

'I will take that now but will ask that you wrap it for me. What else have you got?'

'Sadly, The King James must go into the auction; I expect about three or four thousand pounds, it is a 1611 book, not as old as a Tyndale but still rare. But I do have something rather special. I've come across a Clavicule of Solomon which is for sale by private bidding.'

Pal looked astonished. 'That cannot be? There are only so many copies from the medieval period and they are all well-known and fully documented. Most are in the various classical languages and all are held by big libraries or are in state collections. In what language is it written?'

'Latin, but it has some footnotes and ink additions in French. I am advised by philologists that these later additions are in the language of the 14th century. It also contained a decree of heraldry from the 14th century, written in both Latin and English, which lay between the pages when the volume was uncovered. We would not use that additional insert into the book to date it, but the volume was itself looked at by scholars and they are clear that it cannot be later than the ink written on it. It is almost certainly a century older than Latin, Italian and Greek texts from 15th century, all of which are well-known, inaccessible and do not come on the market.'

Brakespeare continued, 'The present volume is interesting in another way, because it also differs substantially from texts written one hundred years later. All parts of later texts are present, but there are further sections on several rather esoteric aspects of the occult which are present only in the earlier volume. It is as though 'my' commission were the original upon which the others are imperfectly based.'

Brakespeare paused to let his words sink in. 'You will appreciate that this volume is likely to attract a substantial sum; one of six figures. It is being sold privately, by commission of the estate of a former owner. It has not been seen since about 1895, when it entered the collection of a very wealthy family in

Vienna and stayed there, in private hands for one hundred and twenty years.' He paused.

'And it is real?'

'We shall supply it with a written provenance and we vouch for it wholly.'

'Could I see it please?'

'Certainly. We hold it here in a special case. Please would you wait here and I will fetch it in.'

Brakespeare vanished for five minutes and returned with a modern aluminium lockable attaché case, which he set down on a table and opened. It contained the book, bound into two volumes, and packed in layers of archival quality paper within bubble-wrapper.

'As you can see, the bindings are tight and have never been replaced. Please use these gloves to open it and beware of the clasp, by the way. There are small projections on the hasp that are designed to prick the fingers of the unwary, a commonplace protection in medieval books, which were often reputed to be poisoned. See the remains of a bluish encrustation on them; copper cyanide, I am advised.'

'May I spend a few minutes with the volume?'

'Certainly. I will tidy up over here for a while.'

Brakespeare seemed unconcerned and worked quietly while Pal donned gloves and opened the book with care. He spent twenty minutes poring over it and must have examined perhaps fifteen percent of the work. Hastily, he also sketched a diagram from it and could be heard muttering, 'A copy of the Great Pentacle, it is more complete than any other in print.'

Shortly, he said, 'There seem to be a few pages missing. Can you tell me about those?'

'Yes, that fact is, of course, on the sale description. There are some pages currently with our restorers. Restoration work, if is to be done correctly, will take some time, but will be carried out at the vendor's expense.'

'I am keen to bid. How do I proceed?'

'I have been instructed to collect sealed bids from potential buyers, since it is believed that this is a better approach to preserve anonymity and to keep press or media coverage of the sale to a minimum. Such topics attract all kinds of oddballs: soothsayers, magicians, devil-worshippers, TV personalities, perhaps even politicians. I need a written and sealed bid by Friday of next week, the tenth of this month, and by mid-day. Bids can also be emailed to me, but they must first be encrypted using this program' – he held out a compact disc – 'you will appreciate why. Here also is a key to encrypt your bid and this is the destination address. This decryptation key is unique to you, as are those of all the other bidders.'

Brakespeare continued, 'Is there anything else that I can show you today? I have mentioned the King James; perhaps you will bid tomorrow? Of course it cannot compare with the Clavicule, which is a once-in-a-lifetime opportunity. Our other stock, although interesting, cannot really be compared to a volume of national library calibre.'

Pal asked, 'What are the arrangements for the delivery of the book to the successful bidder?'

'Name your preferred means, but please be clear, bids are to be of six figures.'

*

Pal bought the King James in the sale, together with a few other minor purchases. At home he reflected on his trip to Cambridge and considered his visit to have been a successful one. The King James Bible was interesting, of course. Although not rare, it was often worthwhile to reflect on principles it contained and which, in the main, were superseded as far as he was concerned: he would look at it from time to time. In fact, he had actually been after a very old dictionary, an original Webster's perhaps, as a means of understanding the many older dialectal words which might have found their way into local folklore or into manuscripts or herbariums. Perhaps he might be lucky on his next visit.

However he could not keep his mind off the Clavicule of Solomon. As Brakespeare had suggested, it was a once in a lifetime opportunity and the ownership of such a work was an end in itself. Certainly, a more recent volume from another collection might prove useful as a work of reference, but this particular example was an original and as such, must surely contain knowledge that had been lost to more recent examples. And how they were lost – he felt a surge of anger – at the time of the dissolution of the monasteries, when most books were retained in ecclesiastical libraries! He could visualise the soldiers of King Henry VIII as they removed, destroyed and burned all before them. But an original had escaped; it was complete too and very old.

He mused upon what a six-figure outlay would bring. Much of his work was based upon that of Aleister Crowley a century before. Crowley had probably examined a more recent Clavicule, but had seen fit to devise his own rituals. His practices were probably therefore corrupt and likely to be little older than the nineteenth-century. Crowley was venerated by some but considered as a charlatan by many others. What had happened to that relentless self-publicist in Paris? It was well-known that he had failed to bind the god Pan and had ended up in a lunatic asylum, moonstruck and a gibbering idiot. Pal did not wish to be considered as anything less than the most serious disciple and would not make the same mistake.

Brakespeare had spoken of a larger body of work in the older volume, which contained aspects lost to the more recent copies. Was the original therefore any better for his purposes? He was certain it would be. It was a hundred years older, known to be larger, and should contain traditions handed down from an earlier time. With it, he might have access to a very old lore, perhaps even with that of the ancients of a thousand years before. His mind considered the possibilities. He would like to have it, but at what cost!

He would offer a very large sum on the grounds that he could easily obtain more. With little hesitation he wrote down a few figures on paper, considered them carefully and chose the highest to prepare his offer, which he wrote into an email. Encrypting it, he emailed his bid to Brakespeare and printed out a further copy which he enclosed in an envelope. He asked Barrett to send it to Cambridge by courier and requested a receipt from the latter for having done so. Barrett was as tight-lipped as usual and only nodded. Characteristically, he busied himself when his employer chose to display his particular idiosyncrasies.

*

Barrett had taken the envelope when Johan Pal retired to a room which he liked to describe as his study. Although Pal was alone, he closed the door and locked it, and then drew the heavy 'blackout' curtains and sat at a table.

His study would have seemed unusual to an onlooker. Its decoration was of a heavy variety, with an extensive use of silk and satin drapes. Embroidered onto them were designs of a classical form, unusual representations of nature with exotic and imaginary animals and creatures from legend; the unicorn, the leopard, the satyr. They were beautiful, but their form and colour had the effect of satiating the senses so that one initially was drawn fascinated to them, but ultimately repelled.

Sitting, he unlocked a drawer and withdrew a set of Tarot cards. Like many of those who use them, he felt a fateful tingle and the hair rose on the back of his neck as he examined some of the pictures and symbols and began to shuffle them.

As a novice, Pal had tried tea leaves and a crystal ball for divination and they had enabled him to turn inwards so that future events might be seen by the mind's eye. Now, he was no longer a novice and many everyday objects would work in the same way. At his advanced stage, he could foretell simply by glancing at a computer screen or at the surface of water in a basin so that often, and when least expecting it, he was able to overlook events elsewhere or see things which might yet happen. However the Tarot cards were far more sophisticated. They were a gift of the Gods and could tease and confuse. They could be opaque, but they could also foretell with a greater accuracy.

Pal spread the cards on the table, face down, and withdrew only two and turned them over. He often used this very simple spread when in a hurry or when seeking to divine a straightforward dichotomy of paths for the future. There could be many cards together with their diverse and subtle paths, but two cards could foretell a simple best and worst or a 'do and do not,' or perhaps the alternatives of good and ill.

He was disappointed with the first card. It had the title *Lord of Indolence* and showed stagnant water and dead flowers. He guessed that it described his lack of progress, but he had not needed to draw it in order to know that truth. However the second card was the *Four of Disks* and was clearly the more propitious of the two. The card of the *Lord of Earthly Power*, it suggested that an opportunity for power was now close.

The cards were clear; he had longed for a singular opportunity and trivial challenges like the acquisition of wealth were no longer adequate. In past years, he had grown to the extent that he could smooth a path to success for a favoured acolyte or could destroy an enemy, yet there had been no great work and it had now to be admitted he could no longer remain idle.

A forthcoming opportunity, yet what was it? Pal drew further cards but they were opaque. Standing, he resorted to another means of divination using blood, that most precious of liquids. Walking into the garden outside, he collected a cockerel and returning, he killed it with a knife and drained its blood into an ebony dish. Composing himself, he spoke an invocation and looked into its crimson surface.

He was able to see things which the Tarot could not show. He was at the head of a great legion, now goose-stepping and with his arm held high in a salute, palm outwards to hail his many followers. Now a flag was flying: it bore the swastika symbol of Nazism. He also recognised the former Nazi Parade Grounds at Nuremburg and they were no longer derelict. There were great speeches again and cheers and an audience like those of 1938. There was power and purpose in his voice and he was the agent of a great will.

The crimson surface shifted and there was sight of his local landscape with the standing stones and with a great marble gateway. He also saw another flag which he knew to be his own, but it was blank so that he might choose his own symbol for the great work ahead.

The red surface cleared, became settled and he sat down to consider. He would choose such a symbol for his flag while the vision was clear in his mind. It would be the bright sun rising, a Golden Orb, *The Golden Ball*. Thus his great opportunity was now revealed.

Johan Pal felt optimistic. Time had not been wasted and he had read and researched carefully. It could be said that he had actively sought a major work from the dark literature of his masters, as did Catholics in communion with their Saints. Yet few of them became Saints themselves.

Now the Clavicule of Solomon was within his grasp: original, early and uncorrupted and his Great Work had been revealed at the same time; clearly both events were destined to occur together. He would seek that Great Work and would enrol his twelve helpers in the task. Meanwhile he would make a new symbol, the flag of a Golden Orb ascendant on a red horizon to symbolise the dawning of a new era. He would also place the Nazi swastika on that Golden Orb for all to see.

★

Ten days later, Creighton and Ivy Brakespeare were discussing some costly works on natural history which Creighton had added to his personal collection.

Ivy said, 'This will interest you. It is on entomology and you may remember your idea about how we might increase the number of butterflies, many being close to extinction. The author has suggested we might limit the numbers of predators.'

'I bet he has a theory. What does he suggest?'

'He thinks we should keep cats to limit the number of predatory birds.'

'Great idea, I like cats. Oh, and by the way, that man Pal has sent in a bid for the Clavicule of Solomon. He sent an email and a sealed envelope by special delivery so I bet he's keen. All bids close in one hour. What do you think of him?'

'He seems a bit solitary. I'm not sure I like that in a man.'

'Well he might seem that way on the surface, but nobody is very successful in business unless they are clear about how to get along with staff and customers.'

'Granted, he has a lot of money, but perhaps he could he have inherited it?

'I don't think so. He may seem preoccupied, but that is so often the case with successful businessmen; they get called away and their minds are elsewhere. Anyway, he may *seem* solitary, but I happen to know that he holds extensive parties and is probably quite active socially. His gatherings are like large book-groups and are common knowledge in the area.'

'It still sounds odd to me.'

'Well let's take a look then, shall we?'

In due course, all of the paper and emailed bids were collected and decrypted. Once opened, Brakespeare whistled, 'Oh my, our sponsor will be pleased.'

'Who's got it?'

'Pal has. And his bid is very high indeed.'

'How high?'

'Fifty percent higher than what I thought would be the highest.' He made a mental calculation, 'at 7.5% that gives us a clear £112,500.'

'My! That *is* high.'

'Please would you send an email confirming our acceptance of that sum. Don't commiserate with the second highest yet, just in case the funds don't arrive within thirty days as agreed. Please would you encrypt it, he knows the key to open it. I've other customers to deal with right now, so I hope you don't mind.'

Ivy sent off the email and Creighton Brakespeare dealt with a few other matters. Fifteen minutes later, Ivy said, 'There's a reply.'

'Good, that's quick.'

'He has asked us both to lunch on the 31st October. He asks would we bring the book with us and he will arrange for either a bank draft or a cheque drawn on his own account. He suggests we do the transaction at his home; he hopes we don't mind lunch, because he has another social function that evening. The exchange can be done then.'

'Please accept.'

'Creighton, isn't Pal's place near to where Wally Bishop and Amelia live?'

'I think you may be right. Let us have a quick look at the map.'

'It's only twenty miles. We could stay at Wally and Amelia's place if they will have us, maybe for a night or two. I will telephone Amelia today and see whether they are busy.'

'Thank you. That would be very good of you.'

Brakespeare packed the book away very carefully, placed it in his safe and dealt with a few other matters of correspondence. His general sale of books had been excellent. The antiquarian and fine end of the market was buoyant, but it was increasingly difficult to obtain enough fine stock to place, so that with an increasing reputation for placing top-end books he was sometimes approached by buyers more often than potential vendors. That fact could well be a future Achilles heel for the growth of his business; he remembered the expression 'networking' and thought immediately that it would be the key;

some development was necessary in order to match the two more accurately.

He said to Ivy, 'Tell me more about networking.'

'Well, there are professional social media sites, but if you want more, you will have to put yourself around socially. And I mean in person.'

'Yes, there's wine and cheese and chatter. And there are emailed newsletters. But I actually quite like the circuit anyway.'

'Me too. But so many of our personal friends seem be like-minded people in the book and art trade, so it's working in any case.'

'Are you thinking of Wally and Amelia?'

'Oh yes, and quite a few others. But Amelia is a fantastic cook too!'

'Well that's alright then!'

Both took genuine pleasure in good company; it was well-known that Amelia was an excellent chef and that Wally was a connoisseur of the pleasures of the table. They had more than enough excuse to go to Wally and Amelia Bishop's place, where they would talk about old times and about beautiful books and fine art, and would probably eat and drink to their hearts' content.

Later, Ivy spoke on the telephone and was occupied for perhaps ten minutes in conversation with first Wally, then Amelia. Conversations were always informal with Amelia and Ivy need not have asked stay, for as soon as Amelia understood the purpose of their visit to Wiltshire, she and Creighton were invited immediately. Together, they agreed that Creighton and Ivy would stay from 29th October until 3rd November. They would all look forward to this and the party would be large because their mutual friends Peyton and Zenda Oakwood would also be there. Close friends of old, they had all kept in touch over the years and regularly exchanged visits, correspondence and Bacchanalian evenings, an aspect that had never been damaged by talking about the art business they loved.

★

On the morning of 29th October, Creighton and Ivy Brakespeare removed their Range Rover from the garage and added enough clothes and odds and ends to last them for a few days. They locked their home, set the alarm system and went into Cambridge in order to check for any incoming letters, emails or other correspondence at the office. Having dealt with such matters, they removed the Clavicule and other books that Pal had ordered, printed off a formal invoice and receipt, sealed them and reset the alarm and physical security systems. Like most business people, they understood the value of deterrence to the hypothetical burglar: it was best achieved by an intractable physical barrier. Alarms in fact achieved little; few cared about the noise of an alarm system and would not be alarmed or deterred by it.

The drive to Wiltshire took about four hours, but they stopped for lunch in Wallingford and enjoyed a little sightseeing on the way. The B4009 was a country road for most of its length and quite slow. But it was picturesque, and wound through small towns and villages with attractive Georgian architecture that had not been disfigured by modern development. They lingered over their drive, dropped into the occasional antique shop or other interesting feature which caught their fancy and chattered happily throughout. Smiling, they arrived a little west of Oxford by about mid-afternoon and chose to avoid the dual carriageway south. Instead, they continued south west via Burford, Marlborough and the old A4 towards Bath. On the westward leg, they observed Silbury Hill, noted the sheer volume of earth that had been scraped from the landscape for about a mile in each direction and wondered at that feat of Neolithic engineering: as great as any Egyptian pyramid. Half an hour later, they stopped at Avebury, strolled around the standing stones and agreed that it was probably a greater monument than Stonehenge. While they were there, they observed a group of people engaged in an apparently druidic ceremony. Each was dressed in a white costume and the ceremony was a joyous affair; in fact it was a wedding, after which there was Champagne in the village. They watched for a while and resumed their journey west a little later. Eventually they turned south from the A4 towards the village of Peckling, where they arrived by 6pm.

Brakespeare took the Range Rover a short distance off the road and they removed their luggage. Thus on the evening of 29th October, Creighton and Ivy, on both business and pleasure, arrived at Wally and Amelia Bishops' home at Peckling in Wiltshire. They were to meet Johan Pal for lunch on 31st, but saw no reason to view that with foreboding.

Chapter Two

Standing Stones and Strange Tobacco

Callum Dood was the local vicar of the village church of Peckling. He had a reputation for eccentricity, for long walks over the downs and for being the priest whom the Church would ask for help on difficult occasions. A single man, some unkind folk in the neighbourhood had made reference to his friendship with the local Archdeacon, a man 'above him in the Church,' but overall, he was well-liked in the neighbourhood. A grey-haired man of about sixty-five but lively nevertheless, he enjoyed natural history and was reputed to smoke exotic herbs from his garden in addition to the usual tobacco from time to time.

Now, Dood left his own parish church, where he had spent an hour looking at the old parish records. Long before, he had found them to be the most useful, complete and original source of information on births, marriages and deaths in that neighbourhood. After passing the oaken door, he paused at a roughly-carved stone image of a woman, about eighteen inches high and with a small cup-shaped cavity in the crown of her head. The image was green with algal growth and certainly older than the church. It had been rescued from afar in the churchyard and set down just outside of the wooden door, where it had rested, by now, for perhaps one hundred years. There were a few rose petals and a couple of small coins in the receptacle in the crown. Dood himself added a coin, for the statue was probably of Isis, the Goddess of Magic and Life, honoured since time immemorial in that neighbourhood and revered still by some of the locals. None of them felt that its presence was evil, any more than they would feel so about another manifestation or reverence of nature; a rose perhaps, or the fruit of the apple.

As he returned home, Dood was summoned to the telephone. Upon answering, he recognised a familiar voice, that of the Archdeacon, who said, 'Callum, can I please visit soon? We've got a bit of bother for you to look at.'

Dood replied, 'Yes, come over tomorrow if you wish. I've got no biscuits in, but you can bring a cake if you like. Can we say about eleven?'

'Yes, fine.'

The following day, Adam Shilto, the Archdeacon arrived at precisely eleven. They had coffee and Dood divided the cake into slices. They had known each other for many years and Dood now supposed from Shilto's tone of voice that his visit was a serious one.

'Look Callum, we are a bit concerned by one or two bits of bad news in your area.'

'I had thought you might be, but which bits in particular?'

'There have been a lot of reports of lights on the downs at *those* times of year.'

'Frankly, you don't need to tell me about that, because I have seen them myself and the blood on the stones on St Winebald's day, together with a few dead farm animals, big stallions too.'

'Yes, and at the spring equinox there was evidence of feasting and orgies – sometimes I wish they would invite me too! Worst of all on the night of Walpurgis…'

Dood broke in, 'We call that Beltane around here; much of the local legend is still Celtic.'

'Whatever. There were blood rituals and sacrifices. And on St John's Eve, there was more feasting, with an orgy and some nasty sacrifices.'

'Well when you live around here, you get rather blasé about all that. It's been going on for hundreds of years.'

'The trouble is, we've also found a bit more than that. We took samples of the blood from two sites on the downs and took them for analysis. They turned out to be human blood, not from animals.'

'So what are you saying?'

'The Church is saying that we don't mind a bit of paganism. There have always been druids…'

Dood smiled, 'You surprise me. Like what?'

'Like a bit of fur-braiding, or a few young couples frolicking on the White Horse and maybe weddings at Avebury; all harmless and picturesque stuff. You didn't hear me say that, by the way.'

'And the rest?'

Shilto continued, 'We think that there is a fully-fledged Black Magic circle working locally. We don't know exactly what they are up to, but we don't like it. Aside from the criminal aspect of their activities which is very real, and which we can leave to the local police, there is the spiritual and religious effect on those poor unfortunates up to their necks in it.'

'Don't these poor unfortunates do it on purpose?'

'At first, maybe they do. Some of them just want a sexual adventure on the Downs, but they all get drawn in further. With that lot, there can be no perpetuation of the status quo. Their leaders always seek advancement according to their own scheme of things and that means finding a great and evil work by which they can ascend towards their so-called goal.'

Dood smiled, 'Some means of advancing the cause of human misery?'

'Yes, exactly.'

'And you think that they obtain real magical powers?'

'Yes and no. I don't think they can stop a bullet, whatever some novelists may say. But by the force of their will they can probably deflect the arm of the man with a gun before he pulls the trigger. They can also levitate and they can become unseen – I say that rather than use the word invisible, for that is quite different – and they can kill at a distance too. I also think they can make people become sick or very wealthy, the weather inclement, cause general mischief or bring about visitations and raise real demons and devils. We have both helped at exorcisms and know that such things are real.'

'Don't remind me. So what do you want me to do? Confront a devil-worshipping potential murderer?'

Shilto continued, 'A bit of human blood does not necessarily mean murder, at least, not yet. The forensic guys have been over the sites in question and although there is blood, there is no evidence of dismemberment. Knowing *them*, they might even withdraw their own blood with a syringe. But eventually and sadly, we think it might lead to that; a new-born babe maybe. We want them stopped before it gets any worse and we don't want to lose any more farm animals.'

'So where does that leave me?'

'We want you to circulate and find out what they are up to, find out who, what, when and where. I know you circulate anyway, but maybe go a little outside of your usual circles. Have a chat to the folk in the pub, together with the farm workers. They don't say much but they know a lot, especially around here. Also, chat to the illegal badger-baiters and hare coursers. They are out on the Downs at night, amongst the other undesirables, and they quietly see things.'

'I thought you would say that. Do I get this cake for free?'

'It's a deal.'

*

Somewhat later, Callum Dood, deep in thought, looked around his own churchyard at Peckling. All was neat, tidy, and undisturbed; there had been no intruders, no digging and no thefts. He completed another circuit, but looked a little higher, at his yew trees.

There were ten yew trees in the churchyard; several were very large and they were obviously very old. In places, a few older trunks had become divided into new staves growing on the former circumference. The yew was considered to be an immortal tree and those at Peckling had probably been there for three thousand years. Whatever their real age, his church buildings, arising from the prosperity provided by the wool trade of the fourteenth century, were very young by comparison.

The yew trees were growing near to a blind spring and the water, having collected there from the downs above, did not pause in its descent underground towards the River Marden at Calne. Dood had always thought them planted there because of the blind spring nearby. Since yew trees were respected locally and were venerated by some, that site had been one of reverence and devotion for time out of mind and it certainly pre-dated Christianity. As with the statue of Isis, that did not make the place unholy in his view, because the veneration was one of nature, not of dark forces. Now, he looked at the yew trees more closely: there were clean breaks on some of the lower branches as though sprigs of greenery had been collected recently.

Looking at them, he could quite understand why the yew was venerated; tall and evergreen, it whispered in the wind. Oh, the sacred yew tree, with its feet among the bones of the churchyard and its immortal branches stretching towards the sun! Many local words described it; the yew had a diverse lore and symbolism drawn from both Celtic and Anglo-Saxon cultures.

The yew tree; it had its own symbol: ᚔ called 'idad' in the Irish Ogham alphabet. That symbol was unknown in England, but its immortality was universal throughout Europe. Since time immemorial, the undying yew had been used to decorate the face of the Green Man, that personification of the force of nature seen on local buildings of all kinds: country inns, homes and churches throughout the land, and from Tipperary to Transylvania.

The Green Man, a face still seen in the depiction of the Victorian Father Christmas: the green father with beard of green straw and a green hood, beneficent on the day of St Nicholas, although remote altogether from the Santa Claus of today. And locally, he was revered still as the spirit who dies every winter and is reborn in the springtime; the lore of Wiltshire was full of references to him. Local names were many: Jack o' Lantern, revered on All Soul's Eve; Will o' the Wisp, the mischievous spirit whose flickering light could draw the traveller from the safe path; Jack in the Green, the immortal spirit of the greensward, born again and celebrated at Beltane, the start of the new year. It was likely that local folk had removed some sprigs of yew so that the mistle thrush might eat its red berries; or perhaps to throw a sprig onto the coffin of a loved one as a symbol of rebirth. There was nothing here in the churchyard that was less than commonplace.

He returned home and made a few telephone calls. First, he spoke to Pete Rodgers, a curate in the next village, 'Peter, any murders or incest on your patch?'

'No, but we've had another break in.'

'Anything taken? Candlesticks maybe?'

'No, much worse. They took the communion wine and host. Also, the altar was desecrated.'

'Did you clean it up straight away or call the filth first?'

'I got the boys in blue around and then cleaned up after they had finished taking photographs and specimens; fingerprints and stuff.'

'What did they do?'

'To the altar? They turned the cross upside-down and stuck it in the body of a hare. They had cut its throat.'

'I'm sorry. Do you need any help?'

'You mean with the spiritual side or the clean-up?'

'Either way.'

'It's good of you to offer, but I've had a lot of volunteers here, as you might imagine; I can do the other bit myself. Sadly though, the place will have to be locked for the foreseeable future.'

'Come round next week for some whisky?'

'Yes, I'd like that.'

Later that day, he strolled slowly to his greenhouse. A keen gardener, he grew many of his own herbs, would probably choose the more common ones to tear into his salad that evening, and from time to time would also dry a few for medicinal use. Now, he preferred a few dried leaves, chose those which he knew would alleviate stress and improve reflection, tore them into rough strips, mixed them with a little tobacco and rolled them into paper cylinders to make cigarillos in the Spanish style. Lighting one, he took a deep breath of the sweet, fragrant smoke, collected a sketchpad and pencils and went out to look for butterflies.

The late September sun was hot and the air was still and sultry. Hedgerows were laden with fruits; there were rose-hips, haws on the thorn bush, crab-apples, sloes and here and there, greengages too, that finest of the plums. He collected a handful and bit into their sweet golden flesh. For a while, he paused to sketch a large group of painted ladies and commas on a buddleia bush. Their living hues, flashing and moving, made his task difficult, but he drew on his cigarillo again, breathed deeply, and the narcotic vapour made him lose a little sense of time.

Later, he walked higher above the village and ascended narrower paths onto the downs where the air was cooler. A few larks danced and dived high above and he could hear them singing as they sought small pieces in the fields below. He walked about five miles and came to a group of three mounds in the earth. They were burial mounds of the late Bronze Age, probably from about one thousand years BC, but they lacked a tell-tale 'dip' in the middle where earth had been removed and so had not been opened and desecrated. Climbing a few feet, he stood on the top of one and looked around. The air was hazy and the few people in the distance were tiny spots on the horizon. There was some smoke from the fields and the farm trucks were heavy with the autumn harvest of pumpkins, cauliflowers and sweet fruits.

After another mile, he came upon another kind of monument: a long barrow. He had been there many times before and had even ventured a little inside. Yet it had not been possible to go far within, for parts of the roof had fallen and the former passageway had filled with earth, rubble and the collected vegetation of three thousand years. Within the entrance, however, there was some interesting and probably original carving which he had seen on other, earlier visits. Long ago, an upright stone had been carved into the form of a human face with heavy eyebrows, a promontory nose and recessed mouth. It also had a beard and moustache which gave it a sinister appearance and was known locally as the Watcher. That art form, however, was not unique to Wiltshire; similar figures were known to guard tombs elsewhere within the older Celtic range, the best-known of them was Le Guardien du Tombeau, a figure within a barrow on the Island of Guernsey. Here, in Wiltshire, the present face could be seen to guard that burial place still, yet formerly, on Dood's many earlier visits, the carving had been weathered and filled by moss and lichen as though long-forgotten.

Now, the image had been cleaned. All the moss was gone and a light brushing had removed any dirt and decay. Colour, too, had been added and the stone-grey hair fresh-filled with red. The eyes were again yellow and it was as though the spirit of the watcher had been invoked once more, to stand as guardian over the bones of those who lay within. Its appearance seemed to ask for respect and he bowed, turned away and walked on.

Dood walked further along bridleways, parish boundaries and through quiet villages. Many were somewhat cut-off at times; their inhabitants mostly farmers with sheep and the occasional cow, to be met only at local market gardens and occasionally, at the public house in Peckling. They kept to themselves and looked somehow different. They seemed somewhat shorter and darker and their character was a little unlike the taller locals in towns nearby. They often peppered their speech with words of dialect, but were pleasant enough when you got to know them.

At last, he came upon Don Regan, a local sheep farmer whom he knew quite well. Short, dark and rather squint-eyed, Regan moved with the irregular gait of a man with one leg a little shorter than the other and he mumbled a few words, perhaps to his old sheepdog nearby. As he approached, Regan's words became a little clearer, 'ain, tain, tethera, methera, mimp' together with 'ayta, slater, laura, dora, dik' as the sheep passed by[1]. Dood knew that these words were a tired rendition in the former Celtic tongue of that area, words of which still peppered the local speech. Some said that Regan and his ilk still conversed almost wholly in that tongue and there was no doubt that he knew more of it than was often apparent. It was of a form very similar to the Cornish still heard further west and shared very many words with it. In fact, it was probably closer to Cornish than to Welsh and there on the downs, was truly more alive than dead and actually was probably still flourishing.

Dood stifled the thought 'inbred' before it had fully formed; it was after all uncharitable. He hoped that Regan would be a mine, not only of words, but also of local gossip; no doubt Regan could make a living from counting sheep, but he was also a regular traveller on the downs, with the opportunity of seeing people come and go.

---

1 *With local variations all over England and into Brythonic parts of Scotland; still to be heard on the hills even today.*

Entirely without irony, he said, 'mutton day,' an oft-used expression in the neighbourhood and cognate with the Cornish *myttin da*[2], as Dood, an amateur sleuth of words in that dialect continuum of Celtic, was aware. He then lapsed back into Anglo-Saxon, 'Hello, Don, how's business?'

'Fiddler gannets[3], I'm alright, thank you, but business is poor.'

'Why?'

'I've been losing a few of my sheep and I don't like where they've been ending up.'

'Is it bad, Don? What's going on exactly?'

'I don't really like to say, but I try to make sure the sheep are all in the barn these nights.'

'I'm sorry. Why is that?'

'Well, I used to lose one or two to the boys in big SUVs and Land Rovers. They come out with lurchers to do a bit o' coursing and while they are out here, they pinch a couple to put in the deep freeze. Sheep are hard to catch, mind you, so they would need shoot one, or there would need to be quite a few of them at it. A few years back we even had a big cat on the loose. Somebody let one loose from a local zoo. You can always tell if it's a cat, they go for the throat and throttle their catch, but they avoid humans and like to hide down in the woods over there,' he said, pointing. 'The lynxes are not too bad, but the nasty one was the leopard. We also had a couple of wild boar. They grunt to warn you off, but they don't go for sheep. You can tell when boar are nearby from the smell and noise, so you can keep out of the way. Anyway, we lost a few back then.'

'So what's up?'

'Well, we can put up with a big cat or maybe some bad boys in a Land Rover. The cats have to eat too and the bad boys who run the farm shops muck in and buy some of our carcasses off

2 *myttin da; Cornish for 'good morning.'*

3 *fiddler gannets is the Wiltshire form of the Cornish fatla genes? 'How are you?'*

of us. Also, if we get stuck in the snow they've pulled us out in winter. Same as the tinkers: so-what if they are a bit light-fingered, it takes all sorts and maybe I'm no angel myself. But all the same, I don't like seeing what goes on here now and I don't think it's them what does it.'

'What does go on exactly?'

'Blood and guts and it ain't big cats nor poachers, nor tinkers doing it neither. There are sacrifices maybe, and evil chanting.'

'Whereabouts?'

'Over towards the stones, about two mile down from the dewponds and downhill away from the leas.'

'The what?'

'The ley lines, they're strong around here.'

'I suppose you mean by the big dewponds?'

'Yes, we are too high for any other water. There are a few springs, but they are underground and quite small up here. The dewponds were laid down two-hundred year ago with the oxen. They dug the pits out and then ground the chalk round and round with water, then let it dry and set solid. The dewponds collect all the rainwater and some streams course in when it's very wet. They are better than any cement pond even now; they never leak or go dry, even in summer.'

'Those standing stones nearby. Is that where it goes on?'

'Maybe, but they've put it about that there is another big cat on the loose so folk stay away. See them trees yonder, that's where they say it hides out, but I don't believe it, not this time.'

He continued, 'I think that something else happens on the ley-lines in the other direction, up from the dewponds and I don't mean the stuff by the standing stones, neither. Downhill, there are maybe some nasty games and sacrifices too. At one end there is an upset stone or maybe it was placed flat a-purpose. But that was long ago by the Old People. Up the hill by the leys there is something older and maybe stronger, but the new stuff is more evil. Take my advice and stay away.'

'So have there always been a few Druids around here?'

'Yes, but that was just a little hemlock and sunlight until recent. Nobody used to care about the Druids, what mucked about up the ley lines. This new stuff, from nasty folk is unchristian. That's down lower by the water by the fallen stone. The two sets of folks is different, one set of Druids and one set of bad boys.'

'So was there any stuff before, from the Old People, the Druids?'

'Oh yes, there was. Drumming and noises and some of the village folk vanish for the night, and dancing, hemlock and such.'

'What about the newly-painted watcher?'

'That's just the old ways. Whenever some real bad boys come, local people warn them off of digging up bones by reminding them of the older magic.'

He continued again, 'And folks say that there is something nasty that was buried long ago, that is come to life once again.'

'Is that anything to do with the sacrifices by the stones?'

'I guess not. It may have been a *pear-thievin*[4], how do you say, ah, woken up.'

'So whereabouts is this thing?'

'I am not sure, but you needs to go a willow-witching with a stick along the leas until you find it, you know, from the waters up the hill. Cannot miss it, then look down.'

'Willow-witching? Is that like dowsing?'

'*Ea,* yes.'

'So will I find the new boys lower down by the standing stones?

'I doubt it. They come and go and they also hang around elsewhere.'

'Thank you Don, and by the way it's a pleasure to hear you counting in the old tongue. But I must admit that I never understood any of your numbers very well.'

---

4 *Cf Cornish pur dhifun, woken up; Breton dihuniñ awake*

'Aim them when![5]'

'Cheers, mate.'

Somewhat thoughtful, Dood returned home.

On the next day, he collected a hazel sapling cut into the shape of the letter Y. It was about three feet across from end to cut end, and had a small projection of six inches at the union between them: the tail of the Y. Armed with notebook and butterfly net in an apparent effort to catch late-season butterflies to draw, he retraced his journey of the previous day. However, not stopping at his former distance, he walked a further two miles to some well-known dewponds, and so northwards by half a mile to follow the course of a now-dry stream which fed a dewpond in very wet weather.

Shortly, he withdrew the hazel dowsing-rod from a bag and placed its cut ends in each palm and with the tail before him. For a short distance he walked slowly uphill, hazel ahead, but felt nothing. Then, moving his hands so that his palms were downwards, he felt an immediate charge as though the hazel had suddenly become alive; he was reminded of the crystal wireless sets of his youth, with which to obtain a signal, the sensitive surface of the crystal had first to be stroked with a 'cat's whisker.'

Now, the hazel started to twitch up and down as though in response to small variations in induction beneath the surface of the earth and wryly, he reflected that he had not been so 'connected' for quite some time. That had been at his last electro-convulsive therapy session, when his ears had been attached to an electronic device by crocodile clips to cure an addiction to herbal remedies. It had been very successful in improving matters although today, the electrical connection was so sensitive he could almost feel the earth move.

He walked on and it was obvious that he was following a ley-line. The 'Y' jumped up and down and there was considerable

---

5 *'Aim them when;' thought, with a little poetic licence, to be cognate with Amm dhe'm gwen, Cornish celtic for 'kiss my butt.'*

sensation in his palms, although both diminished if he stepped too far to the left or right. As he walked ahead, the electric strength increased and the willow increased its arc. Soon, the landscape rose into a mound of earth and stones, and the willow pointed directly down.

Nearby, the mound was accompanied by one very large stone, far larger than the rest and placed deep in the soil. Walking over to it, he ran the blade of a knife down one side, but it failed to reach the bottom and the stone was clearly very deep-set. The ancient saw marks of the stonemasons could still be seen on its surface and it was regular in shape and had been cut by hand. It was in fact about eight feet long by five wide, had a visible height of four feet and that large a mass would have required much effort to place in the ground. Since it looked rather darker than the local limestone litter scattered nearby, it had certainly been carried there from afar and set down long ago.

Nearby, the landscape seemed to be alive with vibration and electricity and Dood's palms continued to tingle. He dropped the hazel, took a short break to light a cigarillo, and while he inhaled its sweet smoke, the ground underfoot seemed to quake for a second. Or had it been the noise of thunder on the wind? He knew that such sounds were quite important; vibrations and noise were significant in a landscape which he knew normally to be a quiet one.

Further afield and from a perspective of fifty yards, it was clear that the nearby mound of earth could not be a natural figure of the landscape; it was too regular and resembled other Neolithic burial mounds, although it was somewhat larger. It was also a place of considerable disturbance in the ley line. Dowsing for a further quarter mile, the deflection of the hazel returned to a more usual forty degrees but returning, the disturbance increased as he approached from the opposite direction. It was clear that this place was of some significance judging from his dowsing and from the extent of the works there. He seemed to recall that it was called Carn Brea.

Dowsing the outline of the burial mound, the greatest deflection of the hazel was observed at its circumference and, kneeling down, he examined the ground all around. It bore short-cropped grass of a poor quality, marginal for sheep and useless for cattle, and there also were many white-bleached shells of the Roman, or edible snail. The latter was rare and he knew it was associated with former human settlements. It had been farmed by Neolithic and Roman peoples for food, but migrated only locally and relied on being transported in order to extend its range. This was probably such a site, and if so, the present area was almost certainly no stranger to humans.

After some thought, he took from his pocket a pendulum of copper metal suspended on a thin chain, about two feet long. It had a small loop at one end of the chain, which enabled him to support its weight. He held the chain palm upwards so that the links passed between his forefinger and thumb and with the copper weight downwards, so that it was free to swing on the other end. From a pocket he also withdrew a woollen cloth with words and letters embroidered onto it, which he placed on the middle of the grass mound.

Standing on the barrow, the weight was free to swing, but it was not possible to hold the pendulum still. Even with a carefully-controlled hand, the chain magnified the slightest of involuntary movements and made them very much larger. It swung to and fro, but gradually took on a direction of swing between the words 'yes' and 'no' that had been embroidered on the cloth beneath it.

The pendulum was probably of a principle akin to the dowsing wand; both received a stimulus that was derived from some mental process. He did not believe that it was of the paranormal, but its working was certainly below the threshold of sensation or consciousness, so that the result was perceived by his mind without him being aware of the process. The method was such that particular answers could be obtained, which, although not usually incorrect, did require what could only be described as a calibration beforehand.

He asked, 'Was this earth mound made by men?' This was a question to which, by now, he knew the affirmative answer. The pendulum began to swing towards the embroidered answer 'no,' which was therefore incorrect, but turning the cloth around, he repeated the question and the direction of swing was now correct. Satisfied he asked the following:

'Who made this mound?'

The pendulum swung, slowly at first, north to south about ten times and then began to pick out an unusual sequence of letters of the alphabet: 'd-r-o-u-i-s,' which he copied onto his sketch-pad with his left hand.

He continued: 'Are bones buried here?'

'Ea.[6]'

'Have the bones been disturbed recently?'

'Serris.[7]'

'What else lies below?'

'Yet.[8]'

'Are you angry?'

'Ea.'

'Why are you angry?'

'Athulfus.'

'Have you followers now?'

'Ea.'

'I honour you.'

He pocketed his pendulum and cloth and walked thoughtfully back to the origin of the ley line by the largest dewpond. Then, further south, he travelled another mile and approached the collection of standing stones described earlier by Regan.

---

6 *Ea; cognate with Cornish Ea, 'yes.'*

7 *Serris; cognate with serrys, 'angry.*

8 *Yet; similar to Cornish yet, 'gate or portal.'*

He knew them quite well; locally, they were considered to be a former burial chamber from the early Neolithic period. There were six stones still standing, but further stones had fallen to dismantle most of the structure. Long ago a roof stone had surmounted a burial chamber, but now, one upright was fallen and had taken the roof stone down with it, so that it lay nearby, a heavy block six feet in length. It had no recent markings, although it carried green moss on a damp side away from the sun as evidence that it had been there for quite some time. Like the block at Carn Brea it also had a few very old striations on each side; they were very faint but regular lines, almost certainly ancient saw marks made when cutting or shaping it. The upper surface contained a little water in a depression at one end, together with some orange lichen. Had anyone wished for an altar there, it would have been the ideal candidate.

Moving from left to right, he continued to dowse with his hazel and although the ground was alive, there was no ley line. The middle of the fallen chamber was only a little more active, but at the fallen roof stone the hazel spun sharply and pointed straight down. There, he set up his pendulum once more and allowed it to equilibrate above the lettered cloth. On this occasion there was no need to turn the cloth and he continued in the same manner:

'Is there a watcher present?'

'Ea.'

'Have the stones been used for any evil purpose?'

'Na fella.[9]'

'Is there one from afar with his mind on the stones?'

'Ea.'

'For what purpose?'

---

9 *Na fella; this construction is considered to be the local Brythonic for no further. Fella is a mutated form of pella, utmost or further, but mutated after 'na.'*

'Pal aure.[10]'

Thereafter the pendulum swung in ever decreasing concentric circles as though of a mind to talk no further. Once again he made his acknowledgement and packed away his apparatus.

He was home within two hours, where he made coffee and had a smoke.

*

That evening, he paid a visit to the Dog and Duck in Peckling. He settled in a corner with a bottle of Cabernet and a glass and appeared to doze a little. The general hubbub, waxing and waning, took a form in which individual conversation could at times be discerned.

At the other end of the room, Maxton Mawr, an aged hill farmer, but notable in the area with pan pipes and the accordion, squinted at some sheet music on his upright piano. A little short-sighted, he managed to rumble through a few tunes at a moderate pace and then looked around, beaming happily.

Conversation was guarded and the locals: farm-workers with strong cider and darts teams with lager, seemed quite muted. Dood waved to a few and his gesture was returned, but it did not lead to any discourse. Instead he beckoned and the lovely Libby Long, barmaid at the Duck, came over. Libby Long was a very popular figure in the neighbourhood, notorious for being able to balance a full pint glass on her chest with ease.

'What's up with them, Lib? Happy lot tonight!' He gestured towards the bottle of wine.

'Not exactly!' She poured a glass from his bottle.

'If not, then why not?'

---

10 *Pal aure; Golden Ball. Pal is ball in the local Brythonic, cognate with Cornish pel, Welsh pêl, Latin pila. Aure is thought to be similar to Welsh aur, Breton aour, Cornish owrek; 'golden.'*

'Well, mostly they're preoccupied with getting the harvest in on time in case the rain comes.'

'Yes, but they *would* be worrying at this time of year, what with the autumn frosts around the corner and the damp mornings with rusts and smuts! Is there more?'

'Yes, there is. The farmers are worried about something else and so too is anyone who keeps animals. Maybe the Mums and Dads are a little worried also.'

'I think I know what you mean; who is it?'

'We don't like to say, but quite a few people seem to have booked into local guest houses and hotels; maybe they will have had something to do with it. There are also some big cars around these days, large black executive saloons, not the kind of battered-up estate cars that country folk go hare coursing in. And I don't think they go horse racing or shooting clay pigeons, either.'

'Outsiders, then?'

'Yes, I think they are, but because they all come together, they must be coming down by invitation, so I guess they must be visiting somebody local.'

'How long has this been going on?'

'Certainly for more than a year, but I would also say, probably less than two.'

'People come and go, but is there anyone prominent in the area; perhaps someone who arrived about eighteen months ago?'

'There is actually a rich businessman who holds large parties about three or four times per year, together with smaller gatherings every month. At other times, we don't see him; I would hardly call him a recluse, but he doesn't visit the local pubs or restaurants and has a man to do everything for him.'

She continued, 'And of course, there's also Wally Bishop and Amelia up the road. They have guests quite often and they eat here regularly. I like them, they're great fun.'

'So where does the rich businessman live?'

'Go out of the village, turn right onto the main road and then go left after three miles. It's actually the long way back to Avebury. He's supposed to be a German chap with a large Victorian villa in substantial grounds, set back behind a few beech trees. There's been a lot of digging around there recently; maybe he's got a goldmine!'

'Thanks, Honey.'

He poured Libby another glass and settled into his chair once more. After they had finished the bottle, he made excuses and walked home in the clear starlight. His breath was a cloud of mist and the temperature was falling towards freezing point. In the morning there would be a hoar frost.

Two days later he paid a return visit to Adam Shilto. Adam answered his knock on the door and ushered him in. Always the excellent host, he ushered forth coffee and jam doughnuts, which had become traditional at their meetings. Dood liked Shilto and found him a pleasant and amiable companion. Shilto, a tall, grey-haired man with a very pleasant demeanour, looked grave when Dodd recounted his observations.

'Adam, you are quite right, there is some nastiness afoot and everyone seems to know about it: a rumour here and another there. There was a nasty bit of desecration at Pete Rodgers' place recently and closer, there has been some sheep-stealing and blood-letting. But the interesting thing is that someone may be leaking a few bits and pieces of cock-and-bull to scare us away.'

'Yes, I heard about poor old Pete Rodgers. He was quite upset when I spoke to him.'

'He'll be alright. I mean to drop in at some point.'

Dood continued, 'But it's important to distinguish all that from the usual stuff. A bit of hemlock and a few sprigs of yew are quite the usual thing around here, but local folk are against any desecration; they seem to know that something is going on. I think it was local people who painted up the Watcher on the downs. If it was, I think they were trying to warn any outsiders of local practices which are as old, or even older than those which have recently appeared.'

'As old, or older than what practices, Callum?'

'Everything suggests that there is a big and nasty group devoted to Black Magic, working locally as you supposed. They probably meet by those old stones downhill from the dewponds on dark nights. No, they are not like a bunch of teenagers leaving litter everywhere they go; if true, they are discreet and clear up well. Nobody has actually seen them when they are doing it, but old Don Regan is on the downs all the time and I believe he knows what's going on.'

He continued, 'You know those old stones? Their ceremonies need water nearby or they wouldn't work. But, I don't think that stories about a big cat loose in the wood are true; *that* may have been put about to scare people away from the area. Cats hunt at night and any scare stories about howling and shrieking would keep people indoors. But besides the blood we know about, we seem to be losing some farm animals and there is some braiding and maiming of horses. Can you tell me, is that where you found the blood which the police were interested in?'

'No. The human blood was nearer to Avebury.'

'But not far away then.'

'I guess not.'

'Mind you, Regan thinks there may be further activities at a Neolithic barrow up the ley line, further north, about two or three miles from the dewpond.'

'You mean two different groups of people?'

'He seems to think so. But it also strikes me that their activities are quite different, even accounting for my own very limited observations.'

'Why do you say that?

'I believe in my own dowsing. Call it pagan, and magical it may be, but I think it is actually quite scientific; a natural phenomenon maybe. Anyway, it usually works and doesn't tell any untruths.'

'So what did it tell you? I mean can you understand all that stuff?'

'I think I can. A pendulum doesn't exactly give long and stylish sentence construction, and some say it is similar to the Ouija board and should be avoided in case it presents a pathway to an evil spirit, but I have found it useful, albeit with certain safeguards. When I tried it the other day, the results were quite clear.'

'What kind of safeguards?'

'You need to be careful whom you speak to and also exactly what you ask.'

'So these replies to your questions, what exactly did they mean?'

'Having considered my notes and thought a little, I came up with what I think are reasonable translations. I had to consider Welsh, Breton and Cornish words in making reconstructions of the former Celtic tongue of this area, but that hasn't been too difficult; I think it was probably only a dialect continuum. And after all, I asked the questions myself and therefore have a good idea of the context.'

Shilto listened patiently.

'First, I tried it up by the large barrow. There, it seemed to work very well. Of the answers, I think that *drouis* is simply the word 'druid' in the former Celtic tongue and would confirm them as the makers of that large burial (or ceremonial) mound.'

'*Ea* is yes, as old Don Regan still says and would confirm that bones are buried there, but I must admit I have no idea who their original owner was. I also asked whether they have been disturbed recently and the reply, '*serri*' I believe, means 'angry.' Curiously, I also asked what lies below and the answer, '*yet,*' means a portal or gateway. The bit that I didn't understand was the proper noun *Athulfus* when I asked why it was angry.'

'What on earth is Athulfus?'

'I think it must be the name Adolf, but probably of a form used about a thousand years later when they finally met the local

Anglo-Saxons who said 'Athulf.' If so, it might suggest that the entity was describing a more modern experience. It also seemed to be clear that it has followers, even today; but I already knew that.'

'Good Lord. So what happened when you took your pendulum three miles to the south, down by the standing stones?'

'My questions established that there is a watcher present, a spirit entity or warden, but the stones do not seem to have been used for evil purposes because *na fella* is simply 'no more.' However, somebody is planning to use them in the near future or at least has his mind on them. I think that *aure pal* is the old Celtic for 'golden ball.' A similar construction might be seen in Latin, where aureum pila could also mean golden ball. In the local Celtic tongue, the word pel or pal meant ball, but what the significance is, I have no idea.'

'To summarise, I think we still have some traditional pagan practices on the downs, probably druidic, and based on the local Celtic and Anglo-Saxon fusion of cultures, with herb lore, celebrations of nature at certain times of year and mixed Celtic and Germanic phrases, inter-twined and fused into one after all this time. But those answers seem to have an element of anger or worry in them and local people seem to be worried too. They seem to be worried by the activities of a black magic circle, doing Lord knows what, and run by people with money who have moved into the area quite recently. Perhaps they are preparing to do something quite nasty in our neighbourhood.'

'So who are these bad guys?'

'Their names are only conjecture, but the locals do seem to have a few ideas about them and their attitude is quite hostile.'

'Well who are the druids then? Would you regard them as good, or the lesser of two evils?'

'I do not think that paganism is necessarily evil. I think we have to live with the local druidic culture of nature worship. Our own churches are built near, or even over some of theirs and some folk go to both. In the extreme, they worship only nature, sunlight and elementary earthly forces. By comparison, those Devil worshippers are deadly to the living soul and are out to cause human misery for its own sake.'

'So what do we do next?'

'We should go out and look one night when the dates are auspicious. Maybe we could get old Don to telephone us when he hears something.'

'Yes, perhaps we should. Don't forget that All Souls Eve is only a week way. That's a big time for those guys and they would never pass up on some sort of mischief. Perhaps we should think about going out before the big night just to look around.'

'I think you are right.'

Chapter Three

Parties Here, There and Everywhere.

'Emily, would you like to come to a party with me and Freya?' Kayla Raddle said earnestly. 'There are a few of us going along. I managed to get an invitation from a friend of mine, you may know her name, Carol Black.'

Emily replied, 'Is she that tallish girl with short and dark hair? There was a barbecue at somebody's house last year, a sort of fancy dress party. I think I saw her there.'

'Yes, that sounds like her. She invited me and told me to bring a bottle of anything as long as it wasn't Samos. This time, there are supposed to be one or two magicians performing. I thought it might be rather a laugh.'

'Yes, I think I will go. Who else is going and when is it?'

'It's on Saturday and there will be the three of us. Freya Sampson said she would like to go too. We could meet you somewhere, or pick you up maybe?'

'Well I planned to get my hair done in the afternoon, but after that, I'm free from about four. I could go home, get changed and then…'

'We could pick you up at about seven?'

'That would be fantastic, thank you, Kayla.'

'By the way, where is it?'

'I could take you there straight away, but right now I can't remember the name of the street. I wrote it down though. It's just outside Marlborough on the Hungerford road. And by the way, don't eat anything beforehand; Carol and friends are supposed to be pretty generous at the table.'

'Has Freya met them before?'

'I don't think so, but I know Carol reasonably well. Decent sort, though can be a bit fierce at times.'

Emily, Freya and Kayla were three young women, all very pleasant, each fun-loving and all part of a social circle of like-minded party-goers. They were diverse in personality and appearance; Emily Robertson was a tall, willowy girl with long blonde hair, very clever and a student; Kayla, working as a legal executive for a local solicitor, a bubbly brunette with ringlets of curly hair falling onto her shoulders and a ready laugh; Freya an independent-minded, petite girl with fair hair gathered up; she played the violin for a local orchestra and had a very pleasant manner which belied a determination to get her own way when the situation arose. As with many similar friendships, they had first become acquainted when they were all lodgers in the same house together. Now, a year or two later and leading more diverse lives, they had remained in touch.

That Saturday, Kayla Raddle called for Freya Sampson at her place in Calne. She beeped the horn outside and a minute later, Freya came out. She walked very quickly, a gait which suggested a certain athleticism; in fact she swam regularly, ran short and intermediate distances and was very quick over them.

'Hello Kayla,' she said, with a note of gaiety in her voice. 'I'm really looking forward to going out to see a few people. I seem to be so busy these days.'

'Emily said she would come too and she isn't too much out of the way. We can be there in half an hour and the party is only another fifteen minutes out of town.'

'What kind of house is it?'

'Carol's place? Oh well, it is a smallish cottage off the road to Hungerford. We drive along a road to the right and it's a little way down there among the trees. I suppose it must have been a farm worker's cottage a hundred and fifty years ago. It's very pretty, one of those flint-knapped cottages which are quite common in the area. Carol has a large garden and she works out with the spade; she does all her own vegetables and that kind of thing.'

'So what's this party going to be like?'

'Well, Carol has her own circle of course. She seems to throw extensive parties quite regularly and new people are often invited to them. Anyone would think that she's trying to recruit them. She reads a lot and quite often travels away, but her social life does seem to be quite interesting. When I spoke to her about tonight, she said that there might be some kind of magic show, just to spice things up a bit.'

They drove on. Kayla was a careful driver, but the roads were clear and they reached Emily's place in time to see her combing her long blond hair at the window. Emily was just back from the hairdresser, had dressed early for the party and came out shortly, clutching a bottle of wine. She threw her coat into the back of the car, piled in after it and cradled the wine on her lap. Together, they made off along the Hungerford Road and after a while, Emily said, 'Do I take it that we shall be inside for most of the evening?'

'I would guess so, but you can nip out to get your coat if it gets too cold; just ask for the key. But all of us have brought coats along and anyway, there's nothing like a bit of wine to get the circulation going.'

'True,' said Freya. 'Is that the turning?'

'Yes, I think we should turn right here. My, it really is a narrow road, but I like the trees, they make the place look very attractive. Is this a part of the forest, do you think?'

'Yes,' Emily replied, 'there are trees all the way from here to Marlborough. Some of them are very old and there are some great walks there. We must be right on the edge of the Savernake Forest, or perhaps, actually still in it.'

'Savernake,' said Freya, 'where does that name come from, I wonder?'

'Oh,' said Emily, 'that comes from the name of the River Severn, together with the oak trees in the forest.'

'Why,' said Freya, 'are they famous?'

'Yes indeed; some of them have names of their own. The Big Belly Oak is well known in the area; I know people who make a point of waving to it as they pass by. I did hear that 80% of the oldest oaks in Europe are here in the Savernake. Whether true or not, Wiltshire is full of lovely old trees and they seem to have their own personalities as well as names; the King of Limbs, Old Paunchy and the Saddle Oak. And the place is supposed to be haunted as well.'

Kayla said, 'By whom?'

'I am happy to say I've never met her, but Savernake Forest is said to have a headless rider. Long ago, she was a huntswoman following a royal party, but she was decapitated on a branch when her horse ran off into the undergrowth. The forest was a private estate in those days and I believe, still is. At certain times, you can still hear a thundering of horses' hooves along a 'gallop,' which is an avenue of trees. The poor soul returns from time to time and rides a ghostly white horse.'

Kayla replied, 'Ah, this must be it; not the headless woman, I mean Carol Black's house. Good, I can park on the grass verge opposite.'

'Oh hello, Carol.'

'Come in. What would you like to drink?'

'Something with a bit of fizz, please!'

Emily soon said, 'Carol, any guys here?'

'Yes, meet Richard Bascher whom we call Dick or, er, would you prefer to meet Sieghard Trapper? Sieghard is the tall guy over there. He is one of Johan Pal's friends; I may have mentioned *him* before.'

'I would like to, but let me circulate first.'

'Oh yes, I understand, perhaps some other time.'

Emily, Kayla and Freya began to circulate among the guests. Soon, they found that, together, they were chatting to Sieghard

Trapper, who said, 'Ah, meet my friends, this is Macario Vespa and over here, Meinhard Koch. We have quite a few Germans with us, don't we Meinhard? But funnily enough, Macario breaks the mould because he is Italian.'

'Ja, ich kam aus Deutschland erst letzte woche. Wer sind diese schönen mädchen?'

'Meinhard prefers to speak in German until he gets to know someone. And that can make the whole process rather difficult; it makes him seem a bit shy, which rather defeats the object!'

'Is he ever successful?'

'Ah, well maybe you had better ask him. I suppose he manages to change into the local tongue as he loosens up.'

Oh, and Meinhard, these are Emily, Kayla and Freya, girls about town.'

'Bitte schon.'

Kayla said, 'We were just saying that there is supposed to be a headless lady who rides through the forest from time to time.'

'Ach so,' said Meinhard Koch, 'Ve haf such ghosts in Deutschland also. Maybe you would like to see her, ja?'

'Not really,' said Freya. 'And anyway, one could probably walk about Savernake Forest for hours or even days and never see anything.'

Sieghard Trapper said, 'You would need to go at an auspicious time such as on an anniversary perhaps. Or you could go with people who have a connection with her; some kind of similarity, a similar appearance maybe.'

'But even then, a sighting would be unpredictable?'

'Certainly, you could never tell. But Johan Pal could do something to improve matters, I am quite sure.'

'Who is this Mr Pal?' asked Emily.

'Oh, Pal is a clever amateur magician and a minor clairvoyant. He looks into his crystal ball and that kind of thing. He calls it his 'golden ball,' but I don't know why, it's only made of glass. Perhaps he can divine the presence of wealth with it.'

'It sounds, um... so you would expect *him* to be sure of seeing something in the woods?'

‘As sure as anyone could possibly be, which means I’m still not completely sure. Honestly, you never can tell.’

He continued, ‘But, enough of this, he may turn up later. Bring your drinks over and let us see some magic.’

The girls circulated, drinks in hand, but were aware that they continued to be discussed by Meinhard Koch, Sieghard Trapper and the rather quiet individual, Macario Vespa.

Meanwhile, Kayla Raddle continued to chat to Carol Black. She said, ‘There seems to be a preponderance of people from Germany; is that so, or are there lots of local people expected too?’

‘Oh yes, I hold these parties for Johan Pal and his friends. Johan is German, or at least, a second-generation naturalised Briton. His family came from Germany after the war and he has quite a few friends of similar extraction as you would expect. We like to entertain each other and to recruit new people to our circle: people of a like-minded disposition. But I would certainly expect some local people too.’

‘What do you mean by ‘like-minded?’

‘Well, perhaps with a spirit of adventure. An interest in Wellbeing or Yoga is the usual start these days. Then a little fortune-telling or minor magic; nothing serious, just a little bit of fun.’

Freya Sampson joined them. Carol Black noted how pretty she was and how she was dressed to her best advantage. She continued, ‘So, we get together about once per month for a party, and we start with a harmless séance or play about with a few playing cards. This month it is my turn, but we are all very friendly and lots of new people like to join us. Next month we will go to somebody else, maybe Macario Vespa; he is always game for a laugh although a bit stingy with the food. Between us, you might need to watch him a bit and the food and drink is always better over at Sieghard’s place. But if you have any trouble with him, just tell old Vespa to get on his scooter!’

'Is he related to the famous Italian manufacturer of Vespa scooters?'

'Possibly only distantly; otherwise he probably wouldn't live over here!'

'Can we see Johan Pal use a crystal ball? '

'I expect so, but he telephoned to say he would be late. Come through to the parlour! We can see a clairvoyant in action and we can take part, although not to the same extent as a practised medium.'

The girls followed Carol Black and were ushered to an oaken parlour table, large enough to seat ten people around its circumference.

Carol sat down and said, 'My first suggestion is that we might practise some harmless way of becoming more relaxed.' She continued, 'Please make yourselves comfortable and try to release all tension from your body. I find that the best method is to choose a part of the body, an arm perhaps and to consciously relax that, followed by a further choice and so on. Try to control the rate at which you breathe so that it is at first constant and of a speed which you then regulate to make slower. Think of an attractive vista, a woodland scene or something pastoral, cows in a pasture, perhaps and then concentrate your mind on your own wellbeing. I do not use that word frivolously. Ask yourself what simple change to your behaviour might improve your life. Write it down on some paper, or you may prefer to draw a picture of it. Here are some pencils.'

She continued, 'Now test your intuition, a step which is often more natural for women. Consider four possible intuitive answers to a question about which you have had past foreboding. Write the answers down on four scraps of paper and turn them over, so they are face-down on the table. Yes, that's good. Now shuffle the papers around, face down, and arrange them in a row in front of you. Allow your hand to pass over them at a distance of about an inch, although do not allow yourself to touch. No, don't stop, pass your hand over several times and reflect on them as you do. You may find that you are drawn to touch one of the papers only, but if not, carry on a bit longer. Turn that answer over; you should find your chosen paper will carry the most meaningful solution to your question.'

Freya said, 'Do you need to do this every time?'

'No. With experience, a clairvoyant will be able to relax immediately and probably throw herself into a trance straight away. This is for the novice.'

Later, the girls looked up, smiled and compared notes. 'Any success?' said Emily.

'Oh yes, it made quite a lot of sense to me,' replied Freya. 'But can we see something a bit more exciting?'

'Yes, but you may not like it. Only the last time we met here, I invited some new friends and the medium managed to scare them off.'

Kayla said, 'How?'

'She managed to get in touch with the spirit of a child who was murdered in this neighbourhood about one hundred years ago. The case was well-known; the body of a child was found in a well on a disused farm and it transpired that his mother had lodged the child with an aunt nearby, while she worked away in London. The boy disappeared, but the aunt denied any knowledge of the lodgement. The mother was then accused of murder and found guilty, but following a petition from the general public, was sentenced to life imprisonment rather than hanging. The case was known as the Crabtree Cottages murder, after the address of the aunt, who lived here in the forest.'

'And the child?'

'The medium was able to convey feelings of forgiveness.'

'Serious stuff, but surely, not all séances are like that?'

'True. That was a very sad case, but it actually had a positive end to it, as we found out. Would a case like that deter you?'

Emily replied, 'Yes, I think it probably would.'

'Then perhaps we should stick to something simpler. What about the Ouija board?'

'I don't know much about it.'

'Then perhaps we could start there.'

After about an hour with the Ouija board, during which there were various positive messages from beyond, the meeting broke up. They had received assertions of future fortune with regard to members of the opposite sex, together with conveyances of news from alleged relatives: grandmothers of apple-cheeked former appearance; distinguished and moustachioed former great uncles. Soon, they quit and seemed satisfied with their experience.

'I suppose that wasn't too bad,' said Freya. 'I had half-expected to see demons and wizards roaming around. That stuff was tame enough not to put me off a repeat performance.'

'Good,' said Carol Black. 'Then perhaps we can invite you along again?'

'Yes please, and by the way, I'm a bit peckish now. I saw some lovely food in the kitchen and the guys were really tucking in, especially that chap Macario Vespa.'

'Yes,' said Freya, 'and Dick Bascher has been through about four plates already!'

'And,' said Carol Black, 'You must have some of this sweet wine; it is special.'

Later still, there was dancing and the three girls started to feel quite uninhibited; they danced together and the lights were low, but at about one o' clock, they made their excuses and departed. Emily said, 'It's quite a way back to Calne and the boys in blue might catch up with us; not that we have been particularly wicked! But it's not a long way to my place so how would you like to sleep over? Oh, and are you still OK to drive?'

'Oh yes,' said Kayla.

'Yes please!' Kayla and Freya said together.

At Emily's place, safely tucked up in sleeping bags, Freya said, 'I enjoyed Carol's party. She said we should go to Sieghard Trapper's place next month. I said I would let her know, but if we are all free, perhaps we could go together? She did also try to explain why Johan Pal never turned up. He's away on business, but would probably ask friends of Carol to *his* monthly party in two months' time. By then, she said, we might be on the way to becoming initiates into his magic circle.'

Kayla replied, 'Yes, I would like that, it wasn't too scary and we did enjoy ourselves. It wasn't like some parties where everyone stands in the kitchen. Oh, and I did like that sweet wine. It was all kind of heady and made me feel really relaxed. I wanted to dance a lot and I seemed to lose a lot of my inhibitions. It was better than Samos anyway!'

'Emily said, 'Funnily enough, I was going to say exactly the same thing. I seemed to want to lose myself and dance the night away. I even seemed to take a fancy to some of the guys there. I would never have believed it!'

'Let's go to the next one, then!'

*

A few weeks later, Johan Pal spoke to an invitee to his own party. It had been a long summer and a busy one and there was serious work ahead that autumn; but now he meant to enjoy himself as best he could.

'Ah, it is a pleasure to see you, Hedetet.' Pal spoke to a young woman in the fancy dress of an Egyptian Goddess, in the form of a scorpion head-dress and limbs. An ominous-looking sting curved upwards towards her neck, supported by a ribbon in the small of her back. 'Please take some wine and of course, we shall be able to take our fill from the tables as soon as the banquet is brought in. Do I trust that your room is satisfactory?' Pal referred to her hotel room, from which she had arrived by car.

'I am very pleased and grateful for your benefaction, as always, Master. But may I please ask why we are working here tonight, rather than going out to the altar on the downs? Surely it cannot be too cold at this season?'

'I think our wine would have kept us all warm enough to perform well.' Pal smiled a silky smile. 'But there have been one or two spies, maybe police even, looking around by the standing stones and really, that was only a diversion anyway. If we can convince them that a bit of silliness is going on there, then perhaps that will satisfy the one or two interested parties lurking about; they may then ignore us in our greater work here.'

They were joined by a woman dressed as Queen Hell, the old English goddess of the underworld. She carried a staff and her shoulders and breasts were naked. Quite without inhibition, for she wore the mask characteristic of all guests to that party, she joined their conversation. 'Do you think we shall find out much from our medium this evening?'

'That remains to be seen, but of the portents, the sky is clear and there are thirteen of us, so we shall be able to look at the moon, planets and stars accordingly. Our spirit visitor to the medium may still speak to us as we desire.'

'Are there any acolytes and neophytes involved tonight?'

'No, they are present, of course, but they still await the completion of their instruction and cannot receive their new Satanic baptism until All Soul's Eve, a full seven days away. You will know some of them by name but as you are aware, we do not use their newly-baptised name until they have been initiated. For now, they must remain the beautiful Freya Sampson, et al; together with Mr Dick Bascher who is slightly less so. I am concerned by Mr Bascher however. He seems rather repulsive to women and I am not sure whether any of them will volunteer to do what must be done during his ceremony of baptism. I have heard it said that he has a breath that would flatten an ox at twenty paces; I hope that this is not some curse by a former enemy.'

Pal continued, 'Now I have tonight made an arrangement for some entrails and a few other bits and pieces to be found by the altar on the hill. No doubt the uninvited will invite themselves there, but they will return disappointed. We are therefore freer to enjoy ourselves here. How long is it before the spirits can fly?'

'Three hours, Master.'

'Yes, three hours. Now, let us eat and drink our fill. Later we may find out much.'

Later, Pal formed a ring of eleven of his assistants, who knelt on a hard floor to make a circle. Contained within were the twelfth and thirteenth members of the circle, he himself and a keen accessory to the elementary hypnosis which he employed to raise his assistant into a trance. Profanities were offered to their master and then he instructed her to look upon the astral for messages brought from beyond.

She closed her eyes and spoke and although it was not she herself who did so, they learned much from their spirit visitor about valuable new artefacts in the neighbourhood, their potential for very considerable evil and whereabouts they lay. For Pal, this was a very minor magic, but he now knew enough about the placement of a very valuable hidden artefact to begin planning for its abstraction. In fact, he had first sensed the Magdeburg Relic nearby without being told of its nature, and its final revealing delighted him far more than he had supposed it would.

Following this episode, Pal made use of further invocations and sacrifices and as their meeting progressed, he spoke as if in celebration of what he had learned. 'Who would like to fly tonight?'

Several of his assistants spoke in unison, 'We would, Master.'

'Here is my flying salve. You must rub it onto your skin and do not neglect those places where absorption may be fast, such as thighs and chest. Do not swallow it, for failure to regard my instructions may lead to death.' You may sit astride a besom, Miss Raddle, but stay away from the burning coals.'

The young woman, Freya Sampson now asked, 'Master, we are new to your society; what is in it that will make me fly?'

'Ah, Miss Sampson, I am pleased to hear that you are interested in natural philosophy or as we call it today, natural science. My salve is made from the fat of a sucking calf and it contains an infusion of hemlock, deadly nightshade, wolfsbane and henbane. The active ingredients are the alkaloids atropine, hyoscyamine and scopolamine. They are absorbed slowly, but you will feel the effects shortly and they will then make you fly until dawn. Rub the salve on your chest. Here, Mr Bascher may offer to do it for you. And you, Miss Robertson, I must speak to you further please, over here.'

'Miss Robertson your appearance is not wholly in keeping with our magic circle. This may be a relatively minor meeting, with the full Black Mass on the 31st, but your beautiful blonde hair is out of place here and may actually harm our psychic vibrations. Please shake it out into a haphazard mass.'

He continued, 'Yes, that's it.'

'But Master!'

'Now dip the whole into this basin of warm blackened Bear's Grease and tallow, withdraw your hair and allow it to cool so that your hair sets into a black frizzled clump. The colour and stiffness are more in keeping for you as an acolyte and will improve your psychic receptiveness. Yes, that's better.'

'But Master!'

'Do not concern yourself. Bear's Grease used to be a well-known prevention for hair loss; since bears are very hairy, the grease of that animal was considered to promote hair growth.'

'Bear's Grease, Master?'

'Yes, it is very good. That excellent remedy is still made from the fat of the brown bear and marrow of the bull. My own is the real pomade of bear, not the *ersatz* remedy of pork fat. It is quite pleasant, with the essences of lavender and rose, together with a green dye. To this pomade I have added black tallow only.'

'Can the colour be removed, Master?'

'Certainly, you will find that the smell of bear may last for a day or so, but the oil will wash out quite quickly after we have finished.'

'Oh, and Miss Robertson, I would like you to apply for the job of housekeeper at Mr and Mrs Bishops' home. They have advertised for a domestic help and cook and you have very many credentials in that regard. This will give you access to their home while they are away and may give us an advantage in acquiring the relics that we need and which we now know to be hidden there. You will, of course, use your many charms to help with that goal. If you get the opportunity, you must remove the artefact and bring it to me. If you are unable to do so, then I will ask you to place a philtre in their food and drink to provide you with that freedom.'

*

Callum Dood and Adam Shilto met at Dood's place. Both wore jeans and each had a thick coat on, for it could become cold on starry nights at the end of September. Dood, however, also carried a small rucksack with a few odds and ends within, and was confident that it would improve their safety and comfort. He also filled a small flask with brandy just before leaving and locked the door on the way out; his watch indicated that it was ten pm. Closing his front door, the two retraced the former's earlier excursion of a few days before and rose steadily through the village with its sweet gardens and hedgerows, before ascending onto the low chalk downs where the last vestige of the autumn sun had radiated into space and the ground was now cold to the point of freezing.

After some initial doubt as to their direction, they found their eyes were accustomed to starlight and they were able to pick out low hills, rocks and other larger features of the landscape. It was easy to follow Dood's earlier path to the barrows where they observed complete silence and an eerie stillness; eerie as though they were being overlooked or watched with a small degree of hostility. Walking further, they continued to the long barrow which they found cold, damp and chill, with a presence as though it contained the memory of those long dead, and buried within. With a moderate voice, Dood said, 'This way' and changed direction by about ten degrees in order to attend the point of the compass at which the dewponds and stones lay.

As they approached, he called a halt at about a half-mile from the standing stones which now loomed in the distance; they were not great as are those of Avebury or Stonehenge and had only the apparent height of a man. Sitting, he opened his bag and withdrew a set of infrared binoculars, which the two of them were pleased to share. Scanning the horizon, they concentrated their attention on spaces between the stones and around them and behind. They saw no artificial light, nor was there any movement, but they prepared to verify that conclusion at intervals, withdrew groundsheets and settled to watch. After their walk of about six miles, Shilto's wristwatch indicated that it was eleven forty-five.

Neither was able to see any further incursion and by twelve thirty, they were becoming cold, stiff and tired. Shilto suggested that they might move closer and with regard to the complete silence observed by them, together with the apparently uninhabited aspect of the circle of stones, they saw no further need for staying hidden.

Dood mused for a while and said, 'I would like to take a look at the wood over there. It means a short walk of perhaps another mile, but it is not uphill and while we are here, I believe we should see it.'

As they approached the wood, they were conscious of the loneliness of the place and each was glad of the companionship of the other. They were also pleased to have their torches, which they now made ready as they approached the barrier of the outermost trees.

The leaf canopy was high, but it was an effective barrier to moonlight and the wood was dark at ground level. Nearby, beech trees were in fact quite rare on the downs, finding it difficult to become established on the chalk soil. Nevertheless, eventually having done so, they were able to colonise a site more fully, giving a lofty canopy that would permit a passage through it while ensuring that the ground below received little light. Accordingly, neither man had any difficulty in making progress inward, but neither skyline nor outlines of tree trunks could be seen and at length, they were part of the way towards the middle of the wood and paused.

Standing, they listened; un-named animals rustled hither and thither and moss, sticks and last year's beech mast crackled underfoot as they moved. In the stillness, all noise seemed to be amplified rather than dissipated by the uprights and trunks of trees.

Suddenly, a loud screech rent the air; far louder and more alarming than any screech-owl could have made. As though amplified, it sounded like a large animal in pain, but faded to a throaty growl which could only have been made by a cat. Instinctively, Dood grasped Shilto's arm and they both stood quavering. Nevertheless, they recovered their reserve very quickly, and Shilto said, 'Ugh, get off me, man,' and shone his torch around in a wide arc.

Dood made a complimentary arc with his own torch, but nothing was seen. They now moved in opposite directions, in as ordered a manner as was possible in the dark and with the obstructions there. They ranged over much of the middle of the wood and noted the falling landscape as though it contained a slight depression in the middle.

Shilto arrived at the dead centre and stopped still to listen. At first, he heard little, but soon accustomed to the quiet of that position, was able to hear a very faint mechanical whirring, rather like a purr. Immediately, he flattened himself against a tree, fearing that it was the big cat in question, but a clicking soon followed as though some electrical device was working only intermittently. He called to Dood over a distance of some fifty yards.

Dood held his torch low while Shilto checked the damp chalky surface. They observed signs of disturbance low upon the soil, probably made recently. Tracing forwards, Dood reached a small pile of leaves and stones which he kicked with his foot. A group of wires was revealed immediately and with it, a transparent polypropylene box, a solid-state storage device, power pack, further wires and loudspeaker. The power pack was a motorbike battery, enough for at least forty-eight hours and perhaps very much more. Shilto examined the device closely before replacing it as before.

Dood said, 'Clever. See how it powers up the loudspeaker only intermittently.'

Shilto replied, 'We've been had. This is a put-up job. Let me take a few photographs with my mobile and then I think we should leave.'

They tramped back through the darkness with faces set against the cold and feelings of usury. However on the way back, Shilto suggested a short detour to the standing stones on the grounds that, 'Maybe something has been there while we were away.' Dood, ever patient, agreed.

'My Lord,' he said. A sheep's head lay on the altar and a trail of blood was soaking into the ground. Shilto took another photograph from a few feet away.

'No, leave it,' he said. Then, turning their backs on the scene, they walked home.

Two hours later, and after a slower walk than that which had brought them out, they reached Dood's place and within another ten minutes were in armchairs, with a bottle of brandy between them. By then it was three-thirty a.m. and they slept there until eight. Dood rose first and made a large breakfast of bacon, fried eggs, toast and coffee.

As they ate, he said, 'That was a diversion but it wasn't a joke by any means. Someone wanted us to keep our sights on the stones, rather than elsewhere. They tried to scare us just enough with those shrieks to arouse our curiosity and that rumour about a big cat was designed to keep our attention there, not scare us away.'

'Yes I think you're right. And the sheep's head on the stones was probably there for our benefit too. It was clever about the loudspeaker in the wood, though. I don't think we were actually expected to find it and I am glad we left it there. If any of those bits and pieces were removed, the owners would know we are on to them.'

'The question is: what now?'

'Maybe we could find out a bit more about this businessman who holds the parties? I expect he held one last night while we were tramping around.'

★

Wally Bishop's house, perhaps uncharacteristically for Peckling, was made from red brick rather than from the local stone, but it had aged to a soft hue and the rain had made its mark on the outside by means of a matt finish and by the growth of lichen in gutters and downpipes. Wisteria grew over the brickwork but with no suggestion of chaos, and the brickwork had recently been repointed. From the size of the property and its general state of repair, it was clear that it was owned by a person of reasonable prosperity if not considerable wealth.

The rear of the house was interesting. It had a large garden set in a rather formal style instead of the more usual rambling cottage garden found with other homes nearby. There were symmetrical flowerbeds and in the middle, an ornate water feature in the shape of a star, made from a stream of moving water which entered the garden from an underground aquifer and by following channels made from brick. In order to reach a central island, one had to cross moving water by jumping over, but visitors were usually delighted to do so and water continued to flow from the aquifer even in the hottest summer, before the feature emptied into a ditch next to the road outside.

Any guest to the house would have noted the general paraphernalia of the art and antiques dealer. A few objects were placed in downstairs rooms to show them, but they came and went quite quickly and it was as though there was little distinction between home and art gallery; the incumbent clearly liked to enjoy an artefact for a time, before it was passed on. Particularly, one larger room contained a clatter of clocks and automata, together with devices which claimed to offer perpetual motion. It was quite beside the point whether they kept true time or had overcome friction; they were pretty, made a nice noise and were valuable.

In a side room there was also a substantial collection of books. Much of it was concerned with antiques and art collecting, but it also contained reference works on the subject of the rare books themselves. Bishop had many modern first editions and many of them were signed. Although his collection went back to university days it was through these interests that he had kept in touch with Creighton and Ivy Brakespeare and quite often sought their advice or placed some major work in their sale.

It was a Saturday and Wally Bishop bustled about. He was a broad and rather powerful man in late middle age, with grey hair and with a figure trim enough to suggest he was little beset by the pitfalls of indulgence. Athletic and mobile, he was actually a quiet man, little disposed towards giving much away, although confident and purposeful when doing so. At the top of his profession, his business had made him not only wealthy, but had given him that particular opportunity afforded to the art dealer of having large numbers of interesting artefacts pass across his desk. With stock littering the house at all times, he was able to appreciate the scarce and beautiful without needing to deplete his business.

That day, Wally and Amelia Bishop expected four friends for the weekend. They were two married couples and he expected their party of six to be great fun; in particular Amelia, his wife, was an excellent hostess and in her element thus. Now she returned from a shopping trip to Devizes and breezed in with that cheerful way she had.

'Wally,' she said. 'Please say we have enough drink in the place! I know about dinner and breakfast; Creighton and Ivy always have huge appetites, bless them, and the other two aren't far behind, but have we anything interesting to wash it all down? And by the way, how long have you been back?'

'About an hour. Please don't say we might be short! How was it in town?'

'Busy and quite difficult to park, but I managed to get hold of most of what we need. On the drinks side, I was thinking of something a bit different for tonight. How about some of that nice English bubbly which everyone raves about? You know the stuff; the Champagne people are buying up English vineyards because of it.'

'Well in that case, we *are* short, but I know they do it in Calne. I'll pop over in twenty minutes.'

Bishop rattled a box and packet of papers, placed them in his desk and closed it. He would not normally have done so with the small items of professional or academic interest which he had handled that day, but these, a packet of papers which accompanied a box about 30 inches by 12, were owned by a contact and said to be of considerable interest. He had been asked to study their contents by Harry Devine, a contact in the antiques trade, who, having visited Moscow the month before, had returned with a few odds and ends and in a certain state of excitement. No consideration had changed hands; they shared a long-standing friendship and respect for each other's business reputation. They had agreed only that Bishop would keep the artefacts for one month and would prepare a short report at the end of that time. This would count towards the provenance of the piece to any potential buyer, although Bishop would be free to make an offer for it himself if he wished. Now, since elementary security was required, Bishop locked his desk, into the longest drawer of which the collection just fitted.

He drove to Calne and in a wine merchant, bought two dozen bottles of bubbly from a renowned vineyard at West Chiltington in Sussex. Within an hour he was back and picked up a note which Amelia had left. She had popped out for a bit but would be back soon.

He heard a car start outside and assumed that she might just be leaving, but through a window was just in time to see a large black car disappear in the direction of the main road. It was not Amelia's car and he thought little of it, but he heard a rustle and turned again to the room.

Amelia had in fact returned. 'Hello,' she said, 'I've just been out for a few odds and ends. We need to keep this closed.' She referred to the back door.

'I thought it was!'

He returned to his desk, a position which gave him a very good view of his books in a bookcase opposite. None were missing, but the silhouette, which he knew well, was different. He looked at them more closely and without particular concern, to see that some smaller books, which afforded spaces behind them, now lay in different places. It might be that they had been tidied or dusted and he thought it unworthy of further comment. Without any real urgency he turned to his desk and opened it to check that the packet of papers and box were undisturbed.

Both were present, but the edge of the drawer which contained them was marked with abrasions on the edge of the wood. Made with a set square, it had formerly been very straight, but was now rough and irregular and lighter wood showed through the polish.

He said, 'Amelia, come and see. Did I do this? I locked these packages away only about an hour ago and I can't remember seeing these marks. No, here on the edge.'

Amelia said, 'It looks as though we may have had a visitor. Did you leave anything valuable inside, money perhaps? I think you got back before the desk was opened anyway.'

'No money, only that package which Harry asked me to work on. I don't even know what it contains yet. Maybe something else is missing? I can't imagine any casual thief leaving *that'* – he pointed at a full bottle of Scotch whisky only an arm's length away – 'so if there was anyone here, he was probably serious.'

'I agree. There's nothing casual about it. Has anything else gone, credit cards or cash, watches, notes or antiques?'

'I don't know, not from here anyway, but let's look around. Are we actually sure that we have had someone in? We need to find out first, before doing anything.'

They spent twenty minutes going through each room.

'There's nothing disturbed upstairs and nothing at all missing.'

Only downstairs did they have the feeling of any disturbance. Even then, their feelings arose only from the rearrangement of books in the bookcase, slight crush-marks to the edge of the drawer and the position of an upright chair nearby, which had been moved as though to approach the desk. It was all very little.

'There was a large Mercedes outside. Maybe he saw me coming?'

'Or perhaps somebody just walked in and out by mistake?'

'Yes, but what about the marks on the desk?'

'Are you sure about them? Perhaps the bookcase and chair *made* you look for them?'

With nothing gone it was all too little to bother the police with. Their front door *had* been open, or at least unlocked, but nothing had been mislaid or taken. After a while, the topic passed.

Amelia said, 'What time can we expect everybody? Are they coming together?'

'No. Peyton and Zenda stayed overnight at Sandhurst and theirs is an easy road, so they should get here first. Creighton and Ivy are driving down the B4009; I don't think that's a

Roman road and it isn't very straight anyway and has lots of little villages, so I think it will take them a bit longer. Not that they will necessarily start at the same time!'

'Say anything between 5 and 7 for both then?'

Chapter Four

The Magdeburg Relic

In fact, Peyton and Zenda Oakwood arrived only half an hour before Creighton and Ivy Brakespeare. Peyton was a tall, very broad man of military bearing, a career soldier, but unlike some of his contemporaries did not use his army rank of Colonel in his private life. He had brown hair and blue eyes and was good looking and well-dressed off-duty, as he was now. Zenda was similarly brown-haired, a very attractive woman, a careful dresser and with an outgoing, demonstrative personality. She was wealthy, having inherited from her family, but worked nevertheless as a professional sculptor and artist, a trade she had learned in Paris as an art student before meeting Peyton. They had no children, but had an active life of many social contacts within the large circle of armed services couples and the many artisans from Zenda's arena: smiths, wrights and artists; a very diverse bunch. They were very outgoing and were always friendly and very 'easy' with people.

Wally and Amelia looked forward to their company that weekend and especially the prospect of a six-man dinner party that evening. They had known each other since University days and despite quite different paths since then, knew they would instantly pick up their common thread.

The four of them welcomed Creighton and Ivy as they arrived from Cambridge. Their journey, with stops, had taken a little over five hours. Creighton and Ivy, in their own book business, had known Wally Bishop for many years as both client and friend and saw more of them than Peyton and Zenda because of their professional dealings with him.

All three couples were now in their fifties, but there the similarity ended. Creighton Brakespeare was quiet, studious and modest, but firm and disciplined in business. His activities did not usually overlap with those of Bishop, being restricted to the top-end of the collectible books market, whereas Bishop had far wider interests. On many occasions, both couples had visited Creighton and Ivy in Cambridge, had attended their shop and salerooms and had stayed at their home; likewise, a rota took them to Sandhurst also, and they all took it in turns to travel regularly because they shared many similar interests.

Amelia welcomed them and suggested that they 'Might like to dump their clobber in their bedroom…no, that's Peyton and Zenda's.'

Fifteen minutes later they emerged and Wally Bishop said, 'Choose your chairs and let's all have something to drink.'

Creighton said, 'I like this. What's in it and why does it go cloudy?'

Bishop, a moderate drinker, liked to buy gin from small local distilleries. These, in turn, were buyers of specialist local produce and so the local economy was supported. He replied, 'Well, I don't think they cold-filter it, so it leaves most of the botanicals in for us to taste. Some say that if the gin goes cloudy when you add tonic water, then it has more botanicals so it tastes better. Here, try this one; it contains juniper, lavender, citrus and a few other things too. There are thirteen botanicals in all, which makes it is very complex in taste.'

'A bit like raki then? That stuff goes cloudy too.'

'Yes, but without the anise and maybe more subtle.'

Gradually the talk turned to food. Amelia cooked for enjoyment and tried to use seasonal vegetables and herbs from her own garden. On this occasion, she had decided on an idea from further afield. Later, they moved to their dining room with a heavy oak refectory table laid for six, and made themselves comfortable.

Bishop said, 'If you need help with anything, just shout. We've got that new girl starting on Tuesday, she's called Emily Robertson. I hope her long blonde hair doesn't get tangled up with the food!'

'Yes, it would be a shame to get it covered with spaghetti sauce when she's so pretty, but until Tuesday, it's just us!'

The meal was of Turkish inspiration and started with a mixed meze of bean salads, olives, fried octopus and a delightful dish called *baklali enginar*, made from artichokes in oil, with lemon juice and fresh parsley. Bishop asked them to try the local Champagne, bought earlier that day. It was excellent, but Peyton, being very familiar with Turkish food, asked for *raki*, which he mixed with water and ice.

Then, they ate boat-shaped unleavened breads called '*pide*,' made by Amelia that evening, filled with a variety of toppings such as cheese and aubergines. They were light and very flavoursome, but they still had room afterwards and Amelia did not rush the courses through.

She knew that none of them were heavy eaters of meat and she had chosen a simple grilled bass to follow. Zenda remarked on the simplicity and flavour of this king of fishes and the others felt the same way. Finally, they were offered *kayisi tatlisi*, a Turkish dish of apricots filled with cream and nuts.

Both host and hostess rose from the table regularly in order to fulfil requests and distribute the various dishes. Conversation was generally light and concerned family and mutual friends. Eventually, Creighton, who loved to discuss his work, started to talk about his negotiations for a particularly attractive set of signed first editions. He then enquired about Bishop's current activities.

'Wally, I suppose you've been busy recently with your *artefacts*...' There was no wit intended, he had simply used the best word to describe the many kinds of cultural and artistic materials which

Bishop dealt in. '…Anything newsworthy? Russian icons, Greek statues, Hebrew scrolls; nothing looted I hope!'

'Well, Creighton, it's rather funny you should say that, because my contact, Harry, asked me to take a look at a collection of odds and ends which came from his trip to Russia. He often sends me things to do the scholarly angle on. Lord knows why, he is pretty competent himself.'

'Any idea of what they are?'

'I heard they are interesting but not that old. There are a few bits which rattle around in a parcel, which I have not yet opened, and a few papers. Some of them are typed and have official-looking signatures, dated 1946, and there are a few more recent papers too: hand-written, which I suppose are added notes. Harry understands both German and Russian and he's familiar with the Cyrillic script also. He is actually very excited by the collection, but I haven't had much time to look at it yet. It only came into my hands about two days ago and I just locked it away until Monday.'

Amelia said, 'There may have been a bit of interest in it from outside. We think we had an intruder today. Nothing was taken, but a few books were shuffled around in the bookcase and Wally thinks someone may have tried to open his desk. Harry's packet was in it. But we aren't sure and could possibly have imagined it.'

Ivy asked, 'Did you disturb them?'

'Yes, I think we did. Wally came back from the wine merchant a few minutes before I came back from somewhere else. It would have been easy to see a car turn onto the main road at the top of the village; the exit is visible from that window.'

'That would have left whoever it was about two minutes to get out, close the door, run to their car and drive off; or at least reach their car and look inconspicuous for a while before leaving.'

'And Wally saw a large black car pull away on his return, so we think the intruder just missed him. Nothing else was taken or disturbed.'

Creighton said, 'Did you report it to the police?'

'No, they don't do much unless something very much bigger has happened and anyway, we don't know for sure.'

'How do you know that your intruder is linked to Harry's parcel?'

'That's the difficulty, how could it be? Any intruder would have needed to know what it is and where placed, together with the fact that it came here. We don't even know anything about it ourselves, except that it came from Harry. And we've said nothing to anybody, so anyone after it would need to have spoken to Harry first. He's in Oxford or perhaps even abroad by now.'

Dinner had moved to the stage of liqueurs. Bishop distributed Cognac, Scotch whisky and a pleasant and unusual banana brandy which the women chose. The six of them, their interest aroused, moved to sofas and comfortable chairs in a part of the much larger room which served as study and library. It also contained Bishop's desk and its contents, which he now unlocked so that all could examine the edge of the drawer.

Peyton Oakwood said, 'It's a shame about the wood here' (he pointed) 'but *that* can be sanded out and polished. Are you quite sure the marks are new?'

'Totally convinced.'

Ivy said, 'Well let's have a look at this important packet anyway, it sounds like the crown jewels!' She was not disposed towards exaggeration, but she spoke for them all and with some enthusiasm, as though while in business she had discovered a desirable first edition.

Bishop removed the package and brought it over to a low table nearby. He picked up the parcel and shook it. Untying some string and tape, he removed two layers of paper to reveal a box. It was made from wood, had hinges at the back and a simple lock at the front. He was unable to open it since it was obviously locked, but he knew that the key was inside the packet of papers, still on his desk. He showed a small degree of caution when he made the box rattle again; a sound which suggested that several objects were free to move around within.

Bishop used the key to unlock the box. He pulled the lid up and they all peered inside in expectation of seeing an object golden or shiny, but were bemused. It contained only a few small bones, almost certainly those of a hand, together with about six or seven larger curved fragments of blackened bone which, if placed together, could give a spherical sector or part of a hollow sphere, probably of a skull. Several fragments had a brown substance, probably glue, applied to their edges as though they had been stuck together. A little, now hard and brittle, had become detached and lay in the bottom. There was also some indication that wire had been used to assemble the various pieces together; tiny holes had been drilled into suitable positions for wire to pass through and marks had been applied to white surfaces with Indian ink. Taken together, it was clear that the fragments were of a skull; but one which had been burned, broken, reassembled and then dismantled into the package.

The box also contained the long bones of an arm: a humerus, radius and ulna; but each was broken into a shorter length. Like the former fragments, each had a small letter or number inked onto a suitable surface in Cyrillic script, together with marks of glue on broken surfaces and small holes where the bones had been wired together. Bishop replaced the lid and looked more closely at the package of papers.

The first sheet bore a diagram of the bones of a human right arm. Each part was labelled with marks which agreed with those on the corresponding long bones themselves. A further sheet of paper bore a diagram of the human right hand. Individual bones in diagrams were again labelled, but a more complicated script of both letters and numbers had been used so that carpal and metacarpals, together with proximal, middle and distal phalanxes of thumb, index, second, third and fourth fingers were labelled ц,д,е,ф,г and 1-5 respectively, giving 25 possible combinations. Once again, each label was exactly as were those on the disassembled bones of the hand. Looking at the diagrams, Oakwood noted that they had been drawn with a degree of artistic interpretation quite unlike the more literal representation found in modern medical and zoological textbooks, a fact which suggested that they were likely to be quite old.

Bishop turned these few papers face-down and their order was naturally retained since they were numbered and bound together through reinforced holes by means of a treasury tag. Legibility was not difficult; they had been printed with a typewriter rather than a modern printer but there was no lack of ink or worn-out lettering. He was, however, unable to understand them because they were in the same Cyrillic script as that used for labelling. The very few letters which resembled those of the Latin alphabet suggested a Slavic language, probably Russian.

He continued to a further sheaf of papers written in longhand. It was an English translation and pages were numbered and stapled at a top corner. The first sheet was in the form of a letter addressed directly to him. It was signed 'H. Devine.'

Bishop said 'This was written by Harry and dated four days ago'. He read it aloud.

Dear Wally,

I would like you to look at this collection of valuables, although 'relics' might be a better word. I bought them on my last trip to Russia, although I did not realise their likely significance until a bit later. I managed to get the box and papers home without difficulty, but they are not really my cup of tea as you can imagine. I like ivory, but wouldn't know what do with this kind of stuff. I hope that you can make some money out of the collection, but I doubt it.

I bought it from an unusual contact, a dealer called Feodore Alkhimovich who used to be a scientific officer in the Red Army in the late forties, later an official in an FSB records office and now long-retired (and frankly, a bit past it too). He seems to have kept a bit of a personal collection of war memorabilia (you know, the usual things like snipers' rifles and uniforms, photographs of assault troops in action and the like). A lot of his stuff was being sold off and that's how I got it.

He's now in a home for the aged, but this chap is more rickety than senile and he was compos mentis enough for me to get a few answers about the box when I visited him. He could speak English and was obviously well-educated. I understood that he had access to it since about 1991 and had worked on it since about 1995 along with his other stuff, but he had known of its existence as an archive for much longer. He managed to keep quiet about it all this time, and any audit would have revealed nothing missing because he replaced original bones with plastercast copies and kept the originals himself. Eventually, it seems to have faded from the general consciousness.

I wrote down a rough translation of the collected papers which accompanied it. I think that my translation is reasonable, but I am not sure of whether I actually believe it. If shown to be true, I would want to get rid of it pretty quickly unless you want it yourself.

Please don't think I am just dumping it on you! It's probably quite interesting at least, so what I would like is for you to check it over. By the way, you can name your price for it, do what you want to it, borrow it or keep it more or less indefinitely! I am leaving the UK shortly and will be going to Poland for a while on business, so we can speak when I get back.

The best, Harry'

Bishop turned to the sheaf of papers in Cyrillic script. At intervals, it contained references to historical sources and there was a small addendum at the end with photocopies of the originals of these. In places, some text was underlined and there were other marks such as comments which had been applied and question marks, lines or arrows. He examined a few lines from the first paragraph, which ran as follows:

Доказательства, что Гитлер проживал в бункере в Берлине с середины января 1945 года является известный и последовательный из многих источников. По 19 апреля фронт обороны на востоке Берлина, наконец, рухнул, оставив только специальную оборонительную позицию. В течение двух дней (21 апреля 1945), он также известно, что армия Советского Союза достигли крайних пределов Берлине и продолжал обстрел и другие операции против войск, защищающих фашистских позиций.

Sighing, he turned the pages quickly and placed them, face-down, on the covering letter.

Turning to the English papers, he noted that they bore the title 'translation' and a date, but no references and none of the sources of the original. And unlike the original, a composite document made of a mix of type-written and hand-written papers, the translation was of a uniform longhand. He read aloud from it and became progressively quieter as he did so.

Evidence that Adolf Hitler had resided at a bunker in Berlin from mid-January 1945 is well-known and the many sources are quite consistent on that fact. By 19th April the defensive front to the east of Berlin had finally collapsed, leaving only ad hoc defensive positions.

Within two days (21st April, 1945), it is known that the army of the Soviet Union had reached the outermost limits of Berlin and had continued shelling and other operations against the Fascist troops defending positions there. The defensive situation declined over the following six days until by 27th April, Berlin was fully encircled and cut off from any contact with possible supporting forces. However other communications were maintained by the defenders there.

As early as 22nd April, Adolf Hitler is known to have consulted with a physician regarding the most effective method for committing suicide. It is understood that he feared capture by the Soviet Army, the likely trial and the public humiliation sure to follow.

By 28th April, communications had further deteriorated and it was clear that Hitler could not evade capture for more than a few days. It is understood that he made preparations for suicide that day, was wed to Eva Braun on 29th and shot himself on 30th April. These facts are well-documented and diverse authorities have written texts which correspond closely.

Following his death, it is known that the bodies of Adolf and Eva Hitler were taken by their supporters to the grounds of the Reich Chancellery, where they were soaked in gasoline and eventually burned. However this was only partly successful and despite further attempts to burn them, the part-burned corpses were eventually covered with earth in a shell crater.

The fact of Adolf Hitler's death was known to the Allied powers by 1st May 1945, but sporadic fighting continued until 8th May. The Soviet Army captured the Reich Chancellery, including Hitler's burial place, on 2nd May and his remains, together with those of Eva Braun were later exhumed, taken to Magdeburg and reburied in an unmarked grave.

For political reasons the Russians refused to confirm the fact of Hitler's death and on some occasions directly refuted it, preferring to accuse the West of protecting him. However they themselves were quite confident of his death, having been able to check that his dental records corresponded with the human remains. The degree of doubt, however, meant that British intelligence further investigated the matter in 1945-1947.

Soviet agents of СМЕРШ are known to have revisited the site of the original crater in 1946 and to have recovered human bones, which were then archived until examined 66 years later with the more advanced biochemical tests then available. They came to the conclusion that these could not have been the remains of Hitler and as such, are distinct and separate from the bones taken to Magdeburg.

Other sources have confirmed the state of preservation of the remains of Hitler and Braun when recovered by the Red Army; they observed that the bones had been burned to the extent that only a few could be identified, including those that could be matched to dental records.

Twenty-four years after having been interred at Magdeburg, sources have suggested that the KGB exhumed the remains and pulverized and burned them further, before disposing of them in the Biederitz river nearby. This account has been accepted at face value by scholars and historians of the era, who are aware that during the Cold War and before the fall of the Iron Curtain, Soviet authorities were unwilling to risk a resurgence of fascist ideology, for which Magdeburg might have become a shrine.

It is here that my own observations must now differ. The KGB account is substantially correct in its general detail. Human remains of eleven bodies were recovered from Magdeburg and the majority were ground up and burned as was described. However the specific location of Hitler's relics had earlier been recorded by СМЕРШ and they were able to identify the position when bones were later exhumed. They considered it adequate to destroy the majority of the remains taken from the site, but were unwilling to destroy the remaining intact bones thought to be those of Hitler. Privately, these were taken to Moscow, checked against the original dental records once more, and having confirmed their origin, were interred in a further container and retained among other KGB archives. The purpose of this action was not reported, but was held to be that of future academic research, for reasons as yet unknown.

In 1991 the Committee of State Security was dismantled and its functions taken over by the FSK (Federal Counterintelligence Service). In 1995 the function of the FSK was transferred to the FSB (The Federal Security Service of the Russian Federation).

In these reorganisations this former KGB archive was overlooked and its significance was diminished. However in 1995

I elected to further annotate and classify this and several other archives and did so from my office in Lubyanskaya ploshchad, my laboratory and occasionally, at my own apartment. When I opened the archive, a small crate, it contained a number of black and white photographs of the KGB operation at Magdeburg. They showed the site being revealed by raising flagstones, of graves being opened and remains being thrown into water. Each photograph was dated and catalogued and carried a description on the reverse.

I opened the container within the archive in order to study its contents. It contained human bones that were intact enough to be classified morphologically and to be wired into a skull, a right hand and right arm, despite the surfaces of them being blackened.

The archive also contained a copy of a statement that had been signed in 1945 by a dental technician, Käthe Heusermann and by Fritz Echtman, a dental assistant. Together, they had formerly worked for Dr Hugo Blashke, Hitler's own dentist. Blaschke had been arrested by the Americans after the war, but Heusermann and Echtman, who had been arrested by Soviet troops in 1945, had been able to identify the dentition of skull fragments as being those of Adolf Hitler.

A further dental report had been commissioned by the KGB in 1970 and crucially, the peculiarities of that original record still existed in the Magdeburg fragments when I opened the container. In particular, evidence still existed that a bridge over tooth number six had been removed; substantial dental caries was observed in neighbouring teeth and was seen again in a dental report which I authorised in 1999. Taken together, I have little doubt that the bone fragments and other records in the archive are authentic, and those of Hitler himself.

I expected to retire in 1999 but chose to finish two archives in the year following. These works were completed by 2000 but source material was retained by me to augment my own work as a collector and historian of the period. I can therefore confirm that the remains contained within the case which accompanies this letter are those taken originally from Magdeburg. They are the last mortal remains of the Fuhrer of Nazi Germany, Adolf Hitler himself.

The signature of *Feodore Alkhimovich* followed in the Russian version, but not the English.

'I'd like to believe it, if only for the media frenzy!' It was Peyton who spoke.

'*I* believe it!' Ivy answered him.

'Why?'

'What possible motive has a retired Russian civil servant got for making up such a story?'

Zenda said, 'That's easy, money for a start. Or didn't you say he was some kind of academic pursuing research? Perhaps he was after the renown that could have arisen from publicity surrounding the relic. He would be seen as a serious historian. Wally, what do you think?'

'I don't think he could make much out of it; there would be a bit of a stink if it got reported. But I do agree about the media frenzy; everybody hates Hitler. His views have become the very antithesis of those of the modern liberal democracy. It would make a huge amount of news, but it would probably land him in a lot of trouble at home.'

'They have gagging orders like us?'

'Of course. But I can hardly see how such an order could apply to one of their own employees carrying out research on one of their own archives. I can see that the Russians might want to shut him up and would be upset if it got out, but I do seem to remember a case which made the news a couple of years ago. The Russian Interior Ministry placed a gagging order on a chap called Zharikov. They were accused of "regressing back to Stalin's times with show trials, attacks on relatives and gagging orders to terrorise and silence their opponents". With something like this, I don't think they would want the publicity of having made a gagging order. I think they would wash their hands of it, say was untrue, but make sure he didn't get paid in private.'

Creighton said, 'So why has it come out now? If he's not going to make any money, surely this chap Alkhimovich would be better off hanging onto it?'

'Well, Harry mentioned that he's getting on a bit. Maybe he wants to get it off his hands altogether. Elderly people often look on material possessions as an encumbrance or a loose end, so getting rid of it would make his affairs a whole lot tidier. I think we have to take this relic at face value unless something suggests that it isn't so. The relic clearly exists; it comes from the right place and has a provenance in the form of a description and signed statement by a former officer in the KGB. There are also photos, signed and dated, and dental evidence.'

Peyton said, 'That's all very well, but what you need is some kind of proof of...'

'Well, there's DNA...'

'No chance. It would show whether we are dealing with a man or woman and might perhaps tell us a bit about any missing genes, but there would be little point unless we go on to establish links with relatives and I cannot see them being interested in *that*.'

Creighton said, 'Why don't you get somebody to do a Richard the Third on the bones. If there really is enough to wire a skull together, you could get them to wire it up and reconstruct the flesh using plaster or something. I think it works because flesh is always of a known depth over the bone structure. You would obtain a plaster statuette of the individual which could be compared to photographs.'

'Now that's a good idea' said Bishop. 'That is, if we really want to know for sure. What would we do about it afterwards, say Heil?'

Ivy voiced their uniform opinion. 'I know it sounds horrid, but of course we want to know. We can decide what to do about it later.'

*

Creighton and Ivy Brakespeare had arranged to see Mr Johan Pal in order to complete their sale to him, and they pulled up at his large Victorian villa, about ten miles from Avebury. Parking their Range Rover, Creighton withdrew his aluminium attaché case and pressed the doorbell. The door was opened by a stony-faced servant, who ushered them into a reception room. Soon, however, Johan Pal arrived and offered them drinks.

'I must apologise,' said Pal, 'many guests like to come to dinner rather than lunch. I suppose dinner has become the more usual time for entertaining, but when I was younger, luncheon was often preferred, especially in town. But I have another function to attend tonight and so I am grateful for your visit at this time.'

'It is a pleasure, said Creighton Brakespeare. We have been staying with friends locally, so we needed to come only a short distance. You may know the village: Peckling is a small place, but it has a lively community and our friends are well-known in the neighbourhood.'

'Ah, Peckling.' Johan Pal looked reserved. 'I think I may have heard of it. Is it near to Calne? I cannot say that I have been there.'

'Calne, no, that is a little further,' said Ivy. 'But one cannot buy much in the village and I suppose the residents go there regularly.'

'I wonder whether you would kindly come through to the dining room?' Pal pointed. 'Barrett is an excellent chef as well as a very useful housekeeper. He is a valuable man, combining all of the traditional skills of the butler with those of cook, gardener and housekeeper. He knows a lot about wine; here try some of this Chablis, it really is excellent; I don't know where he manages to get it! In these egalitarian days it has become rather unusual to refer to employees as servants, but he doesn't seem to mind and after all, that is exactly what he is, although a very professional one.'

'How long have you been in the area, Mr Pal?' Brakespeare had considered the use of Pal's forename, but had not done so without invitation.

'Oh, I should say a couple of years now.'

'Do you like it particularly? I find that we need a town, not necessarily for the nightlife, but for people who recognise our business presence there. It draws the casual buyer to us.'

'Well, I do quite a bit of travelling myself, so I like to be able to return to a country retreat when I'm off-duty.'

Barrett brought in a terrine of white fish and a green herb, probably fennel. They tried it and it was delicious; the Chablis complemented it perfectly. Brakespeare said, 'This really is excellent. We do a little cooking, but I suppose we've become a little lazy and often eat out. That is Cambridge for you; there are many fine restaurants, some of them very well-known.'

'Yes,' said Pal.' I know of a few locally, but it has become a question of finding the time. I use them mainly for outside catering purposes.'

Brakespeare also considered but immediately rejected any notion of asking Pal about his work. Sensing his interest, Pal said, 'My work is in defence, so you will understand my reluctance to discuss it. I have connections with the British government and act as a consultant for them. My area of expertise is technical, with a background in electronic systems and robots. However, that is only work!'

'Could I please ask about your book collecting?'

'Certainly; I collect, study and describe antiquarian and religious books, many quite old. I run a minor academic circle on the subject and we meet occasionally to buy and sell, and to write articles which we hope will contribute to the literature on the subject.'

'Hence your interest in the Clavicule of Solomon.'

'Quite so.'

Barrett entered, removed the empty plates and returned with dishes of Filet Mignon and a chive butter. With this very rich dish, Pal offered a choice of Mouton Rothschild or Chateau Margaux. He said, 'I hope you like the wines. I thought that you might prefer a choice; not everyone likes very forceful claret and many prefer a lighter, more perfumed style. Or perhaps you would like to try both?'

Ivy said, 'I would love the Mouton Rothschild, please, and I know Creighton is keen on Margaux.'

Creighton Brakespeare agreed, 'We thank you for your generosity; it is not often that we have the pleasure of such wines.'

'I wonder whether you could tell me a little more about the background and provenance of the great work which I bought.'

'We acted as the agent in a sale of the assets of an Austrian collector. I believe they felt they could obtain a better price, or at least a very good price, if they sold it over here. The vendor was the executor of the estate of a deceased individual, we believe quite old. In establishing its provenance, we looked for any last-known records of it and there were none at all within the 20th century. However it was catalogued in verifiable, although obscure library records in the German language in about 1890. It must have been in private hands for about 120 years.'

Brakespeare continued, 'There do seem to be later additions to several pages. They are in the form of black, although faded inscriptions in French, but we have made no attempt to translate them. I did enlist an expert in Romance languages, a Fellow of Gonville and Caius College, to try to date the inscriptions for me. His view was that he could date the ink additions and that the pages could not be younger than the inscriptions on them. The additions were in a style of French known to be of the 14th century, he guessed at a date of 1350 from the meaning and use of some words and from a few words borrowed from Spanish and German. In fact, the book itself may be a lot older, but we have given it our most conservative dating of 1350, from the style of the ink additions only.'

'That would mean that my purchase is a lot older, perhaps by 100 years, than similar texts in other collections and conceivably a lot more?'

'Yes, but he did say that we cannot date the Latin the volume was written in, because it was by then a dead language, preserved mainly in the church and as a medium for scholarly writing. He thought it must have been in an ecclesiastical library for a long time, maybe in continental Europe and throughout the middle ages; thus it avoided the dissolution of the monasteries in England when so many monastic collections of books were destroyed. Like many scholars, he was saddened at the thought of what must have been lost then.'

'Yes, a mere four volumes represent the total known literature of Old English, that flower of the so-called dark ages. Little more than fragments of heroic poetry and a few riddles are left, probably because most the collected work was dissipated by Henry VIII.'

Ivy said, 'So do we know exactly how old the contents of the Clavicule really are?'

Creighton replied, 'No, but if it was written down by 1350, its contents may be far older. We can only guess that there was a far older spoken tradition, handed down by word of mouth and by the practice of its adherents, rather like Christianity before the days of written bibles. The contents may have been well-established for two thousand years, who knows?'

Pal looked pleased.

Creighton Brakespeare continued, 'Would you like me to arrange for a carbon-fourteen test on the parchment? That would give you a date, anyway.'

'No, I don't think that will be necessary, but I would like to know about the leaves themselves. I thought they were vellum.'

'They may be. A parchment is a broad term for an animal

skin prepared in a particular way. Hair and flesh were first removed and the skin was stretched on a frame while wetting, drying and scraping. By such means, the thickness and quality of the parchment could be adjusted to suit. Vellum is of course similar, but was prepared only from the skin of the calf; thus from veal, which is how its name arose. It had a good reputation because the skin of the calf was thin and of a high quality. Your book may be on vellum, we have not ascertained as such.'

He continued, 'Paper became more common when the new printing presses demanded it. By the 15th century it had become cheaper and there were too few animals skins available for high quality parchment manufacture, so paper became the usual material for writing. But most paper is only good for a couple of hundred years unless made to a high standard. The acid content changes it and it will start to crumble and become brown in colour. Proper archival paper will last for 500 years, but you need have no fear of that happening to your purchase.'

Pal said, 'You mentioned that you have about fifteen leaves still to be collected from a restorer. What exactly is the history of those?'

'They told us that a few pages had become detached from the binding. It is inevitable in a volume of that age. They are still being restored in London by our expert. I would estimate another three months before they can be reunited with the book.'

'What was the reason for the damage? I emphasise that I know you to have acted in good faith and I am quite happy to wait. I still wish to proceed as we agreed.'

'Once the pages became detached, they were subject to conditions that were different from those of the leaves within the volume. My expert said they may have become damp; there was an element of friction; the edges became abraded and a little torn.'

'How will these pages look after restoration?'

'The written content can be restored and the vellum mended. They first flatten each page carefully and photograph it with various forms of radiant light; x rays for example. They can easily see where ink was, because elements in it will react to light of a certain wavelength. The problem is restoration of the vellum itself, because it can change a lot with high humidity.'

'My dear Creighton and Ivy, I am neglecting my duties as host.' Pal range a bell and Barrett returned to remove more plates. Both guests lingered over their excellent wines; Barrett noticed and refreshed their glasses. A few minutes later and in the French manner he returned and brought cheese in order to finish the wine with a savoury dish before any sweet dessert. The conversation then continued; all were quite at ease talking 'shop'.

Brakespeare said, 'Creases are repaired by the use of isopropyl alcohol and a little local stretching, while gelatin will fill small tears. Larger tears can be filled with ground-up animal hide or by silk cloth and a gum. I believe that mechanical strength can be enhanced by fine stitching. Once the vellum has been restored, the restorer will then add fresh ink exactly as shown in the photograph of the original. It is very highly-skilled, hence the time necessary to do it properly. He will also need to make a suitable ink to match the original.'

'Originally, a scribe would make his own ink, just as a painter would prepare paints from any pigment available. For example the colour blue verditer was made by suspending copper carbonate in a little egg yolk or olive oil. Therein lies the problem with many old masters; they darken with age because of the primitive paints used.'

'So the inks are special?'

'The inks are interesting, because they can actually help us to date the work.'

'In what way?'

'Before about the 12th century, a scribe would make so-called carbon ink using soot and sticky gum. We do not like to use carbon inks because they are abrasive and rub off quite easily. Your book is not of a carbon ink which, had it been used, would date it before the 12th century.'

Pal whistled, 'So we have narrowed down the date of writing to about three hundred and fifty years; therein lie the benefits of knowledge. But if not a carbon ink, what was it?'

'They used what we now call metal-gall inks. To make them, they obtained tannic acid from the crown gall or oak gall, which is commonly found as a growth on trees. Tannic acid was extracted by steeping it in water or vinegar for a few days and the result mixed with green vitriol, which we now call iron sulfate. The whole mass went black over a period of time and continued to darken; whereupon gum Arabic, the dried sap of the acacia tree, was added to thicken the ink. It is interesting that quill pens do not work with modern shop-bought ink; it is too thin, although suitable for a fountain pen. By contrast, iron gall inks were excellent; they do not fade and soak into vellum well. The original work of the medieval scribe can be seen by modern technology with ease, because it still contains the element iron and can therefore been seen in order to copy.'

The wine and cheese gone, Barrett brought in a desert, a perfect vanilla soufflé and a glass of Sauternes. Later, they retired to a sitting-room and Ivy said, 'We propose to keep you informed of the progress of the restorers, but we would like to complete the transaction now.'

Pal said, 'Of course.'

Creighton Brakespeare opened the aluminium attaché case and leaving the volumes within, passed it to Johan Pal. The latter had a way of looking expressionless, but taking the case, he removed each volume, checked it over and replaced each in turn. Brakespeare said, 'Of course, we will leave the case with you, it is complimentary.'

Pal went to a bureau, opened a drawer and withdrew a bank draft. Satisfied, both parties countersigned contracts of sale and then Pal made further polite enquiries about the book business.

However with time flying, Creighton and Ivy thanked him for his hospitality and left.

*

Wally Bishop knocked on the door of the Department of Forensic Anthropology at a Scottish University. He was ushered in by a secretary and was asked to wait for a few minutes until his appointment five minutes hence.

Since it is not customary to use the title 'Professor' for the status of Associate or Assistant Professor at a British University, Bishop said only, 'Dr Wheatcraft, thank you for calling me into your Department. It is very good of you to help us with our own project; our small museum of palaeontology would love to know what our 'Ancient Briton' actually looked like. We may be a bit parochial down in Wiltshire, but we are keen to place him in our display. Can you tell us whether he died in fire or in battle, or was some attempt made to burn his bones afterwards? We found precious little else to go on; there were no weapons and above all, no treasure! It's probably a little too mundane for your staff to work on, but we would be pleased…'

'Well, Mr Bishop, I can assure you that your specimen has been quite interesting and we have been able to make quite a bit of progress. We started by trying to make a kind of Hand of Glory using the bones of the right hand.'

'What exactly do you mean? Is a hand of glory somehow significant?'

'Well, that is our own little Departmental epithet for a reconstructed hand, but we do reconstruct quite a few, so it is a bit of a joke I suppose. We had to wire the bones together, which was actually quite easy because someone has had a go at them before. Was that you?'

'I think the chap we got them from had already done so, but we are pretty amateurish ourselves.'

'We mounted them on a plinth, see here, in such a way that

the hand can be moved around. You can have it palm upwards, forming a cup, or you can make it point by rotating the hand by 45 degrees and extending the digits. Traditionally, a Hand of Glory was the hand of a deceased person, dried or salted, or otherwise preserved in spirits of wine; ethanol to you and me; or a skeletal hand would have been just as good. Such a hand would have been from an individual hanged for murder. The left or *sinister* hand, was preferred, but it had to be the hand which had carried out the murder.'

'Did suicide count?'

'Oh yes, certainly. Self-murder would have given the hand all the usual powers and I am sure that self-hanging was just the ticket. But I am not sure that a hanging by itself would have been critical: the important point was more that it was the hand of death by violence.'

'What about the bones of the arm?'

'We managed to clean them up and cement them together. The breaks were actually quite clean. We supported them by means of wire as is usual. It would be possible to attach the hand to the arm appropriately, that is to say by the carpus to the bones of the radius and ulna, so that the arm could be seen to point in a particular direction or perhaps even raise a kind of salute. We haven't actually done that yet, but it would be easy to do by means of three wire clips. I can show you later.'

'Tell me more about this hand of glory.'

'In the middle ages, magical powers were supposedly derived from a hand of glory. It was very lucky to have one. Seamen loved them because it gave them the power to defy the elements.'

'Earth, air, fire and water?'

'Yes, exactly; but it gave powers to the owner according to the calibre of the deed for which the individual was judicially hanged. Such beliefs are quite old; they are found in many European cultures and the name itself comes from a French term. Now, we hope that some other of our ideas might be a good thing for your museum: when we cleaned up the long bones of the arm, we used an organic solvent, alcohol in fact, to degrease the surfaces so that our cement would work. Rather than throw away or recycle this alcohol, we evaporated it to dryness and the fat residue, of which there were just a few micrograms, mostly triglycerides, but with a few other bits and pieces if you are a chemist, were incorporated into five candles made to a very simple recipe. They are of paraffin wax, with some stearic acid in them to make the candle softer and less brittle. There is of course a wick right through. Formerly, the wick would have been made from the hair of the deceased, but we were out of luck there. We coloured each candle a dark blue, if only because we had that colour available.'

'Why did you save the alcohol extract?'

'We put the extracted fats through the gas liquid chromatography first, just to see what was there, but the interesting thing is that the bones cannot be more than about a hundred years old, because we know how quickly the fat constituents change with time. They cannot be four thousand years old, for example, because there would be nothing left. My guess is that the fats are up to one hundred years old. Have you debated a call to H.M. Coroner?'

'Well we thought about it, but the criteria hardly seem to apply.'

'I suppose you're right.'

'So why is this useful for the museum?'

'Great powers were attributed to burning a candle which contained the fat taken from a corpse which died on the gallows. The candle was first placed upright in the hand of glory so that the hand acted as a candlestick. The candle was thought to burn to give great powers to its possessor.'

'What kind of powers?'

'It made an observer unable to move, unless directed by the bearer of the Hand. The dark candle also gave out a light which illuminated only the movements of the holder, or made them invisible if you prefer. Above all, and I believe this may have been allegorical, it opened any door that the bearer wished.'

Wheatcraft continued, 'So a suitable candle, placed in a Hand of Glory made from the bones of a really bad criminal, would give the holder tremendous occult power. One might imagine the almost infinite power attributable to a hand of glory made from the bones say, of a mass murderer like Attila the Hun. But I speculate only; we think you will be able to make a nice display from these relics; a kind of witches and broomsticks attraction.'

'Tell me more about the skull.'

'It's incomplete, but we have been able to fix it together so that the jaw articulates quite well. There is room inside for one of the candles, so that light would shine out of the eye sockets. You could even put a small lamp inside.'

'What do you know about the skull itself?'

'Well, it's the skull of a man in his late fifties. Frontal, parietal, nasal and lacrimal bones are all intact, as are the incisive and mandible bones. But the occipitals, hyoids and bones at the back are missing. We have managed to mock them up for you; it's really quite easy. Interestingly, there is a hole through the right parietal bone and corresponding damage to the sphenoid on the left, as though the chap blew his own brains out. But it cannot be, surely; it was probably some kind of damage after death, there's no way of telling.'

'Interestingly though, he seems to have had something approaching useful dental treatment. Tooth number six, I believe it's called, has been removed quite cleanly and there may be evidence of filing or even drilling. He may have had a lot of pain there, maybe enough even to modify his behaviour.'

'Did you manage to model the features?'

'We did. We used markers in the usual manner to indicate the depth of clay to be added to various places on a plaster cast of the skull. We know exactly how deep the tissue should be. We know he was a white Caucasian and we rebuilt the face using modelling clay to the depth of the markers. We used blue glass eyes and short-cropped brown hair as you asked. We made him clean-shaven and with a parting on the right-hand side so the hair could be brushed forwards and to the left. I must say that he looks pretty sinister, no relative of yours I hope! Anyway, we've affectionately called him Johnny after an American benefactor of ours.'

'But here. What we have done for your display is to mount the original skull on a pedestal and to attach the top of the right arm to it so that it can be articulated upwards; raised or waved in a salute, if you like. With the right hand at the end of the arm, this is as near to a reconstruction as is possible, in the absence of any more fragments.'

'So how much do we owe you?'

'Well, we are always after useful material to practise on, so we are only going to charge you for the materials we had to use, not the time taken. That means a bit of modelling clay, the wooden pedestal, a few solvents and some wire. We could do a carbon 14 test on it, but I can tell you, there's no real point. Take it from me that these remains are only 'up to a century' old. Carbon-14 would tell us how many thousands of years old, not tens. I take it that you don't want a DNA analysis done? It would be easy, and it costs very little these days.'

'I don't think so.'

'No, I guess that's taking it a bit far. I doubt whether there's anything odd in Johnny's genes which might make him a criminal.'

★

Peyton and Zenda Oakwood left Peckling after their stay with Wally and Amelia Bishop and planned to return to Sandhurst by the old Bath Road, avoiding the M4 motorway by passing from Calne to Marlborough and from Hungerford to Newbury. In fact they joined the north-bound A346 south of Marlborough and drove northwards through the Savernake Forest before turning right onto the A4. It was dark and Oakwood had turned on his headlights long before.

Zenda looked eastward into the forest and asked Peyton to slow down. It was very quiet and their car was the only one on the road and so it was safe to do so.

'Look, there are naked people dancing and cavorting!'

Oakwood removed his foot from the accelerator and the car slowed. He said, 'Good Lord, my glasses have started to steam up!'

They both looked. There were about thirteen people and a small fire about fifty yards into the forest. The naked men and women were dancing around a huge oak tree at the side of the road, all holding hands in a circle round it. They seemed quite unselfconscious.

Peyton said, 'Look, their backs are to the oak. Now, they've turned around to face it; what fun!'

Zenda said, 'That tree is called the Big Belly Oak and it is famous hereabouts for being over a thousand years old. I would swear I recognise some of their faces, too. I think I saw them in Calne recently. There's a tall, dark girl with short hair and some other, very pretty ones. Poor things, I hope they don't get too cold.'

Peyton retorted, 'I doubt whether they will!'

He pulled away.

*

It was three weeks after their weekend with the two couples and Wally Bishop was at home with Amelia. Their guests had returned home, keen in due course to hear more about the parcel from Russia. They knew that it had been looked at by a forensic pathology department and Bishop had promised to keep them informed of any progress as studies on the relic continued.

In fact, he had returned home with Dr Wheatcraft's results,

but had declined to assemble the set of bones immediately, preferring to keep them in a form more easily stored. As a temporary measure he had placed the box in his cellar, the trapdoor in the kitchen floor of which was lockable by means of a stout padlock.

He had written a brief account of Wheatcraft's findings and had emailed it to the other four and there had been no dissent to the vague idea of 'let me think about what to do next' when later he had spoken to them on the telephone. Since the relic had existed for 60 years, it seemed not to warrant any kind of immediate panic or fuss. Bishop would 'leave them to mull it over,' and would ask for their opinion 'when he phoned again in due course'. He had no doubt that when he did so, they would have come up with a useful consensus for the best thing to do with the 'Magdeburg Relic'.

Amelia said, 'It seems to me that there are several questions. Do we actually believe this story when all is said and done? If we do believe it, should we tell anyone, or indeed everyone; and would *that* really be the same thing? If not, should we hide it away, or could we show it off as something else? Do we own it and if so, can we make a little or a lot of money out of it? Is it dangerous and if so, what kind of danger?'

Wally said, 'At first, I thought it might be a spoof, but I find I cannot argue away the basic facts. Consider the written evidence, fully signed off, which came out of Russia with Harry. And I know him, he's trustworthy. Look at all the physical evidence from the bones: the burning, the bullet hole in the skull and the matching dental records; they all point towards the simple fact that our Magdeburg Relic contains the genuine last remains of Adolf Hitler.'

He paced up and down. 'As for what to do; well, I didn't like to tell Wheatcraft the truth, of course, you know what academics are like: they all have some kind of axe to grind, a pet theory for anything political or sociological or whatever; God knows what he might have done next. He still thinks that we're going to pop the whole lot into a local museum of ancient history; a sort of ancient Briton show. We won't, of course.'

He continued, 'A relic of Adolf Hitler cannot simply be kept in a museum or at least, not in this village. An article of clothing alone would have been sinister enough, but imagine the outcome if something like this ended up in a village display. This just has to be the biggest and most terrible archaeological find of the last half century; there has been nothing bigger since the tomb of King Tutankhamun. It would have to go to a major museum and be kept under strict security. Even then, there would be every kind of crank after it, right wing, left wing, you name it and possibly even bombs. Almost certainly, there would be requests from other countries to have the thing destroyed; deputations asking to have it put it back in the crater and so on.'

'And the question of ownership does arise. We can slip Harry something. He said so, although Lord knows, it is something which nobody could even start to value. But the Russians might want it back although *they* probably have no more right to it than anyone else. They simply took it, like Alkhimovich; at least Harry bought it.'

'The Israelis would want it destroyed, as would the Germans. The Russians would want it back,' said Amelia.

'Yes, but the British or Americans would probably want to put it on display. Think about the Koh-i-Nûr diamond, which we popped into our collection of Crown Jewels, or the Elgin Marbles which we effectively annexed; we do seem to be rather single-minded about keeping our acquisitions for ourselves. I think the Brits would want to gawp at Adolf in a museum.'

'What kind of cranks would it attract?' said Amelia.

Bishop said, 'That's what I'm unsure about. I was hoping to speak to someone with a Church connection and maybe someone with some experience of politics.'

'That's exactly what Peyton, Creighton and the girls thought when I telephoned them; they said speak to someone.'

She continued, 'Why don't you go to see Callum Dood,

the local vicar? He's always been a person the local community could speak to in complete confidence; still further, he has a reputation for a sympathy with unusual spiritual matters. The local WI have accounts of him helping with, shall we say, the spiritually afflicted and some say he is the local exorcist. But I won't say more about that, because I'm not quite sure what it means. Let's just say that I've met him and he seems quite open-minded. I would describe him as a religious conservative; he seems to be almost clerical in character; but I do think he is probably socially quite liberal.'

'How much can I tell him?'

'I think probably everything. He has to know what's going on in order to make his advice sound. If it gets out and goes wrong, we can deny it anyway; nobody would believe all this unless we show them the evidence. It would blow over, just like a UFO story.'

★

On the following Saturday, Bishop spoke to the Brakespeares and Oakwoods on the telephone; they all agreed that 'talks' would be a good idea. A little later, he telephoned the vicarage for an appointment and Dood answered. He said 'Come round straight away and bring an ash tray.'

It was a five-hundred yard walk to the vicarage. Bishop knocked and was ushered in. Immediately, Dood said, 'I got this lager in Calne, it's really good. Or would you like something stronger, whisky perhaps? Or there's tea if you wish.' He seemed unenthusiastic about the last of these and collected two one-pint glasses from a cupboard.

Dood sat down and stretched his legs out. He was a dark man of slight build and longish hair, but it would have been unkind to think him untidy. The walls were covered by prints of insects: butterflies mostly, together with some real ones in glass-fronted boxes. Bishop cast his eyes over the collection and wondered how they were preserved from decay; were they dried? As if reading his thoughts, Dood said, 'There's a preservative in those boxes. I don't know how it works, but one day I'll ask this brilliant chemist I used to know. I hear he fell on hard times, a bit like the insects. They got pickled and I think he did too. What can I do for you?'

'I am sorry, but I have not really paid the Church as much attention as I should, what with the modern pace of life being as it is.'

'Well, it's here when folk need to dip into it. That is rather more often than you might imagine, even for a tiny place like this.'

'Do you get much social damage and degradation, then?'

'A bit, we do what we can, but we don't regard ourselves as being in competition with the Sally Army. Yes, of course, we do the usual births, marriages and deaths, but there is quite a bit of other stuff here as well and we muck in with the degradation side of things when we can. There is a bit of rural poverty of course, here and there, especially among farm workers and these days, dairy farmers. Suicidal lot; can't blame them, I must say.'

'But we also have to deal with a few strange odds and ends too. There's the local countryside and its cultural influences, which are as strong around here as those of any modern cosmopolitan city. There has always been a close connection between the local villages and the farming community on the hills, which is very much more than just the economic connection of course. You do get *that* too, but there is also a profound affinity with the cultural traditions of the neighbourhood. By that, I mean the local folklore.'

'So, what kind of traditions are you thinking of?'

'You might be surprised to hear me say unusual pagan traditions.'

'Very few things surprise me.'

'Good. I think you can forget about people being dragged away and sacrificed in wicker cages, but at certain times of the year, folk seem to vanish for a while and reappear later, dishevelled and rather the worse for wear. That is to say, spiritually the worse for wear.'

'So you are the local exorcist then?'

'Me? Callum Dood the exorcist? Hardly, or at least not unless you can describe as exorcism my assisting with bad smells and knocks in unused rooms, or with the inevitable hooded monk gliding about. But that's par for the course in almost every parish. I *have* helped at exorcisms, of course.'

He continued, 'But there are rumours of something a bit bad, just rumours you understand, connected with some of these old Neolithic burial places on the hills. Such traditions associated with barrows are quite strong in all village communities along the Wiltshire Ridgeway. In fact I have had an interest for quite some time in finding out a bit more. Can't say I have been very successful with it, but just in case you need to ask why I'm occasionally seen strolling over the downs, it's a bit more than just collecting butterflies, believe me.'

'How then would you like a bit of serious trouble on your patch?'

'What kind of trouble?'

'Serious Nazi trouble.'

'I'm not sure it's for me. Why, what exactly is it about? Have some more lager by the way. Oh, and since I'm playing host, I've been growing a little bit of, er, tobacco in my garden and wonder whether you like to smoke? I grow my own because it's organic, you see.'

'I always wanted to smoke but never had the will-power to start. Can I rely on your discretion over this?'

'Of course.'

'Well, this Nazi angle is pretty serious I am afraid. As a dealer in fine art and antiquities, all sorts of stuff comes across my desk, but never anything quite as strange as this. It isn't even a question of money because something like this cannot be valued and it might even have a negative value, with some people paying to get rid of it.'

'I seem to have come across an artefact which appears to be some of the bones of the Fuhrer himself. We have a complete right hand, right arm and most of the skull all wired up to give something which can point, gesticulate or raise its arm to give a salute. Its jaw could move if a motive force were applied, but above all, a light could be made to shine from within the skull and it would be visible through the eye sockets to give, as it were, a fanatical gleam. So all the gargoyle stuff would be there for a nutcase to take advantage of; or maybe someone more serious and quite nasty.'

'The most terrible thing is that a few, one might say, Satanic candles were also made, using the usual wax ingredients but with the addition of fat extracts taken when the long bones were cleaned up for analysis. The whole thing, if you believe in medieval folklore, could be enough to make a Hand of Glory, but out of the Fuhrer himself.'

'A hand of what?'

'The assembled skeletal hand of a man who died on the gallows or by violence such as self-murder; enervated by magical means to give its bearer occult power in proportion to the standing of the criminal. We also have the skull so that a deathly light could shine from the eye sockets, together with the bones of the right arm to make a Nazi salute.'

'And this is no joke?'

'No joke whatsoever. I'm pretty worried, I don't want just to get rid of it, because some other poor so-and-so would have to deal with the same problem.'

'And this has turned up in my village.'

'I am afraid so.'

'Well I think you have done the right thing hanging onto it. It's best kept out of the news. How many people know?'

'Just the six of us know and Harry, my contact, who is shortly off to Poland if he hasn't already gone. Now you know too and there is also the guy from the University who did the facial reconstruction, but *he* doesn't know its history. You know, the forensic paleontology chap who put the bones back together, he did some gas liquid chromatography on the fats, and made the candles.'

'And what did the reconstructed face look like?'

'It looked like Adolf Hitler.'

'Why did your chap put the bones together?'

'We told him it was an ancient Briton and that the bones are going into our museum. He wanted to make us a proper witches' display just to spice things up. You know, it could have been labelled Boudicca's grandpa, but if the guy had a hand of glory as well, it would have added a little supernatural character to scare the kids a bit. They would have loved that; kids are keen on scary things and they would have dragged their Mums and Dads along. The magical angle is this; a candle which contains the fat of a man hanged for murder, burning from within the upturned palm of that same individual, would impart special occult powers to its owner. But he seemed almost disappointed to tell me that the bones were only 'up to' a century old in case we decided not to do an 'ancient Briton' display. We decided not to call the Coroner.'

'Well I hate to say this, but I think that the best thing, for now, is to pop the bones in an Ancient Briton display as though you thought nothing more about it. Personally, I wouldn't want to have them in *my* loft I can tell you.'

'Why, do you think they carry bad vibrations?'

'My first reaction is to say 'yes', but if you want me to say why, I would prefer to mull it over for a while.'

'Perhaps we could entice you to lunch tomorrow to chat about this? I would quite like Amelia to hear.'

'Sorry, but Sunday is my busy day. Can we make it Monday?'

'Yes of course.'

Chapter Five

Intruders at a Garden Party

For a slight man, Dood had a large appetite. He consumed four courses – Amelia had excelled – and a volume of red wine commensurate with it. They ate lobster soup, then poached salmon, followed by roast beef and finally apple crumble with crème Anglais, a homely, but supremely satisfying and filling meal. Their guest ate with relish, as did Wally Bishop and Amelia herself, but finally, when they had slumped into various armchairs afterwards, they continued to talk.

Dood said, 'Amelia, that was a lovely meal. I haven't eaten so well for ages. Thank you again. And it was good of you to give me a bit of time to think before taking up our conversation. But before offering my views on anything, are you sure that this Hand of Glory actually counts? He wasn't a hanged man, surely and so his hand might not work.'

Bishop replied, 'I was told it probably would. Don't forget, he suffered death by suicide, which some call self-murder and he was responsible, directly or indirectly, for the deaths of many millions of people. I should say that despite the absence of a rope, his relics and considering the manner of his departure, would make a hand of glory of extraordinary significance.'

Dood continued, 'And what again does such a hand actually achieve?'

'Legend supposes that the holder or owner can become invisible, that the candle gives a light that will illuminate only those things observed by the holder and that the bearer can open any door, even when locked. I am told that the last of these is allegorical, a way of saying he has the power to do whatever the hell he likes. But of course, such a thing has probably never been tested.'

'Did you say that such power would be in proportion to the sins committed by the bad guy before his execution?'

Bishop said, 'I guess so, which means our present example should have very considerable powers, but exactly what, I couldn't even guess. In centuries gone by the possession of such a hand was actually regarded as quite lucky.'

Amelia broke in, 'Mr Dood, the relic is here. What exactly should we be concerned with, other than the likely series of arguments in tabloid newspapers that we have already been through?'

'I am afraid you are up against two very dangerous kinds of people.'

After a pause for thought, he continued, 'On one hand, there are the revanchists. Since the end of the last World War, there has been a strand of thought in Germany demanding the return of lands in the east; those that were given to Poland by the great powers. Also, the revanchists still want Alsace Lorraine back from France. They could make use of Hitler's relics in publicising their cause; for example they could say that the emergence of the relic is a totem or watershed, a symbol of the dawn of a new age of Germanic freedom. They would try to publicise their cause and might be successful in doing so. With attention on them, they might hold rallies and make speeches and who knows what that might lead to? They might gain some influence over government policy, or make a stable democracy become less stable. That is, of course, leaving aside any question of the object having real and intrinsic magical powers.'

'And the second category of dangerous person is…?'

'The black magician; such a person could undoubtedly make use of the Magdeburg Relic.'

'Do you think the bones have real power which a devil worshipper could use in such a way?'

'Well, that was what I needed to think about; it was the reason I asked to delay before coming over today. I did not feel that I could answer Wally's question properly unless I did so.'

Dood continued, 'When I was younger, I might have been rather scathing about such an idea. But experience has led me to think otherwise. We all have many psychic abilities which cannot simply be explained away. I can remember sorting through a box of old Christmas cards and picking out and reading a card that had been written to me by my Grandmother about thirty years before. By holding the card I was instantly able to sense how she felt on the day she wrote it. There was enough of her 'about the card' to provide a psychic connection with her that was distinct and separate from anything she had written. Unwittingly, I had experienced one of the foremost skills of the clairvoyant asked to link with a lost child; by touching an item of clothing worn by the child beforehand, the clairvoyant can often tell the fate of that individual.'

The others listened with interest as he continued, 'Similarly, I often feel the 'measure' in material objects: the goodwill, the deceit, the love left by other people. I am quite sure they retain at least some part of the feelings of people who touch them; a case in point would be the angry letter: often even an untrained person can feel the anger in a letter before reading it. All of us, I am sure, can easily sense the presence of another person by means of a telephone; despite great distances between us, the wire provides a connection. I have also been aware when the thoughts of friends or enemies are on me and such connections can also therefore exist without the wire. Our language is full of suggestions that this is so; for example, we speak of our ears burning when others talk about us; or psychologists acknowledge this ability as telepathy or thought transference.'

'In my view, these are examples of a very general psychical ability to connect which we all possess. However it varies; with some people it is considerable, to the extent that images of people and their actions can be seen at a great distance. Instances of it are well-documented in psychic literature and in that of the occult. The phenomenon is known as overlooking; it is as though one were looking over another individual's shoulder or into their room.'

Amelia and Wally Bishop listened avidly while Dood waved his hands in emphasis. 'Many people are also confident that they can sense a spirit that is wholly detached from the body by virtue of having passed on. I myself have often sensed a nearby sadness when I have done something wrong, as though a benevolent spirit nearby has become aware of it. At other times, people say they have travelled on journeys while asleep, with the purpose of talking to loved ones or to enemies. Although no sounds are exchanged, thoughts are reportedly visible in the eye or on the countenance of those spirits concerned.'

'In many cases, these occult abilities are highly-developed, especially in older and more introspective people. Although a long training in these matters can develop them, they are really only abilities which all people naturally have. They tell of an ability to connect with spirits elsewhere of the living or dead, of making predictions, of telling fortunes or of divining. There are many other examples of such powers.'

By now, Amelia and Wally were spellbound and not a little frightened. Amelia said, 'Have a little brandy.' Nervously, she crossed the room, poured glasses for them all and sat close to her husband.

Dood took a sip and continued, 'Most people who are highly-skilled in these matters exercise them without the intention of exerting influence on other people, or of doing anything which could be construed as malicious. However, there are a few who do not hold such scruples. If feelings and thoughts can be retained by material objects, then some objects might be better at so doing. If they are then adopted for an evil purpose by means of a ritual, or if that object becomes a focus of evil wishes, then it should logically take on, or acquire malicious sentiment. Such was the essential logic of the so-called devil's potions, witches' potions, or indeed charms, which were an aspect of magic in the middle-ages.'

'How would you like some more brandy before we go on, and maybe some coffee too?'

'Excellent plan, thank you, and oh, are those chocolates? My word, at least I don't have to drive!'

'Certainly, help yourself.'

Ten minutes later, they resumed.

Bishop said, 'You were saying that minor objects can retain an association with a former user?'

'Yes, that's how a clairvoyant will often work. They may ask to touch an object in order to bring about a connection with the individual concerned. I would never have believed it unless I had myself experienced it. Now, I do.'

'Then if that is so, our relic will have an occult association with its past owner, Herr Hitler himself?'

'I am afraid so and in fact, since they are apparently the very bones of the man himself, inevitably so. But it is not necessarily the case that it will cause the holder any unease; in fact it takes two. The unease or sense of evil induced in an onlooker is in proportion to the degree of psychic ability they may have. To some, the relic might be completely inert but to a person of acute sensibility, it might be terrible to have around.'

Amelia said, 'I suppose a big problem would arise if a person of real psychic ability should get hold of it; a clairvoyant in fact?'

'Yes, there could be a big problem, but I was thinking of someone far worse, like a black magician or genuine Satanist. Such people are devoted to the black art for the purposes of power over other men or the acquisition of wealth; perhaps also for sexual gratification or for revenge. He or she would pursue evil deeds for their own sake, because it would not be possible to grow along the left-hand path without carrying out works of an incremental degree of evil. By comparison, a very good man might pursue good works and self-denial in order to progress towards perfection or even sainthood.'

Amelia said, 'But surely, there can be nobody around here who would be quite as bad as that?'

'I would like to say so, but I do believe such practices are commonplace in this neighbourhood. At certain times of the year, vile rituals take place on the Marlborough Downs. And I do mean practices which are far worse than those carried out in the fleshpots of Marlborough on a Friday night.'

Amelia and Wally Bishop smiled.

'Terrible perversions are carried out in secret and at those times, there are places where an observer would be very foolish to tread. In fact, I suspect they are carried out at some of the great earthworks on the downs above Avebury. With their thousands of years of history, some of it probably malefic, the Neolithic and iron-age earthworks there would be the ideal place. However, it is in fact necessary to distinguish devil worship from simple paganism, both of which are known around here. Although the cutting and bleeding of horses, together with the ritual tying of hair are often seen in these parts, they suggest only that a minor pagan circle is working nearby; such low-level paganism has generally been tolerated by the Church because it is not considered fundamentally evil.'

'Nevertheless, I believe that a Satanic circle, with a leader of great ability, currently works near here. I would be concerned for your relic to fall into their hands. They will certainly have the ability to overlook events in this neighbourhood, as I have tried to describe. If so, their routine observation of vibrations and constellations, of psychic contacts with each other and with the demons of their pantheon, all would be affected by the nearby presence of your relic. Its very presence would cause a perturbation of their dreams and thoughts and it is inconceivable that they do not already know that something 'big' is nearby. Having felt it, they would exert all of their abilities to find out what it is and perhaps acquire it. Undoubtedly they would attempt to steal it and use it in their practices. The only real question that would then arise is what they would decide to do with it.'

'In my view, it would provide them with a great opportunity. Your immediate concern would therefore be to keep Adolf Hitler's hand of glory, his candles of dark light, the arm that gave the Nazi salute and his skull with its evil radiance away from the hands of these people.'

'What would they use it for?'

There was a long pause before Dood spoke again, 'They would attempt to disturb the very soul of Adolf Hitler.'

For a few moments a heavy silence followed, but Bishop then asked the very simple question, 'For what purpose?'

'A Black Magician of real ability could use that relic to enable the Fuhrer's spirit to walk the Earth once more. He would be able to bind it to his own purpose; as the soul of a former tyrant of great strength, will-power and fanaticism; and as a director of mass murder, it would give him great and dreadful power. He would be able to use that power, harnessed to the aims of his Satanic circle. Consider the possibilities; modern-day followers of the Nazis; the chanting; the renewed war; conquest, mass murder, disease and darkness made worse by retribution and by recent advances in science and technology. If successful, a new night could appear over Europe and possibly the world.'

'At least twice in the last century, the Harbingers of the Last Judgement were set free to roam the Earth. These, the Four Horsemen of the Apocalypse, were called Conquest, War, Famine and Death. Great wars were the end result, and they must not be loosed again. It would inevitably be the aim of that Satanic circle to achieve their ultimate: the release of the four horsemen once more, so that a perpetual night should return in which their leader would hold sway.'

'How on earth could all this be achieved, even accepting your basic proposition?' It was Amelia who displayed her scepticism.

'Under suitable circumstances and with a black magician of adequate power, a conjuration, with suitable resources and with a living sacrifice, would bring the Fuhrer back to a semblance of life, although not to life as you know it. It would need a coven of thirteen, your relic of bones and a Satanic candle held alight in a hand of glory. They would also need a sacrifice of human blood: it would be the simple trade of a life for a life.'

'Such a ritual would, if successful, raise and probably bind the spirit of Adolf Hitler to the will of the practitioner. Wally and Amelia, can you see the significance? The Satanist would have only one opportunity for success and the life blood of an animal would not suffice. To be sure of success he would need to murder a man or woman in a ghastly ritual and that life blood would act as a direct trade for the life of the Fuhrer himself.'

Amelia now said, 'Callum, if I may be a little more familiar? This is very interesting and not a little shocking, but it does seem rather hard to believe. I must say, however, that if true, we seem to have brought this hardship upon ourselves. My instinct is to destroy the artefact or give it away to a museum, but before we decide, please let me ask the question which has been troubling me: how and why do you, the Reverend Callum Dood, know so much about black magic?'

'Aha, I thought that would eventually surface! I said earlier that I had helped solve 'minor' spiritual troubles on my patch and that is certainly the case. I have indeed helped at several exorcisms and some of them have been quite dreadful: in fact prolonged battles of will. But more than that, herbalism, natural remedies, hallucinogenic drugs and minor magics have been my research interest. In some of them, I have been able to enlist the help of a noteworthy chemist, a man who is very experienced with certain aspects of herb-lore and who recently left these parts, I doubt for good; I may have mentioned him once before. We have indeed experimented together with natural remedies; in my case the hallucinogenic qualities of some plant products; in his case, herbal aphrodisiacs. I cannot say that I have practised as a magician; I am after all a churchman. However let us say that I am cognisant of the natural order of things and regard magical practice as simply the application of natural laws and the exercise of intent. I do not see a little white magic as a danger to my position within the church.'

'Thank you, but to return to my earlier question, can the relics be given away or destroyed and if so, should they be?'

'No, I do not think that you can simply give away your relics; by now their existence must be known and they could simply be retrieved, or stolen from any display and replaced with a forgery. Nor should you destroy them; they do not belong to you or anyone else, but if you chose to do so, what then? I wonder if you burn them, whether the ashes would have a potency just the same. Or what would the ashes do to the ground they are buried in? We do not know. No, it is better that you keep them and reflect at leisure. Keep them in your cellar until you decide what to do. It may be that the Church has a solution. If so I will try to think of one.'

★

Johan Pal had visited Peckling on one earlier occasion, but now stood atop a low hill surmounting the village in order to look at the landscape around and about and at the houses the village contained. He could see several miles in each direction and noted a landscape of great presence, particularly in the manner in which it had been worked by humans over the years.

A little earlier he had passed through the village of Avebury, unspoilt and with few tourist traps and with its impressive standing stones and circles redolent of the many centuries men had lived there. A little further out, other settlements clustered and in them, local people paid due regard to the stones of Avebury with cottages incorporating some of the smaller examples of Neolithic masonry into their construction, so that it seemed as though their homes were slowly changing into ancient monuments themselves.

He had driven a circuitous path and had observed that although its villages were quiet and sleepy, the standing stones gave that countryside a feeling of past civilisations and of magic and a brooding, thinking presence. Other people seemed to feel it also; young couples ascended the nearby White Horse in order to take part in rites of fertility; white-robed druids braved cameramen to conduct their ceremonies; picnics were held among barrows and ramblers walked around hill forts made of great ditches and ramparts. Johan Pal shared these feelings, but Peckling, oddly insignificant in that great landscape, also held a strong attraction for him.

From the hilltop, it was clear how Peckling was wholly typical of the small villages in that county; there were two streets and a crossroads and it contained houses built of the austere local stone. In the middle was a church and tower built from the prosperity of the wool trade, six hundred years before and nearby, a large rectory. There was also a public house and village shop, while several houses seemed to have been converted from former barns or agricultural buildings. Although small, it was clear that Peckling was still a thriving farming community since tractors and trailers were moving around and there were crops and animals in green fields.

About 500 yards from the church lay a large converted farmhouse of brick, surrounded by a wall and with a substantial garden. On paper and by means of sketches in pencil, Pal recorded the position and plan of floors and the outside dimensions of the property, together with the placement of windows and larger trees. He also sketched a street map with parking spaces and noted those houses nearby that had windows which overlooked it. After a while, he returned to his car, a black Mercedes, and drove away.

★

It was three days before the occasion on which Pal had studied the village of Peckling from the hill. Wally Bishop telephoned Creighton Brakespeare in Cambridge and they exchanged general pleasantries, enquired about Amelia and Ivy and then Bishop said, 'Creighton, can we entice you down here again soon? We – that is to say Callum, Adam and myself – thought about going on the offensive in our investigation of possible local practitioners of the occult. We had a nocturnal 'look-around' in mind and would like to have a bit more muscle with us. We thought of you; maybe four would be better than just the three of us. What do you think?'

'I am sorry Wally, but we have three large sales advertised and I just *have* to be here. There are some very important potential clients coming along and we cannot let our people down. The earliest date for a visit of any kind frankly, is three weeks away and then, as I promised Ivy, we have a holiday booked somewhere. But I do know that Peyton is free. I exchanged messages with him yesterday because he was after a book. I think you would be better-advised to telephone him instead.'

'I quite understand. Is he on leave, or just between bouts of being very busy?'

'He didn't say.'

They chatted on the telephone a while longer and Bishop said that he and Amelia would welcome a trip to Cambridge when next the three couples had a get-together. Later, he telephoned Peyton Oakwood at Sandhurst and after Bishop had explained the circumstances, Oakwood agreed to stay once more, although without Zenda, who would be busy with an exhibition. Peyton passed the telephone to Zenda, who agreed, but said, 'You can borrow him as long as he doesn't miss our wedding anniversary!'

A day later, Oakwood turned up on the doorstep with a suitcase and was met by Amelia with a kiss on the cheek. He had taken the M3 motorway to Basingstoke, driven north on the A339 to Newbury and then along the A4 towards

Hungerford and the west. It was a journey of 70 miles only and so not onerous; and the traffic had been light enough for him to complete it in 90 minutes. He knew that had he wished, he need not have stayed the night and could easily have commuted daily, but he liked to stay and so that had been agreed.

Amelia directed him to a bedroom with the suggestion that he might wish to settle in after the drive. After 20 minutes he reappeared, fully refreshed and dressed in a comfortable sports jacket, with dark blue golf shirt and chinos. They all decided that a brief conference would be needed before moving further.

Bishop telephoned Dood, who could be seen in his garden 500 yards distant. After fifteen minutes he came round and knocked on the door. There were brief handshakes and very welcome cups of coffee.

Dood now said, 'I believe that we need to check out this businessman's house over towards Avebury. I have spoken to Libby Long at the Duck. She has contacts in a great many places and knows all about what's going on in the neighbourhood. She tells me this man has actually become quite important to the local economy, because he throws large parties on a regular basis and normally invites many people to them. I do know that Satanists hold monthly celebrations of the black mass and his larger parties would normally coincide with the major dates of their calendar, which are perhaps three or four times per year. The alleged host does seem to hold bigger ones at about the expected degree of regularity and Libby said that one of a particularly large size is planned shortly, with most of the local guest houses fully booked up.'

He sipped his coffee and continued, 'I know it's not much to go on, but a local caterer has been employed to prepare for a big gathering in six days' time. I wonder, do you think that Mr Pal will stay at home for that long? If it were me, I would want to be out and about on errands from time to time. Perhaps we might pay his house a visit despite the fact that we cannot know whether he is there? In fact we know precious little about him at all; Libby tells me he a second generation naturalised Briton with a German background and with many friends likewise, but why would he live around here?'

Bishop replied, 'He is apparently called Mr Johan von Pal, but doesn't use the 'von' very much. It also seems as though he may have spent a lot of money with Creighton and Ivy recently. Creighton was quite the gentleman and didn't say anything, but he deals with quite large commissions as a matter of course. If his meeting had been for a small transaction, one could hardly have expected Creighton to drive down here with a tough, reinforced attaché case. He had a lunch meeting with Mr Pal and seemed very pleased with the outcome. I didn't like to ask any more about him and Creighton could hardly answer anyway, but I can guess that this Mr Pal is pretty wealthy. I do take it that guessing about a friend is OK, isn't it?'

The others nodded.

Oakwood said, 'So, it seems his house is worthy of a visit, if only to look around, but are you actually talking about breaking and entering?'

Dood replied, 'I think such a step would be foolish, but if we spot a genuinely open window, then trespass is a far less serious crime. I do know that my own conscience would be clear; we are, after all, looking for evidence of devil worship and are not out to steal from him. But even then, I would want a pretty good excuse in case we get caught in the act. I hope in fact that we may not need to enter the house. Since he intends to throw a large party, it is just as likely that evidence would be outside.'

Bishop followed, 'So our strategy is just to look the place over, with a view to seeing what there is to see?'

Oakwood said, 'Or why don't we just report him to the police?'

Dood replied, 'That's just it, we only have a supposition and anyway, black magic isn't a crime anymore. There is nothing to take to the police, so I agree, we must just go and see.'

'But sacrifices, mutilation and barbaric rituals are?'

'Yes, but so is breaking and entering, or trespass. We had better be careful ourselves and get our excuses ready.'

Bishop called for Emily, and a bright-looking young woman with long blonde hair appeared from the kitchen. 'We have decided to go out this evening. I don't know when we shall be back, but would you please leave a meal for four people for when we do? Nothing elaborate, just some sandwiches and salads, maybe some cake also, and a couple of bottles of something.'

'Certainly, but you would like a meal for four? There are only three of you!'

'Yes, but I invited Adam Shilto over too. Best not to let the poor guy go hungry.'

'Fine, but will I have to let you in late?'

'No, I don't think so, because although Amelia is away for a few days, staying with family, you won't need any more security than the lock on the front door. You know how to set the burglar alarm if you go out? And there's always the telephone.'

'Yes, I know what to do.'

Adam Shilto arrived at about five pm. By then they had all changed into clothes of reasonable practicality and with some thought, heavy walking shoes in case they needed to explain that they were ramblers, off-course. It was also a damp evening; there might be wet undergrowth and mud, so they each had a waterproof rolled up in a pocket, just in case. They left in Oakwood's car at about 6.30pm and they headed east towards Avebury. At that time of year, dusk fell at 4.50pm, so he put his lights on immediately.

After about fifteen minutes, Bishop directed them off the main road, but they continued in their general direction parallel to the old A4 Bath highway by turning right again very quickly. After another short stretch, a 'B standard' road diverged to the right and shortly, a dip was visible ahead, filled with beech trees.

Bishop said, 'I believe this is the place.'

Oakwood parked his car behind some bushes and said, 'Is everyone sure of what to say if we get challenged? Dressed as we are, we can reasonably say we are lost, but our excuse does get weaker with every step we take into his property. It is much better not to get stopped at all, so we need to keep quiet and try to avoid noise and lights and anybody who may be present.'

All was quiet as they left the road and made their way through the beech trees surrounding Johan Pal's property, where their boots made little sound on the spongy turf. By now it was 7.15pm and the temperature was falling. There was mist in the air and in the semi-darkness of intermittent moonlight and the occasional flash of light from a torch, visibility was only adequate. After two-hundred yards of rough beech scrub, they came across a thick laurel hedge. With some effort they made their way through it and came to an area of grass which, although clear to walk on, was not mowed short to the length of a lawn. Their shoes, by now, were wet through and the grass very slippery.

As they moved, they heard the sound of water from a pipe or conduit. They followed it since they considered it might direct them towards more formal cultivation or to the house itself. Their aim was to examine the property from a distance for doors or windows, before choosing to make for the front, back or a side. As they progressed, they soon found their path was less overhung by branches and they were therefore able to see more clearly by means of the faint moonlight which fell to give the garden a uniform grey colour. Nearby, the sound of water was louder and they observed a large rectangle of grass, shorter-cropped than the rough area they had already traversed. However, around it were human-like figures, standing with sharp shadows in the moonlight; they prepared to run, but a lack of movement soon showed these were statuary and that they had entered an area of garden with a formal lawn and classical sculptures, from which a single pathway directed their approach further forward. In the distance, they then observed the imposing shadow of a property of considerable size against the sky: it had deep gables and bay windows and was a late Victorian house of red brick.

Thus far, they had wondered at the ease with which they entered the grounds and whether security might exist there, or whether it was restricted to the house alone. Shilto proposed the possible existence of a wire, stretched perhaps at calf-height, as a security measure to warn those in the house of intruders; but the others were sceptical. In particular, Oakwood thought it more likely that something 'more up-to-date' would be used and said, 'Wires would not even be considered in this day and age. Any security assessor hired to install garden security would recommend PIR protection.'

Dood said, 'Elaborate, please; we need some advice on this.'

'PIR means that we could face passive infrared detectors. They are activated when they sense a heat source like that from our bodies. When they do, they radio into a main base, generally about two or three hundred yards away, at which point a chime or buzzer would go off inside the house. The owner could then send someone out with a shotgun, or loose the dogs. Some of those Rottweilers are pretty dangerous and would half-tear your arm off; you would be shocked by their power and would have to guard your throat. The only defence would be a baseball bat or long blade. A shotgun would be the illegal use by the owner of an offensive weapon, but that wouldn't stop some people, especially if they have had burglaries before. Later, there would probably be a further PIR system if we break into the house itself, but that would activate a main alarm and make a loud noise. Costly domestic alarm systems can also dial into the local police force. Besides all that, I would expect a pressure mat just inside any French windows and doors, where it would have the same effect.'

'So should we give up now?'

'Of course not; we could be lucky and avoid a PIR sensor. The best way to do that would be to avoid spreading out in the garden. PIR detectors are usually placed randomly and the more paths we take, the greater the likelihood of setting one off. We should also keep our profile low to the ground and avoid passing near to objects where a detector might be placed.'

'Such as?'

'I would fix them to trees.'

'Would we see a mains wire?'

'No, they run on replaceable batteries these days.'

Taking these suggestions into account, they crouched low and kept to the open space on the lawn. Shortly, they came to a path and having got thus far, felt it was absurd not to risk further ingression and they decided to follow its course as far as they could. It became clear that they had skirted quite a large lawn, but their movements were quick and after less than thirty seconds they reached a sunken gallery with a base of porcelain paving.

Reached by four easy steps, the paved gallery was large enough to accommodate a small party of people. It had a pond in the middle, complete with a classical statue representing the god Triton, with conch shell and trident. A fountain issued from the conch shell but the noise was not great because the water fell onto stones below in the form of a cascade. Undoubtedly the level of the water, some two or three feet below ground level, helped the water to flow out without difficulty into a channel beneath, in order to escape.

They walked around, examined the gallery in detail and immediately took note of the floor. Into the porcelain paving, fine artwork had been inlaid and it was clear that the owner had expended considerable time and effort in its design. It was quite unnecessary to step away to view it fully, since the design was simple and a full perspective was available without difficulty for them to see.

The inlaid artwork was of a five-pointed star, augmented by Hebrew script and decorative images. Set directly into individual porcelain tiles and formed from them, the decorative images were of hellish design. They varied in size, but the largest and most significant was of an animalesque face; its form could not be identified, however, because it had the varied characteristics of many species: there were fangs, a beard and snout, and a mane of hair, together with human-like eyes. The latter seemed intelligent and watchful, but Dood's mind disputed what instinct told him: although he recoiled from their gaze, he was able to examine them with the detached manner of the observer of artwork rather than of a living apparition.

The area contained evidence of preparation for a party. On the lawn nearby were trestle tables and a marquee which contained oddments such as musical instruments: there were drums and trumpets in cases. But it was also clear that a substantial meal would be eaten there in due course since chairs, together with assorted knives, forks and plates were piled in a corner.

As far as the question of an alarm was concerned, they now had the collective feeling that their luck was in. They were as quiet as their soft-soled footfall could make them and the loudest sound was that of the fountain-fall. Nevertheless, Dood, after having seen the design in the gallery floor, was imbued with more urgency than before. He stifled a quiet oath and said, 'We may have placed ourselves in grave danger by coming here and I think we need to complete our search quickly now. I would like to take a short look at the house and then I think we should leave as quickly as we can.'

The four men strode quickly towards the house, the side wall of which lay ahead and from which the sunken gallery had been a diversion. Bay windows were visible in four places on a western wall where the property was now seen at its shortest side. Turning a corner to the southern side, they observed its double-fronted aspect, with further bay windows on each of four reception rooms. It was a large house, with high ceilings, but like many Victorian houses it lacked the grace of Georgian architecture: its heavy gables gave it a sullen and brooding look and its curtained windows were like closed eyes with thoughts turned inwards.

Returning to the west side, they looked into two windows in turn. There was nothing to be seen in the first, which had been curtained by very heavy drapes made from dark blue velvet. The second window had similarly heavy curtains, but with a gap between. It was dark and the inside of the room could not clearly be seen. They did not attempt to enter because it did not seem to be a room of any significance and they did not think they would be able to raise the locked sash window without breaking the glass, which they were reluctant to do.

By now it was 8.35pm and they were able to see quite well by starlight and by the light of the moon, now rising overhead. They carried torches, but had used them only intermittently. Quickly now, they returned to the south side and examined windows there, not without trepidation, because they were more fully exposed. There, a single window was un-curtained and they could see it was of the same design as before and could be opened by raising it on its rope sash. They found it unlocked and Shilto opened it without difficulty. He entered the room with ease, looked around inside for a minute, then returned to the window and said quietly, 'This room will do.'

Dood entered too, and they stood in silence for a few seconds, looking at a room without particular significance other than the fact that it had an inner door. This also proved to be unlocked and by passing through, they entered a further reception room in which lamps of low wattage gave a subdued light. It was probably a room that had been deserted only very recently.

They had rehearsed their rather weak excuse of: *'ramblers, lost, caught out in the cold, saw a dark house, so popped in to put the kettle on,'* but by now, were aware that it wouldn't really stand up to much if they were caught. However they had left Oakwood and Bishop on watch outside and they were guarded on the inside by means of a lock to the rest of the house. They felt confident of spending at least a few minutes within and so decided to look around what was plainly a library and domestic office with desk. If necessary, they would be able to vanish out of the same window quite quickly if they heard the noise of someone attempting to return.

The library was small, with two modest glass-fronted lockable bookcases. Within it, there were many reference works on country matters; they saw well-bound volumes on the history, landscape and culture of the shires. There was also a substantial collection of more scientific works such as the origin and history of pharmacology, on botanical medicines, alkaloids and their extraction; and also on the taxonomy of plants, herbaria, identification guides and on mycology. In particular, Dood noticed a book on the chemistry of tobacco, together with several books on the Cannabaceae family of plants. Leafing through one of them with avidity, he was interested to see articles expounding their commercial value in the production of foodstuffs, oils, ropes and medicines. Looking briefly at a further article on the pharmacology of that family, he was drawn to a section on the well-known aroma of the burnt herb: the chemicals the smoke contained and their effect on the central nervous system. He might have continued to read it had he more time; nevertheless, that commodity was now sadly lacking.

The bottom of one particular bookcase had opaque glass. It was also locked, but Dood was able to open it with a sharp tug. Inside was a collection of very much older books; none of which had gilt or other lettering on the spine. He took a couple out to examine.

One was bound in rich leather, but its binding was dry and cracked with age and its pages of vellum had had words applied by a medieval hand. He said, 'I believe this is very old and may even pre-date the earliest use of the printing press. It would seem to be a hand-written manuscript copy of part of the New Testament. And look at this one, I have seen this title in the *Index*

Librorum Prohibitorum, the papal list of banned works from the fifteenth century; it is a copy of 'Hexenhammer,' an original by Kramer and Sprenger from 1487 in the German language. And this…' his voice tailed off to leave a pause '…only an individual interested in witches and the occult could possibly want to own one and then an original volume would cost a huge amount.'

He closed and replaced it, looked at a few more volumes and began to take photographs of them with his mobile phone. Uncharacteristically, the display of his phone began to work sluggishly; then they both began to feel cold and their movements started to feel clumsy and heavy. They began to shiver also and felt unaccountably saddened as though the room had begun to affect their optimism and morale. They were both instantly aware of the change and looked at each other and Dood said sharply, 'We must get out immediately; I think there is some devilry afoot here.'

Quickly, they retraced their steps and found the window. Shilto climbed out first, but as Dood followed, his manner of movement made him face inwards and it was he who first noticed an incipient vapour; effectively a yellow mist forming within the room. It quickly rose to meet his face and seemed to wish to envelope and suffocate; he knew it was evil and not like the clean and gentle mist on the downs nearby. With some force, he closed the window and joined the others who were waiting for him outside.

They had been inside for as little as five minutes, but they had seen quite enough to form a view of the interests of the incumbent. Both now tried to communicate a degree of urgency to their companions and they gesticulated to run as swiftly as they could. Ahead and around, that same yellow mist was rising, as dense and cold as that within the house and as smog-like as any Victorian effluent over the East End. However their return was clear by means of the route they had come in, and they easily crashed through the laurel hedge. There, the path through the beech trees showed them to the apparent safety of their car. Although it seemed that they were now able to run only very slowly, they eventually reached their car, started it without difficulty and were relieved to close their doors to the enveloping opacity outside and pull away.

Moving out, Oakwood remarked on his weak headlights. Fog-lamps, fore and aft, did little to help and he was obliged to drive slowly. Behind them the dense and dark fog was now complete and its unnatural cold seemed to follow them as they splashed through puddles and away. Later, their progress seemed better away from the house and their lights were more effective. They knew that their visit had ended just in time.

Shilto asked, 'What was that dreadful cold and the mist and morose feeling? It seemed to rise from the floor and move around of its own will, even though the air was still.'

Dood said, 'We left just as an occult attack on us was starting. That cold fog was sent to stop us and had we stayed longer, we might not have been able to leave at all and I expect they would have found us with icicles in our veins. I am quite sure we would have had a most unpleasant visitation, probably by some vile entity from the underworld.'

'Is it possible to protect ourselves from such things?'

'Certainly, Adam, but I am ashamed to say that tonight, I was not properly equipped to do so. I shall not make that mistake again.'

They returned to Bishop's house, parked the car and entered. Emily Robertson was obviously asleep because the house was quiet and her room was closed and curtained. After kicking off their outdoor gear they attacked the cold meal she had left for them and had a couple of bottles of claret with it.

Oakwood said, 'What exactly did you feel in that inner room that made you come out again? I saw only mist, but you looked quite alarmed.'

'Someone recently called me an exorcist. I wouldn't quite go that far, but anyone at least helping out at such times would have known the spine-chilling cold of animate evil. There was something bad there and it didn't like intruders. Other than that I cannot say exactly what it was.'

'So what conclusions can we draw?'

'I took some photographs of pages from one or two volumes in his library. It seemed to me that they were exactly the kind of literature I would expect from a practitioner of the occult. Wally, could you send them to Creighton to look at?'

'Certainly, perhaps you could transfer them to me by email. But can we take it that your mind is made up anyway?'

'Yes, I think it is. The unpleasant manifestation and what I think I saw of the books were quite enough to make me decide. The bad guy is Johan Pal right enough, and he has power enough to raise real nasties.'

Shilto said, 'As I see it, our attention was at first diverted towards the possibility of unpleasant activities on the downs. Later, strange noises in the wood were designed to fix our attention there. We also found a fake sacrifice on an altar nearby, but were not fooled by it. Taken together, Pal would formerly have considered his activities at the house safe, with us kept out of the way. However, now, if he knows we were there tonight, that can no longer be the case. Do you think he knows who the intruders were, or could that mist have been a general 'nastiness' left behind to deal with any intruder regardless?'

'I don't think he could possibly act as a psychic guard for every inch of his property himself,' said Dood. 'I think he left that unpleasant agency behind to do it for him, which might explain why there was no noise from an electrical alarm system: he wouldn't need one. There were probably also staff there – Creighton described an accomplished chef – but Pal could have arranged for them to be ignored by it. If I were Pal, which I am happy to deny, I would be inclined to think that our attentions are unchanged and still on the altar on the downs.'

'But surely,' said Oakwood, 'we *are* interested in the altar? What if it's a double bluff and something *is* going on there?'

Bishop said, 'That would be just too complicated. In fact, it might have been preferable for him and his supporters if no evidence were found at all. Then everything would have been much quieter and nobody would have investigated anything.'

Dood continued, 'Yes, a double-bluff would be ridiculous, just too complicated to work.'

Shilto said, 'We think the evidence out there on the downs was a fake. We've seen the house and know him to be active there. We suspect that some kind of big crime is about to be committed, possibly at his house in about six days' time, but we don't know what, except that it may be violent and involve blood. The Police are interested in that too. We have to take all this evidence at face value and cannot construct complex arguments about which bits are more meaningful. Despite that, we may now have a slight advantage because 'they' think we are interested in the hill, but we know otherwise.'

Dood replied, 'And we *do* now know a bit about our important local businessman but he only *may* know we visited tonight.'

Bishop said, 'So what actually do we know about our businessman? I don't think we truly know he is engaged in any business at all. He might be something else altogether!'

Dood said, 'He has money, because his house is big and has large grounds that are well-kept by what must be a team of gardeners. He also has a library worth thousands, possibly millions. That money gives him a lot of freedom to do whatever he wants. However, he is also secretive; very few wealthy businessmen or professionals, of any kind, would be interested in living away from their work, cut off from main roads and railway lines and behind trees and laurel hedges, unless they had something to hide. I believe the expression is *conspicuous consumption*; or *money will out*. He probably tries to avoid that, but the signs are still there.'

He continued, 'He may or may not have a security system, in fact we were unable to find out. However, he showed that he has protection of another kind; one far more deadly to the intruder. It is quite clear to me that he wishes to deter any investigator. And now consider his garden for a minute, that sunken gallery with pond and statue was quite unusual; especially the design on it. I think the inlaid tiles showed a deliberate attempt to represent evil and devilish themes. That, and the presence of water – we all know that their rituals need it – would make it a likely place for a black mass.'

The others were content for Dood to continue summing up. 'Now the library; I opened a bookcase and examined some of its contents. It contained all kinds of interesting and valuable books and in fact, I would love to have spent the day there. The interesting thing is that one substantial section was devoted to magic and esoteric religious doctrines. I saw several priceless books, but my main discovery was a Clavicule of Solomon in the original Latin. Here, take a look at this picture on my mobile. That, by itself, would convince me. It is the one text, in fact the Satanic Bible, from which any such circle would draw its ceremonies.'

Bishop said, 'Yes, he probably got that recently from Creighton Brakespeare. The fact that it was for sale was well-known to dealers. In fact, I think the transaction was completed when Creighton was here, which might account for the fresh round of activity from Mr Pal. But why don't you speak to Creighton about it? I can get him on the phone.'

Oakwood said, 'That's a great idea; he is an absolute mine of useful information on all aspects of books and their contents. It could do no harm at all.'

The next day, Bishop telephoned Creighton Brakespeare in Cambridge. They exchanged pleasantries and then he said, 'Creighton, could you please talk to Callum Dood about a book that we came across in connection with our researches down here in Wiltshire. Callum is our local vicar and he is interested in religious and devotional literature, as you would expect. Callum, this is Creighton.'

Dood said, 'Can you tell me a bit about a book called the Clavicule of Solomon?' The other end of the telephone line went quiet for a few seconds, but the exchange then resumed.

'What exactly do you want to know? You will appreciate that I cannot discuss my transactions with clients. I can only talk about such things on a very general basis.'

'That's OK. We only want to know about it in a very general way, that is, about things that we could look up if we only had the time.'

'Such books are exceedingly rare and therefore costly. The last one, in fact the only one to have passed through my hands raised a small fortune for the vendor. I could not get hold of another if I wanted to…' Creighton Brakespeare coughed and continued, '…but such a book would be the black magician's bible: his best possible working tool. It contains a detailed description of magical practice as it was known in the early Middle-Ages. Any aspiring magician would go straight to that volume for all they might wish to know about things we disbelieve today. They could read about spells, potions, anything the three witches in Macbeth might want to do, and more.'

'Is it the only copy?'

'No. There are several other copies in various classical languages, but it is generally agreed that those in Greek, Hebrew or Middle French are copies of an older work in Latin. The earliest known volume, in fact, would date from about the thirteenth or fourteenth century, before the time of the first printing press, so such a volume would be written on vellum by a scribe. You may have heard that I sold one recently to an individual who lives a few miles from you. I stayed with Wally recently and made the exchange then.'

'Ok, Creighton, but I can take it that the man is a prominent businessman from near Avebury?'

'Since you seem to know already, a straight 'yes' cannot do any harm.'

'Thank you, Creighton.' Dood replaced the receiver.

Dood said, 'He confirmed what I already thought about the book. Pal's copy is older than copies in Hebrew and Greek, or even Middle French, which are known in major libraries of medieval literature. It is absolutely unique and that alone makes it almost certain that the owner is a devil worshipper; I cannot see anyone else being so choosy. From our own observations, he is a practitioner of considerable ability and I believe we need look no further. Now, how do we put him out of business?'

'More particularly,' said Bishop, 'as far as we are concerned, his plans have only been conjecture. What exactly is it that he intends to do?'

Dood said, 'My feeling is that he intends to abstract and use the Magdeburg Relic: how he intends to take it I am sure we will shortly find out. However, more immediately, I believe I owe you all an apology for taking you into as much danger as I did tonight. There is no question that Pal is prepared to use his abilities against his enemies and it is also clear that having entered his home, he will regard us as foes and may try to inflict some kind of revenge. In fact, since he surely knows that we have the Relic still, my guess is that there will shortly be some kind of movement against us here. Before we went out, I should have planned our protection accordingly; I must make sure that we are adequately protected next time.'

Oakwood replied, 'Why just sit and wait? We need to find some way to take the battle to him, not the other way around.'

Dood considered his reply. 'That may be, but in order to do that, I think we need to find out a little more about his plans. We can't expect Creighton to say much more and in any case, we should speak to other, more local sources about our mysterious friend. Maybe I should speak to Libby Long at the Duck again.'

Later over lunch, Dood drew Libby into conversation. They discussed beer, the new style of gastropub and its effect on profits – more labour-intensive and no more profitable than pie and chips – and finally, he asked her straight out, 'Tell me a bit more about that German businessman you were chatting about.'

'Oh yes, he had a smaller than usual party a few days ago but has booked a large catering company for a bigger affair, a Halloween bash, I guess, on the 31st. At least I assume it's a bigger one because all the places I recommend when *we* have no space seem to be full with his guests at the moment. Also, his people have booked up a whole load of costumes in local novelty shops and clothiers; strange costumes, but I suppose no more outlandish than normal for this time of year. There are the usual witches with hats and broomsticks, together with several pagan gods of various descriptions and all with a lot of weird headgear. It looks as though most of them are going in disguise and perhaps that's for the good!'

'You are sure that Mr Pal is the host?'

'Oh yes.'

'Is there anything else on him?'

'Nothing more than before, really; he doesn't come here at all.'

'Thank you.'

Later, the four men were over at the vicarage, where Bishop said, 'Is this a vicarage or a rectory?'

'It was actually a vicarage, so that only a part of the income of the church – of its cash stipend and tithes – was used for the purposes of supporting the priest. In fact, this is one of the few local vicarages which has not been sold off. I don't actually hold with that kind of selling assets myself; I think that the recent egalitarianism shown by the church has caused it to lose much of its social standing, which people disrespect.'

'And you do all the garden yourself?'

'Yes, it's my main hobby. Luckily I have a hothouse – I call it my greenhouse but it's actually a lot hotter – so I can grow all my own herbs. It is huge fun: I planted out some birdseed recently, just to see what would come up: the herbs were great in salads – and you should try smoking some of them, they beat tobacco – and they produce a funny oil which resembles olive oil; it tastes great in cakes and biscuits!'

'So what's your favourite herb in those cigarillos you roll, chamomile?'

'Nearly there!'

'And over there, you seem to have a damp-looking shed.'

''Yes, I am an avid mycologist too. I study the growth and use of mushrooms. Can I show you?'

'By all means.'

'If we go inside, you can see I have a sprinkler system to keep these compost beds damp enough to grow the mushrooms concerned. The bed to the left has these tiny 'shrooms growing: they are Psilocybe semilanceata, a local species which is especially useful for my studies on pharmacology. I have discussed them with my former chemist colleague several times. Pop one into your breakfast and it seems to enhance the flavour of the bacon, somehow…!'

'Yes. And that spotted one?'

'Oh, that's the one they described in Alice in Wonderland. I'm just learning how to grow it…'

'Do I take it that mushrooms have medicinal qualities too?'

'Oh yes. And they seem to concentrate the mind perfectly; many is the time when saying "here endeth the lesson," I have actually felt I've said something worthwhile.'

They strolled back.

'…And anyway, have some more lager: it's from my guy in Calne.'

'Thank you. Now I guess we need to get down to business.'

'Yes, I guess so. We could steal the book?'

'We could kidnap Johan Pal? Threaten to expose him?'

'Not really. There's no proof of anything and the mere intention of throwing a Halloween party would be useless. There has been no crime, only the most vague notion that he intends to commit one. All we could say is that he probably leads some kind of magic circle and *may* have been a bit nasty, but leaving a sheep's head somewhere isn't actually illegal.'

Shilto said, 'In that case, we need to go back and find some proper evidence. Why don't we turn up at his place on the 31st, quite openly, and suitably attired so that we can join in with his celebrations? Half the country will be out at parties on the 31st and all wearing witch costumes.'

Oakwood said, 'Meanwhile, we look around, take photographs, look for anything illegal and rescue any damsels in distress?'

'Yes, that's about it!'

Bishop looked enthusiastic, 'OK, in the absence of a better idea I suggest we go ahead with that. It might even be fun, what with having to come up with a Halloween costume at short notice.'

Oakwood said, 'That's fine, so let's meet up here on the 31st. I hope we will be refreshed enough to pull it off.'

Chapter Six

The Goddess Frige

'Hello Mr Bishop, how did your visit go with Mr Shilto, Mr Dood and Mr Oakwood? I hope my cold table was adequate; it was a rather chilly night to be out – you didn't want something hot? And I hope my choice of red wine was in keeping.'

'Oh yes, thank you, Emily. All was excellent and we tucked in; Mr Dood in particular made his compliments. The wine was a very good choice too, so thank you. But how are you getting on generally? Is your room OK? What about your studies: distance learning I recall?'

'Well the room is very comfortable and I feel very much at home here with you and Mrs Bishop. Also, I like your friends very much, although I must admit that my studies have taken a back seat recently, what with the upheaval of moving and settling in.'

'But you only had a few books to carry over?'

'Yes, that's true.'

'Well anything we can do to make life easier for you, let us know, please.'

'Thank you, that is very good of you.'

Emily went out for the morning and Amelia Bishop came in from her travels around town.

'Hi Amelia, how is your morning?'

'It's looking up. I am still quite busy with village matters, but I have also been able to get into town on a few errands.'

'Good, have you spoken to Emily? I think we need to make sure she doesn't have so much to do that she neglects her studies. I know she is just settling in.'

'Why, yes of course; I'll keep an eye on her. She does seem to be quite active socially, always buzzing about.'

Over the next few days, Emily came and went and although she worked very hard on domestic matters, clearly enjoying and totally fulfilling her brief as home help, both of them noticed a slight unease, as though she possessed divided loyalties between work and study. They also noticed a certain distress when, as the 31st approached, conversation turned to Wally Bishop's requirement for a Halloween costume.

'Mrs Bishop, are you going to the Halloween party with Mr Bishop?'

'Oh no, Emily, I cannot be bothered with that kind of thing. I have decided to keep my toes warm here at home and I want to finish my book, what with the circle coming up soon. One of my friends was quite embarrassed last time, because it turned out she had only read the flyleaf. But Wally and the others said they are going to a friend's place for the night, hence the need for costumes so they can fit in. What about you?'

Emily looked distressed.

'Is everything OK, Emily? You sometimes look a bit worried whenever social functions are mentioned. Are you managing to study here at home?'

'Oh, yes Mrs Bishop. You have made me feel very welcome and I am glad to be able to live in and help you. I do know that you are both very busy with all kinds of business and local interests. I will get back into my studies as soon as I can, but I suppose you are right; I may have let it slip a little.'

'Well, let me know if I can help.'

Emily bustled off and Amelia Bishop bustled off somewhere else.

Later that day, Amelia returned from helping her husband with the business and let herself in. However, as she approached the front of the house, she noted that Emily was standing in the window of her bedroom, with her side facing the window, as though looking elsewhere within the room. Her appearance caused Amelia to drop her keys, for Emily was dressed in a cloak of feathers and over her head was a headpiece formed in the likeness of a bird of prey with a prominent bill. She glanced to the right and noted Amelia's gaze, and quickly withdrew as Amelia entered the house. Amelia said nothing and decided not to mention it unless Emily volunteered to do so.

That evening, Wally Bishop returned from work, clutching an early pearlware porcelain artefact which he had brought home to 'have about the house' for a while. He placed it on a sideboard and asked Amelia's opinion.

'Well, give me time to get used to it. I like the colours. What exactly is it?'

'It's interesting: an early Staffordshire piece by Obadiah Sherratt, completely unrestored and with no damage. It's called Christ's Agony and was made about 1820. Let's keep it for a month and see whether we take to it. Fancy a gin and tonic?'

'No gin now, but maybe later.'

'I wonder what Emily has made. Something lovely, I expect.'

A while later, the three of them sat down to dinner and Emily was her usual pleasant and lively self. They enjoyed her company and she theirs. After a while, Bishop turned the conversation to business and asked for Emily's opinion of the porcelain he had brought home.

'Emily, what do you think about Christ's Agony over there? I bought it recently and thought I might show it for a while.'

She replied, 'I think that it's lovely; no doubt it will end up in a valuable collection and be lost to the majority view.'

Bishop noted that she did not turn her head to look at it. Their conversation moved on, but later he returned to the piece and suggested that she might like to bring it to the table. Again, she showed a reluctance to look at it or fulfil his suggestion and Amelia said,

'Emily, you needn't, but can you tell us whether everything is OK?'

Immediately, her eyes were filled with tears and her guard seemed to drop altogether. 'I'm sorry, I am afraid I have been instructed not to touch religious artefacts like that. Also, I'm very preoccupied by what might happen on 31st. You've both been so pleasant to me and I'm not sure I'm repaying you properly. You see, I'm not really the spying kind.' She rushed from the room and could be heard running upstairs.

Amelia went calmly up to Emily's room and knocked on the door. Shortly, both of them came downstairs and back to the table. Amelia said, 'I'll have that gin and tonic now and please make it a large one!'

In fact Bishop returned with three large ones and thus fortified, conversation flowed much more easily. Emily was now less inhibited and in fact keen to unburden herself with the very gentle encouragement Amelia offered. Wally Bishop said very little throughout, although he did keep the gin topped up.

'I owe you an apology. I am afraid that I had in fact been sent here to find out about the artefact we know you have hidden. When I say 'we,' I really mean Johan Pal, whom we call 'The Master.' We're scared of him because we know the power he has over us. He is unscrupulous, ruthless and can control our destiny. I shouldn't be talking to you like this: I'm very scared of what he might do!'

She continued, 'I know you have been discussing these things with the Reverend Dood and your other friends, which makes it a bit less of a burden, really. He will understand: I am afraid that I have fallen in with a black magician of the worst kind. No I don't mean somebody who joined Wicca and follows the teachings of Raymond Buckland and his cissy magic. I don't mean simple paganism either: the worship of nature, or heavenly bodies or the persuance of herb-lore. I mean something far more dangerous. Mr Pal has real power and he can exercise his will for good or bad over long distances. He can destroy me! Oh, what have I done by telling you? He's bound to know.'

'What precisely did you mean when you said the word spying?'

'Yes, I'm so sorry. The Master knows his destiny is tied to a terrible artefact which you have hidden away. He wants it and sent me here to apply for the job of housekeeper so that I could find out where you had hidden it and obtain it on his behalf. But your home is so wholesome and pleasant and you are both so nice, that I cannot quite do as he wished. Since I was quite young I had an ambition to be of use, perhaps as a vet or doctor so that I could do some good in the world. All that would vanish if I return to him with what he wants.'

'Then refuse to return!'

'I cannot, he could kill me or cast me into the Abyss.'

'What exactly is this abyss?'

'It is an expression reserved for the bottomless chasm which leads to the underworld, to hell itself.'

'And if you stay?'

'All Souls' Eve is soon and he wants me then, because I am to be fully initiated into his circle. I am terrified by what he will make me do that night. I cannot bear the thought of giving myself to a man dressed as an animal. It has been suggested that Johan Pal may do the deed himself, or even worse, Sieghard Trapper, his fellow traveller. My flesh crawls at the thought!'

'Then stay here. I am sure that Callum Dood has the skill to resist Mr Pal.'

'Why, has he some power himself as a white magician?'

'I know little, except that for the Church, he has fought the demonic possession of human beings in all its forms as an exorcist. He has described the battle of wills that has ensued and has also discussed various means of protection against the forces of darkness. How he does it I do not know. It may be with brandy for all I know, but in any case, there is nobody more qualified than Dood, although he can be a bit eccentric at times.'

Amelia said, 'What was that costume you were wearing upstairs? I didn't like to mention it before and I saw it from outside only by accident.'

'That is my costume for the Black Mass on 31st, when I shall be baptised in a new name. I am to take on the name 'Frige,' the Anglo Saxon Goddess of sexuality and fertility. She was worshipped long ago in rites that are still practised today and have been handed down secretly by those initiated into her cult. Her image is one of the head of a bird of prey and her gown is of feathers. After I give myself to Pal, I shall become like her and will have powers myself that are derived from hers. But help me! These are powers over other people that I have never really wished for.'

'Your own powers?'

'Yes, I shall be able to wish ill-fortune on other people, or wish them success or riches. In the course of time and if I am able to advance further, I will be able to leave my body at will or prevent myself from becoming old. But such powers come with a sacrifice. I shall have to pay a tithe to Her every year and She may ultimately choose to take my own soul for herself. Such is the age-old bargain.'

'I thought you said that Pal is a devil worshipper.'

'Yes, but as with Christianity with its many saints and angels, there are many devils in the pantheon, each with its own aims and interests, but united in a common wish to destroy mankind.'

'You are serious?'

'Deadly serious; I could demonstrate some of my present powers but had I offered to show you next week, there would have been many more. In truth, I am actively trying to avoid the attentions of Pal by not showing them to you, because he would immediately know. I have the vain hope that he will ignore me.'

Later, Dood and Shilto came over. After further doses of gin, Wally Bishop explained the situation, whereupon Shilto said, 'I am sure I speak for us all when I say how sorry I am that we have brought you into such danger, Emily.'

'Oh it really isn't your fault. I was trying to get away from Pal long before you found the Magdeburg Relic.'

'But nobody even mentioned that in your presence, so how can you have known about it?'

'That's simple, he told me enough to have an idea of what is at stake. I am sure that he hasn't told me all, but my own clairvoyance revealed more.'

'Emily, you really must not use the powers that you now possess.' It was Dood who spoke. 'Regardless of the question of whether used for good or evil, their use brings a debt which must eventually be settled. It is better for you to avoid having to pay.'

Emily accepted this idea and Dood continued, 'We have actively avoided talking about our relic for a while, half in hope that it would disappear of its own accord.'

Bishop said, 'Yes, it's locked up in the cellar. Its presence sometimes makes me feel uneasy. I had come to the conclusion that I would pass it back to Harry Devine, it *is* his after all. But they would track him down and maybe we can avoid the consequences rather better than he can. Honestly, I still don't know what to do with it and the days are passing.'

'Well at least it's safe for now.'

Emily said, 'Don't you believe it; Pal will exert all of his abilities to get it from you and probably me also. He must know that I am having second thoughts about my future with him and he will never rest until he has me once more. He may even…' her voice trailed off.

'May even what?'

'He needs blood for his purpose and it could even be mine!' Her eyes were huge.

Shilto spoke for them all, 'Here with Amelia and Wally, you have a welcoming and warm home to live and work in. I am sure there is very little risk to you here.'

'I would like to believe that…oh, if only!'

'Emily, you seem so terrified of Johan Pal.'

'Yes, I have seen his powers, or at least some of them. He can overlook from afar. He is probably doing so now. You may yourself have glimpsed, from a distance, an event which concerns you. I certainly have been able to see images from far away that have concerned my own affairs; people talking, gesticulations, places, enemies who turn their back, friends who are concerned. Johan Pal is an advanced psychic and that is nothing to him. He only needs to throw himself into a trance in front of a mirror to view us all, unless…'

'Unless what, Emily?' Dood spoke.

'…Unless a white magician of equal power can place some kind of shield around us.'

There was silence for a while.

'Well, at least we now know what Johan Pal is up to,' said Dood. 'Up until very recently, we had no idea what he intended to do next. All we had come up with was the vague idea of going to his place, so that we could look for some kind of evidence to take to the police.'

Bishop said, 'We must still go. We only guessed that Pal knew about the Magdeburg Relic and were not absolutely sure until tonight. Now, we know his immediate aim, so that is in itself an advance. If we do nothing: if he is left to his own devices, there will still be rites, sacrifices and blood. I do not think that we can change our plans. I take it that the Relic will be significant for him?'

Emily said, 'You will never be able to make anything stick with Johan Pal. He knows that devil worship and witchcraft is no longer a crime, but he would never let himself be found in any compromising position regardless.'

She continued, 'The Magdeburg Relic will become his great work. Through it he will seek to exert his will, try to dominate others and advance some of the Nazi aims that ended seventy years ago. He has the single purpose: to pursue power over people, to bully and crush them, until like a Fuhrer himself, he will rule the world: a new world order of darkness and despair.'

'Then we should burn it!'

'No, it would be pointless; a degree of power would still remain with the ashes. And anyway, we went through all those arguments.'

Shilto said, 'Then let's have some brandy!'

Dood replied, 'Now you're talking!'

After some much-needed refreshment, the discussion continued. They agreed they would try to cut all contact between Emily and Johan Pal. In the comfort of the Bishops' home, her confidence was renewed by the decency and normality she felt around her.

However she now said, 'I am rather concerned by the likely fate of the other acolytes like myself; in particular, my friends Freya Sampson, a decent and lovely girl, and Kayla Raddle, whom we all love. Neither of them relishes the prospect of being initiated and certainly not by the likes of…'

'And you wonder whether we can rescue them?' said Shilto.

She replied, 'Yes. It is one-hundred percent likely that Pal will initiate poor Freya that night. God save her from Dick Bascher or possibly even worse, Pal himself.'

'But he would be concerned chiefly with the Magdeburg Relic on the 31st?'

'We must guess that he will be planning so, but that wouldn't prevent him from carrying out what I have already described.'

'Then we have the simple duty of rescuing her and preventing him from using the relic. The latter part is more straightforward; we have it and he doesn't.'

'Emily, how exactly did you get involved?'

'We went to a party where they had a session on telling fortunes by cards and were then invited to another party the following month. There, they showed us a bit more occult 'fun,' and convinced us that there was still more to see at the next meeting. We always enjoyed it, because there was music and dancing, together with a lovely sweet wine which made us lose our inhibitions. We accepted what we were shown and always wanted to see more. Eventually, we all went to a party held by The Master himself. There, we were shown strange rituals and magical things and let ourselves be hypnotised. Once we were hypnotised for the first time, he could instantly do the same on any further occasion he chose. By then he could also influence us to take part in things against our better judgement. Only later did I realise he was preparing us as acolytes for his magic circle.'

'On one occasion, I had been dancing all night and later, I found myself covered in an ointment made of hemlock. I was dizzy; it felt just like flying on a broomstick and the next day I was rather the worse for wear – no, don't worry about anything – but those occasions were only parties in which we did at least have fun and we only did small things. Unfortunately the next, on 31st, will be a full black mass when we will finally be initiated fully. You cannot think what that will mean; I shall have to give myself to Johan Pal and I can't stomach the thought of it. If I'm to escape, it can only be through staying here. To do that, I shall need protection. Is it true that you have enough power to resist him yourself? If not, I shall have to commit a crime and get taken to a police cell.'

Callum Dood replied, 'I must be careful what I say. I am really only the vicar of our church but I *have* presided over exorcisms and am aware of the power of Christian rituals over the forces of darkness. There cannot be any guarantee of success, however, and I will need to refresh my knowledge once more. Nevertheless, it does seem that we have no alternative than to resist.'

He continued after a few seconds pause, 'However there are things we can do to help. With the 31st approaching, we should try to purify ourselves beforehand. There is a need for abstinence from the pleasures of the flesh and of the table; no wine or beer from now on and only the simplest of food: fruit, vegetables and fish, but no meat. It may also be that some of us have become too cynical, but if we can, we should all try to pray for guidance and strength.'

★

Within his cloak of mist, Johan Pal sat in front of a blank wall and meditated. He began by breathing deeply and closed his eyes in order to remove any outside image that would deflect his attention. He felt no wish to sleep and first concentrated on his right hand, which he endeavoured to relax fully, then successive limbs and head, neck and torso. As he did so, his speed of breathing fell and he became quite calm, with a resting pulse that would have done credit to the finest athlete, and with his mind on the edge of a dream, yet fully awake.

Soon, he sought to project his mind into the void. By visualising a connection of body and higher self as a thin cord of silver, he was able to transfer his thoughts and consciousness to a plane above his body. He had done so many times, was quite confident of his training and knew that he could immediately displace his vision and hearing over long distances.

He now knew that he had been deceived by Emily, whom he had intended to initiate at his next Sabbat. However, she was young and could not be expected to steel herself to ignore the comfort of her hosts' home. He would not destroy her and should still find her useful.

Like the negative image of a photograph, white on black, he could also see the Magdeburg Relic on the very edge of his mind. It was hidden, although not well-enough; and changing, it became transformed into a cupped hand within which was a golden orb that illuminated its surroundings.

Now he heard a whisper in the ether: 'Carn-Brea'[11] and observed a mound of stone on a hillside. Where was it? What

---

11 *Carn Brea: Brythonic Celtic; hill of stones*

lay underneath? For an instant, his dark eyes were filled with desire, but he continued to control himself fully and was calm as he rose from the chair. Where was 'Carn Brea'?

★

Emily was troubled by bad dreams and felt that a pile of stone on a chalk hillside, present since the dawn of time, was now disturbed. Beneath was a pit from which issued a smell as bad as all the smells of age-old corruption. She was naked and stood on the edge, looking down into darkness. Johan Pal stood as though on a ladder within, his torso visible above the rim, and was pulling her towards him. She had little strength of her own to resist his will and was inching towards destruction. She was, however, pulled back by Callum Dood and his friends but their combined strength was barely enough to stop her falling. She knew that only her own strength of will could prevent her final demise, but it was dark all around and her strength could not manifest until daylight.

Silently, she arose from her bed and clothed herself in her head-dress and cloak of feathers. Outside, she met Johan Pal, who had been was waiting for her. He kissed her on her cold cheek and returned to his pocket the silver phial in which lay the lock of her hair upon which he had concentrated his mind. Emily was resigned and for a time could do no more.

★

'Emily has gone! She left everything behind except for a few clothes,' said Amelia.

'When, last night?' said Wally Bishop. 'I didn't hear anything at all; no doors banging, no stairs creaking. She cannot have been sleepwalking. Look, I always lock this door at night and usually put the chain across. It would be impossible to replace the chain from outside and now it's down. She must have gone out in the night, but was it of her own free will?'

'I will telephone the others. They won't mind, Callum usually gets up at 5am anyway and the others aren't far behind.' Amelia made a quick round of calls and could be heard talking quietly from the hallway. Callum Dood came round after fifteen minutes and Adam Shilto only a little later.

Bishop said, 'Well they cannot have taken the relic. I have the keys and it's locked down in the cellar. It would take more than magic to undo that, believe me. Think of the noise of breaking in; but if you like, I will check to make sure it's still there.'

He went to the bedroom, retrieved his keys and then enlisted Shilto in helping him push away the kitchen table. Kneeling, he unlocked a heavy padlock, raised a trapdoor and descended to the cellar with its smell of damp and dead spiders. Moving several layers of old carpet, he then withdrew the familiar box and called out, 'Don't worry, it's all here' and there was a thankful tone to his voice as he rattled the box, replaced it and moved around among the wine bottles and shelves of odds and ends.

A minute later there was a crash and they heard him mumble 'Clumsy today.' After a few minutes more of silence, punctuated by the sound of corks being pulled, his head reappeared at floor level and they spoke almost in unison, 'Is everything alright, Wally?'

Bishop clutched four opened bottles of wine. He said, 'These were on a rack right above the relic. They are sour, all of them.' A smell of vinegar and mice arose from the trapdoor. He said, 'I don't think we shall be able to drink anything from that cellar, or at least, not while that thing is there. I would never have believed it.' He grimaced and pocketed the key.

They said nothing for a couple of minutes, but then Dood said, 'We need to get Emily back. Can we make sure that Peyton comes back for the 31st? He's only a couple of hours away and we shall need all the help we can get if we are to rescue her and maybe the others too.'

'Yes, he said he was coming that day, but I will call him again anyway.' Amelia disappeared and made the call.

Later, they sat and there was little need to elaborate; they spoke and agreed at once, 'We know Pal has her. We know where they are and what will happen if we don't get her back.'

'What he may not know is exactly how much *we* know.'

'Yes, but I think we can count on Emily staying quiet, at the very least.'

'So we are agreed, we go and get her? We lock this place up and go along in costumes?'

'Yes.'

'What, all of us?' Amelia had now returned.

'No, I think you must stay. I don't think that jumping over ditches and fences is quite your strong point and I think we would all be happier with someone holding the fort anyway.'

'That's fine and besides, I need to look after the cellar. Don't worry about me, I'll lock myself in, complete with chain and wait for your return.'

'Then it's agreed, we go in forty-eight hours.'

Dood said, 'In that case, I must move. I need to go to Oxford to do some research and I may also need to go to London. If so, I shall be away for thirty-six hours, but apart from a obtaining a costume, there is little more that I can do here anyway. And please tell Peyton that, despite the law, we shall need a proper weapon. Yes, I'm serious and I don't mean a catapult.'

⋆

In Oxford, Dood sat in a reading room from opening time until the close of day. He was successful in obtaining what he needed from the Bodleian and did not needed to go to London. He asked to see many original writings and journals, made copies of diagrams, labelled them and drew conclusions as to the efficacy of their contents. At the end of the first day he retired to an hotel for the night and on the following morning, after a modest breakfast of fruit and tea which the waitress wondered at, he returned to his studies. Later, he became a little concerned as he looked at his watch, thanked the very patient clerk of records and closed his briefcase.

Driving westwards, he stopped at a small Cotswold town and called at a modest pharmacy there, where he was well-known to the proprietor. Although it was closed, he knocked at its front door and was ushered in. He explained his needs and refused all sustenance other than herbal tea. Taking a tour through the herbarium and chemical store of this long-standing contact, he remarked on the comprehensive nature of the herbs available for purchase and the leading-edge research on aphrodisiacs and hallucinogens conducted there. Later and upon leaving, his briefcase was somewhat heavier and he was careful not to break the stoppered tubes it contained. As he drove south, he thought to himself, 'Some of those herbaceous plants contain chemicals which are probably mind-bending. No wonder that…'

He reached home about four hours before he needed to, ate the minimum fruit and water only, and slept for a while.

A few hours later, Dood called in at his church and collected some holy water. Taking small tubes, he poured a little into each and stoppered them. He also considered, but rejected any notion of taking the host from church; as far as he was concerned there were limits which in all conscience could not be transgressed.

At the Bishops' home, he opened his case and divided its contents amongst those of his friends who were to visit Johan Pal's party. Into pockets, right and left, they placed phials of holy water, salt, and of the element mercury. Around necks they hung charms of garlic and asafoetida grass. He made a ritual seal over openings to the body: nose, mouth, ears and so on, and gave each of them a crucifix and chain which they each placed around their neck. He retained, however, three further sets of each which he planned to take with him that evening.

Satisfied with their preparations, Peyton Oakwood patted his belt with a smile. He had not attempted to obtain a weapon to give to the others, but his waist bulged as though a heavy object hung there. He did not attempt to describe it or the responsibility it held, but the knowledge that he might, if all else failed, protect his friends from some kinds of danger, gave him comfort. Finally, they pulled on the outer garments they had obtained especially for their visit to Johan Pal's place.

Oakwood said, 'What can we expect from this black mass? All I know about it is what my Grandmother told me; that at this time of year, on All Hallows Eve, every peasant in the land used to lock themselves in their home for the night.'

Shilto replied, 'I'm not surprised, but in fact the black mass and All Hallows' Eve are two quite different things. A black mass can be held at any suitable time of year. All Hallows' Eve refers only to what we call Halloween, which is the night before All Saints' Day. The Church doesn't particularly like Halloween and who can blame them? They consider it irreligious at best, damaging at worst.'

'But surely,' said Amelia, 'Halloween has become just an excuse for children to dress up as witches so they can play trick or treat.'

'Yes and it isn't very pleasant. It seems almost a form of extortion; and the sad thing is that it has almost completely replaced 'penny for the Guy' within a single generation. It may have had nothing to do with Halloween, but at least *that* was barter.'

Dood said, 'As far as the Church is concerned, Halloween party-going is the least of our worries. Although partying of that kind is mostly harmless, it has not replaced some of the nastier things which used to go on. Today, secret rites are still carried out in dark woods, isolated moors and in ruined churches, and often in cities where you would least expect. In them, there are still those who are willing to trade their soul in return for the illusion of gain. They make offerings to the devil in return for things we would regard as futile: the ability to place a bane on cattle or perhaps to charm a neighbour's wife into bed. Inevitably, some of the participants bargain for much greater things so their tithe is greater too.'

Grimacing, Dood turned his head away as he remembered those who, referred to him by the Church, had been unsuccessful. Only sometimes had he been able to help them: those weak fools whose rituals had gone wrong; the unlucky ones were in lunatic asylums or struck deaf or blind; they knew only too well the callow nature of the devil's bargain. Yet Pal was a more serious case altogether; he might prove a real heavyweight in that game. Could he, Callum Dood, protect them that same evening? He would soon find out.

The four friends now wore their full party regalia. To mask themselves as strangers at Pal's party they each wore an elaborate costume over simple undergarments. They were, they agreed, completely ridiculous, but they also knew that the more so, the greater their likelihood of a successful disguise. The other guests would be equally outrageous disguised as deities, spirits and animalae; they would be off their guard only with those similarly attired.

Dood had dressed in the character of 'Ai-Apaec,' a god of the ancients of South America. He wore the mask of an old man with wrinkled face, whiskers and the long canine teeth of a cat. A shape-shifter, the cat god had been worshipped in Peru long before the Incas were known there and the disguise caused them much amusement. Dood the wearer was considered to resemble Dood the intoxicated after a hard night at the Duck and they ribbed him mercilessly about his own ability to shift effortlessly from one to the other.

Nor did Adam Shilto escape as easily as he might have hoped. He wore a head-dress with horns to represent the Egyptian deity Khnemu and as a part of that dress, carried a model potter's wheel and clay with which, in legend, Khnemu could mould children and other Gods from the silt and clay of a mythical river source. Oakwood took one look at the horns, chuckled to himself for a while and kept his distance in case of retribution. Eventually Bishop was called to translate words which sounded like 'cuck...cuck...cuck old man' and they all settled to admire the magnanimity of Shilto in the face of direct provocation.

Equally brave, Bishop had taken the likeness of Silenus, the Greek god of beer. His costume made of him a hairy old man, laughing and with a pot-belly, snub-nose and the ears and tail of an ass. While drunk, Silenius in his usual state would normally be carried by satyrs, of whom they agreed, very few would be available to carry him that night. However, Bishop offered to enact a suitable mannerism and given time, was sure that his rendition would improve. In support, Dood offered to help him with extra training at the Duck upon their return.

Finally, Oakwood had chosen the likeness of Hypnos, the Greek god of sleep. He wore a head-dress of hypnotic plants: poppy, hemp, valerian and others, while the Psilocybin mushroom and those of the spotted fly agaric likewise were expressly recommended to him and conveniently supplied by Dood from his mushroom shed at the vicarage. Dressed as Hypnos, Oakwood carried a horn of water to symbolise the river of forgetfulness. However Shilto suggested that in case he should forget to do so later, he should add a few drops of Holy water to it immediately, just in case he needed to partake of a bedtime drink.

Oakwood said, 'I don't like these magic mushrooms, they look a bit nasty to me.'

Dood, who had been waiting to comment, now said, 'I agree they don't suit everybody,' and produced a wry smile.

He continued, 'In case you get arrested wearing them, magic mushrooms are actually quite common. They contain a chemical compound called Psilocybin which, if eaten, the body will change into another chemical which has the properties of LSD. I don't know whether you have tried them yourself, but they are well-known around here. I have grown them only to draw, you will understand, but had I eaten one, I would have had hallucinations, a distortion of time and all the other effects associated with LSD.'

'Are they well-known?'

'Oh yes. In Spain, they are shown on prehistoric rock paintings, and they were part of religious ceremonies in Mexico for hundreds of years. Here in England, the book, Alice in Wonderland, described a psychedelic trip complete with magic mushrooms, which were clearly known at that time. In fact, they have been used here for thousands of years.'

'How poisonous are they?'

'One study said that three pounds of mushrooms would be needed to kill the average male, so they are not very poisonous at all. However that would give an enormous – I believe the term is 'trip' – from which there might be no return.'

'But what about the red-and-white spotted Fly Agaric? Look at this one in my hat!'

'Yes, pretty isn't it! I'm very glad you are interested. As you know, I like to draw wildlife and plants and have made mycology my particular study. I used to go out into Savernake Forest with a former acquaintance – a chemist – in search of various mushrooms and he in particular was interested in species like this. You will understand that my only concern was artistic, but I believe he used to carry out some form of chemotaxonomy on them; a very interesting hobby.'

He continued, 'Like the simple magic mushroom, the effect of the Fly Agaric is like that of LSD and the basic dose for an hallucination to occur is only one mushroom cap. Unfortunately it is also toxic, but the Fly Agaric is not as poisonous as people assume, with a fatal dose considered to be large: about fifteen caps. It can be dried and remain active, my friend says, but may also be eaten as a conventional mushroom since cooking in water destroys both its hallucinatory properties and its toxicity. However eating the fresh 'shroom is clearly a game of chance; a balance between the useful hallucinogenic effect and the likelihood of poisoning. Personally I have always liked my vegetables on the rare side.'

'I must remember not to eat them, then!'

Together, Dood, Oakwood, Shilto and Bishop made a dramatic picture and they were in stitches as they climbed into Oakwood's car. They considered the likely effect of their outfits on the local constabulary and were prompted to rehearse a few suitable replies to any request to 'blow into this bag.' But they did not need to try them out, drove on in good spirits, and reached the main road confident that they would fit in with the party-goers at Johan Pal's black mass, all of whom would have costumes like their own, which despite themselves, they were itching to see.

They made the (by now familiar) journey to the lane before the beech trees and parked their car so that it would not attract interest. It was by now dark and becoming increasingly cold at night, with November only a matter of hours away. Making their way forward, they noted that the chilly air had a sharp chemical tang on the tongue, probably the residue of wood smoke from ahead. Very soon, it also began to carry a rhythmic message like that of an African drum although nearby, it would be unlikely to attract any attention; any straggler walking by would be sure to note the many such parties in that neighbourhood.

More confident of the way than on their last visit, they retraced their former footsteps, broke through the laurel hedge and made across the rough grass on the other side. The noise ahead coincided with the direction which they knew to be towards the sunken amphitheatre. On the way, they considered the possible dangers ahead.

'I think the security system will be held in abeyance tonight,' said Shilto.

'Yes,' replied Dood. 'And we can probably forget that nasty fog also. He expects a whole load of visitors and wouldn't want them all frozen to death.'

'But that doesn't necessarily mean the alarm will be turned off inside the house, so we had better watch ourselves.'

The sound of rhythmic drumming became louder as they approached the sunken amphitheatre where they noted that a musical ensemble had taken up position at one side. Like the other guests present, the ensemble wore masks, but all those with wind instruments had the lower parts of their face uncovered. It was not the case, however, that the extra freedom to play gave rise to better music.

The music was rhythmic but it did not have a precise or logical syncopation. The phrasing seemed to change constantly, but it was not improvised in the manner of jazz and seemed to change only to cause confusion. Instead of a melody there was a series discords and conflicting tones, yet taken together, it was quite unlike the sound of experimental, atonal modern music because it gave a sense of confusion and disorganisation. Each of the players moved their bodies in time to it, or jerked an arm, leg or elbow in emphasis at what they considered to be a significant place. The effect could be described only in an unkind manner as spastic, and it genuinely shocked the onlookers. Nobody seemed to gain any apparent pleasure from the music at all, least of all the players themselves.

The party must have numbered about one hundred and fifty guests. Immediately, Dodd multiplied thirteen people by thirteen covens and with a likely one hundred and sixty nine people in all, it was probably a very significant meeting of magical circles, quite larger than he had expected.

Such a large body of people gave them a disadvantage. How could they identify and remove Emily without exacting some kind of response and once identified, what kind of defence could they put up? They had formed no real plan of action and their phials of magical substances and charms could not protect them from punches, knives or worse. What possible offensive measures could there be against one hundred and sixty nine enraged people? Quietly, Dodd put these points to the others and asked them whether, frankly, they had better withdraw; yet the others were adamant they should stay.

Shilto said, 'I don't think we can leave Emily and the others behind. We must wait for the best moment, stay hidden under our masks, and as long as we don't freeze to death first, we may be able to steal them away without anyone knowing. Then, each man will have to look after himself as best he can.'

The others agreed that this was sound sense and they then concealed themselves among laurel bushes about fifty yards from the sunken amphitheatre, invisible to participants in the riotous party there. The latter, all thirteen by thirteen, were clearly enjoying the occasion and keen to take part to the fullest possible extent. They had decorated the statue of Triton with hemlock, fungi, sprigs of oak and deadly nightshade and in the course of admiring each other's costumes, made adjustments to them or added further adornments of vegetation. Near the fountain, many of them danced with a crazed gyration or when exhausted by their efforts stood aimless for a while. However they did not stand still for long; most seemed to attach themselves to the beat once more and it seemed to Bishop that most were either drugged or intoxicated with alcohol. Few of the throng seemed to tire easily and he was reminded of the stamina of those at some nightclubs where, faced with the prospect of dancing for hours, they consumed Ecstasy or drank Jägerbombs.

However, after a while, some of them turned their attention to the trestle table upon which a lavish banquet lay. It had been laid out with some generosity and there were joints of meat of every description together with bread, cauldrons of hot soup, diverse vegetables, fruit and cakes in abundance. Many now tore bread and meat and ate with their fingers; others ladled from steaming cauldrons and risked scalding their mouths.

There were no individual bottles of wine, but participants seemed happy to drink from open bowls of a wine-based punch. It contained flowers and sliced fruits and they seemed to find it refreshing. It seemed to the onlookers that those who drank their fill were also those who danced with the most stamina and least control; almost certainly it must contain some stimulant or drug. There was also the smell of cannabis smoke and some of the guests had adopted the habit, known to Dood, of making paper cylinders containing a mix of herbal substances which they withdrew from packets within their costumes.

A few of them began to tear away clothing and they rubbed on their arms and chests a liniment with a base of grease. They returned to dance in their costumes, but after an interval, started to make antic gestures with their limbs and to gyrate and spin. Several now stood astride a wooden besom: a broom of ash with twigs of hawthorn, in imitation of a witch in the traditional practice of flying; or alternatively, they seized a besom and began to sweep the ground clean in the manner of their well-known ritual.

Later, the rate of dancing began to subside and the night became colder and considerably darker. Candlesticks were brought forward and a light applied to reveal black candles. The light from them was unusual; it was of a blue incandescence surmounted by a yellow arc, which indicated a fuel containing the element sulfur, a fact confirmed by an acrid smoke which made them cough. The smoke was also rancid, as though each candle contained an animal fat in addition to conventional candlewax. Candles burned down slowly, giving an unearthly light to the gyrating movements of the intoxicated participants, together with a vapour which made them curse and cough.

Throughout, there were outlandish and incredible costumes: a wonder to behold and considerable artistry and expense had obviously gone into making them. There were head-pieces in the design of birds and of snakes and lizards; together with costumes in the caricature of demons, wizards or warriors. All of them successfully masked their owner and most had been colourful before the onset of the uniform grey of night.

The orchestra continued to play, but the four onlookers watched with avidity as a small group of participants entered the pond under Triton's waterfall. They splashed around and were not deterred by the cold or by a poor unfortunate who, while intoxicated, had fallen with his head under water and had not been pulled out. Shortly, the rhythm of the orchestra changed and slowed and the attention of all began to focus on an altar nearby.

The onlookers now saw that a robe of purple had been set over an altar and braziers alight at each corner. Nearby, moving water ran in stone channels and emptied into Triton's pond. One of the revellers then threw a handful of earth on the altar and lit further black candles next to it, so that nearby, each of the mystical elements: earth, air, fire and water was represented.

Three people were then brought forward. However a certain effort was required to pull them and they were holding hands together and hanging back as best they could. They wore unusual costumes and head-dress, but one of them was in the style of Frige, which they knew to be that of Emily. Clearly, the other two were her friends.

Shilto said, 'See Emily there, she looks every bit the bird of prey in that outfit, and that girl, the pretty brunette with curls, is Kayla Raddle. The other one must be Freya Sampson, petite with blonde hair, a lovely girl. They seem to be struggling a bit, all of them. Look, that must be Johan Pal; Emily described him too. How do we get them away from under his nose?'

He continued, 'But look, I think I know that one over there, the one with the broomstick; *she* is called Carol Black. I have seen her around town from time to time. I think she must be one of them: look at how she's cavorting happily with that drunken man over there. I don't think we need to worry too much about rescuing *her*.'

Bishop said, 'What shall we do? Emily's time seems to be getting close. It's now or never, but how can we sneak her away, let alone two others? It's forty to one against us!'

Dood said, 'Let us try to circulate and gradually work our way towards them. We are disguised and so we shouldn't attract attention. Nearer the time, we could try to overpower the few of them who are directly involved. It is dark without the candles and if we could extinguish them we could hide our escape. We can take the girls by the arm and drag them towards the laurel hedge, back the way we came. But we *must* cut that cord on their ankles and wrists. If we do that, they should be able to run as fast as we can, in fact probably faster.'

'Yes, and don't forget that the party-goers are all half drunk and probably drugged up to the eyeballs by now. They look as though they can hardly wait for the rest of the fun to start; *look at them*, cavorting like that!'

'Yes, and so the odds aren't really forty to one, more like four of us and three strong young women against ten or fifteen of them. We should be able to do it. Oh, and by the way, don't drink too much of that wine, it's probably drugged to give them a sensation of flying. Perhaps they also want to make the women a bit keener on the men.'

One by one, Ai-Apaec, Khnemu, Silenus and Hypnos, not altogether ridiculous considering, slipped into the throng and began to circulate in as independent a manner as they could contrive. They decided not to walk towards Pal together, but in as circumambulatory a manner as possible, approached his general direction. Each had picked up some food or drink on the way and they made an affectation of eating or drinking and of enjoyment, while walking with a generally haphazard gait. Dressed as Silenius, Bishop felt that he might actually be having the most fun and he made extravagant gestures which onlookers nodded at with appreciation.

While they were mingling, it seemed to Dood that the throng was becoming slightly hushed and a visible circle was taking shape near to the altar. Thirteen of them were arrayed within it and it was clear that a further ring was taking shape; that of the remaining twelve covens, outside.

Johan Pal was now offered a wicker basket, which he opened and by the neck withdrew a black cockerel. The poor creature flapped somewhat, but its end was quick as he cut its throat. Its blood drained into a silver chalice, but he allowed some to drip onto the altar, made a tracery of markings in the spilt liquid with the tip of his knife and uttered an incantation as he did so. The chalice was then passed around the innermost circle of thirteen, and all were allowed to wet their lips in the precious fluid, which elicited an awe and reverence as it passed.

Next, Johan Pal lifted his garb, knelt on a cushion to reveal his rump and a steady procession of the twelve enacted the *osculum infame*, the devil's kiss. As they did so, a loose end of the remaining twelve covens broke free from their outer circle and joined the queue for that terrible pleasure. Once completed, most rejoined their circle as though by a line around a Maypole, yet nearby, several milled around in a disorganised manner, as though disorder were forgiven or to a point, encouraged.

Johan Pal then stood up and was passed a wooden reliquary by an assistant. He dashed fragments of its contents on the ground and his henchmen stamped on them; however Dood and Shilto turned away in anger and disgust at that terrible sight of the defiling of the Host.

As if that desecration were not enough, Pal withdrew a crucifix, turned it upside down and plunged the short shaft into the soil. Then, he made a space on the altar and placed an object on it so that it stood upright, yet was covered by a silk cloth. To a hushed audience he withdrew the cloth to reveal a reversed swastika, the symbol of Nazism and at its side, his own symbol, a golden orb. That symbol caused the audience to break into animalistic cheers of approval, which he acknowledged with a wave.

The candles gave off their unearthly blue light and the smell of sulfur made Shilto choke. All around it now became colder, but he could see that independently, they had each approached to within twenty yards of Pal himself. Nearer the altar, the cold began to intensify and the radiance of the candles seemed to diminish, yet they were still able to observe their surroundings in the remaining moon and starlight. Soon, on the altar Shilto began to see a dreadful sight; a dark entity was appearing, but it had no luminescence of its own: it was as though the element of darkness itself had begun to fade as a shape, barely discernible at first, was materialising to a hushed murmur of awe from the throng all around.

Nearby, Oakwood saw Pal glance at the girls and knew they would shortly become the object of his attentions. Realising that his own ability to affect matters was tenuous, Oakwood now began to think quickly. He sidled towards Pal and came within a few feet by appearing to encourage and assist in the ceremony. By passing around a few drinks, he helped to encouraged the levity and gluttony nearby.

Now, from his head-dress, Oakwood collected several innocent-looking Psilocybin mushrooms and three large pieces of the fly agaric toadstool. Like all dried mushrooms they were friable and fragile and he rubbed them between his hands into a wooden chalice of red wine. Their fine powder immediately took up the colour and fluidity of the wine and he swirled the liquid gently to complete the process of dissolution.

With his other hand he tore off a piece of meat from a nearby joint, ate a little and then offered some to Pal, who accepted it and ate with relish. Oakwood then held the chalice to Pal who drank the whole lot down without even a grimace. Having done so, Oakwood retired to a distance of about twenty feet to signal his friends.

Shilto, twenty-five feet away and with a head dress of the horned god Khenemu, was grateful for the camouflage, which made him feel less conspicuous in the throng of people since as a very tall man with grey hair, his head and shoulders would otherwise have been visible all around. His height, however, now gave him a clear view of the entity as it materialised on the altar.

Instinctively he moved nearer to Dood, but they were both aghast as the entity finally took ab-human shape. Dood, experienced with exorcisms and hauntings and with at least some esoteric knowledge, had not seen such a materialisation before, was downright terrified and knew that they were in grave danger. As if sensing his distress, Oakwood and Bishop also took up station nearby and they drew as close as they were able without forming a conspicuous, distinct or separate group.

The entity was dark on its altar. It possessed a strange radiance as though not of light itself, or as though seen in the form of an image on a photographic negative. Now, it bent forwards and its features expressed a great weight of pain. There was a ring through its nose and a cloak, made of a loosely-fitting flayed skin, hung in loose folds about it. It gave off a foul smell of putrefaction and surveyed its audience without pleasure.

'My God,' said Dood, 'Pal has raised the spirit of Xipe Totec himself, the flayed god of the Aztecs. We must get out before it is too late.'

'But what about the girls?'

'I cannot. I don't know how, and I do not have the strength.' He could see Pal and a henchman leading two of the girls: sombre and with at least some degree of intoxication, towards the foot of the altar where their initiation must now take place.

Freya groaned; she knew what was in store. Emily too, was whining a little and pulling back, but both of them were pushed forwards by Pal. Behind them, they could see Kayla in the rear of the party, but it could only be a matter of time before his attention turned to her also.

Shilto now shook Dood and said, 'Come on man, you must help or it is the end of them and of all of us too.'

Nearby, Johan Pal tore off Emily's clothes and his henchman, Sieghard Trapper did the same to Freya Sampson. The dark deity looked down in a mixture of apparent pain and pleasure and seemed to anticipate and await the licentious acts to follow.

Yet suddenly, Pal gave a shriek and began to gyrate and utter an incoherent incantation and sentences of doggerel. He turned and pointed to Shilto, but his gesticulation gave way to a general fluttering of hands as though attempting to fly. Continuing, he spun further and faster and collapsed in a heap then, leaping up, he made comic gestures and further strange pronouncements. Nearby, his guests halted for a minute and stared. They seemed dazed and confused and must have considered Pal's behaviour profane even by their own standards. Johan Pal was quite clearly going out of his mind and it was clear that the mixture of Psilocybin mushrooms and Fly Agaric administered earlier had started to work.

Realising his chance, Shilto now grappled with Sieghard Trapper, whom he punched hard on the jaw. From within the guise of the god Khnemu, Shilto now tore some potter's clay from the pouch he carried and shoved it into Pal's mouth. The latter, dumfounded, collapsed and although he continued to breathe, was clearly overcome and unable to shout further. He fell to the floor and lay there, moaning and generally ignored amongst the throng of part-intoxicated people.

Dood now cut the cords on Emily's and Freya's ankles and wrists. Grabbing them both, he shouted, 'Run, run for your life,' and propelled them towards the laurel. However he could feel his legs slowing and knew that a malignant force was dragging him backwards. The girls, past worrying about modesty and interested only in escaping, ran as hard as they could, but they too could feel the same fierce will pulling them back.

Both Emily and Freya had experienced that well-known dream of the 'chase through water,' in which they were unable to make their legs move fast enough to escape a pursuer behind. Their present experience, of running as hard as they could towards the laurel, while pulled back by a malignant will, was unfortunately similar. They started to tire and began to weep, and knew that eventually, the half-drunk and hallucinating mob would understand what was happening and grab them. In turn they slowly and inevitably came to a halt.

Meanwhile Shilto, recovering his balance after striking Sieghard Trapper, observed that Trapper had collapsed, knocked out. As fast as he was able, Shilto now moved to run himself, but was aware that several groups of onlookers had noticed a crisis and were starting to assemble and point.

Like his friends, Shilto's every step was becoming harder and more laboured and like them, he felt the malignant force of the deity on the altar so that his muscles started to fail. With a great effort of will, he managed a short sprint towards the laurel hedge, yet he knew the will of the evil deity was greater than his own. He realised that he could not reach safety in time, knew that he would surely stop and be dragged back, and there would be offered to Xipe Totec. He felt sick and cold, and a sweat broke out on his forehead.

A few minutes before Shilto's flight, Wally Bishop, dressed as the somnambulant Silenius, had been able to approach Kayla Raddle, whose pretty hair hung in ringlets on her shoulders beneath an Egyptian head dress. As had already been achieved for the other two girls, he quietly cut her wrist and ankle cords and despite the danger, told her to sneak the first few feet away and then run for her life. At first she had thought him an invited guest and had turned away, but realising quickly that Bishop was not one of them, had followed his suggestion. Soon, she was speeding over the grass towards the laurel with the odd figure of Silenius in pursuit.

Oakwood looked directly at Xipe Totec, the dark deity on the altar. Since it seemed to possess mainly a presence rather than to emanate light of its own, that entity was easier to see when looking from the corner of one's eye. Its malignancy was a stultifying force on his ability to move any arm, leg or muscle; he felt its call, an insistent demand to walk towards it, which made it quite impossible to move in the opposite direction. At first, Oakwood had been within twenty feet of Xipe Totec, but had involuntarily begun to advance closer. Soon, he began to pray, for like Shilto, he realised that the entity would require a sacrifice and that he would probably be flayed alive to satisfy the desire for pain Xipe Totec demanded.

However Oakwood now had a divine inspiration. He allowed himself to be drawn to within ten feet of the altar, then raised an arm and threw the contents of his drinking horn directly at that unclean spirit from Hell. He had recalled that the horn contained holy water and was grateful for the intervention just in time.

There was a flash of dark light and its grey visage radiated malevolence. Shaking the loose folds of its cloak of flayed skin, the smell of putrefaction reached an unbearable degree and Xipe Totec vanished. All could see more easily, as though a pale dawn had broken.

Oakwood shouted, 'Run,' at his temporarily frozen friends and dashed as fast as he could towards the laurel, overtaking the girls, Dood, Bishop and Shilto as he did so. They crashed through the hedge with a number of pursuers behind and reached their car, piled in and started to drive. Each man offered part of his lap to the three girls who were now shivering with the cold, an effect increased by the wine and by exertion. It was a tight squeeze in the car, but they eventually found space enough for them all, with Oakwood alone having his own seat in order to drive.

It had been quite some time since Dood and Shilto had been in the back of a car with any number of naked girls and had it been under better circumstances, they might have made a joke of it. However they kept their eyes shut – both professed headaches – and while Bishop, who was up in front navigated, Oakwood, managing a stiff upper lip only, drove carefully and not without trepidation to the Bishops' house, where they were greeted by an incredulous Amelia. Offering them brandy, the girls declined and Amelia put them straight to bed: poor things! However the exhausted and frightened Dood, Bishop, Shilto and Oakwood put away a bottle of brandy by the fire and slept quite easily in comfortable armchairs until dawn.

Chapter Seven

An escape from the broken pentacle

Silenius was up first, frying bacon sandwiches in the kitchen at 7am. The fragrance caused Khnemu to throw off his alcoholic haze and drink some coffee and they were soon joined by Ai-Apaec and Hypnos, still in the remains of their outfits, but without their head-dresses to which, despite the inconvenience, they had become quite attached. They all helped to carry vast quantities of toast, butter, marmalade and coffee through to the dining room, where Amelia had arrived, having woken and not without difficulty clothed the three young women.

They all ate well. The girls were quiet and distracted but Emily was more at home since she had her own things there and knew Wally and Amelia Bishop well. She tucked away a handful of toast and the other two followed, saying little. Dood suffered no ill effects at all from his accession to the brandy glass and was quite perky in his inimitable manner.

At last he said, not without irony, 'We had better decide what to do now,' and there was a consensual murmur around the room.

Shilto said, 'Girls, can we take it that we did the right thing in rescuing you from the black mass last night?'

'Oh yes, please don't take us back to him,' was the immediate response from Kayla Raddle. 'You have no idea what he intended to do! He was going to have his evil way with the three of us in turn, perhaps giving us over to Sieghard Trapper or even Meinhard Koch if things failed him. Then he planned to use us in his evil rites and there may even have been a blood sacrifice later on.'

Shilto said, 'You mean you didn't all volunteer?'

Freya Sampson said, in her pleasant manner, 'It was so very easy to get involved with him. We all thought it would just be a bit of fun going to séances and telling fortunes with cards, but slowly and surely he drew us in further. I'm sure he tried to hypnotise me; at one point I thought him attractive and pleasant, but underneath, he was scheming to turn me into an acolyte, well on the way to committing myself irrevocably. Alone, I might have been able to choose whether to become a white or black magician, but with him around, there could never have been any choice about it.'

Bishop nodded, but had quiet reservations about what he might say to Emily, who had been with them as little as two or three days before. Eventually, he said, 'Emily, can you say how you feel about coming back? We were so worried about you and were very upset to find you gone. Did you go of your own free will or did Johan Pal make you?'

Emily was quiet for a few moments and then replied, 'I really wanted to stay with you. Both my head and heart told me to stay. But *he* was waiting outside and he had a lock of my hair which he used to exert his will on me. I suppose it must be a form of psychic bullying; I did not mean to leave but found myself unable to stop. He sent me bad dreams and in a restless sleep I found myself drawn to him in a manner which only his initiates can have experienced. He did not seek to punish me, but can never trust me again and will always be watching. Now, having escaped once more, he will surely change his mind and try to destroy me in some way. Perhaps he will send some evil spirit from the other side.'

'Did he mention his grand project to you?'

'Yes he did. Now that our initiation has failed or has at least been postponed, he intends to take the Magdeburg Relic and use it at last.'

Dood broke in, 'We should remember that last night, we fed him magic mushrooms and fly agaric in huge quantities. He will have had the psychedelic trip of his life – actually, I am envious – and will probably never forget it. He is also usually teetotal, although he did accept a glass of wine – I presume anything less would have been considered sacrilegious. However, taken together: the 'shrooms, the wine: everything that was in the draught, not to mention the cannabis smoke all around, we managed to slip him the *big one*, all in one glass. That stuff seemed to work into him pretty quickly and he couldn't have got better in Calne on a Friday night. However, when he does finally wake up, which cannot be sooner than in 24 hours, he'll have a massive sore head for a while, and I cannot see him getting busy again until at least another day has passed.'

He continued, 'But now we must make some more serious decisions. We *must* resist Pal if he tries to get the girls back; we have a good idea of what he means to do. But Kayla and Freya, do you want to go home or stay longer? We know that you have another life to lead: daily jobs, in fact, and you will probably want to resume them. But Pal may try to get you back from there.'

Freya said, 'No, I don't think so. The black mass is over now, or at least, until the next time. The last thing he wants now is some kind of confrontation in public. He wants to keep his activities quiet and under wraps and would never make a scene. It is of course possible that he might approach us at home, but I live with my parents and they would make trouble if I shouted or screamed. But more importantly, we are only acolytes or neophytes and I don't think he will be bothered by us at the moment. Just now, he probably has more important things on his mind.'

'Such as?'

'His great work, the one involving the Magdeburg Relic.'

'Go on, please.'

Emily broke in, 'I talked to him about that. He wants it and you can expect a visit from him in order to get it.'

Kayla followed in her bubbly, laughing way, 'Yes, he has been talking about it. He hasn't said exactly what he intends to do, but he did mention Germany and that he has plans to "return home with an important object".'

Oakwood nodded, 'Yes, I thought it would come to something like that. However, as far as *we* are all concerned, and with the action probably moving here, Kayla and Freya you will almost certainly be safer going about your normal lives elsewhere.'

Shilto followed, 'And Emily, the choice is yours, but since you lodge with Amelia and Wally anyway…'

'I'm staying here,' said Emily.

The girls all nodded in approval and having agreed, they seemed much happier.

Oakwood continued, 'For the rest of us, Callum and Adam live locally and I have agreed to stay around for as long as I am needed. I may have to drive home from time to time, but the journey is short and I can return easily.'

Shilto replied, 'We have agreed to resist Pal when he makes his next move. He is certain to be weak today, but I would suggest that we convene here, tomorrow morning.'

⋆

By the following morning, Kayla and Freya had disappeared and at about eleven, Dood and Shilto came round. There was a strong and sweet smell of baking coming from the kitchen, and Emily danced in with a plate of jam doughnuts which they all enjoyed with their strong black coffee.

Emily was in a resurgent mood and recounted her version of the black mass. 'Pal dressed me up in the hawk outfit and dedicated me to the goddess Frige. I was cold and scared and knew he'd decided to initiate me first. He made me drink some of that sweet wine, which I knew was drugged, in order to make me more amenable to the idea, but somehow it didn't quite do the job it was supposed to. But when I knew that you were all there, I was happy again because I had a chance to get away from him. Freya and Kayla; well I am not sure what he had planned for them, but I knew they were pleased to get away because their faces lit up when you came along, even though they were freezing cold.'

Together, the warmth and lively company brought about a transformation in the dour manner of Shilto and Dood, both coincidentally rather morose after a sleepless night. Shilto said, 'Did you bake these, Emily? They are lovely, all warm and jammy. And the coffee, well I haven't had the like for quite a while!'

'It's nothing, but I am afraid there's only a light lunch, a chorizo and pepperoni pizza and some salad.'

Immediately, Dood said, 'Well I am afraid I need to stop you there. I am truly sorry, but we can have no meat at the present time or at least, not until our troubles are over.'

'No meat, but why?' Emily replied.

'We made some rather limited attempts earlier, to purify ourselves through denial, so that we could resist Pal the better. I think if we ate chorizo our earlier efforts would be wasted.'

'But we had wine and spirits last night?'

'True, but we were in a bad shape then, and so was he. I said nothing because I took the calculated risk that he was in a worse shape than we were. That cannot apply henceforth.'

'Well I *am* a little disappointed, but I will bow to your knowledge and experience on this matter,' said Emily, rather wistfully. 'I can keep the pizza, though, until later; I think they freeze quite well. It looks like fruit and tea, then.'

Bishop said, 'But I think we can expect an ultimatum from him before he does anything else.'

'Yes, I do believe you're right.'

Bishop had been downstairs into the cellar that morning in order to confirm all was right with the relic. He had felt the same unease as before and knew instinctively that it did not belong in a happy household. He carried the key with him and returning, had placed the heavy kitchen table over the door to the cellar stairs, as before. Lately, he had also been musing on what to do with it and considered that he had more than fulfilled his original brief to Harry Devine. With his friends present, he was about to suggest that it should be returned to its original source; he would recommend to Harry that it should go back to its original archive in Moscow. However, following a light lunch, a knock came at the front door.

Emily went to answer and they heard her shriek. Bishop immediately ran to see what the problem was and observed that Emily was confronted by none other than Pal himself, as large as life, looking none the worse for wear and with a reserved, controlled expression which belied the hostility they knew was underneath.

Bishop said, 'Emily, please go upstairs to your room,' She did so with apparent relief.

He then said, 'Good morning, can I help you?'

Pal said 'I am a friend of Emily Robertson and I would like to speak to you about the events last night at my home. I also have a message for Miss Robertson herself.'

'I must assure you that Miss Robertson is our housekeeper and has no intention of leaving with you.'

'It seems that there may have been a misunderstanding which I am anxious to clear up. There are five of you, so I thought you might at least hear me?'

'I agree to listen, so you had better come in. These are my friends and you can speak openly in front of them. They are the Reverend Dood, Colonel Oakwood, the Archdeacon Shilto and my wife Mrs Bishop.'

From the window they were able to see a large black car parked outside. It characterised Pal as a man of wealth, yet today, his clothes seemed ill-fitting and had been thrown on with haste. He had clearly suffered from the effects of his treatment at the black mass and his anger could be felt below his calm manner. He waited until being asked to sit.

'Now Mr… what can we do for you?' said Bishop.

'We haven't spoken before, but I am sure that indirectly, we know one another quite well by now. My name is Johan Pal. I believe that I need to be frank with you.'

'It may be that you visited a Halloween party at my home yesterday. If so, I must apologise for the behaviour of some of my guests. They may have been intoxicated and their fancy-dress may have seemed a license to over-indulge in dancing, food and wine. I shall forget their behaviour in this instance because they are my friends and it *was* after all, Halloween, when such behaviour can be tolerated. You may be assured, however, that there will be no repeat of what you saw.'

Pal continued, 'However, now I hope to discuss the main purpose of my visit. It has come to my notice that you have a relic stored here, that I wish to buy. In particular my organisation considers that although it will not be of use to you, we would like it for our own display. We are a large organisation, run a noteworthy collection and are nominally a museum in fact, with an interest in classical and mythological materials: books, statues, relics, legends; they are our stock in trade and we are willing to pay a large amount of money for them.'

Bishop said, 'But why is it so important to you? Surely you could buy something else of greater interest. The artefact is the property of our contact elsewhere and we are only custodians of it. We cannot sell it without authority and must either keep it or choose to offer consideration for it ourselves, which we will not do at present.'

Johan Pal's countenance, seemingly pleasant on first acquaintance, began to darken. He looked downwards towards the floor as though he wished to avert his eyes until he had mastered his composure. Now he said, 'We believe that we are a fair and just commercial organisation and thus far, have invested a large amount of time in our research regarding this matter. No doubt your contact is a genuine one, but it may be that he or she, like us and doubtless like you also, would be keen to view this as a valuable commercial transaction. If so, we would like to satisfy your collective wishes in that direction and can more than cover the cost levied by your contact. In addition, we can accommodate whatever large sums are required in commission or brokerage by you.'

Bishop said, 'I can only reiterate that we will not now, nor will we within the near future dispose of our antique for commercial gain. We regard it as a valuable artefact for academic study and wish to retain it as such. Now what was the message you wished to give to Miss Robertson?'

Pal said, 'Yes, I was afraid that you would say that. Miss Robertson has shown a marked reluctance to return to me, having now chosen to stay as your housekeeper. However we can offer her a privileged position within our organisation and are convinced that her financial affairs would be better suited by returning with me.'

Bishop said, 'We believe that she was kidnapped recently by an intruder who influenced her to leave this house. She has told us that it was you, and you cannot now assume to offer her such a privilege.'

'Let me be frank.' Johan Pal stood up and he tried to control himself and made an effort to moderate his speech. Nevertheless, his dark eyes were rock-hard and his presence seemed to enlarge and his physique to grow within his ill-worn suit. 'We are pleased to number Miss Robertson among the members of our, ah, business and we guarantee her safety while she is with us. We mean to have the artefact that our agent has said is with you. You must supply it to us, please, solely for commercial reasons which we do not wish to divulge. Our organisation has a not inconsiderable weight.'

'My position stands, and we will call the police unless you leave.'

'On the contrary, we will not release Miss Robertson from her contractual obligations, unless you sell us your artefact.'

Bishop replied, 'Is that some kind of a threat?'

'Mr Pal, I take it that you intend to use the artefact in some kind of religious ceremony?' It was Dood who broke in, avoiding what had seemed to be a direct confrontation.

'You are a man of some intellect, Reverend. It is quite clear to me, from observing your aura, that you are experienced in spiritual matters and may have some power yourself to influence them. It is true that my museum is of a religious nature; we are an organisation concerned with the retention and preservation of what are called pagan artefacts; some might call them irreligious.'

He continued, 'But I shall continue to be as frank as I can. I *insist* that you will sell me now, while I am here, the intact artefact I seek. We both know that it is the last mortal remains of the former Nazi Fuhrer and it should, on principle, be retained in a proper museum like ours. Like you, I need it to fulfil my research but that, however, is a secondary consideration to follow its proper archival. If you do not release it, then it will be the worse for you tonight. You mentioned the police. You disrupted my party two nights ago and I can advise them, if necessary, of your trespass so the police hold no fear for me. I also insist that Emily should leave with me and if you refuse that, too, will be for the worse. You may see again only a shell of that lovely person.'

Oakwood spoke, 'Never, you are a bully and a fake.'

'Surely not; you saw evidence of my powers at the garden party; do you doubt they were mine? If not, it may be that I shall need to convince you that my abilities are real.'

He took a small wax doll from his pocket, bent over and collected a small object from the floor. It was a single, short brown hair, which he attached to the head of the doll and placed it in his pocket.

'Mr Bishop, this doll is now an effigy of the owner of the hair taken from the floor. Whatever I decide to do to the doll will also be done to the person whose effigy it is; if I were to try to sicken it as if it were a person, so that person would sicken in likeness. I would ask you to observe Mrs Bishop tonight, whose effigy it now is. In fact I may choose not to destroy her, and will decide later on a whim what to show you.'

Callum Dood said, 'How do you know we won't simply imprison you here? There are five of us.'

'Sir, you do not have the strength, either physical or metaphysical.' He stood and within his suit, his shoulders swelled in the fashion of a bodybuilder. In response, Dood rose quickly and crossing the room, slammed the door shut before Pal could leave, then locked it and pocketed the key.

Johan Pal laughed, walked to the door and grasped the handle, then twisted it and pulled sharply. The door seemed to resist at first, but the tongue of the lock pulled away with the sheer force used and he was able to open the door and walk through. As he closed it he said, 'You have fifteen hours.'

Dood closed the door and they all sat in silence for a minute, wondering at the demonstration of physical force they had seen. Then, Bishop muttered, 'I hope that my heavy kitchen table, solid trapdoor and padlock can keep him out of the cellar.'

*

Wally and Amelia Bishop went to bed at 11 pm and the warmth of the bedroom, together with her general fatigue made Amelia fall asleep within twenty minutes. Johan Pal's ultimatum had deferred the sense of crisis until fifteen hours hence and there was little that either of them of them could do to ward off the kind of spell that he had threatened. In fact none of the company had any idea of how to go about it, not quite understanding what he meant to do. Wally Bishop, nevertheless, had chosen to stay awake to act as watchman and so he propped himself up on his pillows and withdrew his toes from the foot of the bed.

The minutes and hours ticked by and finally, at about 2.30 am, he fell asleep himself.

Amelia was in a very light sleep and dreaming heavily. Eventually, her dreams gave way to the curious sensation of a rope being passed around her neck and slowly tightened; but since she was below the threshold of conscious action, was unable to resist. Soon, she also imagined a radiance of light upon her, as though the rays of a lamp were falling, but each ray was distinct and separate and fashioned in the form of an individual cord with its origin a golden orb, so that she was bound to its source. She struggled to breathe as she lay and began to feel a great weight on her chest. The golden orb was above her, and the weight of the orb and its cord-like rays pinned her down, as though the rays were also a force. Like a witch being crushed by great stones – that medieval punishment for witchcraft – she was being punished herself. The Golden Orb pressed upon her; the rope around her neck slowly tightened; and she began to choke.

Her punishment continued for what seemed an indeterminate time. Next to her, Wally was sound asleep. She lay silent, unable to move or cry out; her breathing shallow and in short gasps and she knew she was being held close to death. Caught between sleep and a dream-world, she could not last long if the rope tightened further or if the weight of rays from the golden orb increased. If only the call of a bird, or the dawn would come to break the spell.

Wally Bishop finally turned over and a noise of snoring came to his ear. Gradually, he woke and very gently nudged Amelia on the arm; it was not like her to snore. Feeling thirsty, he swung his legs out of bed to collect a glass of water, looked at his wristwatch and saw that it was now 4.30 am; he spilt some water, said 'damn' and then put on his bedside light.

Bishop could now see that Amelia was covered in sweat and was silent and unable to breathe. Her snoring had in fact been the noise of choking; her throat was swollen to twice its normal size and her tongue was black and between her teeth. He cursed himself for falling asleep, and shook her to see whether she was conscious. Looking at her properly, he could see the terror in her eyes and knew they were dealing with the curse of Johan Pal. He pulled her into a sitting position and called Callum Dood and Adam Shilto, who threw on dressing gowns and came immediately.

Dood took one look at her and rushed to his room. After a minute he returned with a glass, a bottle of Lourdes water and a piece of chalk. He said, 'Get some of that down her throat and onto her face: yes, the Lourdes water!'

As Bishop did so, Shilto helped him pull away the bedroom rugs and clear an empty space on the wooden floorboards. Then, using chalk, Dood made a circle on the floor, asked the others to carry Amelia to it and finally closed the circle with chalk so that she lay flat, but barely comfortable within that very elementary protection.

Dood then entered the circle himself and with Lourdes water washed her face and raised her head so that she could drink a little. By using the glass he was successful in encouraging her to do so although her tongue was still black and swollen. With a little Lourdes water in her throat, she coughed, spluttered and retched with the taste of the calcareous minerals in it; but overall, he was encouraged by the vigour of her cough and knew that she would eventually recover. As she woke more fully, Dood asked her to remain recumbent upon the floor. Then, he soaked a handkerchief with further Lourdes water and swept her body in the manner of the white witch sweeping away a spell: first, from head, down her arms and to her fingers; then, from head, down her torso and to her legs. Amelia Bishop felt the pain ease and the sense of being throttled began to pass. Later, they returned her to bed and Wally Bishop suggested they should call a Doctor.

At seven o'clock, Shilto telephoned a Doctor and they then took it in turns to watch Amelia as she slowly improved. A little later the Doctor arrived, but by then, her throat had become less swollen and she could breathe in an uninterrupted manner. She was also wide awake, although somewhat shaken, but she knew by then that her ordeal was over. The Doctor questioned her, but she was unwilling to say much about the origin of her struggle and the Doctor looked upon her with a frown, first at the marks on her neck, then at her husband and at Dood and Shilto. However it was clear that they were upright citizens and upon consideration there had been no crime; and further, Amelia was unwilling to suggest they had behaved in any way improperly. She seemed content to submit the vague notion that she had experienced an accident with the cord of her gown, and so finally, he gave her a sedative and a salve for a mark on her neck and departed with a promise that he would visit again in due course.

Later on, Amelia awoke from her sedative and was recovered enough to dress and come downstairs. There, while the others had a light mid-day meal, she ate a little and drank some water. They all spoke little and most attempts to start a conversation were unsuccessful. They listened avidly, however, when Bishop asked Dood about his activities earlier that day.

He said, 'Holy water has been blessed by the Church. It is the precious fluid we use in baptism, but it does have many other uses and I was successful in brushing away Pal's spell by using a handkerchief soaked with it. Country folk often still purify their home by brushing-out in the same manner. They use a besom wetted with holy water and a systematic, 'sweeping' movement through floors and over thresholds. Today, I used that same method, a sweeping action over limbs, to remove a sickening spell from Amelia's body.'

'Is Lourdes water any different?' said Bishop.

'Yes, Lourdes water comes only from a spring at the Sanctuary of our Lady of Lourdes, in France, where in 1858 it was revealed to a young girl, Bernadette Soubirous, by the Virgin Mary. As such, it can be described as a holy spring, of which the water is holy if a user first believes it so. I like to keep some myself; at times it helps me believe in the holiness of miracles revealed elsewhere.'

He continued, 'I also used a chalk circle today, which has an ability to contain or protect since it is in fact a material barrier. In the magic of witches, a chalk circle was most often of nine feet across, but we did not have that space today. There are rules which can enhance the value of magic circles; it would be usual to draw them in a particular manner for their most propitious function, which I was not able to do. For example there are degrees of elaboration: symbols and candles, which if used, are placed at the cardinal points of the compass where they represent the four Archangels. However I did not have time; it was necessary to contain Amelia and to deflect, if possible, Pal's interest in her. I think I was successful, but I do not think he intended a major triumph out of it. We shall see what he says.'

They sat quiet once more; they all knew that a direct confrontation awaited them. By the time they had finished their meal and cleared away, they knew that it would be fifteen hours since his last visit and the expectation of having to deal with him cast their morale down.

Eventually, there was a knock on the door and Shilto ushered Pal in. He stood by the window and said quite simply, 'I have come for your answer; I am sure you cannot have forgotten my demands, which remain the same. The only change is that you must now accept that my powers are real. I have come to dismantle the doll in front of you as a gesture of goodwill.'

He removed it from a pocket. There was a cord wrapped around its throat, and its neck appeared to be crooked. Pal made a sign of dismissal over the doll, removed a brown hair from its head, dropped it and dismantled the wooden limbs.

'It is done; now your reply, please.'

Bishop spoke for them all, 'You have caused us great grief. We were very worried about my wife last night and she might have been scarred or worse had the Reverend Dood not intervened. Nevertheless, had you not done as you did, you could have been no closer to your aim; now you are infinitely further away if such a position were possible.'

'We have discussed this in detail today and reaffirm that we will neither sell the relic to you nor give it away. If, as you say, your powers are real then we could not, in all conscience allow you to take away the Magdeburg Relic. You would eventually use it in in your rituals and in a manner that would pervert the wellbeing of all.'

'Nor can we allow Emily to leave with you, since we do not feel that it would be in her interest to do so. Although she might enjoy what could laughingly be called your 'protection,' we feel that her sanity and possibly her very soul might be at stake in the long run. As her friends, we cannot allow this and fully accept the responsibility that our friendship places on us. You may also find that your powers are to no avail against our joint strength if we should decide to use it. Go now, and take your avowed symbol, your Golden Orb with you.'

Johan Pal replied, 'Very well. It seems that I cannot have what I ask for but I will now send a visitor tonight. You fools, after having met him, you may wish to change your minds towards an alternative course of action instead.'

⋆

It was by now mid-day and Callum Dood was contemplating the best way of protecting his friends. Earlier, he had harboured a certain scepticism which even his experience of exorcism had not dispelled and he had been by no means certain that protection would actually be needed. Yet following their confrontation with Johan Pal, he now knew with certainty that they were in grave danger.

It was therefore time to prepare. With the consent of Wally Bishop, he disappeared to look around the house and spent further time in the herb garden outside. After a while, he also returned to the vicarage to obtain more holy water, crucifixes and sundry other items.

While Oakwood stayed with Emily and Amelia, Wally Bishop, Shilto and Dood discussed a pentacle in some detail. There had been no difficulty in providing a suitable room and they spent some time downstairs, in cleaning out study furniture and making certain the place was spotless. They had been quite clear on how to assemble such a structure, yet Dood had a nagging doubt about it at all times.

Nearby was the Magdeburg Relic and at times they had all felt its oppressive presence in the locked cellar below. Just as the spell of a witch could cause the milk to go sour, so the Relic had caused bottles of wine in the cellar to have that same fate. It was evil and its influence might prevent even a pentacle from providing them with the protection they would need.

Yet regardless of such doubts, there could be no other option and Dood finally asked to go ahead. It would take time to assemble a pentacle and he would need the help of Shilto in order to complete it so that they could be *in situ* before nightfall.

Doubt, however, continued to nag him; was there any possible alternative? Placing his chalk and string on the floor, he began to test the empty room with his pendulum. He knew it would mark out barriers and confluences of natural forces and show points of weakness in the room: a gap, perhaps, that would benefit from a cup of holy water or a bunch of asafoetida. Yet the result was disheartening; at all points tested there was a single obsessive swing towards the kitchen. Below was the cellar, the contents of which had so distorted the electrical boundaries around them that their room might be useless. His task, to build a working pentacle to protect them against Johan Pal, could possibly fail.

Eventually, he entrusted his opinion to Shilto, 'Perhaps we could build it somewhere else? We have the time.'

'I cannot see the point of moving. We must safeguard the Relic downstairs as much as protect ourselves. If we leave without it, he will come here to take it away. If we set up elsewhere and take it with us, your pendulum would certainly show the same. We must stay here.'

Reluctantly Dood agreed.

Later, they made a small mark on a floorboard in the middle of the room and drove a nail into its exact centre. To it, by means of a loop they attached a string 8 feet long, so that it could circle the nail by a full 360 degrees. To the other end they fixed a white chalk, with which by holding the string tight, they were able mark on the floor a circle of diameter 16 feet. By extending the string they made a further circle outside, with a diameter greater by nine inches.

On the outermost circle, Dood made a first mark: a spot of chalk which he used as an origin. Using it, he made at intervals of 72 degrees a further four marks around the circumference and checking that the angles between them were exact, used the string as a straight edge; while he held it tight, Shilto drew straight lines in an exact order.

From the origin, a point 1, Shilto drew a straight line to point 3 on the clockwise circumference; then by moving the string, a line to point 5. In turn, he drew lines from points 5 to 2 and from 2 to 4 and completed the pentagram with a line from 4 to the origin.

Within the pentagram and in the area between the two circles, he drew symbols representing earth, fire, air, water and spirit so that the uppermost origin was represented by the symbol for the last of these. Similarly, the twin feet of the star were represented by symbols for earth and fire; and its arms by those for water and air. Between the 5 peaks and at intervals between the two concentric circles he placed chalices; and within the peaks themselves, candlesticks together with large church candles.

As the afternoon wore on, they checked their measurements carefully and made sure they had an adequate supply of water to drink, together with a means of making fire. Finally, they completed their pentacle with further esoteric symbols and with asafoetida grass and garlic.

As nightfall approached, Shilto suggested they should collect pillows to sit on, together with enough layers of clothing to ensure comfort whatever the temperature. Dood made sure that all outside doors were locked, inside lights were switched on and all curtains closed. Then, he filled all chalices with Lourdes water and lighted each of the large church candles. Lastly, all six sat enclosed within their astral citadel, back-to-back, to wait until dawn.

They found waiting itself tedious, but their scepticism had been eroded recently and they were quite content to sit and think. Light conversation also followed and they watched while the candles burned down in their holders. Neither Dood nor Shilto expected any serious psychic attack before midnight, with the most likely time in the cold hours thereafter. Nevertheless, they had church candles of a large size, able to burn for at least forty-eight hours and certainly for the duration of night.

Gradually, conversation waned. They became watchful and by straining their senses, became more sensitive in the process. They began to anticipate; all believed in the psychic abilities of their opponent: there was little question of not doing so because they had each seen the outcome. Yet the silent minutes ticked by and then the hours; their senses were by now razor-sharp, but they felt no tangible interference at all.

Emily said, 'How will we know…?'

Shilto answered, 'It will be designed to make you know. Occult attacks feed on unease and fear.'

Emily's question made Shilto reflect on the difficulty of describing psychic phenomena. Human experience of the occult was in fact quite common, but the discussion of it was not accepted generally. Since it was usually suppressed in polite society, language probably lacked adequate words to describe it properly.

The evening wore on and it began to grow cold. At first, they felt a keen cold as the fire died. The fresh autumn air entered by cracks between window fittings and the falling temperature made them pull on an extra layer of clothing. But it was a clean cold which they knew well: one which could be assuaged by rubbing the hands and feet, or by slapping their sides.

Smoke from the candles continued to rise towards the ceiling and candle flames burned evenly and slowly. They heard several clocks in the house strike midnight and they counted the quarter hours towards one o'clock.

After a while, the smoke began to show movement as though carried towards an exit by a draught of air. It began to circle and smell unpleasant. Outside of the pentacle, they could see frowns form in the shadows; it seemed to them that curtains now hung in a heavy, oppressive manner. They also saw distorted parts of human expressions in the moving vapour. A curled lip, followed by a sneer began to form in patterns on the wallpaper. They at once began to shiver and knew that an attack had finally begun.

At a distance, they heard the noise of a domestic alarm and at that same moment, their own electric lights went out, leaving the candlelight alone. Surely, Pal could not have brought about such a general failure? However shortly, the frenetic sound of the alarm ceased and electric lighting, visible between cracks in the curtains, was restored nearby; nevertheless, of all the houses, they alone were left with candle-light. No electrical supply was restored to them and the room became colder and seemed more hostile. They knew for sure that evil was there.

Emily now felt that she could see Johan Pal at several places in their room; a sneer in the ether; a half-imagined eye in a plaster cornice, black, receding hair in the fold of a curtain; an evil smile in a corner. Nevertheless he was visible only to a sideways glance; any sense of him disappeared when she looked directly, or held that gaze for more than a second. To them all, shadows also seemed more animate; candle light played across the room and naked flames cast moving shadows but their outlines were alive and seemed to contain evil pictures. They also felt that the ceiling had drawn closer and that walls had begun to lean inwards. It was certain that measurements would prove it was not so, but that did not alter the fact that the room now seem to enclose rather than protect. Emily called out a harsh whisper, 'It has started.'

Shapes now seemed to probe their astral citadel; a darker darkness seemed to creep along the floor, moving parallel to chalk lines. Half-seen outlines of limbs, a flapping wing here, the silhouette of a hand there, came into vision as supplementary shadows and vanished after a second. The air grew musty with the sense of decay, rather like that of a pile of leaves in the autumn or a stagnant pond with marsh gas and flickering phosphorescence.

Soon, they also began to hear squawks and animal noises; the snort of a pig, the screech of a crow; and after a while, a low chuckle which in particular made them recoil. What spirit was that; was it Johan Pal himself or some ab-human confederate?

Shilto said, 'I seem to remember our last exorcism when we went on the offensive and found it worked. We can do the same again now. Our combined efforts will be stronger and Pal will make mistakes if we get him angry.'

They began to insult him and refute his aims and views. They were not completely sure that they would be heard, but thought that unimportant.

'Johan Pal, you lack chemistry,' called out Bishop, using a colloquial expression.

Emily said, 'We called you *'Master'*. That was a mistake.'

Shilto began to sing 'Rock of Ages' in his strong bass voice. Emily sang harmonics in her own sweet voice and they began to cheer. Gradually, the room seemed to lighten a little and Pal's ethereal chuckles, still heard, now contained an angry note.

Oakwood called out jovially, 'Come on Johan Pal, you can do a bit better than that. You don't scare us one bit!'

As if in answer, a whisper could be heard in a sudden wind. 'You will do things my way.' The room was filled with gusts of air and the sound of a sigh and one by one, the candles guttered and went out. In a deeper darkness lit only by the glow of cooling embers in the grate, Pal seemed stronger and his presence contained a deeper malice. They now huddled together and sought to gain strength from each other by holding hands. In some cases this did not come naturally and as Dood grasped Oakwood's hand the latter said, 'Good God man,' and pulled away. In the dark, the room was increasingly cold, but it was no longer the cold of autumn gales or drafts through the window. It was a bitter and spiteful cold, one which made them aware of the approach of a new and deeply malevolent, evil presence.

In the corner of the room, a large torso materialised as if from a vapour. Its eyes were green with spite and its hands clutched a trident, the three-pronged fish spear beloved of classical mythology. There was a smell of decayed fish and entrails and of seaweed and fermented corruption. The folds of an ethereal garment covered its body, if indeed it could be said to have had one.

Amelia thought that had she been able to touch it, she would have felt nothing; it seemed to have no material substance or physical body, only a vacuous shape. Nevertheless it grew larger as though empowered by its own malevolence – or was it that of Johan Pal?

Its upper body had muscular arms which clutched a conch shell, but one twisted in a parody of the symmetry of the living conch. This it blew to give a sound which struck terror into listeners; all other degrees of malevolence were now insignificant in this new rendition. It wielded its triton and conch with muscular dexterity; its chest and shoulders were powerful and gave vent to an enormous volume of harsh sound from the conch shell.

Below its torso, the apparently human form gave way to something less than human. As the eye passed downwards, its body could be seen to possess Piscean scales of a putrescent lucidity; they lacked colour, but they were lit from within by a grey-green spiritual non-life. As the eye continued, the monster could be seen to have a bifurcated tail like that of a fish.

It moved, leaving behind it on the floor a trail of foul-smelling slime, in which small particles of its body, like fleas or sea-lice, were left behind. The smell was appalling, like the rotten smell of all dead fish yet encountered, and then fermented for a thousand years. It wore an enveloping gown of a semi-transparent material which deflected the direct gaze; yet when the eyes were averted and it was viewed indirectly, shells could be seen at its shoulders.

The entity stood erect to reveal its full height and they were able to see that its fish spear, a trident of three prongs, was as tall as itself. Barbed, and with a heavy shaft, it jabbed the weapon down towards them. They had at Pal's garden party experienced the stench of Xipe Totec, the Aztec god, but although as foul as the present visitation, it was as though he had appeared only to be supplicated by his audience. By comparison, this new devil seemed to have come to wage war.

Emily said, 'Pal has sent us the god Triton to battle with.'

As they waited for the three-pronged spear to fall on them, any doubt which they had earlier managed to dispel by their joint efforts: singing, bravado, jesting, now returned but magnified tenfold. In particular, Dood and Shilto began to regret placing them all in danger in this manner; were they not safer in bed at their respective homes? Logic said no, since Triton was outside, but what if he managed to enter?

Dood's eyes passed restlessly over their astral citadel of chalk circles, Lourdes water and symbols; his eyes tested every inch. It had been difficult to build and its construction had taken time, surely it was safe… but suddenly, he sat up in horror as he thought through the manner of its construction; it was *wrong*!

His doubt now communicated itself to the others; they sat up also and looked around in alarm. As if their predicament were understood by the entity outside, it now began to examine the circumference of the pentacle with its malevolent green eyes. They knew that if it could only break in, it would exact a dreadful revenge on them all.

He dared not tell his friends of his mistake, but sat in a cold sweat, looking down at his shoes. He considered it further: all marks on the outer circle were correct and made at the right intervals. They had also been joined by good chalk lines made with a straight edge; this was no playground hopscotch of a construction. Yet the points had been connected by lines made, in turn, between numbers 1, 3, 5, 2, 4 and 1. That was incorrect; he should have connected, in turn, points 4, 1, 3, 5, 2, 4 since such pentacles were entirely different. The correct form was a banishing pentagram, perfect for protection and positive force; instead he had made its mirror image, an invoking pentagram. He had made an absolute danger to them, a pentacle that would encourage a spirit to enter and enable it more easily to appear!

Restlessly, now, Triton began to slither closer and his putrescent trail of slime was left just outside the walls of their supposed citadel as he tested its strength. Repelled by the chalices of holy water and by the sprigs of asafoetida, his pathway was of a zigzag shape, but they could sense his satisfaction as he jabbed his trident across a pinnacle of the five-rayed star and was unrepelled there. Triton now turned his attention directly to them and his evil, green gaze held each of them in turn. He raised his arm and the shaft of his trident rose above his head, ready to stab. It was as though he were a fisherman on some forgotten sea in a time long past; but today he was fishing for the souls of men and women.

Dood began to pray for guidance and as if in answer, the thought came to him of a solution to their mortal danger. However, just at that moment, the trident was thrust forward for the first time and a barbed prong pierced his calf. As he had feared, the pentacle was useless; again and again the trident thrust forward and he, Shilto and Oakwood began to bleed from puncture wounds from each successful thrust while only the very nimble girls and Bishop were successful in dodging them.

Dood, in pain, asserted all his will power and tried to think clearly. Picking up one of the chalices of Lourdes water from the breached pentacle, he threw it towards the figure outside and without waiting for the result shouted, 'Run. Follow me for your life.'

Following him, the others left the house in an instant and ran into the garden after him. He made for the water feature, which he knew consisted of a central paved area surrounded by running water in brick channels, fed by a stream from the local hillside. They made the paved area without mishap, but continued to leak blood from their wounds so that dark trails could be seen in the moonlight.

Nevertheless they knew they could not be reached by their evil enemy except by crossing running water, an anathema to the powers of darkness and so a natural protection from that which they had experienced. As he stood watching, Dood immediately wondered at his own decision to make a pentacle indoors. Why had he not strengthened this natural citadel outside?

Emily and Amelia now took charge. There was no alternative: they made the bleeding men remove their trousers and Bishop helped them tear strips of cloth from each leg. This revealed some serious puncture wounds to calf muscles, but the girls were quick to bathe them in pure, ice-cold water and apply pressure by tying wounds with their primitive bandages. After having done so, they were unable to suppress smiles at the appearance of the trouserless men, but modesty was eventually restored when remaining 'trouser-shorts' were pulled on once more.

In fact Triton was a malevolent spirit, yet the wounds were real and debilitating. The three sufferers in bandages were required to sit silent because they could not afford a further shock to their small group that night.

Behind them, they heard a disappointed chuckle and a hiss like that of a spent firework. They felt the malevolence diminish and knew that Triton had passed. Now, the night seemed altogether more wholesome with a fresh smell of aerated, running water instead of the former putrid staleness. They were within a new citadel of flowing water and Pal would be as exhausted as they were. But it was cold, very cold in the small hours before the dawn.

However despite the cold and his wounds, Shilto said firmly, 'We shall stay here until the cock crows.'

Chapter Eight

The Nazi Parade Grounds at Nuremberg

It was dawn by seven-fifteen at that time of year and they heard at last the noise of birdsong and from a nearby farm, the crow of a cockerel. The sky began to lighten in the east; it was a cold, pale light, but welcome after their ordeal the night before. They had waited patiently for the first sign of dawn or that magical crow of the cockerel, a call they knew would break any dark spell. They were very cold inside their citadel, where running water, icy and pure had prevented dark things from passing. Now they were safe from un-named, unclean spirits: the bat with yellow fangs, the wer-fox, the slithering snake; but above all, from the evil Triton, sent by their enemy Johan Pal by means of his dark skills. Three of their party were wounded, but they were now safe to emerge and recover.

Their breath made clouds of condensation in the icy air and they were stiff and shivering in the little clothing they had brought from their breached pentacle; and further, with stab wounds to calves and thighs, the three men found movement difficult with tight bandages and the throbbing of damaged muscles. Their bandages, formerly ice-cold with spring water, had prevented the loss of much blood, but they were now dry and constricting.

They had huddled together until dawn, but the time had come to move. Gingerly, they tried to stand; the girls first stretched, leapt up and swung their arms to make a little warmth. Then together with Bishop, they hauled Shilto from the ground and Oakwood, a heavy man, followed by Dood. The wounded made a comical picture with their trousers shorn at the calves and makeshift bandages drawn tight and Amelia was unable to resist another giggle.

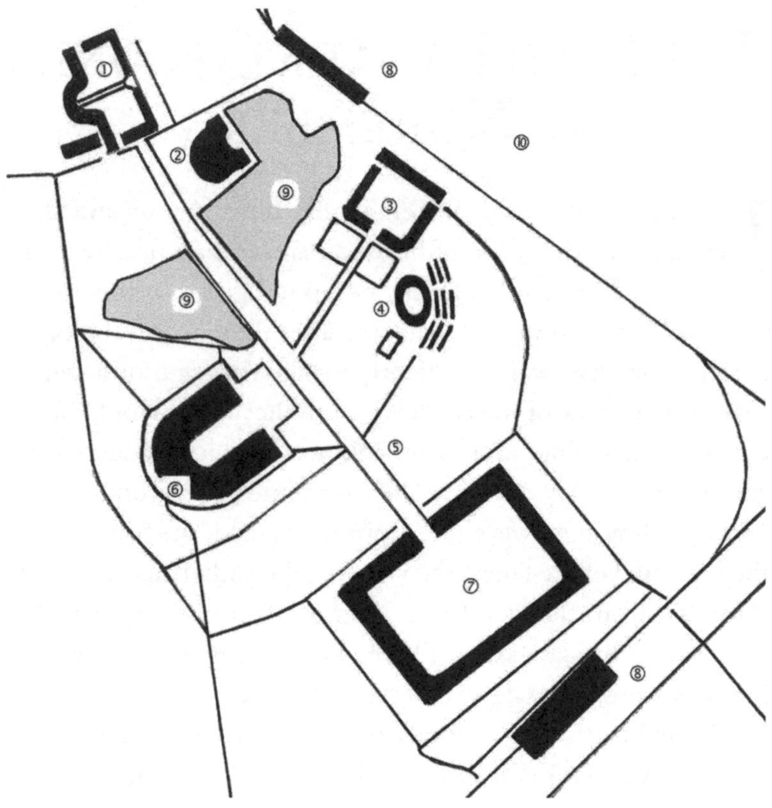

Nazi Parade Grounds at Nuremberg

1. Luitpold Arena; 2. Congress hall; 3. Zeppelin Field; 4.Municipal Stadium for Hitler Youth; 5. Great Road; 6. German Stadium; 7. March Field; 8. Railway Station; 9. Lake; 10. Kraft durch Freude Field

Callum Dood pulled from his pocket a mis-shapen cigarillo – what had it contained? – and lighting it, he let the sweet smoke circulate while he considered their fate. He was pleased; it contained frankincense, that beneficent resin from the Boswellia tree, known to enervate and repair. Calmer, he considered their escape. It had been through momentary inspiration that he had repaired his earlier mistake and their escape could not be considered to be a real victory. Why then had he made such a serious mistake in the first place? Perhaps there been too much beer or too few vigorous walks over the downs? He dismissed such thoughts quickly; he knew that compared with Johan Pal, he was no expert practitioner of magic himself and deserved at least some small accommodation.

They all knew that he was full of remorse. Oakwood said, 'You found it necessary to make decisions without certain outcomes and we are alive after all.'

Alive, certainly, yet evidence of the risk they had taken was manifest in the form of not inconsiderable puncture wounds to calves and thighs. And still they waited for his next suggestion.

They now stretched their stiffened limbs and tried to walk around a little, an excursion which required the help of those with undamaged limbs. Limping, a few steps seemed to restore a semblance of circulation and despite the pain, there was no rush of blood or fainting. No major artery or vein had apparently been breached.

Wally Bishop said, 'Perhaps we need to be careful before we call out the Doctor. It seems only a few hours since he came here to see Amelia. I can't help thinking he would start to question a series of similar puncture wounds to three different people. '

Oakwood replied, 'We do need some form of medical treatment; these puncture wounds are painful but they will soon heal if we keep them clean. But I agree: I would rather not see your doctor here so soon.'

Bishop added, 'I would half-expect the Doctor to call out the police, so why don't we just go to the casualty department at the local hospital instead? If so, we shall need to decide on an excuse beforehand. How about an accident with a spiky farm implement? '

They examined the effects of the trident and Oakwood said, 'Yes, we had better do that. But look at these stabbing wounds: the trident is a fisherman's tool. It would have been much too unwieldy on the battlefield. I don't suppose we could say that we had a fishing accident!'

Shilto followed, 'Yes, the trident is still used for catching eels and fast-moving sea fish in southern Europe to this very day. In Greek mythology it had a symbolism associated with the seafarer. The spear of the warrior was a different thing altogether; it was a cutting tool with sharp sides.'

Dood looked glum as he remembered their opponent, 'The fact that Johan Pal had the ability to raise such a demon simply confirms what we already guessed. His status as a big-league black magician is assured. I know it is no comfort to Amelia, but his trick with the wax doll was only a minor magic. Last night, he sent an entity which I can only describe as a devil of the major division. That kind of ability does not "come cheap" and he must be very advanced in his studies.'

'Do you think he meant to dispatch us completely?' said Emily.

'This time, yes, I think so. There would come a time when his interest in revenge would be greater than his interest in you as an Acolyte.'

'Yes,' said Bishop, 'Or his interest in the rest of us.'

Shilto said, 'What now?'

Amelia replied, 'Its light now. Let's go inside and get warm. We can clean up, get something to eat, and we can also take a closer look at those wounds. In fact, we may even be able to treat them ourselves. Let's face it, if we go the casualty department at the hospital, they will probably only do what we can do here. Those injuries look like punctures only and we have antiseptic and bandages here, after all.' They nodded in agreement and followed her indoors.

They checked the house over and found no trace of the atmosphere of the previous night. With doors and curtains open, the autumn sunshine shone in, weak but welcome. They replaced carpets and furniture, rearranged cushions and other oddments and soon had a presentable room. There was no trace of the presence of Triton, nor of evil shapes, or of sinister smiles in curtains or cornices.

Amelia and Emily now removed makeshift bandages and with warm water bathed the various wounds until clean. There was little further release of blood, and it was the general verdict that while not inconsiderably deep, there had been no cuts or tearing of tissue of the kind that would require stitches. They dried all wounds carefully, applied an antiseptic and lint, together with a proper crêpe bandage. Amelia said, 'See that crimp in the cloth? It gives a little spring to the bandage. The tension should support the wound underneath so that walking won't reopen it. But go carefully; it will be stiff for quite a while.'

A little later, they had washed, and dressed in their warmest clothes; the girls from their own wardrobes, Oakwood from his suitcase, Dood by walking the 500 yards to collect replacements from home and Shilto by borrowing Bishop's spares.

However, they were still very hungry, having had to tolerate the partial abstinence of the past day. Whether it had worked or had been irrelevant, they were now in need of a proper breakfast.

They prepared a table with knives and forks, coffee cups and plates, but after a few minutes, there was a muffled oath from the kitchen. Amelia emerged with a bottle in her hand.

She said, 'This milk is horrible and everything else has gone sour as well.'

Wally Bishop replied, 'What everything?'

'Come and see.'

One by one, they removed all items from the refrigerator. There was no exception: milk, butter and cheese were rancid; meat, vegetables and salad were sour and slimy; everything had to be thrown away except for those pickled in brine or vinegar.

Shilto said, 'Well, I've heard the expression "your face would turn the milk sour," but I would never have believed it…'

'I believe it,' said Dood, 'and folklore suggests that in medieval times, any practice of magic by witches was supposed to do just that. Country folk were always suspicious that one of their own number was secretly casting spells against them and sour milk was the foremost evidence that it was. One could assume they had sour expressions too!'

'Does this mean our home is now unclean?' said Amelia.

Dood replied, 'This is your home and you have to live here. We all saw what happened last night and if it would make you feel more at ease, we can enact a ritual of purification.'

'But it hardly looks any different from last week!'

'That may be, but in my work, I sometimes come across rooms and indeed, whole homes that have become difficult to live in, often for unaccountable reasons. A few quick questions of the owner will often provide some kind of insight, but not always.'

'Then I think it might be wise to go ahead. But please tell me more.'

Dood continued, 'Homes and in fact, all buildings, keep an aura: a 'psychic recording' or image of dwellers and events there in the past. The memory of a bright and happy young family will impart a caring and pleasant aura to a home, which a new incumbent might feel. But violence, cruelty and falsehood can leave an oppressive atmosphere instead.'

He waved his hands in emphasis, 'Sometimes, upsetting disturbances can then take place. They arise from the recording of events left there, in the very fabric of the building itself. A simple cleansing will often clear this in the same way that a videotape can be wiped clean. It is these circumstances that I have been asked to attend many times.'

Emily asked, 'Are they hauntings, then?'

'No, a true haunting is quite different. It arises from the presence of a troubled spirit, unable or unwilling to pass on from this life. It may be that he or she does not wish to leave a former home or may prefer to relive happy memories there. They require the help of the Church also, but are often harder to deal with. That is where an exorcism may need to be applied. I do not think we need to concern ourselves with that here. I think we may need only a ritual cleansing.'

He asked them to take out all moveable furniture and any general junk and detritus. Carpets were removed throughout; floors were cleaned thoroughly and dried; then carpets, cleaned and beaten in fresh air, were returned. While they did so, he officiated in the preparation of liberal amounts of holy water by using fresh spring water from the garden. He said, 'I can bless my own from first principles, but I would like to show you a method for making the homeopathic preparation instead. Adam and I have discussed this often. I would like to use serial dilutions because it illustrates a principle of which I am a strong believer.'

Shilto said, 'Callum has been keen on spiritual homeopathy for a while. He is quite sure it works despite the criticism levelled against it by its critics.'

Emily queried this, 'Why, what's wrong with it then?'

Dood replied, 'Many homeopathic remedies – and magical ones too – are made by the serial dilution of an active ingredient. In our own example, too many dilutions of Lourdes into spring water might mean the final preparation would contain no active ingredient at all. That argument would accept the notion however, that Lourdes water must contain a formal active ingredient, which in fact I doubt, and therein lies my point.'

He continued, 'The homeopathic art – it is not science – *actually suffers* by those who propose an absurd law, which they call the Law of Infinitesimals. They argue without logic, that the lower the concentration, the more potent the ingredient must become. This is self-evident nonsense because by analogy with sugar-water, the less sugar it is diluted to contain, in order to taste it the sweeter it would need to become. This is absurd; they are trying to present homeopathic medicine as a natural science.'

'My old friend, a chemist I must introduce you to when he is sober, explained this reasoning to me. He said that Avogadro's number describes the number of particles in a *one mole* quantity of a substance: a huge number (6×10^{23}). Dilutions in homeopathic medicine, such as the typical '12C' dilution – twelve serial one-hundred-fold dilutions – would be unlikely to contain even one particle of a homeopathic ingredient, because the concentration would then be one part in 10^{24}. A further dilution to say, a '30C' concentration, which is common in our art, would give one part in 10^{60}, so that a diluent would contain none of the original substance with a certainty of 10^{60} minus 6×10^{23}, a final concentration of one part in 10^{37}, therefore certainly containing none of the homeopathic remedy at all. Yet homeopathic and magical remedies still work.'

'So why do supporters of homeopathy talk about a Law of Infinitesimals?'

'It is clear to me that they are right about the worth of their medicines, and if so, they must be wrong about their law. They would be better-off by presenting their remedy as a minor magic, cause unknown – but possibly psycho-somatic – rather than as a science. All I know is that my blessings work, as do the adequate preparation of herbal remedies, although not incorrect ones. By *that* I mean preparation by disbelievers. I support the herbalists and homoeopathists as much as I support the chemists. My friend the chemist agrees with me, just as he believes in homeopathy. Believe me: he has monkeyed around with some odd stuff over the years.'

Dood summed up thus, 'None of our dilutions of holy water could have diluted out the original Lourdes water completely, but had they done so, I would still have had no worry about its efficacy; there are stranger things in Heaven than Earth and it would still have done the job regardless, simply because one had wished it to be holy in the appropriate manner.'

Interested and still thoughtful, the party continued their cleaning, dusting and purifying. All remaining surfaces were dusted and wiped down with this new holy water. Windows were opened and gusting winds were allowed in to replace the air within the house. The kitchen and bathroom were thoroughly cleansed, degreased and appliances such as the refrigerator also cleaned, turned off and left open to the air. Any trace of dust and of depleted air or dirt was removed from all upper rooms, including the loft.

After two hours, salt was added to some holy water and blessed, before being smeared with the forefinger over all closing surfaces of doors and windows, and on walls, ceilings and floors. Then, an invocation was spoken in each room: "May this blending of the elements salt and water now preserve the sanctity and holiness of this space".

Then, in all approaches to outside doors, the remaining salt and water was placed in a line across the ground and the names of all those invited to enter were spoken while doing so. Lastly, holy candles were lighted in each room and Dood spoke prayers for the invocation of protection as he allowed a little dried sage to smoulder in the flames. All was then replaced: windows were closed and fresh air enclosed within rooms. However by then it was 11.15am and they were very hungry. The Bishops went with a few more-than-willing helpers to the village shop, from which they returned with replacements for those foods discarded earlier.

On Shilto's advice, they again avoided meat, but made an excellent breakfast of fresh bread, butter, cheese and fruit, together with coffee. An observer might have noted a certain perkiness return to them all, despite their wounds which, bound though they were, made them limp around at times. Later, they cleared away their plates and were pleased with the house, clean and sanctified as it was. They were still together, musing over their fate, when Wally Bishop returned from the kitchen area, where he had been clearing things away into the cellar.

Bishop walked in quite calmly and sat down on a vacant chair. He said, ‘It’s gone!’

The others turned to face him.

‘What’s gone, Wally?’ Amelia said.

‘Our friend the Fuhrer. You know, downstairs: the relic. We have been so busy recently that we had quite forgotten about him. The box with its contents has been taken in the night. Johan Pal must have entered the cellar while we were busy elsewhere and removed it.’

*

They were all in conference. ‘Adam and I have a special dispensation from the diocese to carry this work forward and there is a roving locum who will be taking my place in church for a while. Personally, I would call him raving loco. But we had better put our heads together over the next day or so to decide what to do.’

‘Do you need me for a while, Callum?’ said Oakwood. ‘I can dip back in when you do, but I must see Zenda and I don’t want her being left alone for too long. She has her engagements, as I do, but I need to spend more time at home for a while to support her.’

Bishop said, ‘Good Lord, Peyton, it has been a pleasure to see you and we couldn’t have done without you. Perhaps the difficult bit is over now, but by all means come back when things settle down. That applies to you all, of course. Emily, you are based here for now, but are you still happy?’

‘Oh yes! I don’t want to slip back into my old ways with you know who!’

Wally Bishop spoke again, ‘Well I think that settles our movements for a short while. Can we drop over to the vicarage later today to reconvene?’

'Yes, I was going to suggest that. Say by about five, so we can build up to something to eat at about seven?'

Later, they all walked over to see Callum Dood and Shilto, who had joined him about an hour earlier. Oakwood had telephoned home to let Zenda know he would return there the next morning. In the meantime, they discussed what they should do.

'The basic problem, as I see it, is that we have to find Johan Pal and put a stop to his activities once and for all. There is also no doubt that we must relieve him of the Magdeburg Relic. We can guess that his intentions with it will not be very pleasant.'

'But what will he do, and where will he go with it?'

Emily said, 'When I was with him, he said he would take the relic back to its proper place. I understood him to mean that he would return it to Germany.'

'What, immediately?'

'No, but very quickly; he's probably getting ready to go right now. But I would point out that I've managed to keep clear of him recently, so for more news it would be better to speak to some of the other acolytes. I'm not saying they know more than I do, but they may know about *other* things.'

She pulled a face, 'Like me, they were sworn to secrecy, but they soon knew that they had taken on the wrong kind of magic when they joined him. We all thought it was just a bit of harmless foolery on the downs at night; you know, like a magical disco. Why don't you speak to Kayla or Freya? They are under no illusions at all and would be certain to help you. But avoid Carol Black; she's much too far down that road now to change.'

'Where can we get hold of them?'

'They all have perfectly respectable day jobs. You can reach them at their work-places.'

'Where can I get hold of Freya?'

'Freya Sampson works in some kind of professional or secretarial post but she might meet you in a lunch-time. Here is her number; I know she will see you.'

Dood picked up the telephone and switched it to speakerphone.

'Oh hello, Callum, I *am* pretty busy but I do have half an hour. We could meet in Devizes. Do you know the Bear?'

'Yes, I have been there very many times. What time can we meet?'

'I can be there by twelve-thirty today.'

Later, they sat at a quiet table at the Bear, each with a sandwich and something to drink. Callum Dood explained the situation. 'The thing is, Freya, we need to know what Pal intends to do with the Relic, now that he's managed to get hold of it. Emily said he would go to Germany, but we don't have much to go on.'

'No, I expect you don't, Johan Pal is pretty quiet about his intentions at the best of times. However, I *can* tell you that his family background is from Germany, as are some of his friends, all of whom will be completely at ease there. If they return, it will be to take the Relic back to the place of some former rally in the 1930s, or some other place of special significance to them. Hitler himself actually said that the home of Nazism was Munich, but I don't think they will go there.'

'Why not?'

'Because I heard them speak of Nuremberg. I can only assume that Pal considered he was in safe company when he said it.'

'To Nuremberg?'

'Yes, think about it. Once there, the Relic would have returned to at least one of its former homes. Nuremberg was the place of the great Nazi rallies of the 1930s.'

'What will he do then?'

'He will try to raise the soul of Adolf Hitler and bind it to his own purpose. However, such a task will not be easy because he will need to create a suitable ceremony. That will in fact be very difficult; the recreation of a life or the raising of a resting spirit would require the sacrifice of a living soul. It would be a formal exchange, which in practice means murder. I often felt he intended that doubtful privilege for me.'

'But Nuremberg is pretty busy isn't it? So how will he get enough seclusion for his grand project?'

'I don't think by any means, that he would just hire a hall for his work; there would be no '*affinity*'. He would need to return the relic to the old derelict Nuremberg parade grounds, where the Fuhrer preached. There, in a suitably secluded place, I expect he would carry out a ritual at night and at some particularly effective time in the Satanic calendar. But in case you didn't hear what I said earlier, he would need to murder somebody to achieve his aim.'

Dood nodded, 'Yes indeed; that is the age-old law: a life must be spent in order to buy a new life. I wonder who will be the unlucky one…'

'Some babe snatched from its mother, or maybe one of his former neophytes in revenge for allowing themselves to be rescued.'

'But what would this ritual be like?'

'There would need to be the usual exhibition of licentiousness and gluttony and a coven of thirteen people present.'

'Why thirteen? I know the significance of the number, but for what reason?'

'Thirteen has a general importance in such rituals. It is an optimum for many kinds of magical ceremony and they tend not to work with other numbers. A larger number is usually worse, but thirteen multiplied by a further thirteen is exceptionally good. Don't expect 169 followers, however, because that would present huge difficulties in terms of security. Some fool would be bound to give the game away. No, you must look for thirteen followers only.'

She continued, 'There would need to be the four elements earth, air, fire and water nearby, but they can easily be improvised. He would also need to raise a demon of some kind;

he has recently been successful in raising some particularly nasty ones as you will know. In fact it is the devil he may raise that would grant him the earthly power he needs. It will ask for blood as an offering and in return, will grant enough power to restore life to the Magdeburg Relic. Blood would need to be spilled onto a dedicated altar within a circle made from chalk or of followers holding hands. The ceremony would also need to be held at a suitable place; that would be vitally important. But make no mistake, a minor demon would not have enough power to grant him. It would have to be a devil of considerable renown and one that had been appeased properly.'

'What about that deadly demon which he raised at his last Sabbat?'

'I doubt it. That particular devil was sufficiently damaged not to fall for him a second time. They are vengeful, you know, and don't like Lourdes water thrown at them. I doubt that he could raise it twice. I would expect some demon known to the Roman Catholic Church, with a description in medieval literature.'

'You speak as though life can be restored to a few bones.'

'Heaven only knows. I hope you can stop him. He is seriously wicked and plans to rule the world.'

'So where do we pick up the chase?'

'As I said, you can expect him to alight at the old railway station, not necessarily by train of course, but just to retrace the former route of the Fuhrer.'

'When, please?'

'I doubt he will wait until 22nd December, which is the feast of the winter solstice. That would be a big day, but too far hence. I would say four weeks from All Souls' Eve or Halloween, just passed. You would have about three weeks to catch him.'

'Why wait at all?'

'Well, normal gatherings on the Downs or at his home are at monthly intervals. If he decides go straight ahead, he would still need to prepare everything and by that, I mean procure a sacrifice. Then he would need to get his followers out there, put them up at an hotel and get them ready. In the meantime, he would need to avoid the German police, Interpol, the newspapers, conduct his own business affairs and allow his followers to conduct theirs too.'

'Freya, you have been a great help, thank you.' Dood kissed her on the cheek and watched her depart, fair hair gathered up and very pretty, and as always very graceful and composed.

Later, Callum Dood described the outcome of his meeting with her. 'We need to find out how and when Johan Pal intends to go there. I don't think that we can just go out, book into an hotel and wait. What if we have to sit there for a month before he turns up? Think of the practicality.'

Amelia said, 'I doubt whether he could take all his paraphernalia with him on a train, nor would he have it crated up to go by air.'

'You are right. I can hardly see him booking an extra seat in a plane for the Magdeburg Relic. No, I can only see him going by road, and he would need a fairly large vehicle too, not just a car. I would suggest a Ford Transit or something of that size.'

Emily said, 'I do know that he owns a Mercedes Sprinter, he uses it quite often. You know, it is one with blanked-off windows at the back.'

'Yes, a panel van. What colour is it?'

'It's actually black. I think most of them are white.'

'Well, I think we could look out for that leaving the area. If only we knew the registration number.'

'How would that help us?'

'Well, Peyton Oakwood knows a chap who works with road traffic control. As soon as that van is on the road, the traffic cameras would pick it up on the motorway.'

'What would you do then, follow it?'

'We would need to leave ourselves and go straight to Germany.'

'I bet I can get its registration plate,' said Emily.

A day later, Emily danced in with a piece of paper. 'Here it is!'

Bishop smiled; she had a slight air of triumph about her. 'How did you manage it?'

'Oh, they keep service records at the garage where he gets it fixed. I went round there, quoted the name and address of the owner and asked to see the service record and whether it needed another visit. They've seen me before. I said sorry, I couldn't remember the registration number but I knew when it was last in. The manager recognised me and showed me his record on the computer.'

'Well done, Emily. I will phone Peyton and get that number hooked up for a warning when it goes down the M20 motorway to the coast. He will let us know when to go.'

'But doesn't that count as the illegal use of police road traffic cameras and their computer?'

'That would normally be the case, but Peyton will explain to his contact that Johan Pal is a suspected abductor of young women, that is to say *you;* and you can give a statement if necessary?'

'Oh yes!'

'Then it becomes a wholly valid police issue; but a not-too-complicated one: a simple recording of who comes and goes, together with when and where. And Peyton is a member of H.M. Services too, although not the usual service of course, but we won't say that, now will we?'

Over the next few days, the four friends made ready for their overseas trip. They made sure that their passports were in order, adequate money distributed – Shilto made it known that the church would provide for a limited underwriting of expenses, given the importance of the current project – mobile phones were working, adequate clothes obtained and as far as Dood was concerned, suitable psychic protection procured or made. Once more, Amelia declined to come, preferring to stay at home with the business and other domestic matters. Waiting, nevertheless, proved to add its own tensions; there was no news of any movement and after four days, they had fallen back into their former routines of studying, ecclesiastical matters and antiques dealing.

However on the fifth day, Peyton telephoned to say that a Mercedes van with the required registration had been spotted on the move, travelling from London towards the coast on the M20. Immediately, they booked a flight from Birmingham to Nuremberg. Bishop indicated that they would let Oakwood know how matters were progressing in Germany and they made ready to leave. Oakwood suggested that he could follow at a later date if need be, but would be committed for a week or ten days.

They caught the train from Swindon the following day. It took a little over two hours to get to Birmingham via Bristol, whereupon they booked into a local hotel for the night.

On the following day, their flight left just before two in the afternoon. They travelled with Lufthansa, in an A320 Airbus: a comfortable twin-engine craft with a single aisle. They had a short stop at Frankfurt after an hour and forty minutes of flight, changed aircraft and completed the final leg of their journey to Nuremberg in a Boeing 737. They enjoyed the short-haul flight with plenty of room for their legs and no change of time zone, but preferred to eat nothing on their journey and accepted coffee only, having had their main meal at the airport earlier.

On the aircraft, they discussed Johan Pal and his likely timetable.

'Well, I think we can discount the overnight ferry from Newcastle to Amsterdam. That would have given a sailing time of about 17 hours but only 6 hours driving time at the other end; call it 36 hours, what with comfort stops and so on. The journey would have been easy, with other people doing the navigating and steering for most of the way, but there would have been no reason to be on the M20 going south had they done so.'

'I agree; we can be pretty certain they went from Dover to either Calais or Dunkirk, which is a two hour crossing. And that would give them about seven hours of driving time at the other end. All in all, we could expect the whole journey to be of about 12 hours duration, but again, they will surely have wanted to stay somewhere comfortable on the way, so let us call it 24 hours.'

'So when they finally get onto dry land, which way by road?'

'The route is really quite easy. They would drive along the coast towards Bruges and then veer off towards Ghent. They would then use the E40 motorway, drive around Brussels, head south-east towards Liege and so towards Cologne. Just east of Cologne, they would veer southwards to Bonn, but would go around that city to Frankfurt. They would have followed the same high-speed motorway for a considerable distance, but by then would be heading towards Nuremberg, which is actually quite far south and in fact in Bavaria. It sounds straightforward, but the distances are considerable: a little short of 600 miles, so they would arrive wanting a bit of rest. In fact, they would not be so far short of the border with the Czech Republic; Prague is almost due east and only about 200 miles further.'

'I believe we should arrive at roughly the same time, but probably in a better state of repair. I would expect Johan Pal to get organised within a few days of arriving, but probably not directly. Does this leave us any time for sightseeing, do you think?'

'Perhaps on the way back!'

Passing through baggage handling and customs, they went straight to their hotel on the Bahnhofstrasse, a large, six-storey building in a traditional style and with impeccable décor and furnishings, in which they had taken rooms for fourteen days.

That evening, upon a recommendation from Bishop, a regular traveller to that part of Germany, they went to the Adlerstrasse and ate at a restaurant there which he knew would provide many local specialities. They were tired after their travel, but were fully able to do justice to the excellent dishes they ordered. Emily and Dood chose meatballs with fried potatoes and cabbage, while Shilto chose the excellent Nuremberg sausages with sauerkraut and potato salad. Always his own man, Bishop chose the pork shoulder with dumplings and cabbage.

After about half an hour, Emily said, 'That was lovely, but my savoury dustbin is full and my pudding dustbin completely empty!'

It transpired that the others also had empty pudding dustbins, so they all had pancakes with apple sauce and powdered sugar. Overall, they delighted in their first Bavarian food, which had a spiciness absent from much traditional English cooking. Rather sleepy after the beer which had accompanied it, they returned to their hotel bedrooms and slept soundly.

★

The four friends were installed in a good city centre hotel, the Hotel Bayern, a few minutes' walk from the main railway station. At any other time they would have been keen to look at the great art collection of the Neues Museum, with free entry for guests to their Hotel. That day, however, they were rather preoccupied.

Emily relaxed in her marble bathroom before venturing downstairs for a substantial buffet-style breakfast. She met the others there and they delighted in their pleasant surroundings, with a wood-panelled dining room and very comfortable furnishings. Nearby, traffic moved at a moderate speed on the Konigstrasse, although directly outside their hotel the wide road was busy at all times. They were perhaps half a mile from the Germanisches Nationalmuseum and a little less from the Neues Museum, both of which contained prominent collections which they had decided to visit as soon as they were able.

Downstairs in the restaurant, Emily was met by the others. Soon, Callum Dood turned the conversation to business, 'By now, Pal will have arrived and no doubt will be staying at some suitably pleasant place with one or two of his closest followers. But I doubt whether they will all be staying together because that might attract attention, certainly from *us*, anyway. I would expect them to be distributed amongst the other hotels in the city, probably posing as businessmen or holidaymakers. However, tracing him shouldn't be difficult. We could simply phone the dozen or so top-end hotels in the city and ask them whether they have his vehicle in their car park.'

Bishop replied, 'It's worth a shot, but don't count on it working. He may have left it somewhere else, much further away. At least, that's exactly what I would do.'

'Perhaps, but I would imagine he would want to keep a close eye on its contents.'

Bishop continued, 'Let me phone around, my German language is quite good – I often come here to the Christmas markets – and I can pose as a businessman hoping to re-establish contact with him. Business and sight-seeing have been the purpose of my former trips here anyway, so there is no reason for anyone to consider anything amiss. Why don't you look at a few of the local attractions this morning, while I try to find him?'

He managed to make himself understood, but was met by a cursory response in his first few calls:

> *„Guten Tag, mein name ist Wally Bishop. Ich hoffe, einen Mr. Pal, die mit Ihnen leben wird gerecht zu werden."*
>
> *„Es tut mir leid, aber wir können nicht geben Sie die Namen der Gäste auf dem Telefon. Allerdings kann ich eine Nachricht an ihm zu geben, wenn du willst."*
>
> *„Danke, später werde ich Sie zurückrufen."*

Later that day, he spoke to them over coffee in the lounge.

'Unsurprisingly, hotel receptionists were unwilling to give out the names of their customers, but I eventually managed to locate him at an hotel on Jakobsmarket. I think the young receptionist there may not have been quite as experienced as the others and she eventually said, *„Ja, wir haben Herrn Pal mit uns. Er hat zwei Begleiter mit ihm, Fräulein Schwarz und Herr Trapper.“* 'So that makes three of them; and as we thought would be the case, he has access to the hotel's own parking facilities nearby.'

'Well done, Wally; that makes it a lot easier to track them as they come and go. If we know where *he* is, then we don't really need to keep an eye open for his friends.'

Bishop said, 'We need to take a look at what we think is his intended place of mischief, but why don't we hire a private investigator to help us with Pal while we look about? Obviously, it makes more sense than to have to chase around after him ourselves. He would immediately see us and he knows what we look like by now.'

Emily followed, 'And I think he would know, even if he didn't see us; he throws himself into a trance to 'look around' on a regular basis and would observe us following him.'

Later that afternoon, Dood called in at the 'Heinrich Detektei ab Nürnberg' based on Äußere Bayreuther Str.

'Guten tag, Herr Heinrich,' said Dood.

'Please may we use English? Good afternoon to you Mr Dood. What can I do for you?' Heinrich was a tall, slim man with large hands and short brown hair.

'Thank you, I do have to confess that my German is not what it should be. I would like to put that right, of course, and would be pleased to come again on a longer visit to your beautiful city.'

'That is very kind of you and you would be welcome here at any time. I must recommend the old city for tourists.'

'Yes, thank you. Now turning to business, I would like you to track and report on the movements of a former business associate of mine, Herr Johan von Pal, while he is staying in Bavaria. Despite his name he is a British citizen, but he is of course at home here. He plans to use some of my professional ideas as his own; publicity, you understand, involving major German historical sites in this city. I think he plans to visit them soon, to use them as film sets in opposition to our particular agreement to work together. He is likely to try to carry out his work in secret, so I require a discreet observation of his movements and of any personnel he works with. I need photographic evidence in case I need to press a case. Here, this is his Hotel.'

'Ah, the Osterreichisch on Jacobsmarkt; I know it well. Herr von Pal has very good taste, which is very convenient because I haf not been seen inside for a number of years and my face there is therefore unknown.'

'I expect that the work will finish within a week, but may I retain your services for longer, if need be?'

'That would be very convenient. May I show you this brochure for my fees and further expenses?'

'Yes, of course. You will please remit your weekly account and invoices to me at the Hotel Bayern? '

'You will please to supply me with your credit card details today?

'Er, yes of course, here they are. I need an opening account with your headed notepaper, please.'

Transaction completed and authorised, Dood returned to the Hotel Bayern. In the meantime, Emily and Bishop had gone sightseeing, while Adam Shilto was sitting in the bar with a brandy and soda. Dood, a renowned beer drinker at home, asked to try a large glass of a local style of beer and received a *Maßkrug* of *dunkel,* a traditional dark lager of about 6% alcohol. He remarked to the barman on its pleasant malty taste and the barman replied that he should visit some of the local beer cellars where a very wide range of traditional beers could be obtained. Dood continued to test the recommendations of the barman and he and Shilto reflected upon their progress.

Shilto said, 'Well, Herr Trapper and Fraulein Schwartz are clearly Sieghard Trapper and Carol Black. I wonder where the rest are staying.'

'In all likelihood they won't come out for a while. They don't need to be here until the big day itself, or perhaps only a couple of days before in order to get things ready. I did ask our friend to keep an eye on Johan Pal and record any contact with the others. He's bound to notice the other two at the same hotel, but I didn't ask him to track down any more of them.'

'I wouldn't have thought they would need to concern Pal at all. He doesn't need an army of workmen; all he needs is the lightest of gear to carry about; no more than clothes, suitable drapes and other 'religious' paraphernalia. The rest of his friends would probably only convene with Pal himself on the day. They would probably simply respond to a signal from him and so naturally turn up when needed; all we need to do, therefore, is to keep our eye on him and his movements.'

'True, but leaving aside the question of whether he notices our private detective, have you thought whether he will be keeping an eye open for *us*?'

'I do say that it has been at the back of my mind. As we know, Johan Pal is quite well-established on the road, one might say, to perdition. He is sure to be a regular traveller in the ether; able to set free to wander on the astral plane, quite at will. He will surely also make contact with his spiritual guide at the earliest opportunity.'

'Guide, or guides?'

'Guide only, I am afraid. We all have two of course, one busily engaged in trying to lead us on the straight and narrow; the other on the broad pathway to ruin.'

'God or mammon!'

'Exactly, but in his case, the former will be have been constrained completely through his declared allegiances. He, she or it will be wringing his, her or its hands, while the evil counterpart will be celebrating. The point being that Pal will be in communion with his evil spirit guide and will undoubtedly be directed to look around for us. If so, then we will probably be seen.'

'Is there any way in which we can hide from him?'

'We could surround ourselves with what might be called a psychic smokescreen; erect a pentacle maybe, or go to sleep in a church. I don't think that we can do that here, but at very least I think we should carry a bit of protection with us. That might deflect a casual glance at least. Johan Pal cannot like to look at things which seem, to him at least, as unpleasant as an ugly demon would be to us. He might quickly look elsewhere.'

Emily and Bishop came in at about 5pm in the afternoon. They had been to Nuremberg Castle.

'Well, Emily, what did you think of it?' asked Shilto.

'It is quite an imposing place actually; a huge fortification, all on a great sandstone rock and distinctly different from most English castles in appearance. I loved the view of the city from above; I found it very interesting indeed and I would love to come back again someday.'

Bishop said, 'Well there you are, then! I enjoyed it very much, too.'

Dood said, 'Where do you all want to eat tonight? I've room for about two more beers and then I will need to get something more solid down. What do you say if we go to the Restaurant Albrecht-Durer-Stube?'

'Why do you recommend it?'

'It's got food there. Come on!'

Later, Dood had more beer with his appetiser of three Nuremberg sausages with sauerkraut. They were small, seasoned with marjoram, had been grilled over beech charcoal and were very tasty. They were attractively served by pleasant staff and complemented his beer perfectly.

Shilto said, 'I believe it is a good idea to choose food to go with a particular beer.' Enthused by his idea, he started with a corn salad with fried goose liver and said afterwards 'I was right about that combination.' While he was choosing again from the menu, he complemented the waitress on his appetiser. She appeared not to understand his German, but he gave the thumbs up and *vereinbarung* was restored; the food was very good and the beer excellent.

In turn, Emily chose a pumpkin cream soup with pumpkin oil and röstbrotwürfeln – cubes of roast bread – but she declined beer and stayed with a glass of hock; as she said, 'All the better to leave more room for the next course,' to which they all nodded sagely.

Like Emily, Bishop started with a lighter dish and so had the horseradish cream soup with smoked salmon and röstbrotwürfeln. He also chose a glass of wine rather than beer; a 'wise decision that would leave room for beer later.' His friends complimented him on his wisdom.

After a short break, the waitress cleared away and further dishes arrived.

Shilto, having admired Dood's earlier dish, chose three loin and two Nuremberg sausages cooked with Frankish wine vinegar and served with local bread.

Although Emily disliked cats, she nevertheless chose catfish fillet with horseradish sauce, parsley potatoes and salad. She said 'fangs' to the waitress, managed to stay a whisker ahead of the others throughout and told a tail or two as she ate.

Bishop chose a ragout of venison cooked in the Frankish manner with cranberries, together with red cabbage and *spaetzle*, a kind of soft egg noodle well-known in that region. He wondered whether it was indeed the Germans who had first invented the noodle, rather than the Italians or Chinese and referred to the long-standing argument between the latter nations. He was certain that the success of his meal pointed towards a clear German ascendancy in the noodle department.

Having taken a while to choose, Dood opted for the rump steak Strindberg, together with seasonal vegetables and roasted potatoes. He said, *'The steak has been with seasonings and mustard covered, then in a brunoise of shallots, flour and egg dipped and then on both sides fried.'* The others waited for verbs to end clauses,

German-style and agreed that it was his best way of keeping their attention until the end of his speech.

They continued with their levity and between them shared two bottles of Schloss Sommerhausen: a dry black Riesling and two of Castle Wuerzburg, a dry Champagne-like wine; there was absolutely no doubt of the complete excellence of both.

About an hour later, Dood chose the warm *zimtzwetschgen* or cinnamon plums, a dish of that noble fruit supplemented with cinnamon liqueur and vanilla ice cream. He proposed that it would be churlish to decline the glass of pear brandy offered by the house, but the others took the risk, declined any more food or drink and had coffee only.

The bill was moderate, the food excellent and the four friends decided to walk home. They were encouraged by the sky, which was clear and with stars alight, and by the air, now cool. As they sauntered back to their hotel, the city was still alive since it was as late only as 11pm. Dood, having eaten and drunk substantially more than the others and possibly dreaming that this was a night out in Calne, was unsteady on his feet. Of the others, Emily had been moderate in her intake of wine and the remaining two somewhere in between.

But what sorry soul would actually blame Dood for being rather worse for wear? Hey! He was on holiday, the company tremendous and the food and wine outstanding. It was just that, in truth, he had developed a little bit of a headache. Declining further companionship that evening, he returned to his hotel bedroom and flopped, fully-clothed but shoeless, onto the bed. Quickly, he was asleep and snoring a happy, but slightly drugged sleep redolent of an evening at The White Hart Hotel.

The others stayed up a little longer in the lounge, chattering idly about that lovely city and the general excellence of its food, drink and hospitality. Had they not come on an errand, they were sure that they would wish to pursue its sights and sounds more fully; nevertheless, they agreed to see all they could in the undedicated time available to them. Soon, after coffee and the occasional yawn, they felt it would be better if they, too, were asleep and each returned to his or her room and went to bed.

Outside, the moon had risen from a point a little north of direct east. It was a full moon, its light was bright and it shone directly into any room with curtains undrawn. Sharp shadows crept slowly across the floor and it was easy to see without the need for a lamp. Slumped on his bed, the fluorescent face of Dood's wristwatch was alight in its energising rays.

In his room, the moonlight shone directly onto his face, but in his subconscious mind, part overcome by wine and only part asleep, he felt the impact of its pale, cold light. It was a baleful, sinister presence in which, as the hours wore on, his sleep became lighter. By 3am he was dreaming, but his dreams were strange, eerie and fateful.

Shortly, moonbeams seemed to penetrate his closed eyelids. To his semi-subconscious mind, they appeared to take on a solid form as though they were made according to the same principle as the rings of Saturn with component parts of individual bands or phases. In one of them a band of white light seemed to take form as though made of crystals of ice, sparkling and moving; or as of a white powder of moon-dust, settling gently onto his closed eyes.

The effects of the wine began to wane and he reached a point at which he began to wake. As he did so, he felt a constriction on his chest together with fingers around his throat. Astride his chest was an old hag. She was prostrate upon him and his limbs were pressed down onto the bed, his body crushed.

He drew each breath slowly, feeling an increasing weight on his chest. The weight made it easy for breath to be expelled, but difficult to draw. As he lay there, he felt cold fingers explore his throat and find his windpipe. They exerted still more pressure and he writhed in an effort to avoid their bony grasp. She lay upon him, now fully-formed, a dark part-clothed female full of cold life; a deadly life who needed to withdraw his own from him; thriving on his warm breath while he waned in the cold of hers.

And he knew her; she was *The Hag*. He had heard of her from parents who had spoken of their child's night-time terror; *The Hag,* a dead life from beyond the grave: she was known to many cultures and had lived many centuries.

Language contained memories of her; she was *hægtesse* in Middle English; or in this very land, the word *hexe*. People disbelieved in her today; instead of the 'hex on you,' she was known by the more modern term – the more foolish – 'sleep paralysis' as knowledge had waned. In times past, evil people knew of spells that would raise her.

He was unable to move and drew a rasped intake of her cold breath; he was weak with the effort of breathing and of drawing life from her depleted air. She had become a great and terrible weight, grown larger by malice; an evil presence wishing to take his life for her own while he was immobile and weak. For three hours they lay together, by now he was cold and bathed in sweat; she was corpulent and refreshed. He felt close to death; she, close to life.

The moonshine at last waned. Finally, there was a noise of birdsong and her anger, malice and regret vanished in the emerging sunlight. Drawing sweet air into his lungs once more, he was weak, shaking and tearful. A pale dawn approached and a warmer kind of light came in through the window. At last, he was free.

Shaking, he pulled the quilt over his still-prostrate self and slept for an hour. Eventually, he awoke to sunshine but lay, eyes open in a continuing paralysis, for half an hour. Falling from the bed, he dragged himself to the bathroom and lay in a warm bath. By then, he had not yet been missed by his friends at breakfast but desired their company the more.

Walking slowly downstairs to the dining hall, he joined them at the breakfast table. Adam Shilto said to him, 'Callum, what's the matter with you? You look hag-ridden this morning, or is it just a hangover?'

Dood nodded and sipped some tea in silence, until, after shedding a tear at one point, he was a little revived.

*

Later, he recounted his experience and they were shocked, although not surprised. Shilto said, 'We have to assume that Johan Pal sent it?'

'I expect so, but my assailant is also well-known to the church and has been described many times in the medieval literature of several countries. I am sure there are *some* cases of clinical sleep apnoea and paralysis, but this was a real visitation and she was a foul spirit, believe me.'

'Does she kill?'

'No, she feeds on fear and just like a parasite, takes what she needs while leaving her victim alive. I expect she was a strangler aeons ago.'

'Then my bet is that she was Pal's work. I expect he was trying to warn us off or was out for revenge.'

'We shall never know, but what I do know is that we need to carry more protection. We have allowed a bit of a holiday to enter in to all this. Last night could never have happened had we done so. The dreadful thing is that Pal might have sent something far worse than she was. Maybe he was too preoccupied to muster the extra effort.'

'Extra effort?'

'Certainly; the higher in the devilish pantheon, the more the sacrifice to raise.'

'So what protection should we carry?'

'Come to my room in an hour. I need to get some coffee down.'

Later, he lined them up and gave them small envelopes of Asafoetida grass and garlic. The foul asafoetida could be smelled immediately through the porous paper. He also gave them a crucifix to wear, together with vials of salt, mercury and holy water. Distributed about their persons and with prayers offered by them all, he asked them to carry these strange substances which he assured were a potent protection against evil.

Emily said, 'Must I really carry the asafoetida?'

'Yes, you cannot suppose that garlic will be enough.'

'What exactly does it do?'

'It is a resin which comes from the root of a plant of the *Ferrula* family. They look like fennel plants, have yellow flowers and grow in places like Afghanistan. In medieval times, the smell was supposed to be so foul that even the devil couldn't put up with it, hence its use today. In fact, asafoetida is also a valuable spice which is used sparingly in Indian cooking; it gives the 'poppadum smell' to poppadums and funnily enough, is closely-related to muskroot, another very useful medicinal herb.'

'You seem to be a mine of information on the subject of herbs,' said Emily.

'Ah, yes. I have found that herbs of all kinds can be taken by mouth, or smelled and often beneficially smoked.'

'Have you ever smoked asafoetida? said Adam Shilto.

'No, of course not, but I did break a bit of poppadum into my cigarillo once upon a time!'

Later, he ordered more coffee and cakes from room service. Then, he said, 'All this begs the question of whether, having had a day or so 'off task,' we can now go on the offensive in finding out a bit more about what Johan Pal intends to do. I am due to hear from Herr Heinrich at the detective agency today and we may soon have more to talk about.'

That day, Dood took a telephone call from Herr Heinrich. 'Ah, Herr Dood, I hope you are well today?'

'Yes indeed, thank you. I am still enjoying your beautiful city and plan to continue doing so. How are your researches?'

'I have been able to observe Herr von Pal at his hotel, the Osterreichisch, with some success. He seems like any other tourist, although a rather busy one.'

'Busy, in what manner?'

'Herr von Pal occasionally returns to his hotel for lunch, but at all other times he seems to be busy elsewhere throughout each morning and afternoon. During the early part of his stay, he transferred some large cases, perhaps heavy, from his Mercedes van to his own bedroom. I am advised by a cleaner that the cases are locked, but she became unwell after cleaning his room so no further information will be available from that source for a day or two.'

'Could there be any connection between the act of ascertaining whether locked and that of becoming ill?'

'I cannot see how that could be.'

'No, I guess not. So where does Herr von Pal go to?'

'He has avoided most of the usual tourist places; the toy museum; the churches.'

'And?'

'He has shown more interest in the many icons of German culture and history. On successive days he visited the Schöner Brunnen: the gilded fountain, you may know it, on Hauptmarkt.'

'I am not sure I do.'

'It is near to the Old Town Hall; if you have ever been inside, it has some dungeons and a torture chamber, ja? Also, it's very near to the Gänsemännchen, a well-known fountain in the form of two geese with water issuing from the bill of each bird.'

'Yes, I remember passing that.'

'He was also seen visiting Albrecht Durer's house, which is now a museum to Durer's life.'

'But these are just short visits perhaps?'

'Yes, but he did spend a whole day at the National Germanic Museum.'

'Can you tell me what that museum contains, which might attract him so?'

'It is a very big collection of German art and culture, especially of Franconian artistic and cultural history; it contains old documents on parchment; a collection of 17,000 seals and other fine arts.'

'Could he study or get close to any of the documents?'

'Yes I think so, but by appointment. Do I take it that he may have an interest in our very recent past?'

'Maybe.'

'Ah yes, I thought so. In that case, it might explain why he also went to the Documentation Centre at the old Nazi Rally Grounds, a very ugly, boxy modern building, next to the hall where the Nazi Party rallies were held.'

'Did he stay long?'

'Yes, a whole day, far more than enough to view the exhibits inside.'

'Did your agent follow him within the building?'

'I cannot describe my methods, although I do know that Herr von Pal also took some interest in the rally grounds themselves and in other buildings open to the air.'

'I thought they were derelict.'

'They have not been actively preserved, but they are not derelict to the point at which they are in danger of falling. There are limestone facings missing from walls, weeds in corners, that kind of thing, but the main symbols are still present. So it seems that he may have a connection with such places?'

'Yes, perhaps, but exactly what connection, I have no idea.'

'That is good, now I know what kind of connection to find, is easier, I think.'

'Are you able to describe his general outlook and demeanour?'

'Herr von Pal seems very preoccupied and he has been unusually systematic in his approach to Nurnberg. It is as though he were researching the past of the city or planning some forthcoming activity. He does not seem like a casual tourist, much more a businessman with a tight schedule.'

'Pease, would you kindly carry on with your surveillance as before?'

'Yes of course.'

Later, Dood chaired another get-together in the bar. He

said, 'Johan Pal has visited some Nazi sites and has, as likely as not, researched Germanic themes in a local museum.'

Bishop said, 'Which Nazi sites?'

'He went to the Nazi Parade Grounds and Documentation Centre.'

'Then perhaps we should also go there,' said Shilto, 'but what would we look for?'

Bishop replied, 'I think he would need to find a suitable place for his activities, a place inside a hall, and quite secluded. Also, he would need to be able to furnish an explanation if caught there. As far as we are concerned, we need to look for evidence of preparation; alterations perhaps, or fresh paint and so on.'

'Well he can hardly sleep there!'

'True, so he would have to get things ready bit by bit, by visiting the place several times. One way to do it would be to pose as a workman; very few people question a man in a hard hat, carrying a paintbrush or ladder.'

'Not just one man, surely?'

'I guess not; he would probably need several men in hard hats.'

'Or maybe a total of thirteen on one visit!'

'Yes, or he may only be looking around.'

'Our detective fellow is still on his tail. Do we really need to go too?'

'Herr Heinrich knows me,' said Dood, 'and he would probably wonder a little if he bumped into me again in such a place. I don't want to think of an excuse right now, especially if I absolutely need to go there a further time. But I'm sure it would be fine for any pair of you to look around; that would give us two teams. You would be able to walk about together, looking for signs of unusual activity.'

'We can't be certain, but the chances are that Johan Pal knows we are here.'

Dood replied, 'No, we can't be certain, but it is likely; my visitor of last night would indicate that it is so. She is a well-known 'nasty', but exactly why she should have chosen to visit me on this one day out of the last twenty-odd-thousand, I cannot imagine. So I am pretty sure that Herr Pal sent her, damn him; I wouldn't have minded a half-decent succubus! But anyway, yes, I'm forced to agree; he is probably waiting for us to move.'

'Do you think he would be likely to delay, put off, or alter his timetable? I mean, why don't we just turn up on the right day when everything is propitious for demonology and general nastiness?'

'Nice idea, Adam, but have you any idea of how difficult it would be to find him if we do that? The Nurnberg Nazi Parade Grounds are six square miles in area! It is a very big place indeed.'

'Yes, I have heard as such. But can we not narrow that down a bit? He would want to conduct his ceremonies inside a building, surely.'

'I think you're right; and there are parts of the site that we can discount for several different reasons.'

'What does the site look like?' said Emily.

'The site was designed by Albert Speer to glorify the Nazi Party and its ideals. Although they originally intended to use about eleven square kilometres, the project was never really finished and it covers about half that area today. Nevertheless, many impressive buildings still stand.'

Bishop said, 'So what parts can we assume Johan Pal will leave alone?'

Dodd continued, 'I think we can forget the Luitpold Arena, which has a stone grandstand in front of a former arena which is now a recreation park. It would be too open to interest him, and it is too far from water.'

'Similarly, there is the Zeppelin Grandstand. It was built on the so-called Zeppelin field and had rows of columns flanking the individual parts of a spectator stand. The field was huge: it could contain 100,000 people and the stands a further 60,000, so the whole construction was like a large soccer stadium. Parts of it were blown up by the Americans after the war, but in any case, it would again be too open to interest him. There were some displays there, but they were later transferred to the main Congress Hall.'

Emily said, 'Please can I see that map?'

'Yes, certainly.'

'And see here; for the same reason the Sports Stadium, intended originally for the Hitler Youth: that would be much too open. Likewise, a long road known as the Great Road, which linked the Luitpold Arena and the March Field – formerly a Parade ground for the Wermacht – can be discounted for similar reasons. There is a lot of housing development near the March Field and the Great Road is often just a big car park. Like the other places I mentioned, anyone could see him there because there is no real cover.'

'And so, what is this bit on the map?' said Emily, pointing.

'Ah, that is another open area: the Kraft Durch Freude Field; it was formerly a funfair and cultural area with many wooden buildings, but I don't see how it could interest him. All of the wooden buildings were removed and the area is now under housing estates and sports fields.'

'And see there?' said Dood, 'that horseshoe-shaped area of water? It is the Silbersee lake, a site excavated to make a large stadium that was never built. Instead, they filled it with water to make the present lake and I cannot see him being interested in *that*.'

Bishop said, 'As I see it, large open areas would be useless to him, so we need to look for enclosed areas, with the further requirement that he needs to work near to water for maximum effect. To put it simply, we want a building near water. That narrows it down quite a lot, surely.'

Shilto said, 'So what buildings do we need to consider?'

'Aren't there former barracks?' said Emily.

'Yes, but those, the former SS barracks, were used by the United States when they occupied that area after the war. More recently, they became German Federal offices, so you can forget them altogether. There is, however, one point we have not yet thought of; the question of whether a place has the particular 'potency' that Pal would need for a successful ritual. For example, there is an abandoned railway station, but I cannot see how it would have any connection with the Nazis.

'So what kind of place would he need?' said Bishop.

'I think it would need to have been used for a Nazi parade; especially good would be a place where the Fuhrer actually spoke to his supporters. I would imagine that such a place would be particularly propitious; his ceremony would probably have more chance of success.'

Adam Shilto said, 'So that leaves only that very large building which all tourists see on promotional literature for the city.'

Dodd followed, 'Yes, the building in question is the main Congress Hall.'

Bishop replied, 'So what exactly does it consist of?'

'The Congress Hall is a large horseshoe-shaped building which encloses an open area. The horseshoe isn't open, however, because each open end has a further block erected there. It has a general similarity with the Coliseum in Rome, which is hardly surprising because the Congress Hall was modelled on that earlier building. There would eventually have been a roof over it, through which light would have passed, but it was never finished and so the only enclosed spaces today are rooms within the walled construction. Those within the upper level contain a museum of that era and you can also see the document centre; a funny box stuck on the side.'

'And didn't you say his magical ceremonies need the four elements?' said Emily, 'see here, there is a huge lake on two sides of the building, so water would be taken care of at least.'

'Well,' said Bishop, 'I vote that we look at the Congress Hall.'

There was a general murmur of agreement and then Shilto said, 'Yes, I think we should, but let us choose our teams. I reckon that Wally and Emily should leg it around the place first. Tomorrow, Callum and I can spend a morning there. That way, poor old Callum, feeble bones an' all, can have a bit of a rest today after his experience last night.'

Dood smiled and said, 'Nobody has mentioned my hangover either! Oh, and by the way, if Emily and Wally are starting out after lunch, then I think we had better get on and have some.'

After a quick chat together, Emily said, 'Wally and I have decided to push straight on and visit the place as planned; I for one have had quite enough to eat for a while. Did you see how much I put away last night? But I've taken a banana and popped it in my pocket, just in case, and Wally has some chocolate, so we can munch those if we get short. That way, I can save myself for something larger this evening.'

Bishop said, 'But we'd better go back to our rooms to collect our coats. I don't want to freeze or get too wet, if you don't mind. Can we see you here at supper time?'

'Please be careful,' said Dood, as they disappeared.

Later, Shilto and Dood had a pleasant lunch at the bar and they both relaxed for an hour afterwards in armchairs in the lounge.

Shilto said, 'Was it a real evil spirit or some kind of bad dream? Perhaps you ate too much sausage?'

'Oh, it was real enough, and exactly as has been recorded by hundreds of other people over the years. Believe me, she was real; I have had to deal with many cases of unpleasant visitations in my own parish and a few of them have been pretty nasty.'

'So where was this one on the scale of general nastiness?'

'About in the middle. Visitations are not uncommon. In most cases, people experience them from relatives after they have passed on. They usually offer words of wisdom or comfort, but sometimes, matters are a lot worse.'

'Are those the only circumstances?'

'Certainly not; in some cases a visitation can be from the spirit of a living person. Under such circumstances it is usual that something important remains unsaid between them.'

'So what does that tell you about the human condition?'

'It is quite clear that the human spirit is free to roam, most often when a person is asleep. Other than in those circumstances the spirit will stay close, usually within or by the body. One of my parishioners recounted a state in which her spirit remained anchored within her physical body while her spiritual head and torso stood watchful above.'

Shilto said, 'I guess we have all experienced the things you describe although some still feel their experiences derive from electrical networks and nerve cells. But that doesn't alter what I intended to be my question. If your 'friend' last night was only half way, that is to say, somewhere in the middle between good and bad, then what would be the whole way?'

'There are sundry demons and devils, just as there are the souls of the good or very good.'

'Like whom?'

'I am sure they had names at one point. They were probably people just like us, but they may have become embittered by their experiences of life and unable to forget. Who knows, perhaps over the years they continued to remember in a resentful manner and their hatred grew so that it has consumed them. They now think of little except revenge, but they must also hate themselves for it. It may be that they lived lives long ago, but with the aeons of time they have grown ugly to those they visit. Who knows, the Hag may once have been a living person who liked to throttle people.'

'And so they are your everyday evil spirits, demons and devils?'

'Yes, I think so.'

'I know you have exorcised a few back home. What do they want?'

'I have to say that I have never quite established that. They just seem to have become intrinsically bad, almost as fundamental forces of nature. They will probably be there until the end of time. Almost certainly, more will enter the pantheon for both good and evil over the years.'

'Was Adolf Hitler good or bad? He is known to have been kind to animals, for example.'

'I am not competent to answer that. He believed in the nation state and may have considered that his aims were good as far as his country was concerned; today, we think otherwise. Certainly there were dreadful crimes, but how do we know on what basis they were calculated? It has been said that his motivation was one of natural vengeance for the betrayal of the German Army at the Treaty of Versailles. If so, I myself have punched someone who tried to steal my wallet. Clearly, both were revenge, although my action could not be held to mitigate his. Similarly, we all have the potential for good or evil in diverse ways.

'And he can really be raised once more?'

'Yes, I think he can.'

★

Emily Robertson and Wally Bishop entered the foyer of the exhibition entitled Faszination und Gewalt. There, they were immediately impressed by the work of the architect Günther Domenig: clearly visible ahead. They commented to each other upon the theme, that of a glass corridor which cut diagonally through the building and which, as a brochure made clear, disturbed the rectangular stone structure of the former Nazi Building and was therefore a counterpoint to the beliefs which led to its construction. Later, in galleries within, they spent several hours examining its contents. The brick arches and subdued lighting complemented the exhibits perfectly and their effect was exactly as they had expected; there was little moralising and the exhibits were adequate in their own right.

However they did not lose sight of their mission and after a while, Emily said, 'I do not see how this place could possibly be of use to Johan Pal.'

Bishop replied, 'I was thinking the same thing. The floors are too smooth, too clean. The inside has been restored and he could never use it for his own purposes; it's just too pristine and 'high-tech'. It would be like holding a Satanic ritual in a bank or maybe in the middle of Marks and Spencer's. Besides, someone would see him and call the police.'

'I agree, it would be crazy; and anyway, he's certainly not here now. Tell me, what about one of those secret rooms that were thrown open to visiting Nazi dignitaries?'

'I think they are down a level, but I do not feel that we could visit them all in any case. Let's have a look around here.' He pointed in a direction that would take them through to a further gallery.

Later, they strolled around the large enclosed space within the horseshoe-shaped Congress Hall. There was sunshine, but underfoot it was damp and the moss, small stones, cracked concrete and the occasional low-growing daisy or dandelion reminded Bishop of a deserted airstrip. However, no aircraft could possibly approach over the walls in order to land; there were at least four storeys of the stone and red brick Coliseum, which loomed over.

Emily said, 'Too exposed, too visible and not special enough. It would lack the requisite symbolism. Johan Pal would be looking for something more secret, more powerful, and something less given to apology.'

Bishop said, 'I know what you mean. Let's go back to the Hotel.' They were back within the hour.

Later that day, the four friends sat down in Callum Dood's room to decide what to do next. It was clear to them from

Emily and Bishop's description that it would be pointless to drag around such a large site, day after day and in the cold.

'And besides,' said Shilto, 'we have been paying somebody to do it for us, haven't we? I am pleased to say that following our discussion about the financial side of things, I can confirm that the Church will pay our legitimate costs. There has always been a modest fund of money for cases like this, but we still need to account for it and must make sure we use it wisely. But I can tell you that we had to pay for this hotel ourselves, by the way. They wanted to wish bed and breakfast places on us, but we insisted on something at least half-decent. Luckily, we have reached a stage in life where that is no longer a problem and so they said we only had to pay the difference.'

'Well, I am quite sure that 'using our time wisely' cannot consist of simply strolling around idly, hoping to bump into evidence of Herr Pal and his preparations. Even if we did, what would we do about him?' Bishop voiced their thoughts. 'And how long have we got, now, anyway?'

'A week, maybe,' said Dood, 'before he moves.'

'Are you sure about that?'

'No. He may decide to press ahead with his ritual regardless. It is so important to him that the most propitious date, desirable though it may be, might not loom large in his calculations. However I do base my opinion on other factors – he is undoubtedly very clever – such as the time he might take to complete his researches, get his hardware ready and procure a sacrifice.'

'What do you mean by sacrifice?'

There was a pause. 'He needs to arrange to kidnap somebody.'

To some extent, the four friends were taken up by their new and very pleasant surroundings. Nuremberg was a lovely city and they had thoroughly enjoyed its Gothic architecture and the local Bavarian culture with its museums of art, restaurants and nightlife. However the reality of their purpose was again brought home to them; they had only a little time to prevent their enemy from carrying out kidnap and possible murder. They must also prevent the darkest magical rites imaginable: not just necromancy – the magic of communication with the deceased – but something far more sinister: the act of raising the spirit of Adolf Hitler himself, a rite to be conducted within a place as yet undiscovered.

Bishop said, 'We must inform the police if we think someone's life is in danger or if we know they have been kidnapped. I am not quite sure about the local laws on witchcraft, but I still doubt whether we could make it stick. I would think that kidnapping and threatening behaviour would be the best we could throw at him.'

'But isn't there a law against promoting Nazi ideology? Surely that would include trying to bring him back to life?'

'It wouldn't hold water in court. Nobody believes in necromancy in this day and age. But they would certainly get upset by flags and Nazi regalia.'

The next day, and therefore two days after their earlier conversation, Dood took a call from Herr Heinrich.

'Guten morgen, Herr Dood.'

'Oh, hello again.'

'This time I haf sent my associates out to follow Herr von Pal. It is as you supposed. He has visited the Nazi Party Parade Grounds and Congress Hall, but spent very little time in the Congress Building itself. He went around it, of course, but lately, he has shown more interest in the old Zeppelin Grandstand. I am surprised because most of the interesting exhibits from that era were put on display in the Congress Hall some time ago.'

Heinrich continued, 'There are empty chambers and some interesting architecture, but how could that amuse a man for a whole day? He looked up and down the field also, and strolled around it; there were three of them; a large fat man with a huge stomach and grey balding hair; also a woman with dark hair, a

Fraulein Schwarz I believe. She seemed to be doing quite a bit of talking and one might say "she wears the trouser," ja?'

'Are you sending out the same associate tomorrow?'

'No. We follow in turns so no suspicion. I haf other associate tomorrow and maybe I go after her. I mean, the day after her.'

'I quite understand. Can we agree that you should telephone back again when you have some more news?'

'Ja, is fine.'

Dood returned the receiver to its pad and mused for a while. Then, suggesting to the others that they should enjoy themselves elsewhere that day, he pocketed a few odds and ends: wallet, mobile telephone, camera and a small polythene bag containing a map of the site under survey, together with a number of the protective devices which, by now, they routinely carried with them. He also collected a rather heavy overcoat and hat and caught a taxi.

Upon arriving at the Nazi Parade Grounds, he avoided the main Congress Hall and noted that the main throng of tourists was there and upon the grounds outside it. He walked on and at the Zeppelin Field, made for the grandstand area – the Zeppelin tribune – and noted the few stragglers loafing around. The seating areas, which resembled old-fashioned football terraces in the UK, were fenced off from the field but one section of fence had fallen and some youngsters scrambled up and down the weed-festooned grandstand where plants flourished in the rain and weak sunshine.

He was pleased to be alone. Had he gone with one of the others, he would have felt responsible and did not wish to be so. On that occasion, he was also reflective to the extent that he would have been concerned by the need to be companionable.

Strolling around like one of the other stragglers, he stood about fifty yards from the front of the grandstand and looked directly towards it. It was of three tiers of beige stone, on the top tier of which a swastika had sat until blown up by the Americans after the war. The first tier was a little taller than head height, while standing areas extended to the top of the second tier. The whole building contained a door and various other apertures, but denied its original purpose and without flags and banners, it was a sad, miserable-looking and block-like affair.

Walking round it, he noted two large *feuerschale* – fire shells or braziers – made of cast iron. They were waist-high, scalloped shells about ten feet across and on four short legs. One of them, behind the Tribune Building, had been painted orange and used as a child's paddling pool. It now lay empty and had recently been cleaned out.

The Zeppelin Tribune building was not normally open to the public, its display inside having been moved elsewhere. Nevertheless he was fortunate to see that access, although reserved for particular days only, was not denied that day and he entered to find he was alone. There he observed a further feuerschale on display, but unlike the first it was painted a grey colour. Both had formerly been used for open-air gatherings in the Nazi era, where a large cauldron of fire symbolised the significance of that gathering, as does the Olympic Flame today.

Despite its emptiness, the Zeppelin Tribune Hall was of considerable grandeur inside. Floors were made of stone and walls were of marble; its ceilings were high and had an intricate pattern of golden lines on them and spaces from which swastikas had been removed. The lofty space was at first quiet; later a couple arrived and their shoes made a clicking noise on the stone. However they left quite quickly in order to return to the main tourist areas and silence returned. Looking around, he felt quite sure that the place still contained enough of its former history to find favour with Johan Pal.

After a while, Dood left the place himself and as he did so, he passed through a set of double doors, complete with cuts and abrasions, ink, paint and anti-fascist graffiti. Their message was clear and justifiable, but their respect for the record of history a sorry one. He read a few sentences as he stood there. The silence was ominous.

In that sinister, portentous quiet, he suddenly felt that Johan Pal had stood there recently and that he had been very angry. He continued to stand at the double doors without breaking the spell he felt. He was quite sure that Johan Pal had also seen the painted graffiti on the door and wished to exact a revenge on its perpetrators. Walking on, he felt an ominous, tangible trail of anger continue on with him until it vanished into the ether after twenty yards. He now knew for sure that the Zeppelin Tribune Hall was *the* place. About an hour later and deep in thought on his return journey, he walked around, bought a newspaper and some postcards and looked for a quiet place to deal with them. Finding some time on his hands, he decided to drop into a beer cellar called the Mata Hari. Descending the twelve or so stairs to the lower floor, he entered a very small bar that was clearly also an occasional venue for music. There were advertisements on the wall for a performer of blues called EvilMrSod, together with posters and photographs of past performances. Here and there, a few customers were also chatting, but he made for the bar and spoke to a bald man behind it, who wore black T-shirt.

He was anxious to improve his German and said, 'Bitte, könnte ich ein paket von nachos und einem großen glas bier.'

The bar had a white surface of some man-made material atop a pedestal of red brick. The barman leaned forward with his elbows on it and his T-shirt proclaimed the term 'paloozah.' Nearby, another man ate an excellent burger made of no fewer than six layers of beef, cheese, tomato relish and bread.

The barman said, 'Ja, was für bier?'

Dood replied, 'Ein Münchener bier, bitte.'

The barman said, 'Hell oder dunkel?'

Dood, now pleased, concluded, 'Ein leichteres bier, bitte.'

Taking the glass of beer and packet of nachos to a corner, he sat down, opened the local paper and took a swig from his glass. It turned out to be a very good beer indeed, but he was disappointed to find that he was able to make only limited progress with the newspaper. He fell into a reflective mood and made a mental note to take lessons in that language to use them in some future trip to Bavaria.

Somewhat absent-mindedly, he considered the events of the last week and with the corner of his eye, watched the other customers come and go. As he drank his beer, he swirled it and allowed the froth to settle once more; the head was thick enough to write his initials in, following the manner of publicity for a well-known UK bitter stout. As the beer swirled, his initials spun and his eyes naturally followed them. Although he did not feel dizzy or confused, the spinning beer had a natural hypnotic effect. For a second, the spinning froth and slowly-dissolving initials took on the shape of a boat and a line of bubbles its frothy wake. He took a sip and swallowed much of the froth, then stirred with his pencil and watched again. The storm of froth disappeared so that the beer seemed flat as of the surface of a millpond. In it, a momentary eddy took on the shape of a coracle: oval and with a shape like a hollowed-out walnut shell.

He was immediately reminded of the shape of the feuerschale and thinking of it, became wholly sure that Pal had been there only just before him. *And having felt Pal's anger there, he was quite certain that there would be no reason for any further delay on his part.*

He drank the rest of his beer down and bought a small bottle of Marillenschnaps, which he placed in his pocket. Ascending the stairs once more, his mobile phone obtained a signal and he called Bishop. 'Wally, you must all come quickly. Can you meet me outside the Mata Hari on Weissgerbergasse?'

'Is that far?'

'No, but I suggest you get a taxi. It's about fifteen minutes away. Please can you bring Adam and Emily too?'

'Are you sure it's OK for Emily?'

'I doubt whether we could keep Emily away. Anyway, she's no safer at the hotel than here with us. You know what that man can do. And please wrap up warm and bring all the bits and pieces of protection and some torches too. I think I'm on to something.'

They arrived in a taxi about twenty-five minutes later. Dood opened his schnapps and took a swig and that, together with his coat and the effect of an earlier little dance on the pavement, ensured that he did not feel cold despite the wait.

Chapter Nine

The Ceremony at the Zeppelin Tribune

In the taxi, which they had retained, Dood explained how useless to their enemy he felt the main Congress Hall would be, 'We all agreed that the Congress Hall is too frequented by tourists and that any odd goings-on would be noticed straight away. There is security there, and despite his abilities, I cannot see how he could avoid that. Or at least, the rest of his people probably couldn't. But leaving that aside, I legged it around the quieter areas today and it so happened that I came upon something else more eminently suitable.'

He continued, 'The Zeppelin Tribune is a grandstand, but it also contains a hall of moderate size. Inside, there are still some original Nazi memorabilia despite the fact that its main display was taken away some time ago. For example, its ceilings still have most of their original decoration and there are the original marble walls. But the essential thing is that it is usually closed to the public . At night, with its reasonaby secluded location, it would be ideal.'

Shilto said, 'So what do you have in mind?'

'I think he will now move. Out of all the places we have seen, *that*, in my view, is the most likely. Call it intuition, but I somehow feel he has very recently come to the same conclusion. I think we should stake out the Tribune area and keep our eyes open for him because once decided upon, I doubt whether he will wait around.'

'Stake out with a view to what?'

'We might come out on top in a scrap with Pal and twelve half drunk, semi-capacitated followers, but even if not, we could certainly disrupt the proceedings. We might be able to grab our relic back and get on our way home. But the next best thing would be to get clear and let the police know. They won't like what he intends to do, that's for sure. Do I take it that you all still carry elementary protection with you?'

There was a general mumble to the affirmative.

'It's seven o'clock now. Nothing serious will happen here until midnight, if it does at all. However Pal and his friends could normally be expected to indulge themselves a bit before that; and since there are probably only thirteen of them it can be done fairly discreetly. I think we can expect the usual display of gluttony and licentiousness, following which, at about midnight, Pal will start to get serious and we can then expect to see some sort of depraved ritual, there in the Zeppelin Tribune Hall. I suggest we go off somewhere warm for about three hours and sneak back in at about ten pm.

'Er, I know a nice bistro,' said Bishop. 'We can get some franks and saurkraut there and maybe some beer.'

'By all means let us eat, but very simply, please and no meat as before.'

The meal took them an hour and a half and they ate only salad and fruit and had soft drinks. Dood remembered his earlier beer and schnapps but felt recovered from it, said nothing, and the bottle of schnapps sat unscrutinised in his pocket. Therefore of clear thought, they returned to the Nazi Parade grounds by nine-thirty and were *in situ* near the Zeppelin Tribune by 10pm. It was now quite dark and the night had become still, with a clear sky. Heat had radiated into space and both ground and air were very cold. They were warm within their *Thinsulate* clothing, however, and fortified by their supper.

The Zeppelin Tribune Building was now closed, but one by one, they flitted away quietly into the night to scout around, keeping distances of about one hundred yards from the front and sides of the grandstand. Its imposing façade and terraces were clear in the starlight, but its inside spaces were behind closed double doors. All was silent and soon, three of their number returned, taking up station at the end of one particular terrace, some two hundred yards from the main grandstand building.

'There are windows,' said Emily, 'but they are too high to see into and although not closed or blocked in any way, there is no suggestion of any light inside.'

'No,' said Bishop, 'I saw nothing.'

After a while, they began to miss Shilto. He was absent for a further twenty minutes before returning.

'I've seen something. You know that big brazier or cauldron behind the grandstand, you know, the one painted yellow?'

'Yes, what about it?'

'Well, there was a shadowy figure cleaning it out. I watched him – not that it's dirty or anything, it's just got a bit of water in the bottom – use an ordinary brush with bristles on it. It was very effective in pushing water over the side. Then he loaded it up with what appeared to be a small pile of kindling and some heavier wood. Also he stuck a few paraffin firelighters in it too.'

'Then I left him and nipped up the side of one terrace; you can get past the fence and go up to look in the window. See over there' – he pointed – 'the fence is down. The window is of a height which makes it difficult to see in at ground level, but you can look in from the top of the terrace. I saw a faint glow inside from what appeared to be a storm lantern with a cover over one side and a filter over the other, so they have a very weak source of light which is unidirectional. The interesting thing is that there is another brazier inside…'

'Yes, a feuerschale,' said Dood. 'A literal translation would be 'fire shell' but brazier would be a better. What about it?'

'Well, another fairly dark figure was pouring water from a large flagon into it.'

'Ah, so we have fire in one and water in the other. I wondered how they would make sure they had the essential 'elements.' What next?'

'He struck a flame in the first one. The flame isn't big or conspicuous; probably no more than the size of a small hearth fire, but it *is* present and it looks rather symbolic.'

'That's interesting. They need the four mystical elements present and often perform their ceremonies next to a pond or lake. However the significance of two elements within separate feuerschalen, formerly used in the Nazi era, is considerable. I have no doubt that there would be extra potency in their ritual because of it.'

'Why is that?'

'The ritual of necromancy is more propitious when carried out in places and with symbols, trappings and artefacts which connect with the spirit they wish to raise. It becomes as though that era were still present.'

Shilto continued, 'They have blocked off the back area with the feuerschale in it, by using a length of barbed wire. I could not get in without heavy wire cutters. Is that symbolic too?'

'Perhaps, but we must go. Can we get in?'

'I doubt it. They are all inside and the double doors are locked, so any notion of getting in and starting work on them is out. But we can look through the window I used earlier, and there are several openings nearby, all about five feet apart. No glass, of course, just openings.'

Quietly, the four friends returned to Shilto's former window and made ready to look inside. At first they could see little, but their eyes became used to the dark quite soon and after a couple of minutes they were able to see more when a part-covered lantern was turned to light their field of view.

Events unfolded before them. There were thirteen people inside the hall within the locked grandstand of the Zeppelin Tribune. Looking up, they noted that ceilings had been 'refreshed' with swastikas to replace those removed by the

Americans after the war. They lent the hall an ominous and sinister tone.

In the middle of the floor were concentric circles of chalk, the outer one larger by a diameter of some three feet and in the space between them, esoteric symbols, some of which Dood recognised from his own books and recent researches on the subject. The whole construction was clearly a form of pentacle with circles as a barrier to any malevolent force raised within. However in it, a naked man was tied, face down and spreadeagled, by his arms and legs. He was silent and still, and Emily thought, 'Probably drugged to keep him quiet.'

They considered the likely fate of the drugged man but knew they could do nothing. They could not get in, and any noise would only precipitate an earlier conclusion to his fate.

Emily nudged them and pointed to a corner of the hall. Johan Pal and Carol Black were eating and drinking heavily. There were also shadowy movements from other people within, and they made the occasional trip to a trestle table to refresh their plates. They were not yet in the full throes of their magical ritual, only the necessary gluttony and licentious activity beforehand. Despite being enrobed in gowns, it was also possible to recognise the short and paunchy figure of Dick Bascher and the tall, bespectacled Sieghard Trapper from their outlines in the dim light.

The feast continued from four large hampers which now lay open. One hamper was promptly upended on a portable trestle table and the participants tore wings and thighs from a roast bird and slices of meat from a joint. Unsated, they also collected hunks of bread and handfuls of cheese, together with pastries and slices of extravagant cakes. There were also bottles of wine and spirits which they opened without difficulty and drank deep. They continued to eat and drink until the contents of each hamper were depleted at last.

After half an hour of engorgement, Johan Pal belched and hitched up his robe. Like the others, he wore a robe with mystical symbols only and it was clear that they had forgone the elaborate outfits seen at Pal's garden party. Nor were there head-dresses and they had clearly not attempted to represent figures from the underworld that night. Perhaps, thought Bishop, it had been impractical to bring elaborate costumes there.

At his signal, the others stopped eating and drinking, removed their robes and woman upon man and in other combinations thereof, they threw themselves into wild copulation. At intervals, they fortified themselves with wine and by swapping partners; then they continued for at least half an hour. Outside, Bishop remembered the mushrooms slipped into Pal's wine at his garden party and regretted that now, they were unable to do the same.

The lantern was now turned off and a deep darkness descended within. Any primeval noises now ceased and mumbled sounds of awe were heard instead. On a small stone pedestal a familiar yellow-black light slowly began to illuminate the darkness. The four friends knew that a devilous shape was appearing before their eyes.

A vague, diffuse outline slowly assumed the height of a man. As it materialised, they could see that it had hair over its whole body, cloven hooves and was of a yellow or brown colour. It also had a long and pointed tongue which lolled out to the side as it moved its head, leaving droplets of a stinking spittle. Its height was further increased by the horns of a goat, which curved upwards above its goat-like head.

The emerging entity had a chain manacled to one wrist and when moving, it seemed to rattle on its pedestal. Soon, it raised a hairy, muscular arm, and a crack emanated from the chain as it swung like a whip. As it did so, its other forehoof clutched a handful of birch branches, which it used to swat its own rump. Throughout, its malevolent eyes of green-yellow contained a perverted, human-like intelligence. It now surveyed the scene and showed satisfaction with what it saw.

Dood whispered, 'A goat. They have raised the devil here.'

Bishop, familiar with German folk-lore, replied softly. 'They have raised the demon Krampus.'

'Who or what is he?'

'He is an evil man-goat who likes to receive sacrifices. He carries chains, which symbolise his binding by the Christian church in the middle ages. Birch rods or *ruten* are used to torment his victims, who are often children, as he carries them to the underworld. He is probably a demon from the Germanic pantheon, just as Queen Hell is in England, and is threfore pre-Christian. Over here, he has much of the significance of the Devil himself, and as far as we are concerned, they are one and the same.'

The yellow-black entity radiated malevolence and impatience. It cracked its ruten, rattled its chain and looked towards the middle of the circle. The four friends, paralysed with fear, were unable to call out or otherwise move. They felt condemned to observe only, as though a punishment for past sins. Their paralysis meant that, had they wished to raise the alarm, they would have been unable to run.

Johan Pal now raised his body from that of one of the female participants and adjusted his clothing. He stood, entered the circle and the twelve other members stood in silence around the outside, looking inwards. He bent over the prostrate figure on the ground and in the darkness, his hand flashed through a small silver arc next to the throat of the unconscious man. It brought no consolation to the observers outside that the figure was drugged into silence, but the dreadful crime was not yet complete.

Pal now continued to bend over the figure of the dying man on the floor and he wetted his finger in the blood, made a mark on his own forehead, and collected the precious blood in a steel chalice. Standing, he made similar marks on the forehead of each of the twelve observers, invited them to sip from the chalice and then did so himself. Finally he flicked blood towards the evil entity on its pedestal. Satisfied, Krampus seemed to settle and become less impatient; but still observed the proceedings with further expectation.

Johan Pal now defiled a crucifix, holy wafer and water and threw them onto the stone floor. He planted the inverted crucifix in a wine bottle and spoke words in Latin, '*...dimittere anima exercitu nostro dux Adolf Hitler et adduc eum ad nos iterum in his magno opere...*' – Dood thought it some form of invocation; it continued for five minutes – '*...Hitler complebit suo magno operi... et efferes foras vasa quatuor equitum...*'

Rooted to the spot outside, the four friends began to feel very cold. It was a cold they had known before, the cold of fear, paralysis, evil and desperation; but they were unable to draw their eyes away. They knew that they were witnessing a dreadful ritual there, but they could not imagine how they might be rescued: it was clear that nobody would see the flames in the feuerschale; it was well-hidden and there would be no other people nearby at this time of night. And they alone would witness the events inside the bunker and could not stop them from proceeding.

Now, Krampus turned his head towards an object at the far end of the circle. It stood about five feet tall and was covered by a silk cloth. There were symbols and devices on it: swastikas and more; but their outlines were vague in the yellow light and momentarily hidden by the broad figure of Pal as he whisked the cloth away.

Immediately, there were further expressions of awe from the twelve participants outside the circle. Johan Pal had revealed the Magdeburg Relic, exactly as had been delivered, upright and supported on a stand, on Bishop's visit to the Forensics Department a thousand miles away. The skull and bones of the right arm had been assembled in proper conjunction and the arm was now raised in a token salute, supported by a cord.

Pal lit a candle and the audience saw that it was one of the blue candles that had been made for their Hand of Glory exhibit; it burned with a demonic glow and he placed it upright in the skeletal hand before him by means of melted wax. Immediately, it became difficult to see his outline; he now failed to form a proper shadow in the light of that unholy relic. However shortly, he could be seen to move the candle so that a little light was given from within the skull itself; yet throughout, he seemed himself to be of the very vaguest of outlines in the dark.

The thirteen participants now said 'Heil Hitler'as candle light issued from the eyes of the skull. Spilling the rest of the blood in the steel chalice at the feet of the devil Krampus, Pal now uttered,

'Ich frage Krampus, mir zu helfen. Wieder leben Adolf Hitler. Führe uns auf dieser Erde.'

Immediately, Johan Pal cut the cord which held the hand aloft. *However the hand did not fall and as though spring-loaded or animated from within, it slowly rose to a position of salutation.*

Johan Pal then withdrew the candle and placed it before the newly-animated relic. It continued to burn to give a low light all around, *but the luminescence within the skull did not cease*. A light continued to shine from the empty sockets of its eyes and Johan Pal now bowed low in front of his new master, 'I have brought you back, mein Fuhrer,' he said.

All now heard a whisper, *'Sie müssen das tor zu öffnen für meine Wehrmacht wieder zu steigen.'* The identity of that voice was recognised by all; consonants were crisp, vowels precise and words articulated slowly and carefully. Despite its very little volume, it contained power, strength, anger and will.

Johan Pal replied, 'Ja, mein Fuhrer.'

Shortly, the candle now burned low and Krampus, having presided over the proceedings, began to fade. The skeletal figure of the Fuhrer was covered once more with a cloth; devices and hampers were packed again and quickly and efficiently the fire was extinguished.

Outside, the four friends felt that they were at last free to run and as they did so, they shed tears for the things they had witnessed.

'We must inform the police,' said Bishop.

'Yes, but we cannot afford to be caught up in this. We must telephone them but leave no name. Our job is to follow Pal and stop him.'

They arrived at their Hotel at three o'clock in the morning, having first alerted the police by using a public telephone. They turned in to bed, but were beset by dreadful dreams: contorted and twisted representations of things they had seen.

'The following morning they met at the breakfast table. Bishop said, 'Have you seen the news? Take a look at my phone.'

'Mord an der Zeppelin-Tribüne. Ein Detektiv, Herr Heinrich entdeckt, mit durchschnittener Kehle...'

'That was our friendly private detective. Is there any more?'

'Yes, its made the international news. Here's the New York Times:'

> *'A private detective, provisionally named as a Herr Heinrich, was found dead last night after a suspected satanic ritual in a hall at the Zeppelin Tribune building, at the former Nazi Party Parade Grounds, a major tourist attraction at Nuremberg, Germany. Local police have said that his body was discovered following a telephone call from a member of the public who observed the ritual, which is alleged to have had connections with the Nazi past. Inquiries are continuing, but police are anxious to trace the caller, who left no identity, but spoke with an accent and may be a tourist. Police are also keen to trace a black Mercedes van that was parked nearby at the time according to CCTV cameras.'*

Shilto now said. 'We need to leave. I think we may be in for a long grilling if we stay here any longer. The police generally release only yesterday's news to the newspapers and I bet they are well on our trail. If we stay, we might have quite a bit to explain if they catch us and I don't expect them to be lenient because it would be a huge political embarassment for them if they don't catch the perpetrators. At the least, we would have to help with their inquiries and at worst, we might implicate ourselves in some way. As we have said, our job is to get after Johan Pal to put an end to his plans once and for all.'

Emily said, 'Yes, but where will he actually go?'

'I telephoned the Hotel Bavaria this morning and asked for him,' said Shilto. 'I was told that he had left separately. He seems to have left his Mercedes in the car park and gone by car.'

Dood said, 'If the police were after a black Mercedes van with a known British registration number, then you can bet that Pal would dispose of it here, or maybe just leave it. The police must know there is a British connection and it won't be long before they've gone through all the hotels in the area, looking for him. Of course, Pal himself will have pushed off hours ago.'

He continued, 'I would have thought he would head straight home, but that black Mercedes van will be a dead trail. He will have decided to buy or hire something else and could be half way to Holland by now. Adam, your telephone call confirms he has new transport, which doesn't surprise me because it's a safe bet he won't leave any of his paraphernalia behind, especially his Master, nor leave his closest followers.'

'And the rest of them,' said Bishop, 'they seem pretty independent and more than capable of getting back under their own steam. But why straight home?'

'As far as the police are concerned, he is a suspect in a nasty murder, so it's hot for him here. Also, if they have a vehicle registration, then they may have a name and other identity details as well. At home, he would be on his own ground and it would be easy for him to vanish, or at least get up to his usual tricks.'

Bishop said, 'I agree with Adam. We must all leave this morning. If they know Pal is British, then they may also expect the telephone caller to have a similar background, a fact confirmed by the foreign accent of the telephone caller last night. In turn, that would mean looking through the local hotels. To avoid that, we need to be on our way.'

Emily said, 'And didn't we start the investigation in the first place? We hired Herr Heinrich and the police only need to go through his records to get names.'

'Oh, my Lord,' said Dood, 'I paid by credit card!'

'You are right to be concerned,' said Bishop. 'Even if we could show we are innocent – which would take time and involve many witnessess – he would have disappeared and could avoid us and get on with his big project. Let's finish here, pack up and head off. We can be out within the hour.'

They were all visibly upset after the events of the previous night, but in an attempt to introduce a little cheer, Dood said, 'I must say that I was just starting to enjoy myself here. I love this Hotel and I like the German people and their city. Also, I could get used to this beer, it has a distinct edge on the stuff we get in Calne!'

Nevertheless, an hour later, with breakfast over and their packing done, they met in the hotel foyer with their suitcases and paid in cash. The exceptionally pleasant and polite staff wished them well and commented on their stay, and the four friends promised they would one day return. Collecting taxis, they returned to the airport and invoked their open-ended tickets back to the United Kingdom. Although conditional on vacant places for the flight, they were lucky; at busy times they might have expected to have to wait for the second flight of the day, but this was not the case. Nor was there any disturbance on the way back; there was no car chase, nor police sirens. Bishop said, 'I think we may have given them the slip.'

At the airport, there were a few more news bulletins and the case was making considerable impact. Tabloid papers, especially, had prominent headlines as though they made a speciality of such stories. One prominent British tabloid ran the headline :

Nazis murder detective in Satanic Ritual at Parade Grounds.

The four friends observed wryly that the tabloid in question may have had an unfair reputation for hysteria. Other papers, however, had a more circumspect manner and they read a large number of them whle waiting to board their aircraft. They were in the air by mid-day and continued their discussion in the departure lounge and on the aircraft itself.

'What exactly will Johan Pal do now?' said Bishop.

'That's been troubling me also,' said Shilto.

Emily replied, 'Didn't we hear something about releasing the Fuhrer's former followers from a gateway?'

Dood replied, 'Yes, but we need to think a bit, before deciding what he meant.'

Actually, he had had a small fragment of an idea, but wished to consider it in more depth. Lapsing into a somnambulent reflection, his chin dropped onto his chest and he closed his eyes. However within, he turned his mind to their enemy and tried to imagine what he would do next. The aircraft engines hummed away; the stewards made a trip with coffee and after thirty minutes, he opened his eyes, strolled up and down the gangway two or three times and then sat down.

'Yes,' he said. 'I think I know what he meant by a gateway, but let me think about the details for a while longer. We have got the Munich stopover to worry about.'

At Munich airport, the plane landed for a short stop in order for passengers to be exchanged.

Bishop said, 'My Lord, there are police outside.'

There was nothing they could do except wait. A policeman boarded the aircraft and looked at some papers given to him by the Pilot and Stewardess. He then walked down the aisle, asked to see passports and tickets and stopped for a minute at the seats of the four friends.

'Touristen? Ich hoffe, dass sie ihren aufenthalt in Deutschland genossen?'

They said, 'Ja, danke' and the policeman passed on. Bishop thought, 'Probably looking for someone with a guilty conscience.'

Shilto replied, 'Well it wasn't us he was looking for anyway. Maybe the other guy.'

'Yes,' said Emily, 'After this time I would have expected at least some attention to have been directed towards us, but they obviously have other priorities. Look at that plane over there; they are ignoring it altogether so I bet they are only interested in UK flights.'

'And I wouldn't be surprised if they are more interested in the roads given that Pal probably left that way.'

The policeman left the tarmac altogether, and Emily said, 'Well, tell us!'

Dood replied, 'Ah yes, gateways. The Fuhrer's order was to release his former supporters. Pal will want an opening from the underworld through which to achieve it. The underworld is a place denied by atheists, but we instinctively know it exists.'

'Who did he want back?'

'He meant members of the Party and units of the Schutzstaffel, the SS. Perhaps he also meant individual supporters from his staff, who knows. But Borman, Eichmann and the like would be prerequisites.'

'But they are all dead, surely!'

'Yes, long since dead and their souls are who knows where.'

'Can he bring them back?'

'Yes, we saw that ourselves. But I don't believe he could do ten similar rituals if that is what you mean. However, I do think he could prepare a pathway for them. With an open gateway, who knows what might happen.'

'Can a suitable gateway be made anywhere?'

'No. In Satanic manuals, a gateway can be made only at certain places. One might call them pre-established by virtue of the human activities which have taken place there. A gateway might be a temple which has been used for dreadful rites for centuries, or a place where a terrible crime has been committed. Castle Bran in Romania, the castle of Vlad the Impaler, whom we also call Count Dracula, is reputed to be such a gateway. Even today its name has dreadful connotations as though it cannot escape its past history.'

'Esoteric doctrines suppose that there are places of great holiness where a few individuals can achieve great advancement by contemplation, abstinence and by doing good works. It is often held that one such place is an inaccessible valley in the Himalayas, hidden except from the very few. By contrast, there are places where terrible evil has been committed and they would naturally facilitate the activities of people like Johan Pal. I think he will try to make use of one.'

'I believe he will attempt to make use of a gateway in England. There are several he could consider and they are on his home territory, so he would know how to evade those after him.'

'You don't mean Stonehenge or Avebury?'

'No. Those places were great temples of devotion to the sun. There are other places.'

'Such as?'

'There is a place called Carn Brea on the downs. It isn't marked on a map, even though it is very old. Local lore suggests that it is a kind of gateway and the stones there are venerated, if usually avoided by local people. On my last visit, I dowsed the place; it has big and powerful vibrations and a feeling of anger, as though something will try to interfere with it in the near future. Johan Pal, with his antics on the downs, may actually be seeking it. Nevertheless it might also be that he will now prefer to disappear rather than go back to Wiltshire. If so, there are other places he could use.'

Just at that moment a message came over the intercom of the aircraft in German and English, *'Due to weather conditions, the departure of the aircraft is postponed by two hours. Please leave and go to the departure lounge where your agent will meet you.'*

They stood up and made ready to carry the personal effects they had with them. At the barrier, they were met by a travel agent and by the German police. 'Please would you kindly step this way, Sirs and Madam,' they said.

Later, they were taken to the Munich Police Station, a large imposing six-floor building made of soft beige-coloured stone. They were interviewed individually, and with a translator present.

'Mr Callum Dood, you may know that we are speaking to as many British tourists as we can, so there is nothing to worry about. We regret stopping your passage home and wish only to exclude you from our enquiries. Please would you give us an account of your recent stay in Nuremberg.' The translator pressed a switch to record the conversation.

'Certainly. There are four of us on holiday in your beautiful city. We have visited many of the usual tourist attractions, castle, restaurants and architectural works. Our holiday has now come to a natural conclusion, but we love your city and would be pleased to visit again at some point in the future.'

'These tourist attractions, are there any others that you may have failed to mention?'

'You want a complete list? That would surely vary, depending on which one of us you are speaking to.'

'Well let me be specific. Have you visited the former Nazi Party Parade Grounds?'

'Yes. In fact they are so large that I failed to cover the whole site on a single visit and went twice.'

'When were your visits?'

'Yesterday was the most recent, but I also went a few days ago.'

'Did you see anything unusual yesterday?'

'I would point out that I *have* seen today's newspapers and am aware of the crime there, but as far as seeing anything connected with it, the answer is no.'

'Is this your credit card number, Mr Dood?' He produced a series of numbers.

'Yes,'

'Can you explain why it was found amongst the transactions of Herr Heinrich, a private detectve who was murdered at the Zeppelin Tribune yesterday? You will understand that this has grown into a most embarassing case for us. We cannot afford any suggestion that Nazi sympathisers are active at the Parade Grounds.'

'Yes, I can give an explanation for that. I have been trying to trace my uncle, who remained in Germany after the last war when he was a member of our armed forces. He was reputed to be working in Bavaria and I wished to get in touch with him before he became too old to do anything. You can rest assured that I have no Nazi sympathies of any kind and am not connected with the events reported in the news.'

'We do not dispute that, but you will understand that we need to speak to all those who may have had dealings with him.'

'Of course.'

'You will of course furnish us with details your alleged relative?'

'Again, yes.'

'Thank you, Mr Dood.'

Later, they spoke to Emily.

'Miss Robertson, have you carried out any business activities with your sightseeing?'

'No, I am a one-hundred percent tourist, as are my friends. I am Mr Bishop's housekeeper and otherwise a student. It would have been foolish to pass up the opportunity of a free holiday!'

'Mr Bishop is a lucky man. But have you knowledge of any other dealings which members of your party may have had while here?'

'You would need to ask them. To some extent, we have remained independent and have had different interests. For example, I do know that Mr Dood has a particular interest in the restaurant life here. Myself, I don't really eat that much.'

'Have you visited the Nazi Party Parade Grounds?'

'Yes.'

'Did you observe anything out of the ordinary?'

'Nothing. It was cold, wet and rather miserable. There are better things to see.'

'Miss Robertson, until we have completed our enquiries, we will need to ask you to stay in Munich at our expense. You will not be kept in a cell, but if you stay at an hotel, we shall need to keep your passport. We apologise, but hope you will understand.'

'Yes, I can see your point of view.'

Later, the friends met in a very pleasant hotel on Neuturmstrasse.

'Can we get home?' said Emily.

'Yes,' said Bishop, 'But not easily, and we must face the fact that if we do a runner, we will lose our passports.'

'And my credit card,' said Dood.

'How long will they keep us?'

'I don't think we can expect to get away within the week.'

'We have to assume that Johan Pal will get home easily.'

'Why any more easily than us?'

'We know he has a car; so he will be near Calais or Dieppe by now.'

'So do we have anything of real value to lose?'

'Aside from passports and credit cards, which can be replaced easily when we are home, we would be unable to get into the UK without proper documents. But we do have money, together with our cases and clothes.'

'And if we stay here, we would have let Johan Pal get clean away.'

'Do they think we did it: the murder, that is?'

'No, of course not, but they probably do think we know something about it. Perhaps they think we could lead them to the person involved.'

'So this hotel is a pleasant way of giving us enough freedom to take advantage?'

'Yes, I think it probably is. We could disappear while sightseeing in Munich and they would try to follow us.'

'So why didn't they just leave us on our flight?'

'We would have been home sooner and harder to pick up. Or they might have considered that we know of some further place that Pal intended to go to over here. *We* think Pal is going home, but *they* don't know that.'

'If we abscond now, how then can we get back into the UK?'

Bishop said. 'We telephone Peyton and get him to pick us up at Calais.'

'Are you serious?'

'Very. All he has to do is to get over in a motorboat. I happen to know that he is a competent boatman with the Yachtmaster qualification and in fact, has actually water-skied right across the Channel. He could cross over, bring four sets of skis and then we could all go back. I am not suggesting that we actually water-ski. That would just be an excuse in case we get stopped; the water is too cold and the shipping lanes are dangerous, but a high speed boat could do that run in a couple of hours, it's only twenty miles.'

'If we get stopped, the coastguard would never believe us. They would think we are drug smugglers or people smugglers.'

'Certainly they would, but they would find nothing and we would co-operate fully. We would be as English as the Queen and could give valid names, addresses and other personal details. They would have to let us go. They could hardly discharge us back onto the beach at Calais, could they?'

'But wouldn't they be in cahoots with the German Police?'

'Perhaps they would. But that wouldn't change matters. We would be back home, where we could get our old passports cancelled as 'lost' and apply for new ones, together with new credit cards. The police might follow us, hoping we lead them to Johan Pal. But that would hardly bother us.'

'Well, let us do it then. How can we get to France?'

'Via Postbus, *"der bus für Deutschland"* which goes from Munich to Frankfurt, Cologne and Calais, although we may have to use local bus routes after Cologne.'

'What about travel papers?'

'We are already within the Schengen area and do not need to show a passport to cross into another country within it. We only need one to get in from first principles.'

'Where do we book?'

'Strangely enough, at the local bus station. Let's get packing'

*

Two hours later, an official from the Federal Detective Agency spoke to Polizeidirektor Helmut Bruns regarding the four friends.

'Herr Schmitd , haben unsere Freunde angebissen?'

'Ja , fing sie die 12.45 bus nach Köln und wahrscheinlich planen, über einen Kanal -Anschluss zurück zu bekommen.'

'Sicherstellen, dass sie nicht behindert werden.'

'Ja, Herr Polizeidirektor.'

*

Bishop dialled a number, 'Hello Peyton, this is Wally.'

'How are you? I heard that there had been a spot of bother over in Nuremberg and hoped that you were not caught up in it.'

'Well you had better hope again! Unfortunately, we are on the run from the police and would appreciate your help in getting us out.'

'I would love to, but I am busy with my unit for another twenty-four hours.'

'That would be fine. We don't expect to get to Calais until tomorrow morning anyway.'

'What had you in mind?'

'We thought you could bring a motorboat over and pick us up from the beach.'

'That simple, eh? It's a big beach. How do you know I won't miss you?'

'We thought that you could meet us by the Blériot-Plage monument on Bleriot's beach. There are plenty of concrete bunkers there, all from the war, or satnav would get you there easily. But you have to watch the ferry; it's big and in the way. Do you think you could sport something like the Jolly Roger so that we can recognise you? And can you aim for midday tomorrow? Oh, and please can you bring some brandy with you?'

The following morning, a bus approached Calais along the A26 motorway; then, via the A216 and N216 roads, it reached Calais town centre. The four friends alighted at the Boulevard Lafayette and quickly approached a small brasserie, Le Regent, which appeared to be a good place to eat and above all, was open. They had a late breakfast and were also able to freshen up after their bus journey. Later, they telephoned for a taxi and the driver seemed completely unworried about their destination; it had become commonplace for people to journey to the Calais seaside with suitcases.

At the Blériot-Plage monument they waited. It was clear and very cold, but not blustery. A low breeze sent small waves scudding and tumbling, but the sea was light and boats did not look distressed with the swell. There were a few small fishing vessels offshore and on the hinterland behind the beach, the occasional tent and stall. They waited in the cold for about 90 minutes, stamping and swinging their arms to stay warm.

At midday, Bishop telephoned Oakwood using his mobile and was connected straight away. 'Hello Peyton, this is Wally, we are on the beach, how about you?'

'I am about two miles offshore. There is a rather official-looking cutter a little east and I don't want to step on its toes. Can I telephone you back?'

'Sure, we are ready and waiting.'

An hour later, Oakwood telephoned back. 'I am coming in now. Can you walk down the beach in about twenty minutes?'

Later, they walked down the beach, looking rather incongruous with their cases. A man of Arabic appearance saw them and dashed off. Later, a small group of five Arabs was observed running over the beach towards them. However by thc time they were close, Oakwood had run his boat up close to the beach, the four had waded out, thigh-deep in the cold water to join him and he had pushed off again. The five Arabs were a hundred yards away when Oakwood, fearing his mission might be compromised, gunned the engine and made out to sea. Looking back, they felt for those left behind.

'Where did you get this boat?' said Shilto.

'From a friend of mine, who lives at St Margaret's Bay. We used to go water-skiing together. In fact, he took me along, and that's how I got used to it. He is quite a keen motor-boatman.'

'It is now about one-thirty. What time should we hit England?'

'If all goes well, in about two hours. We cannot go too fast and I do not intend to go straight to Dover. That would be about twenty one miles, but I would prefer to go a little further west, say to Folkestone or Hythe, which would make it about thirty miles.'

'Why Folkestone?'

'There is no cross-channel ferry now and the harbour is a bit quieter. Most continental traffic actually goes through the Channel Tunnel, so coastguard patrols are mainly concentrated there. In fact it may interest you to know that the local townspeople actually wanted to restart the cross-channel ferry; it would have done a lot for the town. But it was not to be, and the end result is that Folkestone is a quiet town these days. If we call at Folkestone, or if we go on to Hythe, then I can let you go there and can tie up and sleep at a pub. I have actually left my Range Rover and a trailer at Hythe and could drive back to St Margaret's bay tomorrow morning.'

Peyton proved true to his word and they reached mid-point after about an hour and a half. At about that time, an official-looking cutter could be seen in the distance and Dood began to fish around in his pockets and transfer articles to a small bag. As he put it, 'Just in case I need to get rid of contraband. This stuff is only a remedy for seasickness, but I wouldn't want them to take offence.'

After a while the cutter disappeared in the haze and Dood relaxed somewhat. It had taken them a little longer than they had expected, for it was rather choppy in mid-channel, but they were near to Dover by 4pm. When about a mile offshore, they turned west and passed Capel and Folkestone easily. By 4.40pm, light was starting to fade and Oakwood approached the beach at Hythe. Together, they raised the outboard motor and pulled the craft up the beach. With four helping, it was easy to raise the craft onto the single-axle trailer by means of a hand pulley. However once in the comfort of his Range Rover, Oakwood said, 'I think I will head straight off now. I can be back in St Margaret's Bay within the hour and there's no point in sleeping here for the sake of it. I will probably stay at my friend's place. Can I drive you anywhere?'

'Please could you take us to Folkestone Station?'

'Certainly, Adam.'

Half an hour later, the big sports utility vehicle pulled up at Folkestone Central Station and the four friends disembarked. They bought four tickets to Swindon and upon arrival took a taxi to Peckling. They were there by ten pm.

Dood said, 'I'm going home.'

'Me too,' replied Shilto.

Bishop exclaimed, 'What an adventure! See you tomorrow or maybe later!'

Emily said, 'I'm a bit sick of travel and fancy food. What I want is a good night's sleep, a plain boiled egg and soldiers and a cup of tea. See you sometime!'

So they all went to bed.

Chapter Ten

A place of great Evil

Herr Johan Pal, Carol Black, Sieghard Trapper and Meinhard Koch sat down on comfortable chairs in Pal's suite of rooms at the Savoy Hotel in London. It was a month since they had successfully returned from Germany and Pal had decided not to take up residence in Wiltshire again; at least, not for a while. The cost of the hotel was considerable, but not more than he could accommodate with ease.

'Master, we must continue with the great work and I have wondered whether we can return to complete it soon.' It was Carol Black who voiced their thoughts.

'No, we cannot return. We saw how the German police used Bishop and Dood. They were arrested and later released, but it was with the intention of gaining a means of tracking us and they were of no real interest to them. The police first caught them at the airport, then let them escape and in fact I have little doubt that their path home, via Calais and the channel, was smoothed by the Bundesministerium des Innern on purpose. No doubt, Dood and his friends are being followed by the German and British police as part of a joint enquiry. Poor fools; it has gone 'big' in the newspapers, more for its cultural content than the nature of the so-called crime. They just *have* to find us to satisfy their 'politically correct' masters and we cannot return to the standing stones and ley lines, however helpful they might prove to be, at least, not just yet. That place would be the ideal one for them to catch up with us and Bishop and Dood are their only real lead.'

'Do they know who we are?'

'It doesn't matter whether they do, we have gone to ground anyway. I expect that the various branches of the ENFSI, the pan-European forensics department, are happily co-operating together, sharing and conferencing what they know.'

'What do they really know?'

'Their forensics men will have worked over the mess we left when we had to leave in a hurry. They will have traced Bishop and Dood via the dead private investigator and will have searched his offices. There will be records of their commission for him to follow us. If not, they will have records of all foreigners who left Nuremberg hotels on that day and the police will have searched and analysed our hotel rooms. There may be DNA traces on things we touched and in our bedrooms. They will have traced our Mercedes van by now and will certainly have examined that. I think they may know who we are, but I doubt whether they have any photographs of us and I believe we are safe in our new identities. Certainly, most German hotels do not routinely have internal CCTV cameras at this time. The only word of caution is that we cannot afford to be seen in our former haunts, at least not yet. Later, after we attain our goal, it will be irrelevant.'

Black said, 'Then is there somewhere else, or have you decided to shelve the great work, Master?'

'The great work cannot be shelved.'

'Can it be completed here in London?'

'No, certainly not, we need a place where strength has been shown; a place of great standing; our opponents would say one of evil. This I have been considering for a while, now.'

'Am I at liberty to propose the site of Borley Rectory?'

'At liberty yes, but Borley Rectory, no. That place has a history of psychic phenomena, but it is hardly suitable. We would find nothing left in any case, because it burned to the ground and many of its collected vibrations were dissipated. By itself, however, it was not wholly evil enough.'

'We could return to a former Nazi shrine?'

'No, those places, formerly of great evil, have now become places of apology and regret. It is now as though they have become synagogues or churches.'

'Then have you an idea?'

'Yes, there is one such place, far from prying eyes, with a history of works conducted there; some similar to our own. Parts of it were burned down, but the evil was never dispersed. Its vibrations were such that great fires were oft-repeated and the evil nature of its psychic vibrations grew over the years.'

'Where is this place, Master?'

'We must make our preparations for a trip northwards.'

Pal continued, 'Herr Koch, you are well-known to be good at logistical matters. I would like you to organise sympathetic and confidential places of residence for us in *this* neighbourhood.' He passed over a piece of paper. 'We shall also require an adequate source of victuals for one month and the ability to live rough; also suitable costumes, appropriate salves, potions and chemicals and a means of mixing them to our requirements.'

'Miss Black, you are known to be successful at influencing young women to join us. Do you think you can influence to rejoin those, who through outside influence, departed from our circle?'

'No Master, I cannot recommend it. The price to pay for a lack of security would be high and I doubt whether we could easily persuade them via the usual run of 'parties' without it getting into local conversation.'

'You are wise. We shall conduct our experiments with thirteen members.'

'And you, Mr Trapper. Although we shall have a base, we shall also need to be mobile. Please lease, using the utmost confidentiality, a transport to house all of our apparatus, supplies and equipment. You may convert the inside as you wish. I suggest that the transport, perhaps a Ford Transit van, could be decorated with flippant slogans in the manner of a party of students seeking enlightenment. Lease it for at least one month using this credit card and these details.' He passed over a package of documents.

'And Herr Koch.'

'Ja, Herr Pal?'

'We shall need to be equipped to dig with spades and hydraulic hand tools; if necessary to remove certain amounts of earth. Also, we shall need a quiet method of generating electricity to provide lighting. Investigate and acquire a powered generator that will not suffocate us with fumes, so no diesel.'

'Ja, Herr Pal. Should it be rechargeable, and if so, from what source?'

'We need a source of propane or natural gas in cylinders. Such devices produce a haze when they burn and could be passed off as a camp fire with care, but they also make little smoke or fumes and above all, no mechanical noise.'

Carol Black now spoke, 'Master, are you ready for this challenge, or can we aid you further? I recall that we need to have access to some of the pages that were missing from our ancient treatise of magical rituals. You were successful in Nuremberg but cannot guarantee further success without them.'

'I shall rise to the occasion. Leave such small details to me.'

*

'Ivy, I have just heard from that fellow Johan Pal again. You know, the wealthy individual who bought our magic book by sealed bid.'

'Yes, I remember, but that was quite a while back, maybe three months, wasn't it?'

'Something like that.'

'And we have not heard from him for quite a while?'

'No, Ivy, but he seemed to have a certain element of urgency in his voice, as though he wanted the repaired stuff back regardless, maybe to read or use or something.'

Creighton Brakespeare closed his computer down and prepared to lock his office once more. He placed a plastic dust-cover on his priceless machine and momentarily mused on its value. It contained data on all his business transactions: estimates of value of stock, scanned receipts, contracts of sale, income and expenditure accounts, details of all his clients. He was more concerned by reliability than security because all his records were continually encrypted, but would need to examine reliability again. More immediately, he must look again at estimated dates for completion of work in order to put pressure on his sub-contractor; perhaps the next day.

'Has something happened?'

'Not really, but Mr Pal wondered about the progress of the repairs to the few missing pages. I will need to check up because I haven't heard for a month.'

'Pal wants his missing leaves back ASAP?'

'Yes, but why the hurry? He struck me as verging on the obsessive about his books, although book-collectors very often are. But I don't think that he is quite the same kind of obsessive as many we come across.'

'In what way?'

He said, 'Well, a lot of them are in love with the chase. They scour old bookshops for a long-lost first edition and when they finally get it on their shelves, the chase is over and their interest is only for the next book on their list. Other collectors are totally obsessed with originality and wouldn't be seen with a priceless book without its cover; a reproduction cover might actually improve it, even if didn't enhance its value; but not to them.'

'And Pal?'

'Well, he seems almost like a scientist or artist, engaged in some kind of research project. I get the sense that he is collecting for their contents rather than monetary value or aesthetic quality.'

'But if so, what would the contents of a Clavicule of Solomon make him?'

'That's just the point, I don't like to imagine. When I do, the combination of a secretive, solitary man, certainly very wealthy, with an interest in herbal lore and esoteric religious doctrines make me sweat, rather.'

'But you wouldn't want to strike him from your list of clients?'

'Good Lord, no! He has done a lot for our turnover this year. And also, what folk do at home is their own business. But I'm rather wary of things which I know some such persons are alleged to do, at least in films. I wouldn't want to get involved myself.'

As they closed down, it was six o' clock. The phone rang as they set the alarm but Creighton and Ivy were very careful not to let their business dealings intrude into their leisure time. They knew from past experience that if the twain should meet, the line between business and pleasure would become blurred to the confusion of both. Now, they ignored the telephone and went out to dinner at a small anglicised Greek taverna in the middle of Cambridge.

'Creighton, can I start with a few bits and pieces, please! No, those there at the top of the menu. I would like melitzanosalata and tirokafteri, please, with some warm pitta bread.'

'Sure, but they will probably fill you up a bit. I shall have avgolemono, a lemon and egg soup. I think it will soup me, ha ha. And then?'

'I'll have a gypsy kebab. I shouldn't, but I love it!

'In that case, I am going for an escalope vesuvio!'

'Retsina?'

'Well just for a laugh. I once heard an unkind man compare it to disinfectant and add that it was oddly appropriate with Greek food.'

'Did you agree with him?'

'He was a well-known critic, so yes, but when I actually tried it, it seemed a little unkind to disinfectant. Anyway, now I'm all for it.'

The waiter came, went and returned and they both had a sip from their bottle. It was in fact very good but as they relaxed a little, Ivy noted a preoccupied expression on Creighton's expressive face.

'What's the matter, Creighton?'

'Nothing. Anyway, I don't want to talk about business.'

'So what do you want to talk about?'

'Alright, business.'

'But it's good! We are doing so well. It's old Mr Pal, isn't it?'

'Maybe. Oh, alright, yes!'

'He wants something else?'

'Actually, some time back, I heard that Wally Bishop had some dealings with him. You know that business about his strange relic when we were down there? I think that old Mr Pal is interested in it.'

'I bet he is.'

'Well, a bit later, I had a call from Wally and he passed me over to Callum Dood, you know, that chap who works for the church. I think he's more than just a vicar, the local exorcist perhaps – no, I'm serious. He started to talk about Mr Pal. I tried to keep quiet because of client confidentiality, but I got quizzed about him. It seems that old Pal is connected with something odd. Or, more accurately, is connected with the Reverend Dood, which is more or less the same thing.'

'So you are worried that our book may have led to some dodgy practices which Wally and Callum Dood are having to sort out?'

'Maybe. Now what with Pal appearing again, perhaps I should speak to Wally once more. And by the way, Pal seemed keen to phone me rather than the other way round. Maybe his address has changed. Anyway, my mobile recorded the number of his call so I can get hold of him if necessary.'

He continued, 'Ach, there's a lot of chilli in this!'

'But you love it!'

'Very true, and that's why Retsina is the stuff for me!'

*

'Is that Medieval Parchment Restoration?'

'Speaking.'

This is Creighton Brakespeare here. We spoke about a month ago regarding the restoration work on fifteen very old pages of a magical treatise. How's progress?'

'Ah, Mr Brakespeare, we have made very good progress, but we have one page left to complete. It was in an advanced state of decay and had become creased and damp, probably many years ago. What is worse, it had undergone an attack by a fungus. You may not believe this, but the fungus was akin to ringworm and had grown into small circles leaving a middle area of parchment that had become quite crumbly. You must appreciate…'

'I do. Now tell me, can you recover the script from the remaining crumbled areas?'

'I believe we can. We took all the usual scans before we started work. Then, we dampened it at the creases using the usual methods. As we opened it, we repeated our scans and held the page flat between glass to examine it further. We shall have to sew in new vellum to replace the crumbled areas but we estimate that 75% of the original skin will be reused. There is very little displacement of the script, which is in Latin. Once new vellum is in place we can embark on replacing the script.'

'Is a knowledge of Latin significant?'

'Yes. It helps us understand the bit which says *'utque glisceret legionem mortuum'* and we think the contents are really rather unsavoury. We don't like some of the things it seems to encourage.'

'What does that mean?'

'It means "to raise the legion of the dead"…'

'Is that a problem?'

'No, but believe me, we want to get it back to you as soon as we can. My girl doesn't like going anywhere near it.'

'How long now?'

'Give me another fourteen days.'

*

Carol Black, Johan Pal and two others drove along the northern side of Loch Ness. They passed slowly through Drumnadrochit and Invermoriston in the direction of Fort Augustus. Their direction was towards the south west and they had the afternoon sun on their left. The A82 road was of sufficient size to make good progress and they had chosen the north and west side of the Loch for an initial survey for that reason; now they drove quite slowly in their van and many heavy lorries passed them with ease on that arterial highway.

To their right lay the heavy, brooding presence of Meall Fuar-mhonaidh, a hill of about 2,300 feet in height. Its name, 'cold rounded hill' was apt; it was black against the sky and reflected no light from the afternoon sun. To their left lay the grey water of the loch itself, its surface with only a few ripples to spoil an otherwise grey mirror. The landscape, grey, green and black and with clouds and sunshine, was by the same token beautiful, bleak and sad.

At Fort Augustus they stopped at the behest of Johan Pal, who now said, 'You may wish to refresh yourself.' There, they ate a modest meal at a loch-side restaurant and afterwards, carefully paid with cash. The proprietor thought little of their appearance; the side of their van carried slogans, hastily daubed, such as 'Nessie here we come,' together with various encouragements towards alcoholic drink and promiscuity. His guests were dressed in jeans and hoodies and were unshaven; they resembled the many hundreds of students who visit that neighbourhood regularly.

Resuming their journey, they turned left onto the B862 and at Whitebridge turned left to use the B852 through Foyers. They were now on the south-east side of the loch, driving northwards with Loch Mhor on their right and Loch Ness on their left. At Foyers they stopped once more and bought further bottles of water; there were a couple of tourist establishments and public houses and suitably refreshed again, they again continued.

Johan Pal now said, 'We are approaching our destination and can make camp off the road. We must not impinge upon farmland or leave mess and detritus, but we can deter any casual inquiry quite easily.' He withdrew cameras and stands for them and they trained their lenses towards the loch. 'It must be clear we are interested in the monster which we believe lies within. It is wise to proclaim that we have seen something; here are photographs of a school of dolphins that we can dismiss with cynicism; and here are some which purport to show an aquatic creature with elongated neck and flippers, some thirty feet long and our supposed relic of the Cretaceous. We can, by contrast, use it to express our enthusiasm. However, I would like one person to stay with the van and that individual, in the first instance, will be you, Mr Trapper.'

'Master, I shall show appropriate cynicism and enthusiasm when describing our photographs in any casual conversation,' said Sieghard Trapper.

Carol Black, Johan Pal and Meinhard Koch looked at a low house with a single-floored construction, painted off-white. It had two half-turrets at the front and in total, eleven windows facing forwards under a conventional tiled roof. A lawn sloped towards them and the house was about one hundred yards from the road. On the other side of the road and behind them, they could see an old cemetery with gravestones and mounds, some of them at least three hundred years old with stones that had now fallen.

'We should not the approach the house,' said Pal. 'In fact, we do not need to. Our interest lies in the remains of the chapel which are deep underneath its foundations.'

Carol Black said, 'So that is Boleskine House, allegedly a haunted house and place of great evil, beloved of aspiring magicians and rock music fans and which itself has suffered fires on several occasions?'

'It is. I am told that in this neighbourhood, susceptible people still feel its brooding presence; a presence which they say has increased over the years following a series of suicides, self-mutilations and fires, either in or nearby. As you say, the house itself is alleged to be quite evil, although some say that the evil quality arises from an old kirk below it, which in legend, was burned to the ground long ago. It is rumoured that the congregation was burned alive inside and that their spirits are unstill. The house above was owned by the magician Aleister Crowley about a hundred years ago and much later, by a musician called Jimmy Page: I am told he was also a devotee of the magical art and ran a bookshop on the subject in London.'

In a didactic mood, Pal continued, 'It is also rumoured that a tunnel connects the burial ground, behind us, to the cellars or kirk beneath the house. That is where our interests lie, not in the house itself. My intention is to enter the tunnel at the cemetery end. Both entrances were sealed long ago, but many chambers are thought still to lie below the cellars of the house and they may have been the site of magical ceremonies similar to our own, although not always successful.'

'And we can dig unobserved?'

'I doubt it. We shall bring our van near, of course, and if necessary we can lift flagstones from within the Mort House in the cemetery, to act as a diversion from our main dig nearby. The Mort House, too, is a place of some symbolism because bodies of the deceased lay there before being buried nearby. We shall erect signs which advise passers-by to avoid the place during council renovation.'

'But where is the entrance to the tunnel?'

'I have looked amongst the records of Aleister Crowley himself. The tunnel starts only fifteen feet from the Mort House: I have carried out ultrasonic scans which confirm that fact. While we are there, I doubt whether there will be any intrusion upon us since although this area is normally plagued by aficionados of contemporary musical culture, we can deter them easily. If there are more serious questions, for example from public workmen, I can produce suitable papers' – he withdrew them – 'and we can wear high visibility jackets and other suitable gear.'

Meinhard Koch said, 'Unt ve shall start soon, ja?'

'Certainly; let us return to our residence in Inverness now. We shall need to fortify ourselves for the work ahead.'

Black said, 'How long do you feel it will take to break into the tunnel?'

'No more than seven days. We can decide whether to return to Inverness each evening. I may ask you to go but remain myself in order to absorb the local vibrations and to prepare for the ordeal ahead. Once our access to the tunnel is complete, we can work towards the galleries under the house which connect with it. Only then, with the stars being propitious, can we proceed with the remainder of our task. I would remind you that this is not a holiday.'

'No, Master. We have come this far in order to release the legions of Adolf Hitler and then we can march at the head of a great new Wehrmacht. Their spirits will roam the earth once more, grown more powerful by previous ordeals; ordeals that by then will have finally been overcome.'

*

Two days later, Shilto and Dood entered the office of the Diocesan Bishop, the Reverend Bertram Taylor. 'Sit down, please, gentlemen, I hope you will find these chairs comfortable,' he said. 'This is Chief Superintendent Nicholby, who has come a long way to speak to you. Would anyone like coffee and cakes? We may as well make ourselves comfortable.'

They talked pleasantries for a few minutes and an elderly man brought a tray with a coffee pot and doughnuts. They each had a cup of coffee and Dood tucked into a jam doughnut; finally, Taylor said, 'How are you getting on with your investigation into ritual practices on the Wiltshire Downs?'

Shilto replied, 'Quite well, thank you. As you know, we came across evidence of some nasty Satanic practices on the Downs and we investigated a businessman and his followers via the characteristic network of parties he was known to hold in this neighbourhood. I believe he considered his activities were discreet, but in fact there was a considerable 'vapour trail' for us to follow. He went to Germany, having first procured an antique relic from Wally Bishop, a local dealer in antiquities, which he believed would be an aid in his magical practices. As you know, we followed him there, but the trail went cold about a month ago, when we returned to the United Kingdom.'

Dood brushed some crystals of sugar from his fingers. 'Our visit actually coincided with some distressing news in the local media. It concerned a murder at the former Nazi Parade Grounds in Nuremberg. We were stopped by the local police on our way home and they interviewed us and let us go.'

Nicholby shifted in his chair. 'Yes, quite.'

Dood continued, 'I assure you that I am not a cynic, but I got the feeling that we *just might* have been allowed to leave, in the hope that we would lead the authorities to Mr Pal and his cronies.'

'Yes, they didn't think for a minute that you did it yourself, don't worry. And they didn't want to keep you there, either, just in case you 'broke out' into the news somehow. Better to keep suspects and leads nice and quiet. Our friends the Germans were quite amused at your escaping antics, believe me. It was just like Colditz.'

Nicholby continued, 'Now, the important point. We hoped that Mr Pal might reveal himself to you upon your return. We know who he is, of course, but he has quite disappeared. He has the means of causing everyone immense political damage unless he is found; the German authorities are quite beside themselves because they just *cannot* allow black magical rituals to take place under these circumstances, complete with Nazi graffiti and murder, in the place that it did, without the offender being caught. They are being hounded by the Americans, the Israelis, the Dutch, the French; the only ones not hounding them are us.'

Shilto broke in, 'And so, where exactly does that leave the rest of us?'

'That is what I would like to establish.'

Nicholby continued with a question of his own. 'What exactly was Mr Pal's interest in the two of you, and in Wally Bishop and Miss Emily Robertson?'

'Emily is a former member of his 'circle', but I think we managed to extricate her from his clutches before she and a few others were initiated.'

'What should I understand by the term initiation?'

'They – three young women – would have been required to surrender their bodies to Pal and his male friends in a ceremony. In return, they would have been baptised into their Satanic circle, within which they would have been a beneficiary of its privileges.'

'Are such privileges real, or is it just an excuse for a frolic in the woods?'

Dood said, 'Yes, it is indeed an excuse for a frolic, but I would like to dispel your cynicism here, because they would have received tangible powers in return.'

'Returning to my question, can you tell me about Pal's interest in you all?

'Adam and I are on leave from our usual daily routines for the duration of this investigation. The Church has taken the view that there are some nasty goings-on and we are their ground troops. However, Wally Bishop's position is quite different. He is a businessman, no more, who had an antique relic stolen from him, which was later used for occult purposes. It was taken to Germany and used in the magical ritual in the news.'

'And what actually was the relic itself?'

'The relic was of the last mortal remains, in fact the very bones, of Adolf Hitler. Their provenance was wholly verifiable and authentic.'

'My God, that cannot be. If *that* gets into the press, there will be total chaos. And it was *that* which ended up in the Nazi Parade Grounds?'

'Yes.'

Nicholby continued. 'This is a very nasty new piece of information and it will complicate matters enormously if it gets out. But regarding its worth let me ask you whether its advantage to him is real. I will bow to your undoubted knowledge of spiritual matters, but I do need to understand the implications of what we know.'

The others raised a collective eyebrow.

'Don't worry gentlemen, you can be quite frank; I have an open mind and understand that you speak as men of the church. However I need to make an informed judgement of the dangers that we face. Please enlighten me.'

Shilto answered, 'Johan Pal has stolen the bones of Adolf Hitler, together with a few other odds and ends. He used it to raise the soul of the Fuhrer in the Nazi Parade Grounds. His ritual was successful. We witnessed a murder but felt we had no option but to try to escape. He has since fled, we presume back here, but in fact he could be anywhere. Callum can tell you more accurately about his abilities.'

Dood said, 'He intends to use his powers to release the legions of the SS from the underworld. Make no mistake, the danger is real. He was successful with his experiments in necromancy; he has the ability to raise the devil himself and is prepared to do so. His aim is to gain enough power to dominate the world and he has successfully raised the soul of the Fuhrer to help.'

He sighed and continued, 'He intends to carry on the unfinished work of the Nazis. However, from our point of view, he needs a place of great former evil in order to complete his invocations. There, he will enjoin with the spirit of Adolf Hitler to create a gateway through which the SS hordes will come forth, although they will not be as you might imagine them. They will be shadows from the past, evil ghosts who will influence the minds of politicians and pervert justice. They will release death, pestilence, war and famine, but made worse by the ease with which modern technology can harvest data or create weapons.'

'Are you sure this isn't just the antics of a sect of nutcases?'

Dood looked weary. 'Do I need to convince you by showing you some kind of counter-magic myself? Let me be frank: in my own little village there is enough collected mythology: paganism, folklore, general magical practice, herbalism, distillation of whiskey, to give any policeman a year of sleepless nights. Even *I* can do some simple things.'

He tore a scrap of paper into two and said to Nicholby, 'List all the contents of your pockets on this piece of paper and give it to Adam.' As he did so, Dood withdrew a small bottle of Indian ink from his own jacket, dipped a pencil in it and with closed eyes and a minute of contemplation, began to write on the second piece.

Dood listed ten items and passed the paper to Shilto, who said, 'These lists are identical.'

The others were silent. Eventually, Nicholby asked, 'How did you do that?'

Dood replied, 'Call it magic if you wish, but in fact we all have such abilities. I used a simple method of divination; the Indian ink was no more than a device to apply my own clairvoyance. It might have been tea leaves; they work too. However you must remember that anything I can do is nothing compared with his ability.'

Nicholby said, 'I am sorry; you will forgive how disbelieving and cynical I must have become. You were quite right to challenge me. But in fact the main reason for this interview was to work out a way of finding him; he has simply disappeared and could be anywhere.'

Shilto said, 'Callum described a need for a portal or gateway. Does that still hold true?'

'It does,' said Dood. 'There are probably many places which would be suitable, but as it stands, I have barely thought of one or two. I mentioned Bran Castle in Romania, still a place of great evil; but none of the former Nazi places are any good; they are too closely watched.'

He continued, 'I thought of the Tower of London, but changed my mind; it was only a gaol. I am afraid we still need to find the proverbial blasted heath. Sorry, I'm completely in the dark.'

Nicholby said, 'Here is my card with my own telephone number. Please can I ask you to let me know as soon as you have thought of something?'

'Yes, of course. I hope I didn't scare you with my little trick.'

They shook hands and Dood and Shilto left.

Shilto closed the door and as they walked, he said, 'I had actually thought we were quite clever in escaping. But regardless, I think we need to talk to the others pretty quickly.'

On the following day, Shilto telephoned Oakwood and gave a brief account of the meeting with Nicholby and Taylor. Oakwood offered to drive down, but Shilto felt his help would only be needed once they had decided what to do. He would telephone with updates and would consult at all stages. Oakwood, otherwise satisfied, made no further comment other than to voice his wonder that, despite a feeling of satisfaction in 'having managed to get away with an escape,' they had in fact been facilitated in doing so by the German and British police.

He made a further telephone call to Wally Bishop. 'Wally, can you, Amelia and Emily come round this morning, or are you hopelessly busy?'

'Amelia and I are pretty busy during the day, I'm afraid. Can we come over tonight instead? I know that Emily is out and about today, but she said she would be free this evening too.'

'Yes, fine. Please could you make it at about seven?'

Shilto telephoned Dood with the same question, 'Callum, the others are over this evening. I take it that you can make it at about seven, too?'

'Are you cooking?'

'No, but I thought we could nip out for a takeaway; a curry perhaps.'

'I'll be there.'

That evening, Shilto, Dood, Emily Robertson and Wally and Amelia Bishop sat down to chicken Vindaloo and prawn Bhuna. Shilto had supplied some wine, and Dood his favourite Calne-bottled lager. A man of considerable largesse when it came to beer, he shared several flat-packs with the others. It took about an hour to finish their meal, but at length they slumped into armchairs.

'I would like this to be a proper party,' said Shilto, 'but I am afraid we must take stock of the matters we filed away at the back of our minds.' He then gave an account of the conversation which they had held with Nicholby the day before.

'We haven't really let matters slip, have we?' said Emily. 'Surely it's just that there has been no lead for us to follow. I thought we might pick up some kind of scent, you know, perhaps on the party circuit.'

'I take it there has been no rumour?' said Dood.

'If there had been, you can guarantee that I would have mentioned it. But there has been no Carol or Sieghard, no party in the woods, no dancing around the oak tree: nothing!'

'And,' said Dood, 'I have strolled over the downs quite a few times. Old Don Regan and his mates say that everything is totally quiet. Not a single sheep has disappeared; there are no noises, no disturbances; everything suggests that Pal has moved on.'

Shilto said, 'Nicholby did say that Pal has vanished from his big house. No visit there, no car, although his servant is still there. The man has apparently been quizzed and followed also.

However he was completely inscrutable and from Pal's point of view totally reliable. He just said that he has a brief to look after the home, is able to cash modest cheques for its maintenance and draws a reasonable salary each month. There are adequate funds in a domestic account to enable him to continue with that for a while, but the bank has had no contact with Pal recently. He – Barrett – hasn't made any attempt to get in touch with Pal either, and it seems that he "expects to hear from Pal when he is ready, but not before". Therefore it looks as though Pal cannot be traced through his domestic arrangements.'

'Can we go hunting for Mr Pal ourselves?'

'Good idea, Emily, but unless we have a better idea of his destination, then that would probably be fruitless.'

'You mentioned Bran Castle.'

'I did, but I don't fancy going on a massive expedition unless we hear something a bit more positive.'

'What other leads do we have?'

'None, unless…'

'Go on.'

'…Unless we can get a clue from his domestic correspondence or library.'

Shilto said, 'We can't really just call in and go through his papers. Best to get Nicholby involved in that.'

Dood immediately telephoned Nicholby using the number on the card he had given them. 'Chief Superintendent Nicholby, please.'

'I am sorry sir, but out of office hours the Chief Superintendent cannot be reached here. If urgent, I can pass on your number.'

'Yes, please.' He left his name and a couple of numbers. 'Could he get in touch?'

Fifteen minutes later, the telephone rang and Shilto took the call. 'Ah, Chief Superintendent, thank you for telephoning so soon. Can you arrange for us to take a look at Mr Pal's papers and library? We think it might possibly contain a lead. No, there's no need for you to come down, but we thought maybe you could arrange for a local police car to accompany us. We wouldn't want to burgle the place after all.'

There were affirmative noises from the other end of the telephone line and Shilto replaced the handset. 'We can go tomorrow morning at ten. A car will come for us then. He asked whether we had some idea of what we are looking for. I said not yet.'

★

'Mr Barrett? We have a warrant to search the premises. Here is our identification.' Police Constable Smith entered Pal's house by the front door. 'Please direct us to your library in the first instance.' he said.

Dood had come without the others; it seemed fitting that only one of them accompanied the policeman. Now Barrett pointed and they traversed an entrance hall to a reception room and via an internal door, passed to the library.

He recognised the room and its furniture from his earlier illicit visit. Crossing the floor, he approached the bookcase which contained volumes he had examined before. Most were there, but three or four had been removed by their owner. He opened a few of those left behind and found them to be nineteenth century volumes on botany and herbalism, some of them illustrated. There were also very old religious tomes and other works in classical languages. Next to them was a sheaf of papers which proved to be receipts and correspondence. The policeman watched his actions carefully.

'Nothing of interest here,' said Dood.

Barrett watched them as the policeman opened an unlocked desk. It contained further papers; mostly correspondence of a household nature such as domestic receipts and expenditure accounts. There was, however, a scrap of paper with a telephone number. Dood glanced at it and observed that it had a Cambridge dialling code. He replaced the wad of papers.

A general search of the house then followed. Barrett accompanied them and introduced them to various rooms. All were tidy, with clean and presentable furniture and with empty wastepaper baskets. Barrett looked on with sentient approval.

In one particular downstairs room, they noted very rich furnishings and to Dood's trained eye, the satin curtains were of a style of décor found in churches that had – in these egalitarian days – the increasingly rare high service; they were an emphasis on splendour which made him look more closely at his surroundings. It also contained a few chairs, a table, and against a wall, a small kneehole desk. Testing the drawers of the desk, he found them unlocked and inside was a set of tarot cards.

He examined them closely and had an immediate thought: like all users of tarot, Pal would shuffle the pack immediately before use; it would be inconceivable to use them otherwise. And after having pondered on the result, it would be pointless shuffling them again for future use; he would rehouse them straight away and probably without further thought. If so, they would still be in the order of his most recent hand.

Pal had used a deck of cards with artwork in the style of Dame Freda Harris, painted after suggestions by Aleister Crowley. It was a beautiful deck, with the influences and symbolism of several distinct occult disciplines and natural sciences. However, among them, two cards had been returned to the deck together; they were face-down in the pack.

The first of them, the Princess of Wands, bore a picture of that Princess within the background of a northern vista; its interpretation was one of brilliance, enthusiasm and the desire for power. The second card, well known and fateful, was the Blasted Tower. It had an eerie aspect: a tower blasted by lightning and still burning; it was alight with yellow and red flames against a vista of grey mountains. It described the coming of a new aeon, but had an associated aspect of warning.

What could they mean? Could he indeed interpret the hand of another user? He took a photograph of them with his mobile phone, but hardly needed to have done so; their pictures and symbolism were clear in his mind's eye: 'Pal... would seek power...was within a northern quadrant – a place in the north...? within a tower – a building...? that had burned...' Dood considered them carefully as he continued his search.

No other room revealed anything of interest. The house had an almost museum-like quality about it and his attention strayed elsewhere. His companion, the policeman, continued his search for firearms, knives, twists of silver paper; he returned disappointed.

The police car dropped Dood at his home. Dood thanked the officer and emailed a quick note to Nicholby. He knew that a further report would follow from the Police Constable in due course.

Then he telephoned Shilto and the others, 'Not much luck; the house is more or less bare. There were a few books gone, but nothing we could take as evidence of his whereabouts.'

'Anything else?'

'Just a few tarot cards, but we cannot go on those, can we? Let me mull things over for a while.' He replaced the handset.

⋆

'Do you believe in fate?' asked Shilto.

'I don't know. I had always thought that the great issues were decided for us; you know, God's wind, and so on.'

Shilto looked at the photographs of the tarot cards. 'Johan Pal didn't know you would see these. Could they contain something the fates intended *you* to interpret?'

'I really couldn't say. Even if there is something in that idea, I'm probably not up to the task. Unfortunately, I see only the literal message: that *Johan Pal is seeking power within a northern tower that has been burned.* Make of it what you will.'

'So what towers do you know of in the north?'
'Only the Blackpool Tower, mate.'

★

In the old burial grounds opposite Boleskine House, Johan Pal and his confederates dug down into the soil. They had made a few diversionary repairs to the area around the Old Mort House; it had 'repairs to' notices nearby and was roped off. However it was not their main activity, only an excuse for their presence if required. They were confident, therefore, that their efforts would pass unnoticed elsewhere in the grounds.

The earth was dark and dank, but it was not compacted and he was able to make some considerable progress. After the first day, a period in which there had been no outside disturbances whatsoever, he was three feet below ground level and at 6pm, he signalled a stop.

Pal and his co-conspirators held a brief conference. 'We need to use the hydraulic auger. Please make general progress in the morning, but use the auger when no strangers are near. Start with the auger after 1pm, when it is quieter; you will find that it will drill out a lot of earth which we can remove very easily. Using it, I estimate that we can dig about four feet every day, but the difficulty is in moving the soil away, which is why we need shovels. I had considered taking the whole lot elsewhere, but I realise now that we will be gone from this place for good within ten days. Therefore we need only find a temporary home for our soil for that time. If we need to cover our entrance, we can install the steel sheet and a foot of earth on top. Let us enlarge our pile over there' – he pointed – 'and we can cover it with the tarpaulin at all times. It will not be conspicuous under the tree.'

Meinhard Koch said, 'Excellent idea. The logistics are simple; there is not much earth in terms of sheer volume. After 6.30pm I suggest we replace the metal sheet over the hole and re-turf. At this rate we should reach the required depth within three days. Thereafter, we shall need to clear out and support a horizontal tunnel of some fifteen feet, which I estimate we can clear within a further three days. Taken together, we should be in the main south-east to north-west shaft within six days.'

Three of them replaced the metal sheet over the hole and Carol Black replaced the turf. Then, they retired for the night and were unobserved at their usual parking space overlooking the loch. On the third day they returned to Inverness to refresh, slept in soft beds and ate a large breakfast.

They continued to avoid observation and comments from strangers and on schedule, drove their tunnel in a horizontal direction on the fourth day. By then, although tired with the physical effort of clearing out the shaft, they were pleased with their progress. Each passing day enlarged their tunnel by a distance of four feet and the roof, which stood three feet high, was supported by means of timber. As they had planned, they broke through into a very much older shaft on the sixth day.

Before finally entering, Pal and his servants carefully tidied up the site of the old burial ground and made sure that the area around the old Mort House was clear of diversionary notices. There was no trace of loose earth anywhere, nor any trampled plants or rubbish. However, they left a single sign near their main shaft, which proclaimed a danger due to gas. Then, after descending by means of a short ladder, their last entrant was able, with some effort, to cover the opening by means of a steel sheet of the kind used to cover excavations on building sites. They followed Johan Pal as he broke away a few roots and entered a main shaft with a height of five feet, and with sides and roof made of old brickwork.

The old bricked tunnel was of a dark red colour and ran south-east and upwards, towards General Wade's Military Road; the B852. There was a dank atmosphere, redolent of musty, damp blankets, stale mushrooms and the general decay of vegetable matter. They were unsure whether the air was safe to breathe; it had been enclosed for many years and was cold and unpleasant; nevertheless they continued forward.

Walking slowly, they could see that the design of the tunnel was of a perfect circle. There was no lintel-stone and each brick acted to support its neighbour. It therefore resembled a brick drain or sewer, without an identifiable floor or ceiling. It was clearly strong and stable; nowhere had there been a settlement of earth large enough to bring about even a small fall of rubble.

Carol Black chose to walk first and following her, Johan Pal said, 'We can find out how far it goes. I shall be interested to see whether it goes all the way to Boleskine House on the other side of the road. If so, that would suggest a reason for the history of psychic disturbance in the place and might also give a reason for Aleister Crowley's base there. I hope we find a pathway right to the ruined kirk underneath; if so, it will be very interesting.'

They continued forwards and were obliged to stoop a little, but by means of rechargeable fluorescent torches they obtained adequate light. As they walked, the tunnel rose and it became slightly warmer. Black guessed that after one hundred yards, they would have broken through the surface had it remained level. Nevertheless, since they did not do so, it was clear that the ground itself was rising.

After about 150 yards, they came to a brick wall and in it, a small door. Its hinges were rusty, heavy and full of grime. Despite some effort they were unable to open it and it seemed to be locked from the other side.

Pal said, 'This will need a lot of effort to break through. We shall need proper leverage from a long handle, or a force from some kind of power tool. Let's hope it doesn't bring the wall down.' They turned around and retraced their steps.

Later, Johan Pal said, 'Judging from the distance, we seem to have reached an entrance to the foundations of Boleskine House or the kirk below. The tunnel may continue on the other side of the door, but I doubt whether the door has been opened in one hundred years. Whatever we find, legend has it that the tunnel was built to connect the burial ground with the kirk, not with the house itself. We are not, of course, interested in the house; to enter it would be an act of trespass, but it would be difficult to say that the same holds true of the remains below its foundations.'

Pal continued, 'For now, we must try to get past the locked door, but we need to be discreet since the house may be occupied. Nevertheless it is the kirk we are interested in; its remains were buried long ago. I believe the tunnel will enlarge into a chamber and within it the remains of the kirk, left exactly as it was on the day it burned down long before the house was built. If that is so, it may still contain the last remains of the congregation who were burned alive there.'

'Master, why did the kirk burn down?'

'Such details are lost in the mists of time; some say it was arson; others say it was accidental. However our own tradition suggests that the priest was engaged in a quest similar to our own. It is held that his experiments ended in failure and that he lacked sufficient strength to control the forces raised. Eventually the kirk was consumed by flames, which onlookers described as like the very flames of Hell itself. Observers heard screams from the tormented souls within and they are reputed to scream there still. Such are the mistakes made by those without enough knowledge of the old ways.'

'And this place is sufficiently evil?'

'Consider the evidence. It is the site of devil worship and the mass burning of many people. Centuries later, Aleister Crowley is known to have owned the house above to conduct his own magical rituals. Some of his work was undoubtedly corrupt: he made up many of his own ceremonies; nevertheless he made genuine progress in the cause.'

'And recently?'

'After Crowley, the house passed to a succession of owners and it became associated with the paranormal. It was owned by Jimmy Page of Led Zeppelin, a rock musician interested in magic and is still a place of pilgrimage for the adherents of a form of music called heavy metal. There was a further fire, a suicide, a self-amputated hand and so on. It is a place of genuine evil, an evil which has grown from the kirk below and festered unsated by the passage of years.'

'And the tormented souls, bound to the underworld, can they be of use to you?'

'Yes of course. Their torment will aid our ritual. We can open a gateway of consummate evil, and Adolf Hitler will welcome his followers who will come through it. They are those who followed him to the very end and whose release can be obtained only through a portal of adequate worth. However we must prepare quickly now, because I sense that minds elsewhere are now upon us.'

*

'Hello Creighton.' Wally Bishop spoke to Creighton Brakespeare on the telephone. 'How long is it since we last spoke; two weeks maybe? I had been meaning to speak to you again. We seem to have led parallel paths recently; both of us have had dealings with Mr Johan Pal.'

'I am sorry Wally, but you know how things stand with clients; I cannot discuss him.'

'Yes, I know, but unfortunately, Mr Pal may have been rather a bad boy in the eyes of the police and although there is normally no question of discussing the business transactions of clients, nor for that matter their personal lives, the boys in blue went through his affairs in some detail. They found he had dealt with a large sum of money recently and that it had been handled by your business. They also know that we are friends and I thought that, on a casual basis, I might introduce you to them. I believe it would be in everyone's interest for all parties to meet, because Mr Pal's actions have probably become extreme enough for the normal rules governing client confidentiality to be shelved. At least, that is what they told me.'

Brakespeare made a statement rather than a question, 'And this is as gentle a way as possible for you to bring about an introduction.'

'Yes, that's about it. If I don't come with them, they will probably visit you anyway.'

'Well, Wally, I have known you a long time and I know that we can trust each other. When would you like to visit?'

'Can we, that is Adam, Callum and myself come tomorrow? We will be with Chief Superintendent Nicholby.' Listening, Nicholby nodded. 'Everyone else will be otherwise engaged, so it will be the four of us and a driver.'

'How about lunchtime?'

'Love to.'

'It is a Friday tomorrow, but I can close at mid-day. Home or office?'

'We will come straight to your office and then decide what to do.'

Nicholby smiled and nodded.

On the next day, a large and powerful police BMW arrived at 9am and both Nicholby and his driver declined refreshment. They departed within ten minutes and the driver drove at a consistently high speed and with great skill. He chose a motorway route and they proceeded via the M4, northbound M25 and A1M, a distance of 135 miles. Other drivers showed the police car due deference and they were in Cambridge slightly ahead of schedule. Parking was easy for them; the driver stayed with his car and Nicholby accompanied Bishop, Shilto and Dood to Brakespeare's combined shop, office and warehouse.

'Creighton, you know Callum Dood and Adam Shilto,' said Bishop. 'And this is Chief Superintendent Nicholby, who has kindly agreed to accompany us today.' Brakespeare returned the pleasantries and introduced Ivy, who promptly asked whether they would all like coffee. They answered 'Yes, please,' in unison and a few minutes later she brought in a large, steaming pot and six cups.

Ivy enquired after their journey and Bishop explained that since they had been driven by a professional driver, their trip had been as easy as such a journey could possibly be. Other light conversation followed but after a few minutes, Bishop turned their conversation towards the topic which they all knew to be their main purpose.

'Creighton and Ivy, Chief Superintendent Nicholby is a notable figure in our local constabulary. We have been advised that the police have attached some importance to this investigation. As a friend, I know that you have had some dealings with Mr Johan Pal, but had I not done so, I am advised that you would have been interviewed anyway, as part of a combined operation which they are carrying out with the German police. It was with some trepidation that I came today, because as a friend I did not wish to interfere in your private or business affairs. Yet regardless, we had become involved with Johan Pal as you have, and the investigation has become so serious that by now we had little choice.'

'Why is Johan Pal the target of a police investigation of this nature?'

Nicholby spoke, 'Mr Brakespeare, did you hear about a nasty murder in Nuremberg a while back? A Satanic ritual was carried out in the former Nazi Parade Grounds and a murder was committed there. To make matters worse, it was committed with some very unpleasant Nazi regalia and trappings present. I understand from Mr Dood that these were part of the ceremony and had to do with a resurgence of Nazi beliefs by Pal and his followers. The whole event got into the newspapers and the tabloids especially had a field day.'

He continued, 'Callum, Adam and Wally had previous dealings with Mr Pal and decided to follow him to Germany, where they witnessed the murder. We know that your friends here have had no direct involvement in it, apart from as witnesses. The German police allowed them to tell a few white lies in order to escape, which they did. Together, we hoped they would help us to trace Mr Pal. In fact we have been trying to catch him since his return to England, but without success.'

Brakespeare said, 'I see. So you went over Pal's affairs in the hope of finding a lead of some kind and came up with me?'

'Yes, we did. We know where Mr Pal used to live, but he organised his affairs with a caretaker there. He is a man of considerable financial means and quite obviously can come and go as he would please. You dealt with him in business and we wonder whether you have had any continuing contact with him?'

'First of all, why so senior a policeman? I would have thought that my little world hardly merited a visit from a Chief Superintendent.'

'That's easy to answer. A murder is big news anyway, but the whole Nazi background makes it very embarrassing for the Germans and for us too. Neither of our police services nor our political establishments can put up with being seen to be ineffectual in the face of such a culture. Nazism is anathema to our modern political and social consensus. If nothing is done, well, I can leave you to imagine.'

'I can see that faced with the possibility of a crime having been committed, I cannot withhold anything. The politics, well, I shall have to leave that to you.'

Brakespeare continued, 'You will know that Pal has been a regular customer of mine over a period of about two years. He visited me at my shop a couple of times and made a purchase of auction items, general display items, and on one occasion, bid in a private sale. We delivered that to him in person; Wally will remember the occasion because we stayed with him in Wiltshire. The transaction took place at Pal's property and he gave us an excellent lunch.'

'What was the sale item?'

'It was a book of an aesthetic and magical nature. It was very rare, the only one of its kind I have sold in my career. Mr Pal paid without difficulty: it was a very large sum.'

'Does he stay in contact with you? If so, how do you converse?'

'Normally, I send emailed newsletters and lists of forthcoming sale items to my clients. This is because many are collectors and together, they usually swallow up the majority of my more costly sale goods. Of course, folk wander into the shop, but such customers are mostly interested in cheaper things, usually modern fiction up to one hundred years old.'

'So you have his email address?'

'Yes, but I expect that like most people, he has several.'

'What about by telephone?'

'Yes, I have also phoned him on business. I used a number which I believe is his domestic number in Wiltshire.'

'Of course we cannot be sure that Mr Pal has opened his emails recently. He might be engaged in some other mischief.'

Dood said, 'You can count on it.'

Nicholby said, 'Can you reach him any other way?'

'No, if he has moved out, I have no further idea where he lives. He usually contacts me. He has my number.'

'Can I have his email address please and I must ask you to telephone me personally if he contacts you again. Here is my card; I must stress the importance of this.'

'Yes, of course.'

'I am afraid that I cannot leave my driver waiting any longer. I must get back home as soon as possible. There are meetings to attend, together with paperwork.' Nicholby looked glum.

'Well, thank you for coming all this way just to see me. I was about to suggest lunch, by the way.'

'That is very good of you, but I'm afraid that lunch would slow me up somewhat. I do know, however, that my companions today,' he indicated Dood, Shilto and Bishop, 'had hoped to stay rather longer and said that they would prefer to find their own way back.'

'Well, in that case it looks like lunch for the rest of us.'

*

Back at their favourite anglicised Greek Taverna, Ivy ordered the Special Mixed Meze for them all, followed by chicken Espagnole. Dood was the only one who asked for something spicy; he had the escalope vesuvio, a dish suggested by Brakespeare... 'Although I do myself like something different occasionally.'

They all tucked into their plates of food; for them all it had been a long morning and one not without its allocation of distress. Ivy soon said, 'What do you think Nicholby will do to Mr Pal when the police catch up with him?'

Dood replied, 'This is just what I had been thinking about.' He looked concerned.

'Why?' said Shilto.

'Well, the plain fact is that they can't really constrain him for very long.'

'What do you mean by constrain?' replied Ivy.

'They can arrest him, put him in handcuffs and take him to a police cell or he might even end up in gaol. But they would not be able to keep him there, or at least, not for long. How do you keep a man who can influence a jury by force of will? By night he can levitate or cause a guard to drop dead! He can cause a police car to break down or foretell the future. Constraining him is just not a practical proposition. He cannot simply be shot either, we don't do that any more. They might hand him to the Germans, but that would simply pass the buck. I bet you he would be out within a month and up to his old tricks again.'

'So what can be done?' said Bishop.

'Johan Pal needs to be damaged or weakened.'

'What's the difference?'

Dood continued, 'His power must be stripped away.'

'How?' said Shilto.

'He needs to carry out a big magical ceremony and it must be made to fail.'

'How could we make that happen?' said Brakespeare.

'He would need to be opposed by a white magician of equal or greater ability, in which case his invocations would be neutralised. Or alternatively, he would need to make some kind of mistake in his invocations so that any devil he raised would retrieve the occult power granted to him.'

'Do we know anyone who can stand up to him?'

'I know of no white magician of equal power, let alone greater.'

'Then he must be induced to make a mistake.'

Bishop said, 'Is such a mistake the sort of thing Nicholby could induce him to make?'

Dood replied, 'Good Lord, no. If Nicholby catches up with Johan Pal, there would be an instant arrest. That would be *his* potential embarrassment taken care of. Johan Pal would be back in Germany within 48 hours and the British police force could then wash their hands of the case. They would get the tabloids off their backs and everyone would be happy, at least for a while.'

'I didn't say so when Nicholby was here,' said Brakespeare, 'and I had quite forgotten about it, but I did have a brief contact with Pal earlier this month. It may have been two weeks ago, I cannot quite remember.'

'What kind of contact?'

'He telephoned me about his book. I sent a few pages away to be mended and he wanted them back as soon as possible. In fact, I am due to telephone the restorers again about now. They were on the last page, which had to have some stitching done to the vellum, you know, new material sown in and the lettering restored or reapplied.'

'Do you have his telephone number?'

'Yes, but it's a mobile telephone. He usually keeps it switched off, but I don't know why. I did leave a text message for him and he called back soon after. That was two weeks ago. He probably leaves it off to keep the line secure from callers. But I cannot see how he could connect me with any of his pursuers.'

'If he leaves it on, then the location of the telephone can be traced easily by means of triangulation, just as targets were tracked for bomber aircraft during the last war. Where two radio beams crossed was a target; similarly, a mobile telephone can be traced by its signal.'

'But I thought you said it would be foolish to try to get Nicholby back in?' said Ivy.

'I did,' said Dood.

'Then how can we trace where he is?'

'We could get you to send him a text message, and when he signs on to reply, we could triangulate to get his position.'

'But *we* can't do that, surely?'

'In fact, I think we can. Let's finish this delicious lunch and then go back to your place, Creighton and Ivy, that is to say, if you will have us!'

'As always, it will be a pleasure.'

⋆

At Creighton and Ivy's home, a spacious Georgian-styled apartment on the outskirts of Cambridge, Ivy made some tea and Creighton started up his precious computer. He typed a question into a search engine: *track a cell phone*. There were many hits and he went into one of them and read aloud:

> *'If you wish to find your cell phone or are an intelligence agent trying to obtain information on the whereabouts of a criminal, we can help you. We can easily track a smartphone or often an older phone too. The GPS location software in a smartphone can*

enable you to locate it easily. Just download and use the 'Catch' app and a smartphone can be traced to within a few feet. Alternatively, you can send an instruction to take a photograph of the user and send it to you.'

He said, 'That of course depends on whether Pal has such a service on his phone.' He read further and said, 'Some of them enable you to install the app remotely.'

He continued, 'Here's another.'

'Tracker & Co: A GPS Phone Finder Using Just a Mobile Phone Number. We run a website for tracing any phone signal by means of the number only. Try it on your cheating lover or your business partner! The Tracer app can locate your cell phone in less than 30 seconds! Try it online without the tracked person knowing. Just enter the phone number you want to look up, and obtain its location on your Windows mobile machine!'

Another website said:

'With GPS Phone Search you can find or trace a mobile phone. Each phone gives a radio signal that we follow via public satellite records. Although not as accurate as GPS tracking systems, we can locate a phone to as little as 150 yards in large towns, which is more than enough to know where you cheating lover is or whether your employee is in the pub!'

'So,' said Brakespeare, 'we can probably locate Johan Pal from his phone number, if only to within about 200 yards. I would say that within half a mile is probably enough; we can use our intelligence to work out the rest. The only snag is that they want a mobile number and a credit card!'

'We can use this one,' said Shilto, 'no, it isn't my own; the Church gave it to me for the duration of this investigation. However everything must be fully accountable, of course.'

'Stop, stop!' said Creighton Brakespeare. 'The first thing is for me to telephone my restoration people; I owe them a call anyway. It would be absurd to send a message to Pal's mobile telephone only for it to contain no news.' He picked up his own handset.

'Hello, this is Creighton Brakespeare. Yes, the book guy. How's my commission getting along? Yes, the Treatise on Magic. When we last spoke, it was to have taken only fourteen days to finish.'

There were reasonable replies at the other end.

Brakespeare continued, 'Yes, excellent. Please package it up in your usual manner and send it by courier. By Monday? Yes, very good; please also include your invoice. I will settle it in my usual way.'

'Creighton, can we take it that you will have a package ready for Pal early in the forthcoming week?' said Shilto.

'Yes, I shall have fifteen repaired pages to send him. But I don't expect him to fall into the very obvious trap of calling to collect them himself. He will send his own courier.'

'Yes, and with a destination address supplied only when the courier is on his way back.'

'The police can follow such a courier?' said Ivy.

'I'm sure they could, but that is not our aim. We want to damage him permanently. We agreed that the police would only arrest him.'

Bishop, who had been quiet for a while, now said, 'Actually, it seems to me a golden opportunity. Why don't we scan the pages and offer to email the scans to him, with the real pages to follow later?'

'So what would be the point?' replied Dood.

'We could introduce some errors into the pages in question. As a backup, we can try to locate him using the gps mobile triangulation method and lastly, if all else fails, we announce to Nicholby that we have traced him – we give Nicholby the latest contact details – with the suggestion that he should pick him up as soon as possible What do you think?'

'Wally, darling, you make it all sound so simple,' said Ivy.

The others nodded in agreement and Dood said, 'It's brilliant. I think it may succeed. But, what kind of errors could we add to our fake pages?'

Bishop replied, 'Perhaps we need to wait until Monday to find out exactly what is in them. In the meantime, you have been fantastic, Creighton, but we cannot expect you to put us all up. Can you suggest a half-decent hotel nearby?'

Shilto said, 'And I fancy taking a punt on the River Cam!'

★

Shilto, Bishop and Dood made telephone calls to the effect that their return would be delayed. A locum was arranged to take church services for the Sunday and in the meantime, on the Saturday and Sunday, Ivy and Creighton Brakespeare showed them around Cambridge. They visited Great St Mary's Church, toured the Colleges, strolled along the Backs, and finally on the Sunday, took a trip to Ely in order to visit the beautiful cathedral there. Of all the cathedrals they had seen, Ely quickly became the visitors' favourite for its simplicity, light, and for its cold stillness. After, they had tea in a tea shop and returned to Cambridge in the late afternoon.

Later, talk returned to the question of how to place a mistake in a copy of a page of Pal's magical treatise.

Ivy said, 'We must make sure our page looks like the real thing. In the first instance, we must scan a blank piece of vellum, perhaps a reverse side with nothing on it. That would give us a 'canvas' to which additions could be made.'

'Yes, that would be easy. We could then superimpose some scanned words or symbols onto that,' said Shilto. 'But we do need to wait until we see the real thing, so we can decide on what to remove or alter.'

On Monday, a courier arrived from *Medieval Parchment Restoration* and Brakespeare signed a few papers and took delivery of the work. A packet contained fifteen papers of vellum, which they examined closely. Overall, it was clear that restoration had been carried out with a view to retaining the originality of the work and that the commission had been executed to a high standard. Thus although many pages showed stitching or flattened creases, new ink had generally been applied only as an aid to legibility and not to supplant older text. On the final page of the fifteen restored, however, more extensive repairs were present.

Brakespeare examined the work of the scribe and said, 'There is no obvious start or end to the text, so it should be possible to rewrite a section of it. Perhaps we can redo two or three pages and introduce some significant mistakes. But what does it all mean?'

He made a telephone call to a Cambridge number. 'Ah, is that Jim MacDonald? This is Creighton Brakespeare. Can I come and see you please?…What about?…Can I ask you to look at and maybe translate a few pages of Latin?…Yes, I know where your rooms are…yes, Tree Court. Could you let the Porter's Lodge know?…What about ten thirty?…Yes.'

In Jim MacDonald's rooms in Caius College, Brakespeare said, 'Jim, it's worth a couple of decent bottles of fizz – name your poison – if you translate these pages for me. I have a customer who wants to know what they mean and I'm pretty useless at Latin. It is Latin, isn't it?'

'It looks like it. Well I'm not a greedy man, so I'll stop at a bit of Jameson's. It would be for my chest, you understand.'

'Thanks, Jim, how long?'

'For you, a couple of hours. Go over the road to the cake shop, buy a cake and eat it, buy a highbrow newspaper and read it and it will be done by the time you come back.'

Brakespeare walked to a newsagent and bought a magazine and in a café bought coffee. The magazine contained a section on Italian food which he read with avidity. One particular part, an article written by an 'Italian grandma,' was concerned with a dish called 'anelletti pastina with ricotta salata.' It enabled him to keep his mind off the translation for a full thirty minutes and he made a mental note to take Ivy to Italy in the very near future. However eventually, he finished the article and walked back to Jim Macdonald's place. The translation was finished and Macdonald was sitting with his feet in front of an electric fire.

He said, 'Where did you get this stuff? It's all about necromancy and bringing the dead back to life!'

'So what does it actually say?'

'Well, come over and look at my notes; I hope you can read my writing. See this: page one. It starts by suggesting that the reader will wish to communicate with the spirits of the dead; it tells one how to do it.'

'Go on.'

'The reader will carry out an invocation in order to seek knowledge, but must first throw himself into a trance. Suggestions are made on how to do this: the writer has suggested several herbs which can be applied to the body. Interestingly, there is an addition to the script on the side of the page, written in ink and dated 1350, which proposes *'folk petersilie.'* This may mean hemlock, I am not sure, but it may also be fool's cicely or fool's parsley. The user, regardless, will end up in an excited state and will howl and gesticulate; in so doing, he or she will speak in a deranged state to the dead, or perhaps even in a trance.'

'The ceremony should be carried out at night,' it says. 'And there should be a pit of fire, together with a sacrifice of blood, the nature of which will depend upon the status of the spirit to be raised. Blood must be drunk and it says, '*Invocations praecessisse dicenda est deos mortuorum*'. I believe that would mean an invocation to the Gods of the dead should be spoken.'

'The script goes on to describe the appearance of the participants. They should wear the clothing of the people whose spirits they wish to raise. A further section deals with food and drink; all participants should consume a feast similar to that which a spirit of the underworld might expect to receive while there: namely, a flat, unleavened bread made of course grains, together with the unmatured waters of the vine. It sounds pretty nasty to me.'

'It also talks about other ways of facilitating the intended outcome, see here,' he pointed. 'Spirits can be conjured from the bones of the dead by a passing through fire or flames and in suitable temples of invocation, such as those with a pit or chasm of flame. I think that means grinding up a bit of bone and burning it in a suitable receptacle within a larger fire; a fire-pit in fact.'

He continued, '*Ceremonias magicas'* were, of necessity, carried out within a circle traced upon the ground and with letters of power traced therein, in order to contain the spirit in question. One particularly effective circle involved the use of strips of animal skin, with a ring of *annulum salis*, which translates as a ring of salt within it, to deter the egression of any likely demons. So that is about it. The rest of it is concerned with the preparation of oneself by means of fasting and supplication, together with the use of herbs or – as is written in the margin – worts. Overall, a nice piece of work, eh?'

'Look, Jim, I want to speak to my customer later today. Can I have these papers to take away, please and of course, I still need the originals. Depending on his verdict on them, he may ask me to arrange for something to be written into Latin: a reply for the purpose of an academic foray or a spoof to go into a student magazine. If so, would it be possible for you to pop something into Latin if I came back at the same time tomorrow?'

'I don't see why not! Maybe we could have a bit of lunch on it, or a few beers?'

'You can bet on it.'

⋆

'So Creighton, what did your mate find out?' said Dood.

'Well, a whole load of mumbo jumbo, basically.'

'That's just what I had hoped. Can I have a quick look at it, please?'

'Sure. It's a bit of a mish-mash with lots of notes in English as well as the original Latin, but you can rest assured that with Jim doing the work, the idiom will be perfect.' Brakespeare passed the sheaf of paper.

'Spirits…conjured from the bones of the dead…? Well, that would tie in with what we saw in Germany, when Johan Pal invoked the ghost of Adolf Hitler using the Magdeburg Relic.' Brakespeare looked stunned, as if he had only just realised the extent of Johan Pal's endeavours.

'And here, we know that his adherents, if not Pal himself, smeared themselves all over with hemlock in order to simulate the sensation of flight on a broomstick. At least, that's what I was told by the girls after his Garden Party.'

Dood continued to chatter to himself, 'But how to make his ceremony go wrong? Let me think… we must somehow alter it fundamentally…find a way to ensure that it doesn't work.'

'Look here, it seems to recommend abstinence and suggests that rather basic, unpleasant food should be consumed beforehand. Perhaps we could rewrite it in such a way that Pal will eat and drink to excess; he is used to that.'

'And here, the invoker seems to be protected from danger by a ring of animal skin and by salt. If the necromancer must raise a spirit from within a pit of fire, perhaps we could change matters so he or she stands within the circle instead of outside. They are simple changes, but ones which could make things go badly for him.'

Brakespeare now said, 'I have promised to take my suggestions back to town tomorrow. Please would you kindly write down your ideas on a scrap of paper? I will never manage to remember them unless you do.'

*

'Ah, Miss Black, I have had a text message from Creighton Brakespeare to the effect that my pages are ready. I had been meaning to get in touch with him again anyway. Brakespeare has suggested that he should, in the first instance, scan and email the restored pages to me; I think it is a rather good idea. First of all, we would obtain the pages on approval and secondly, we would not endanger our security by meeting with him in person. I have therefore agreed with his suggestion. With them, I can start to plan our invocation in more detail. To that end, how are we getting on down below?'

'We have made some progress towards clearing the door in the brick wall at the end of the main tunnel. We are not through it, however; the door will require force. We thought we might use an hydraulic tool, but were concerned by the likely noise and wished to draw it to your attention beforehand.'

'Again, Miss Black, you have been wise. However, we can make an attempt forthwith and I propose to do that during the day. By doing so, I think it less likely that we shall be disturbed; it is naturally more noisy during the day and residents are more often elsewhere.'

'Do you wish me to alert the other nine?'

'Ask them to make themselves ready. We are of course, only four so the others should prepare to arrive upon notice of 24 hours.'

*

'Good morning, Jim,' said Creighton Brakespeare. They exchanged further greetings. 'This is what I would like you to say. Please would you write down your revised copy on this bright, white paper? I would like the script to match the original if possible. I can then scan it onto something more suitable for our student magazine.'

'Yes, it will be about an hour or two's work; I have nothing else to do this morning.'

'Should I come back, or would you like me to wait?'

'Have a stroll around town. I will text you when the document is ready.'

Brakespeare went to the bank, bought a trade journal, read it in the park and was just about to consume a sandwich when his mobile telephone rang. 'Hello, Creighton, this is Jim. Your document is ready.'

'How has it come out?'

'I think it looks pretty authentic, just don't smudge the ink! I am quite sure your friend will find it useful.'

'I will be round again in fifteen minutes.'

On the way back, Brakespeare bought a couple of bottles of Jameson's and a decent bottle of red. He carried them into MacDonald's rooms and the latter smiled. 'Let's have a drop, shall we?'

'Ok,' said Brakespeare, 'just a drop.'

Macdonald, formerly a little asthmatic, seemed to find it easier to breathe and he removed his feet from the fire and replaced his socks. An hour later, Brakespeare returned home, clutching a buff-coloured envelope with papers inside. Callum Dood said, 'Please can I see?'

Four pairs of eyes looked over Brakespeare's shoulder as he withdrew the papers. He said, 'Here are our notes and here is our ancient document, suitably revised. Last but not least, this is a translation of the revised paper, which Jim made for me. What do you think? If the work is OK, I can scan the Latin transcript onto the blank page of vellum. It will take only ten minutes.'

'Creighton,' said Ivy, 'I have had a return message from Johan Pal. He agrees that we should send copies of our scanned pages by email. Here is an email address; it is a completely new one.'

'That's fine. When you reply please send him some kind of question by text. I want to make sure that his phone stays on. Say that his email address doesn't work; we can always apologise and say we left out a dot.'

A little later, Callum Dood said, 'Alright, Adam, you can enter your credit card details here. Now look for the drop-down menu; yes, that gets you into the screen where you can enter the target telephone number. What was the mobile number, please, Creighton?'

'Here,' said Creighton Brakespeare, 'I have written it down on this piece of paper. How long will it take?'

'Well,' said Dood, 'if he keeps his mobile switched on for a while longer, they can do the deed immediately. Yes, press send. The website said that tracing is instant.'

The screen said, 'verifying credit card details,' and about thirty seconds later, there was a melodious beep as the computer received incoming data.

'Ah look, they have sent me a reference showing the location of the phone on a map. See, I have saved that into my browser; but where is it, a place called Inverfarigaig? But that's in Scotland. What on earth is he doing up there?'

Dood said, 'Ah, at last, I can see some kind of sense. In fact, it ties up with what the tarot cards revealed when I was over at Johan Pal's home: they revealed a desire for power, placed somehow within a northern quadrant. Not only that, but they showed the Blasted Tower: a house or fortress burning down.'

'I don't understand how those tarot cards could be connected with Scotland,' said Ivy.

'No, but in my line of business we hear about such connections. In fact, that area is very well-known for having been one of the haunts of the devil-worshipper Aleister Crowley, who was active about one hundred years ago. He bought a large hunting lodge there for his researches and the area became somewhat celebrated by his fans and those of certain rock and roll bands with their culture rooted in black magic. The house burned again recently and has been the centre of many alleged psychic disturbances over the years. Perhaps that is why the tarot cards showed what they did.'

Dood continued, 'All that remains is for us to go and challenge him.'

Shilto said, 'It might be better if Creighton and Ivy were to stay here in Cambridge. Don't forget that Pal may have further queries about his manuscript and may call at any time. There is also the question of the original pages to deal with.'

'Yes, that's OK,' said Ivy. 'We can also deal with any query from Nicholby. Who else would rather stay?'

Bishop and Shilto both suggested they would prefer go to Scotland, but after a minute, Bishop said, 'Would you like me to get Peyton Oakwood up here as well?'

'Oh yes, that would be great.'

Chapter Eleven

In the Crypt

Herr Koch, please would you insert the end of this lever into the gap we have made in the door there; yes, that is fine. Now we shall need to exert all our strength on the lever; Miss Black, if you take my shoulders here, I will grab Herr Koch around the waist and we can all pull together. Harder, yes, that's it. Very good, see how we have moved the door on its hinges. But they are tearing away from the wall. Can we improve matters, do you think?'

'Yes, Master, I can heat the hinges with this portable blowtorch. It runs on a small cylinder of propane gas and has a very hot flame; stand back, please. Yes, that is it, and now the lower hinge. Good, now we can add some easing oil. It is a very light oil that will penetrate the spaces made when the residue of iron oxide and dirt was heated. No not yet, I must let the hinge cool first so that we do not have smoke.'

Koch continued, 'Ach, the oil has gone right in, so we can try to exert some force on the door once more. Here is the lever; as before pull, and pull again; excellent.'

With a creak the door swung open.

Johan Pal picked up his lamp and Meinhard Koch, Carol Black and Sieghard Trapper followed behind. On this occasion they had chosen not to leave a sentry behind at the entrance; it was far too wet for the curious to be out. As they walked, they were able to light the tunnel to a considerable degree with their four fluorescent lamps.

The tunnel continued upwards and remained of brick construction. After a further distance of fifty feet, the walls began to look darker and Meinhard Koch stopped to run his hand over the wall. His fingers left a trail and he said, 'Dies ruß; how you say, this is soot.'

Shortly the tunnel widened into a chamber of brick. The floor of red brick was uneven and of an irregular 'drystone' style, without cement. It was about two inches below the level of the tunnel outlet and a small amount of water lay thereon. The walls showed evidence of condensation and there was an all-pervading atmosphere of dampness.

A little further, the brick floor and walls gave way to material of an older construction. There were small flagstones, irregular in outline and they had many cracks in them. Carol Black scraped the blade of a knife across a flagstone and was able to confirm that they were hard and probably of a local stone. The floor continued to walls of the same material, but there were no gaps for windows. Johan Pal said, 'We are still underground.'

They looked upwards, but a dark ceiling was out of reach, probably eight feet from the floor. It was made from thick floorboards mounted on very sturdy wooden joists. There was a considerable amount of caulking between the boards and no light from above them.

Carol Black said, 'This is a cellar. I think that the floorboards above are quite old, perhaps over 100 years old. If so, we are probably below the house itself. These flagstones look ecclesiastical; I think we are on the floor of the former kirk but there is no evidence of older use of the kind we wish to see ourselves. That surely cannot be.'

Johan Pal replied, 'Look closely around the room. We must look for closed passages in the walls; perhaps this cellar leads to an extension.'

They walked slowly around the cellar, looking closely at the walls. At one point there was a wooden step ladder leading up to a trapdoor. Meinhard Koch, who first observed it, mounted the step ladder carefully and pushed at the trapdoor above. It would not move.

Elsewhere there was no mark in a wall to suggest a door. Johan Pal finally said, 'It seems there is no other way out.'

However Seighard Trapper began to look at the floor in detail and after a few minutes of observation, well away from the others, he said, 'This may be of interest.'

Trapper began to rock his right foot on a group of small flagstones at the rear of the cellar near to its entrance. There was not a great amount of movement and the flagstones were well-fitting; nevertheless it was clear that they were loose. His efforts attracted the others and they began to imitate his movements. As they did so, a surface layer of dirt was dislodged. It contained dust and soot and was very black, and its dislodgement revealed a gap between the stones.

Black inserted the blade of a knife between two flagstones and enlarged the gap between them. Finally, she was able to exert sufficient leverage to raise a smaller stone. Below was a dark space, from which the smell of damp and decay came forth.

Now, the four of them began to work on neighbouring flagstones and together, they got a jemmy below the edge of a larger stone. Working it, they were able to raise a single flagstone which they laid down on its back and with fluorescent lights looked down inside.

Johan Pal said, 'This is a remnant of a very much older building below the house. Look, the construction is quite different. It is made of worked stone like the flagstones here.'

He continued, 'It is a crypt; a burial chamber. It lies below the cellar floor and was therefore beneath the former kirk. I agree that we are standing on the floor of the old kirk and if so, its foundations would have been at the level of the cellar floor of the modern house with walls rising above ground – although we cannot now say what it looked like. However look below, the crypt is blackened on its walls, floor and ceiling; in fact this flagstone floor is also the roof of the crypt.'

'We must pass into this space below and carry out our ceremonies there. However we cannot go below our present level until we are properly equipped to do so. Let us replace this flagstone and retrace our footsteps; unfortunately our fluorescent lamps are depleted and we do not wish to be caught in total darkness. I must also travel back to Inverness in order to open an email from Brakespeare. I understand it is of the repaired pages of the magical book that we need for our ceremony.'

'Can you not open such an email here, Master?'

'It would be possible, but I wish to do so only from an internet café; I cannot take the risk of staying online for too long while we are here. I assume that Brakespeare acts in ignorance and I therefore trust him, but there are also individuals whom I know are plotting against us, even as we speak.'

*

Later, Johan Pal and Meinhard Koch exerted their strength and opened the flagstone leading to the crypt once more. They had with them recharged fluorescent lamps but they held these in reserve. On this occasion, each had brought a paraffin storm lantern of the 'Tilley Lamp' design, giving abundant light and very little hiss. They suffered from the disadvantage that they gave a characteristic odour of spent paraffin, but the combustion warmed the icy crypt below, which had made them shiver at first.

They looked around with interest. There were shelves let into two walls, made of stone and supported by narrow pillars of stone at each end. On them were coffins or sarcophagi. At one end was a raised altar, devoid of ornament and reached by three low steps. A floor of flagstones was uneven and had names and dates carved into it in evidence of further tombs below. Where such dates were legible, they suggested that burials had been made in the 16th century.

On all sides, the walls, floor and ceiling were blackened and Pal took this to be evidence of fire. At intervals there were also piles of blackened organic material on the floor, which, although possibly of burnt wood, were of indeterminate origin. In the middle of the crypt was a space on the floor, also blackened but apparently swept clear. There were no items of furniture, nor signs of ornamentation. It was an austere space, dark, dank, foul and without grace. Pal surveyed it with satisfaction; they would accomplish all they required there.

Later, they dropped the flagstones, closed the cellar door and retraced their footsteps once more. At the exit, they made their shaft safe with signs, a steel cover and a tarpaulin. Then, Pal bade his followers to return to their Transit van while he made his way alone to Inverness in order to investigate further the messages that had been sent to him.

The next day, Pal printed out his emails, made a brief acknowledgement and closed the computer quickly. Then, he made a minor diversion to a pharmacist and a supermarket and obtained several items he needed. Returning to his assistants, he suggested they should fortify themselves by means of a break in town and asked them to return with the remaining nine members of his circle. 'By then,' he said, 'I shall be ready.'

*

Dood, Shilto and Bishop were without their own transport and they were grateful that Peyton Oakwood had agreed to join them. After a brief lunch they were refreshed and Oakwood, a skilful driver, said, 'The total distance is a little over 500 miles and it should take about 9 hours. Our route is the A1(M), M74 and A9. We can decide what to do on the way.'

'I would like you to find space for this case,' said Callum Dood. 'It contains several important elements that we may need to ensure our safety if we venture into dark places. Make of that what you will.'

They set off by 12.30pm and made good progress by cruising at 70 miles per hour. On the way, Oakwood asked them of their recent fortune. 'When we last spoke, it was with the intention of introducing the police to Creighton and Ivy. The police knew there was a connection between the Brakespeares and Johan Pal. How did you all get on?'

Dood said, 'Creighton agreed that he had done business with Johan Pal and Chief Superintendent Nicholby went away with an email address and the promise of a telephone call if Pal got in touch.'

He continued, 'After the police went away, Creighton remembered that he had been expected to contact Pal upon completion of some repairs to the pages of a book. We were pleased that he had so skilfully diverted the attention of the police from our main lead! He sent a text message and Pal replied. That enabled us to trace Pal by triangulation of his mobile phone signal. *We* didn't do that, of course, but we managed to find people on the internet who could. Meanwhile, we sent Pal copies of his pages by email, but we had subtly changed them in the hope that his magical ceremonies might go wrong.'

'Can you guarantee that?' said Oakwood.

'No, but we are also working on two further options. First, we hope to find him and stop him from working. I have an informed guess of where he will be, but I am very hazy about what to do if we catch him.'

'And the last option?'

'We have tried to keep the police out of things because we think they would arrest him, which would probably only delay our plans for his demise. However our last option is to give the police enough information to arrest him regardless. Although less desirable, it is just possible they would keep him in circumstances which might prevent him working.' He smiled. 'They might lock him up in a church!'

'Let us hope one of these ideas bears fruit. Now where would you like to stay when we get there?' said Oakwood.

'Well, I have taken the liberty of booking four rooms at an hotel in Fort Augustus. The place is rather austere, but it is comfortable and clean and the views are excellent. However it remains to be seen what Scottish food is like; I have heard some conflicting views about it.'

'Ah, yes,' said Oakwood, 'that should give us a very convenient base. It isn't far from that house – what was its name again?'

'Boleskine House. But of course, that isn't our objective, nor his; he can hardly break into someone else's property and carry out a ceremony of black magic there. No, he is interested in what probably lies below.'

'How did you work out where to look for him?'

'Well, we managed to get a mobile phone triangulation to a 'box' with sides of about 1000 yards. We also knew he was looking for a place of supposed evil in which to take his work forward. We made a cursory search and came up with name of *that* property. It is quite famous in the neighbourhood.'

'Famous?'

'Yes, among followers of magic, heavy metal music and the like.'

'So if Pal isn't going to attempt a break in, what can we expect him to do?'

Shilto said, 'We think he will try to find a way into whatever lies below the cellar of the house. The house is privately owned so that entry to the cellar would itself be trespass and more significantly for him, his activities would probably be disturbed there. However, below it are reputed to be the remains of a former kirk which burned down before the house was built. I doubt whether the owner of the house could do much about that.'

'Why not?' said Bishop.

Shilto replied. 'The Land Registry is concerned with the surface ownership of land, which is taken to mean no more than the depth required for reasonable enjoyment of your property.

You can dig a foundation to a depth required to keep your house stable, but no more; such a depth would depend on the nature of the property in question. You would need planning permission for a basement or cellar, but once obtained, you could live and work at that depth or go as deep as you need for adequate foundations to be installed.'

He continued further, 'However, underneath your foundations, ownership falls away. For example, all utility companies have statutory rights to their service tunnels and cables and they enforce them regularly. Similarly, tunnels for underground trains or deep sewers are owned by the company which runs them. In fact you cannot dig any deep mine indiscriminately; all rights to coal, oil, gold and silver are owned by the Crown; and even if a mine is under your home it cannot be yours.'

Shilto summed up thus, 'Taken together, if Boleskine House is built above the remains of a former kirk and if the two properties are discontinuous, then it would take a lot of argument in court to prove that you had broken the law of trespass. Further, if there is a tunnel to the kirk from a burial ground across the road, the owner of Bolskine House could not conceivably claim ownership of it unless on the title deed. So I think Pal and his minions are in the clear.'

'And of course,' said Dood, 'his best defence is discretion. If he sneaks in via the tunnel, does his business and departs, then nobody would be the wiser.'

'And this tunnel: is it well-known?'

'No, it exists only in legend. The kirk was well away from the cemetery and in fact the two are on opposite sides of the present main road. There may be a connecting tunnel between the cemetery and the kirk, but nobody knows where it starts or finishes. The kirk was supposedly burned down and its former existence is itself only a rumour. Later, Boleskine House was alleged to have been built on the site of the kirk, which would mean, if true, that a tunnel still connects the cemetery and the kirk below the house. I say 'kirk,' but nobody knows what remains of it. It might be a few bits of rubble and nothing more.'

Dood summed up, 'The whole area is one of myth, alleged Satanic practices, alleged paranormal activity and more. There is also a connection with fire. The kirk is thought to have been burned down well before the original house was built in the eighteenth century, while a significant fire burned the house itself in 2015. The famous black magician Aleister Crowley lived there between 1899 and 1913 and is alleged to have carried out terrible rituals there. Later a further owner is known to have committed suicide and there are supposed cases of the disappearance of people and of others going mad. Jimmy Page of Led Zeppelin bought the place in 1970 and although he owned it until 1992, spent only six weeks there – and that was in a period in which he is said to have been interested in the occult. There is no doubt that Johan Pal would be drawn to such a place.'

'When he gets there and starts his own experiments, what do you expect him to do?'

'He has already been successful at invoking the spirit of Adolf Hitler and can now command that ceremony to the extent that a repeat would be easy. Probably, he would need only the cursory release of animal blood to reinvigorate the Relic rather than commit outright human murder. Nevertheless having done so, he will try to open a metaphysical gateway into this world through which the deathly remains of the Fuhrer's former servants can pass.'

Shilto said, 'What would the observer actually see?'

Dood answered, 'If you were present, I doubt whether you would see an animate body, but you would certainly sense the presence of a manifold and terrible evil. Many hundreds of his servants would return in spirit form; doubtless they might be seen as demons by the sensitive; or alternatively you might see a vision of their former works: barbed wire perhaps, or the image of a flattened city. Perhaps one might have a vision of marching hordes in SS uniform, who knows?'

He looked grim, but continued to speak, 'Once released, they would work to alter the judgement of politicians and remove morality from the experiments of scientists. They would cause harvests to fail and create disease, famine and discord. Johan Pal would effectively control the ghouls he had released and would grow in power and influence. He would be the new Fuhrer in a great new world order: an order which draws its influence from Adolf Hitler and his SS supporters.'

Oakwood said 'I may have had a tendency to sound cynical in the past, but is all this real?'

'I am sorry to say that it is.'

*

'Miss Black, are we ready? I hope to move all our devices and tools into place tomorrow, so we must first remove all the detritus and waste of former years. Once done, we can decorate our crypt using suitable drapes and then dedicate the altar to our master. We must also mark out our symbols upon the floor and the thirteen of us can make ready for our ceremony the following night.'

'Yes, Master. We have met with the remaining nine of our circle and have provided them with suitable clothing and lighting equipment to work underground.'

'Good, then I shall now descend the shaft. I would like you to leave two members in place at its opening, those of suitably strong personality who can deter any interest from the public or from council contractors.'

'Yes Master.'

'Herr Koch, please pass me that Tilley lamp,' he said, as he descended.

Later, in the crypt, he placed the lamp in a prominent position above the floor so that it gave the greatest distribution of useful light. Then, he collected a besom and began to sweep the floor, not however with an arbitrary pattern of movement; he swept from the mid-point to the circumference along many radii. As he did so, he uttered guttural words in a tongue that none recognised.

Around the walls they hung drapes of patterns like those of Johan Pal's own home, rich in colour but infernal in design; he looked on them with satisfaction. Later, he dedicated the altar to his infernal master and as he did so he said, 'I feel this altar may have been dedicated before into a use like our own. However I shall renew that dedication with my own offering.' Upon it, he placed a profane image, sprinkled it with blood and set black candles made from pitch and sulfur.

Then, he began to clear out a depression in the floor in front of it. To a depth of two bricks below the floor, he made a cavity large enough to hold several large black candles and a plate of pewter upon which the candles were impaled by spikes. By its side he placed an urn and all knew that it contained the holy water of a church, stolen earlier and defiled into his purpose. With it, he placed a brazier of a design akin to that of the *feuerschale* used in Nuremberg, although very much smaller.

Around the altar and upon the floor so that it enclosed both urn and brazier, Johan Pal placed concentric circles of chalk and between them, chalk symbols: a mixture of Germanic runes and other forms of lettering. Within the innermost chalk circle, he placed strips of animal skin and lastly, a ring of salt. His design then complete, he set down cushions for their comfort, together with a small table for a feast. Nearby he placed thirteen uniforms and associated flags and insignia. Carefully, they removed outwards traces of their visit, closed the door and tunnel and replaced signs at the entrance outside.

However, as they passed along the tunnel, Carol Black placed her hand on Johan Pal's arm and he stopped and turned around. He said, 'Come now, Miss Black. We cannot let any feeling of affection or passion cloud our judgement; this is our great destiny. We are preparing for the future of the world here.'

Miss Black touched his cheek, nodded and they passed on.

⋆

Bishop, Dood, Shilto and Oakwood were particularly interested in their forthcoming Scottish breakfast and trooped happily down to the dining room of their hotel.

'I want a pair of deep-fried Mars bars with black pudding on fried bread,' said Dood, 'Or maybe deep-fried pizza with brown sauce and salt.'

'Forget it,' said Oakwood, 'not enough calories there. I want a roll-and-pie with brown sauce, followed by a deep-fried butter bomb in Irn Bru batter.'

However they were in fact given a truly excellent traditional breakfast and faced with the general munificence of the table, ate heartily. Then, wearing casual clothing and practical footwear, they drove to Foyers where they parked discreetly. Pleased to walk after their breakfast, they stretched out and walked the mile or so to their destination.

Once there, they made a cursory investigation of Boleskine House from the roadside, without any ingression upon the property itself and then turned their attention to General Wade's Military Road, which they crossed towards the cemetery. They found it tidy, although damp and cold in the morning air. Walking amongst its stones and paths, they could see no evidence of recent human activity and all was apparently peaceful. After a while, Oakwood gesticulated towards the old Mort House. They looked inside in turn, breathed in the damp air, tapped its floor and walls and strolled about. However it contained nothing which attracted their attention.

A little further from the road, they observed some signs which forbade their approach. Approaching nevertheless, they saw a small work-site enclosed by a portable fence and within it, a tarpaulin and metal sheet. Without much debate, they crossed the barrier, removed the tarpaulin and sheet and stared down into a shaft in the ground. At its foot they could see that the shaft changed direction to the horizontal and it was clear from footprints and other marks in the soft soil, that people had been along it. There was also evidence of wooden supports to the horizontal tunnel and a sign which said 'Danger: gas leak.'

'I think we may have found what we are looking for,' said Dood.

'Yes, I believe you are right,' said Shilto, 'but what to do?'

Oakwood said, 'People have clearly worked here very recently. I am happy to climb down and take a look, but we do need a ladder and it will be quite dark in there.'

Dood replied, 'We have most of what we need in the car, no ladder but we do have a knotted rope and lights. I suggest we should leave things as we found them and return in half an hour.'

The four agreed on this course of action and had replaced covers, barriers and signs within five minutes. They returned to the car within twenty minutes and decided to drive it closer to the cemetery. Having done so, they parked once more and with rope, torch and waterproof clothing, Oakwood descended to the bottom of the shaft.

Shilto elected to guard the entrance from passers-by. Dood and Bishop followed Oakwood and stooping, they entered the tunnel into the hillside.

Oakwood said, 'This part has clearly been made within the past couple of weeks; see how the roof has been supported with new timbers. It is muddy too, with seepage from the side. But from here on,' he pointed, 'the walls are made of brick and are far older; and dare I say it, probably more stable too.'

'Yes,' said Bishop, 'the whole tunnel does in fact look stable. There is no subsidence and apart from a bit of condensation, it looks as though drainage is good: see here,' he tapped with his foot, 'there are small holes at intervals in the floor.'

‘Who’s in favour of following it upwards?’ said Dood.

Bishop replied, ‘Well, I think we all are, but mind your head.’

In line, they followed the path already taken several times by Johan Pal and his followers. Eventually, they reached the brick wall and door which he had forced with a lever and passed into the space identified earlier as the remains of the kirk. Like him, they noted soot on walls, general evidence of broken and disused stonework and agreed that a great fire had burned there, probably long before.

However it was clear that they were the only intruders present. ‘Since we are alone,’ said Bishop, ‘we should look around a bit. The entrance has clearly been forced and I am quite sure that people have been here very recently. We are lucky not to have disturbed anyone.’

Oakwood said, ‘I am pleased that we’ve come out into what must be a building; I was concerned by an earth-fall blocking the only way out.’ The others nodded.

‘I know what you mean,’ said Dood, ‘but if this is the kirk, and if there’s no evidence here of Mr Pal, then we need to look elsewhere. There are no other openings to the side and the house must be right above. In fact there may also be something below our present floor level,’ he pointed, ‘So I think we should be looking at the floor. If I look around over here, can you please try over there?’

They looked around until Bishop saw some marks on flagstones of the floor. He said, ‘Look at these scrape-marks and here, this stone is rocking a bit. Mind where you stand, it may not support your weight.’

Within a couple of minutes they had removed enough paving stones for a dark space to be seen below. From it came the characteristic smell of burned paraffin.

Bishop said, ‘This smells rather recent and it’s also warmer down there. I think Mr Pal has been down below only a short while ago. If only we could lift these flagstones up, one of us could get down there.’

'If the two of you get that side, then we can probably do it. These smaller ones are easy,' said Dood.

Slowly and with a few scrapes to their hands, they made a space and were able to enlarge the opening to reveal flagstones below. Bishop shone a light around and saw the brushed flagstones, markings on the floor and the altar with its profane relics.

'My God,' said Dood, 'they have already installed a complete Satanic temple down there.' Nearby were a trestle table, piles of strange clothing and a plate of pewter with black candles. 'And they intend to use it very soon.'

Dood considered the candles and said, 'They need a source of fire, but it looks as though that plate of candles will be placed directly on the brazier. I suppose they could easily make something bigger, but I don't think they could deal with a lot of vapour and smoke underground. Let me nip down for a minute to take a closer look. No, I'll keep my case, thank you.'

He was in the crypt below for no longer than five minutes before he returned. He whispered, 'There's water in that vessel next to the candles and bottles of wine on the table. We have probably disturbed them only a little time before their party. But I have made a few adjustments.' He seemed lost in thought and unwilling to elaborate.

Oakwood now said, 'I think we should replace the flagstones and withdraw quickly. Am I right in thinking there are thirteen of them?' Dood nodded. 'Then for the sake of our safety we should get out now. I would not like to have to wrestle with that lot in the dark. Who knows what might happen.'

'Yes', said Bishop, 'and we need to get ready to crash their party in a better state of preparation.'

They replaced the flagstones in the floor, made good any marks and left via the cellar door and brick tunnel. Rising from the shaft they were helped out by Shilto, who reported no intrusion. Quickly, they replaced the steel sheet, tarpaulin and signs, returned to their car, repacked it and made for the hotel. A little later, their car was replaced by a Transit van which approached slowly and parked at the same spot.

★

'Please carry these hampers Herr Koch and you too, Miss Black. Mr Trapper the wine and Mr Bascher the bag of pitch candles. Senor Vespa I am quite sure I can trust you with the food; I will lead the way with this storm lantern. Would the last of you pull the tarpaulin over the shaft, but do not attempt to move the steel sheet over; it is very heavy and we cannot afford to have difficulties on the return journey. I do not think that there will be any travellers here at this hour, but to be on the safe side I have raised a malevolent spirit at the approach to the Mort House and any trespassers within the tunnel will have the most unpleasant shock. Come now; let us celebrate our destiny in a new world order: the order of the new Fatherland!'

★

'Don't forget,' said Dood, 'we cannot really do much to them at this stage. They are thirteen, let alone any other entity they might raise from beyond. We need to keep quiet, let ourselves in and watch and if we can disrupt their work, so much the better. I must say I am glad I went down into the crypt when we were there. Who knows, perhaps the best I could do has already been done.'

They parked their car a little further away than before and once out, Dood opened his attaché case and distributed herbs in small sacs of muslin. They hung them by small loops around waist and neck and noted the pungent scent that each gave out. Oakwood smelled the combination of asafoetida grass, garlic, copal resin and rue and said, 'This is bad enough to scare any demon away.'

Dood then gave instructions on how to seal the openings of the body with holy water and gave a crucifix to each, together with further phials of holy water, mercury and salt. He also gave each man a powerful Tilley lamp and torch, together with the means of making and keeping fire. Thus armed, they walked towards the opening of the shaft.

'I have an uneasy feeling that we are being watched,' said Dood. 'I believe we can expect a visitor, but there are four of us, so we shall not be so easy to get rid of.'

They began to feel cold; the unearthly chill they had all feared. Oakwood spoke for them all when he said, 'He's trying to scare us. Let's get on with it; I want to get this over and done with.'

Dood took up the rear and Shilto the front. As they walked forward, Shilto saw in their path a greenish glow about five feet from the ground. It hovered, expanded a little and contracted and seemed to radiate malevolence. As they drew closer they could see it had a diffuse outline without a definite boundary, but with an increase in luminosity towards its centre.

Dood whispered, 'It feeds on fear. Without fear, it cannot properly take form. Hold your head up and walk forward.'

It remained a vague and amorphous character with features that were only part-formed. There was a pair of hideous eyes and a crack for a mouth, but neither was of a constant shape. As they approached, their general determination became clear and the entity seemed able to assume a physical presence only by an effort of will. Eventually, it seemed to shrink in anger.

Dood said, 'That thing may scare off a child or a curious individual out for a stroll, but it has the ability only to scare. Johan Pal left it behind as a present, knowing that it would seem worse in a cemetery.' He withdrew a small bundle of dried herbs, set light to one end and threw it. There was a hissing sound, the green light was extinguished and a dissipating green vapour left instead. As they grew near to its former position in front of the shaft, there was only a fading smell; the sweet smoke of burning St John's Wort and the smell of the charnel house had cancelled each other.

Bishop said, 'Callum, give me a hand with this tarpaulin.' He continued, 'Look, the steel plate is already to one side. I bet they are down there now.'

'Yes, and they will want to get out quickly afterwards and will be half-drunk when they do. And as for the sober half, well, that will be a bit 'hemlocked' and won't take too kindly to heavy work for a while.'

Dood continued. 'I had better go down first.' He descended, switched on a torch and went forward.

As they walked in the tunnel, they became unaccountably weary. The electric torches they carried seemed to grow less vigorous as though the batteries they contained were depleted quickly. The tunnel felt increasingly cold and dank and finally, their legs became heavy and their hands awkward and numb. Aware of this, Dood stopped them and said, 'A strong will is attempting to prevent us from passing. We must continue. I will light a hurricane lantern.' They paused while he did so and the increased level of light, the reassuring hiss and slight warmth seemed to dispel their doubt for a while.

After about five minutes they came to the brick wall and saw that the door in it was closed. There, try as he might, Dood felt unable to approach the door further: by raising one leg to take a step, he managed only to place it down at exactly the same spot. His hurricane lamp now became dim and the electric torches gave out completely. They knew that an evil force waited on the other side of the door. It was infinitely greater in strength than the malevolent green glow outside and its will repelled them, yet it wanted them to come to their doom also. For a minute, they contemplated turning around but knew that they could not do so and must go forward. For a while they remained, halted in indecision.

Dood now took his phial of holy water and placed a few drops on the palm of his right hand. Raising his hand, he flicked its contents in the direction of the door and immediately, as if it had been the negation of a curse, they all felt the press of will lessen against them. The hurricane lamp became brighter and at last they were able to advance towards the door. They now exerted their combined physical strength and were able to lever open the door as they had done before and pass through.

On the other side, they advanced towards the kirk. Soon, it became an effort to move forward once more; the battle of wills recommenced and the hurricane lamp gave forth the most feeble light; it also became very cold and the stench of the charnel house returned. They stopped and looked forward, but could see very little.

Suddenly, Oakwood looked behind, gesticulated wildly and grabbed Shilto's arm. There was a hissing sound from behind them and in front and they froze in horror. In the tunnel around them were large snakes.

The serpents moved closer; each was about eight feet long and two inches wide. They were black, but visible in the dark by an eerie phosphorescence and by yellow eyes lit by an evil intelligence within. Slowly, they slithered forwards, with heads raised from the ground, their mouths open and their fangs dripping a foul venom. Their bodies became contracted into coils with a muscular tension: they were preparing to strike. The four men withdrew into a smaller circle and faced their foul opponents.

In the pale glow of the lamp, Dood fumbled for his case with some considerable urgency. His hands shook with fear from the all-pervading sense of evil around them. His movements were slow and it seemed to the others that he did not feel their own sense of urgency. Slowly, the snakes inched closer and were now as little as three feet away. They gave forth a feeling of evil triumph as though they knew their victims were trapped.

Dood opened a small tobacco tin, prised open the lid and laid a thin barrier of powder on the floor behind and in front of them. At its end, he lighted the powder with a match and a flame quickly flourished to make a glowing trail. As it approached the vapour and glowing embers, the rearmost snake reared up and its triumph seemed to fade as it found itself unable to pass.

Bishop whispered, 'What *is* that stuff?'

'It contains dried osha root with a little saltpetre to help it burn. Osha was used as a magical herb by North American native tribes to ward off evil. It was also understood to have great potency against poisonous snakes such as the rattlesnake. Smell the vapour; does it not clear your mind and remove the fear? Now consider what it has done to them. However, we must go forwards.' Dood cast some more osha root in front of them but the second snake could no longer be seen.

Shortly, they reached the kirk and were immediately aware of a subdued noise from below the floor. The incumbents of the crypt had replaced the flagstones in order to lower the amount of noise released above, but they could be observed from cracks in the floor through which a little light could be seen. The four intruders therefore lay upon thc floor in order to peer below.

As they had expected, there were thirteen members of the Satanic group and they were holding hands, facing inwards in a circle. They wore Nazi uniforms and Pal himself had the full regalia, complete with armband and swastika, jackboots and SS insignia at the collar. The onlookers were concerned to see that he also wore a holster. Was it only symbolic or did it contain a real firearm? The circle then broke up and its members made ready to eat and drink.

It was clearly an early part of the ceremony because members of the coven had arrayed a considerable spread on the trestle table and in a considered fashion were now starting to collect platefuls of food, which they took to convenient corners of the room in order to eat. There was an ample supply of food, but it was rather simpler than the usual fare on such occasions; there was a broth and black bread and bratwurst sausage, together with dumplings and a frothy beer; it was clearly intended to emulate the rations of those they wished to raise. Although simple, they ate it with great gusto and barely a morsel was left afterwards.

Oblivious to the dank, cold air, each participant now removed his or her shirt and applied a liniment to shoulders and chest. Its effect was observed with five minutes; Johan Pal and his twelve associates began to sway from side to side or twirl like a top; some fell prostrate and raised themselves; they all howled like the demons they wished to become.

Shortly, they removed further clothing and a period of licentiousness followed, during which the onlookers above removed their gaze. It was a while before they were sated, but eventually they replaced their clothing in order to continue.

The thirteen now reformed their circle and faced inwards. Johan Pal lit the large black candles on the altar, together with smaller ones on the plate of pewter. Dood had been correct in his guess, because Pal placed the whole plate on the brazier rather than light a larger fire.

Shilto whispered to Dood, 'Do they need to raise another demon?' To which Dood replied, 'I think not, Pal has already raised Hitler and can do so again.'

As if in reply, the thirteen now droned an incantation and Pal spoke words which they had heard before. The sinister words of the ceremony of necromancy were guttural, as was the reply, an evil whisper in that evil place, *'öffnen sie das tor und lassen meine anhänger'* and as before, they observed a glow in the outstretched skeletal hand of the former Fuhrer.

Pal then killed a small animal, which squeaked away its last moments while blood dripped into a metal bowl. He passed the bowl around and all made a mark in blood on their forehead. The remainder, a few drops in Pal's hands once more, were dashed into the candle flames.

Dood whispered, 'The description of this ceremony spoke of a portal arising within a place of fire. Look, the flames are increasing in size above those candles. And there, Pal is grinding a small piece of bone with a pestle and mortar. He has just thrown a little powder into the flames.'

As he whispered, the candle-light grew to a new height and Pal looked around in triumph as an ethereal spectre began to form in it; it was the reverse of Dante's vision of Lucifer eating the treacherous Judas Iscariot and they imagined for an instant that Lucifer had now disgorged a treacherous soul. It was clear that a gate was now open and the thirteen members of the circle muttered in fear and bowed low.

Dood and his companions felt the same awe and waited for the legions of Hitler's supporters to come forth. They felt they had failed to influence matters and were now in danger of their own lives. Nevertheless, Dood patted them on the shoulder; the others knew that he was not quite ready to run. They settled once more to watch the conclusion of the ceremony.

Johan Pal now raised the water flagon from the floor and dipped a ladle into it. Withdrawing the ladle, he began to flick defiled water around the crypt. It fell onto the altar, onto the participants and into the fiery portal itself. But suddenly there was a scream from one of them. A large flame, dark red and very hot, billowed outwards and engulfed him. Something had gone wrong and a panic ensued; they all knew in legend the result of a magical ceremony gone amiss: there would be pain and retribution. All semblance of order within the crypt now turned to chaos.

Above, Dood, Shilto and the others seemed to see another version of Dante's vision. The portal closed and those evil spirits previously disgorged were engorged again. Fire was released everywhere and the crypt began to burn.

Dood said, 'Run.'

The four onlookers now fled back the way they had come. As they ran, Bishop said, 'What happened?'

Dood, somewhat breathless, replied, 'Yesterday, when I went down there, I threw out the contents of the water flagon, cleaned it and replaced it with undefiled holy water. I also removed some salt and replaced it with sand. They defiled their own ceremony with holy water and the circle of salt was broken so they had no protection from the forces they raised. Their work went wrong and now they are paying the price just as Aleister Crowley and his antecedents probably did. We must get out quickly.'

The four of them fled down the way they had come, but they heard shouting behind them and knew that their enemies were aware of their presence and were trying to climb out and follow them. Despite the heat of the fire, Shilto, at the rear of the party, began to feel a new cold behind him. It was the cold of embodied evil and as before, his legs became slow, heavy and difficult to move. Very soon, the others felt the same sense of trying to run through seawater, their speed dropped and they knew that Pal was exerting all his remaining strength in order to prevent their escape. For an instant, Bishop mused on being able to feel the heat of flames and the cold of evil together and was quite unable to explain how, although able to feel them both.

Suddenly, Shilto heard a diabolic hissing and at the same moment, he felt a bite to his leg. Turning, he saw a snake – one of the pair seen earlier – slither out of the way, its job done. He tried to run, but felt a numbness in his ankle, which, together with the will holding them back, made his progress slow. At length he slowed to a stop and said, 'You go on, I am afraid he's got me this time.' He felt Pal's satisfaction, very close behind.

The others stopped and Bishop said, 'Never. You're coming with us, it's all or none.'

Now Dood took up station behind and as the others inched forwards, he stood, ready to confront their pursuers. A gap opened up, so that Bishop, Oakwood and Shilto, slow though they were, drew ahead. They knew that this final confrontation was that which they had all supposed would one day take place.

They could still hear screams behind them as some members of the coven tried to flee from the flames. There was smoke also and a draught, so that hot air and embers drifted towards them as they fled. Dood thought, 'There was very little down there to burn; those flames must be the heat of Hell itself.' If so, it was terrifying.

Shilto began to feel the numbness spread up his calf and his breath came in gasps. The three escapees could smell smoke and found it increasingly difficult to draw their breath, which became laboured and more painful with the increasing temperature. Eventually, they came to the foot of the upright shaft and mounted it by means of their knotted rope. Shilto found it difficult to do so and he collapsed on the grass at the top. Lying down, he pulled up his trouser leg and examined the puncture wounds made by the serpent below.

His leg had started to become swollen and the two incisions were weeping a yellow trail. He knew that unless he could obtain treatment quickly, his time had probably come. The numbness too, was now spreading towards his knee.

'Here,' said, Bishop, 'we can use a thin section of rope.' Using a knife, he part-cut the rope and unwound a section. Then, placing it around Shilto's calf, he made a loop, passed the loose end through and tied a further loop in the emerging end. Finally, he chose a stout peg from the edge of the tarpaulin nearby. By passing it through the vacant loop, he was able to twist and make the rope constrict about Shilto's calf muscle. Since it was dark, they were unable to see how successful they had been in restricting the spread of poison, but with Shilto's leg quickly becoming stiff, they helped him reach the car, left him with the ignition key and returned to the shaft to help Dood if they could.

*

With his three friends waiting above, Dood turned to face the direction of the crypt, from which he could see a human figure advancing. There were screams there and he guessed that several participants had been caught by flames and by the black smoke now filling the tunnel. However coming towards him was Johan Pal himself. To Dood's consternation, he carried with him the disassembled remains of the Magdeburg Relic and running, thrust it into a canvas bag as he moved. He muttered to himself, 'I can't afford a direct confrontation; can only slow him.'

Dood's attaché case was still heavy in his hand and considering it, he decided to use as many of its remaining contents as he could. Quickly, he grabbed a crucifix and thrust it into a drainage hole in the brick floor. Then, grabbing handfuls of the various impedimenta in test tubes, he sprinkled barriers of salt, holy water and asafoetida in the tunnel. Pal was by now close and Dood turned and ran as soon as he could.

As he ran, he heard curses and shouting and at the entrance to the shaft, looked upwards and saw Bishop and Oakwood waiting for him. As he grasped the rope, they pulled him up bodily, but as he reached the top, he looked down and saw the dark shape of Pal below. It had probably taken a great effort of will to cross the barrier he had made in the tunnel – had that saved him from Pal? It was perhaps so; he would probably have been caught had he been delayed by another thirty seconds. However, since the rope was now drawn up, there was no longer an opportunity for Pal to reach him. He felt the anger and hatred in Pal's voice as he heard him say, 'We shall meet again and when we do…'

They ran over the grass to the waiting car and Oakwood started the engine and pulled away. They arrived back at their hotel at two o'clock in the morning, let themselves in and were silent and shaking when they reached their rooms. At first, Oakwood offered to sit with Shilto while the other two rested, yet after an hour of watching, it was clear that Shilto had lapsed into a semi-conscious state and was on the verge of becoming delirious. Shortly, Oakwood decided to wake the other two and was pleased to find that they were refreshed. Returning to Shilto's room, Dood examined his wound.

He said, 'His leg is starting to swell and turn black. We must help, but we don't know how. Up here in Scotland, and at this time, it might be six hours before we could find any conventional antidote, even if we knew what kind of anti-venom to use. All I can say is that whatever kind of snake it was, it certainly wasn't Scottish.'

Oakwood said, 'It must be two hours since he was bitten. What could we tell a doctor anyway? Was it real venom? Do we call a doctor out, only to tell him that Adam was bitten by a ghostly snake from Hell?'

Dood countered, 'It was an evil elemental: the ghoul of a snake. It had enough low intelligence to kill or maim and the puncture wound is real, but we cannot know what the venom was.'

He stated the obvious, 'Someone could make an incision with a scalpel and suck the poison out…'

They all sat and thought further for a while. Eventually, Dood sat up and said, 'I will try…' but his sentence petered out. He sat in silence for another minute and then became more animated: 'Get me some boiling water, a knife and saucer.' The others obliged.

He opened his attaché case and withdrew a small piece of a dried root. Cutting it with the knife, he recut each part several times and by grinding the fragments with the serrated edge, eventually obtained enough grated fragments of dry root to immerse in boiling water in the saucer. The root absorbed a little water and immediately, the room filled with a bitter medicinal smell. He held the saucer close to Shilto's face and the vapour seemed to make him stir and become more at ease.

Next, he collected the damp, finely-divided root and applied it as a poultice to swollen or dark areas of flesh and tied it in place with a handkerchief. Lastly, he grated further dry root, mixed it with a little saltpetre in a dish and using a cigarette lighter, played a flame over the mixture. There was a crackle and splutter as the mixture started to burn and they smelled the same bitter smell as before, but more pungent and probably more efficacious.

Holding the plate a few inches only from Shilto's face, he said, 'Better to cough and splutter than to die of snakebite. That's the best I can do for a while.'

'What's in that stuff,' said Oakwood, 'isn't there something more scientific we can try?'

Dood replied, 'Aspirin was only a folk remedy until its value was understood by science. Country people first used it as a painkiller by chewing willow root. They also used a liniment of willow on a swollen fetlock.'

'But this wasn't willow?'

'No, it was snakeroot. A poultice of it was used by early Americans to counter rattlesnake bites. Also the Chickasaw people used the smoke of white snakeroot to revive the unconscious. They were closer to nature than we now understand. I was able to burn the dry root successfully because I mixed it with saltpetre, a substance which I also used earlier tonight. It breaks down when heated to give oxygen, which is essential for combustion; it is very good at giving smokes and useful vapours and I even use it to keep some of my cigars alight. But your point remains, what are the smoke and poultice doing to Adam? The answer is nothing yet; please give him time.'

Dood finally said, 'I've had a bit of sleep and can happily stay here for the time being. I don't think we need to worry about Mr Pal tonight; we know he has devilish powers and could do us harm if he chose to, but I think he will leave us to another occasion. Also, he will need to recover after his ordeal and will probably take stock after having lost so many of his henchmen.'

'Yes,' said Bishop, 'many perished.'

'I am sorry if they were burned or smoked out, but I've no plans to go back immediately. In any case, we must stay here until daytime. I would suggest both of you should return to your rooms and sleep as best you can.'

When they had left, Dood stayed to watch Shilto. Before, he had been semi-delirious, sweating, and with involuntary movements and strained breathing. Now, he was properly asleep and more relaxed. The vapour of snakeroot was still in the room and its acrid, medicinal quality seemed to bring him ease. The poultice also seemed to adhere to poisoned, darkening flesh and where it did so, surrounding areas were pink as though the flow of blood had improved. However, despite all, Dood now closed his eyes and slumbered until dawn.

When he woke, it was to the smell of coffee. Both Oakwood and Bishop were present, but Shilto was still asleep and the smell of snakeroot was gone in the fresh air from an open window. After a cup of coffee, they looked again at the snake-wound.

The poultice had stuck to the wound, but it could be removed easily and underneath, they could see only the brown colour of bruising. They smiled and poured more coffee. Dood then said, 'We should investigate this herb further; ten thousand years of hand-me-down medicine cannot be ignored.'

Sitting up, his eyes open, Shilto smiled in agreement.

Later, and fortified by another generous breakfast at their hotel, they compared notes. Shilto said, 'Johan Pal left those snakes in the tunnel to get rid of intruders. That bite was very painful and had it not been for snakeroot, I think it would have finished me.'

'Yes,' said Dood, 'but now it may be Pal who is finished. I think he may have lost his coven in that crypt.'

'Lost them all?' said Bishop.

'Many anyway; did you hear those screams?'

'Yes, I did. But he was single-minded enough to collect all of his important bits of hardware: book, candles, relics; you mentioned a canvas bag. Do you think he went back for his friends?'

'I doubt it.'

'Can he work without his coven?'

'Debatable. If he recovers enough, he might.'

'So he's probably still in business. What will he do?' said Oakwood.

'I don't doubt that he will find somewhere to lie low and recuperate. Later, well, I am sure that he won't just give up. He will probably work towards a repeat performance, but somewhere else.'

'But going back to the crypt, what actually happened to them?' said Bishop.

'As I said last night, I managed to switch his pitcher of defiled water for sanctified holy water. That alone might have stopped everything working, but don't forget, we also sent him some carefully altered pages of his magical treatise. One change was that the coven was within circles of salt and chalk instead of outside. It may be that Pal and his friends were imprisoned inside with whatever forces they had released, but I also broke the circle when I was down in the crypt beforehand. Either way, I don't know quite what happened then, apart from the fact that there was a sudden release of fire. Perhaps they released the mythical fires of Hell through their portal. Anyway, they set light to the crypt and probably themselves also.'

Later, Bishop and Dood took Shilto out for a walk in the grounds of the hotel. Shilto looked a bit grim and limped a little, but he had taken on board a good amount of breakfast and was of a strong constitution. The Scottish air was clean and filled their lungs. After a couple of turns around the grounds they were warm and comfortable, although still in need of sleep.

Meanwhile, Oakwood turned on the television at 9.00 am and he and Dood watched a local news programme for a while. There was some general news, but after a few minutes the reporter introduced a more local news feature. They recognised the scenery around Boleskine House immediately and sat up to listen.

The reporter said, 'Last night, there was a fire below Boleskine House, the well-known former home of the magician

Aleister Crowley – the self-dubbed most evil man in Britain. This house has been a magnet for the adherents of magic over the years and was also owned by Jimmy Page, the guitarist of Led Zeppelin. It is not known how the fire was caused, but we can now speak to a spokesman from the local Fire Services, who will be able to tell us more.'

The spokesman said, 'The fire was probably caused by faulty wiring in an electrical conduit underneath the property itself. I would like to emphasise that no part of the house itself was at fault. There was some smoke damage to the cellar below the house, but apart from a lot of smoke, no flame reached the main fabric of the building, which was completely undamaged. We have not yet gone into the cellar or foundations, but thus far, have been content to pump water into it.'

'The house has a chequered history, does it not?'

'That may be, but I am afraid I cannot comment on a lot of superstition. I am quite sure that the antics of previous owners can have had no bearing on its susceptibility to fire last night and the house itself does seem to have been quite resistant.'

'But there have been two major fires there in the past!'

'That is well-documented, but this does seem to have been rather different. We do not think that anyone was present at the time, so we are not expecting any bad news when we clean up.'

Somewhat chastened, the commentator moved to another story and Oakwood turned the television off.

Later, they drove to Bolskine House and watched the firemen work, but the smoke had gone and when Dood asked one of them about the fire, the fireman said, 'It wasn't serious. There was little damage and it will be easy to clean up.' He looked weary, 'And we shall be giving advice about fire prevention, just in case.'

To his friends Bishop said, 'Someone is trying to keep the worst details out of the newspapers.'

A few minutes later, Dood and Oakwood crossed the road and ventured towards the cemetery. Behind the old Mort

House, they found no trace of signs, barriers, steel sheet or tarpaulin. Oakwood said, 'Look, the shaft has been filled and even the turf has been replaced. I wonder by whom?' Then he said, 'If that was Pal and I bet it was, what do you think he will do now?'

Dood replied, 'If I were in his position, I would probably go home, although I doubt to my own house. After all, he knows the area and has to find somewhere familiar in a hurry. I think he will try to use the local features there. That is, if he still has all his paraphernalia saved after last night.'

Oakwood said, 'Yes, but I think he will also want revenge. Success with his grand project will give him all the revenge he needs. If he moves quickly, he can avoid attention and still get what he wants.'

'Are you talking about those stones on the downs? One of them was supposed to have covered a portal or gateway.'

'Yes, I am.'

Chapter Twelve

Carn Brea

Johan Pal and Carol Black had returned to the shaft and filled its entrance at four o' clock in the morning. It had taken an hour to replace the earth, but that had been a task made easier by the fact that underneath its tarpaulin, it had been placed on a wooden board which, by being tipped, sent its burden down the shaft, leaving only a few tracks on the grass as evidence. It had been messy, but they had made good and were away by half past five in the morning. Rain had made the ground seem less disturbed, had flattened a few unattended perturbations here and there, and the fire services had not arrived until they were long gone. In fact, the fire had been restricted to the crypt where it had been hellish hot, and smoke only was revealed in the cellar above.

Carol Black mused upon the events of the previous night. She said to Johan Pal, 'How many of the others escaped?'

'There are now only two of us; the others were unable to escape the fire and smoke. We were tricked. Our researches went wrong and I know why. We lost control because somebody had been down into the crypt beforehand. Obviously, we have an adversary who knows more about magical practices than we had given him credit for. I am severely weakened and will not be able to conduct another ritual for a few days until I recover my powers. At the moment, I cannot even divine the future, let alone seek guidance from my mentors on the astral or bring influence to bear on the lives of other people.'

'And who was that adversary, Master?' She put her hand on his arm, as if in comfort.

'He is called Callum Dood. We have met before and I know him to be an investigator of occult phenomena for his church. I also believe him to be a white magician of considerable power himself; well-versed in herbal lore and in the devices and charms for defence against us.'

'But he has confederates also?'

'Yes, that is certain. At one time, he was helped and aided to a degree by our own neophytes, sadly, our influence over them waned; they seem to have returned to their former lives and are now removed from our world; I shall desist from further involvement with them. Dood, however, is ably assisted by his Archdeacon, Adam Shilto, by a local villager Wally Bishop, and by Peyton Oakwood, an individual whom I have certainly observed on the astral plane several times. We must also consider that Creighton Brakespeare, our dealer of antiquarian books, may himself have been influenced by Dood. However I still find Brakespeare's services useful and I shall restrict my attention to Dood and his friends.'

'And the police?'

'Yes, it has not escaped my attention that they are interested in us, yet they are no closer to finding us than before.'

'What now?'

Johan Pal checked that his canvas bag still contained the Magdeburg Relic and the other useful items: magical treatise, candles and costumes and upon establishing that it did, placed it in his Transit van, newly-painted and unadorned by slogans. He said, 'We need to pay a visit to our friend in Cambridge,' and started the engine.

That evening, they booked into a costly hotel in the city and ate a meal together. Later, Carol Black said, 'Master…?'

'Very well, Carol.'

*

A day later, Johan Pal called unannounced on Creighton Brakespeare at his shop in Cambridge.

'Mr Brakespeare, you appear to be quite busy today?'

'Certainly I am busy, but as always I would be pleased to show you our latest stock prior to sale. We do have some interesting…'

'That will have to wait. I would like to collect the last fifteen pages of the Clavicule of Soloman and I do mean the originals rather than pages that were copied. You will be aware that they are overdue now and must be inserted into the volume itself.'

'Let me get rid of these last few customers and then I can close the shop.'

Fifteen minutes later, Brakespeare went to his safe and withdrew the package marked with Johan Pal's name. He passed it to Pal, who opened it and carefully counted out the pages. Then, picking up one particular page he said, 'Please can you tell me why this differs from the corresponding page you emailed to me?'

'I had no choice. I received a visit from the police and from a gentleman by the name of Callum Dood. They asked me many questions about my relationship with you. I had no alternative other than to answer truthfully about having dealt with you. They asked how we corresponded and I said, truthfully again, by email.'

'Thank you. Please continue.'

'My email was the only way of contacting you. When I told them why I needed to, Dood said he would transact the email for me. I had no alternative other than to do as they asked; I could not realistically refuse to cooperate, despite the rule of confidentiality which I always exert with clients.'

'Yes, I see.'

Pal continued, 'It is clear that you have been open with me, a fact which I respect. Further, I agree that you had no alternative in your actions; it was not your fault that the police investigated our relationship or that Dood made disappointing alterations to a page of text. However, now that I have my properly restored pages, my immediate concern has been removed and I may now leave. Nevertheless, I must ask that upon my departure, you do not yourself contact the police or Dood for a period of twenty-four hours. I remain willing to patronise your business and I do not try to make it a condition of business that you do not contact them; I know that such a step would destroy the basis of equality upon which business is transacted. I also know that you are friendly with Dood, Bishop and the others and cannot be dissuaded from being so. However my request arises solely from our own personal dealings and the consideration that is engendered from it.'

'Yes of course; I cannot promise that Dood or the police will not *get in touch with me*, but I have not seen either for a few days now and have no expectation of them doing so. I cannot therefore imagine that I will be a nuisance to you.'

'Thank you, Mr Brakespeare,' said Johan Pal, and left with his restored pages of vellum.

*

Two days later a Transit van stopped at the premises of a plant hire company near Devizes and Pal, confident in his outfit of hard hat and blue overalls, entered.

He said, 'I would like to book a digger.'

'Yes, Sir, what size and for how long?'

'I have to move a number of large rocks from my own land because they are impeding its allocation to agricultural use. I would expect the work to be done in a day, but I can book it for longer to make sure.'

'Well, Sir, we have a 1.5 Ton Mini Digger, which is great for most digging work and in fact it is also capable of serious concrete breaking if you use the breaker attachment.'

'How deep can it go?'

'It will dig to a 3 metre depth and we can provide a driver for the day too, for an extra hundred. My operator has a standard post-1997, 3.5 Ton driving licence and he can tow it for you as well.'

'Very good, can he start in two days time?'

'Let me see my computer. Yes, that's fine.'

★

Somewhat later, Don Regan was with his sheepdog on the downs and once more counting sheep in the manner of those parts: 'ain, tain, tethera, methera, mimp, ayta…'

His dog raised an ear as Regan stopped at 'ayta.'

Loosely translated into English, Regan said to his dog, 'We must go a bit further to find them.' The dog apparently understood his tone of voice and growled.

Striding over the downs in a purposeful manner, they came to the ley line and walked upon it since Regan knew that sheep, as with other animals, are often sensitive enough to follow electrical stimuli or other natural perturbations they may find.

In the distance, Regan observed three people, one of whom was in the cabin of a digger of moderate size. It was not wholly unusual for a mechanical digger to be so far away from main roads; there were ditches to make and channels by bridleways. Nevertheless, it was unusual or even remarkable for ancient stones, probably of the Neolithic age, to be dug around or possibly even dug up.

As the driver drove, the onlookers gesticulated so that the bucket ran square along the side of the stone. It went deeper and broke ground that had not been broken for three thousand years. That stone was notable amongst local people, who spoke of it in hushed tones, but as he watched, the trench was continued around a corner and along a second side.

Regan stopped in order to tell his dog what to do. It set off rather gruffly to round up sheep with the names – or numbers – dora and dik. The enterprising hound then sent them towards the main flock a short distance away.

As Regan watched, earth was piled neatly on the ground and the trench enlarged to a depth of at least four feet. At length, the digger placed the edge of its bucket underneath the stone and exerting a considerable force, raised it on one side. The stone toppled onto the grass and the two onlookers peered down into the space it had left with some satisfaction.

It was clear there was some feature within the trench which they wished to cover, because they placed a board of marine plywood over it and some soil on the edges. Still, as long as his sheep were away, it was not Regan's business to ask. As the light started to fail, he made sure his sheep were enclosed by a fence and the ewes were in the barn. He had to consider that there were still a few people about in big SUVs.

Later, after his evening meal, he relaxed in an armchair and considered the stone and digger in more detail. After a while, he felt rather thirsty and decided to walk down to Peckling village for two or three pints of cider. It was a decent walk but he did not take his dog with him; better to let it rest.

At the Dog and Duck, Regan sat in the corner and sipped his scrumpy, a pleasant concoction of 8% strength, but without the sweetness of some modern proprietary brews. He chose to drink from a traditional quart pewter mug which Libby Long kept for him behind the bar. Not far away was Callum Dood, who turned to wave. Dood was talking to Libby, but later on, he joined Regan.

'*Fiddler gannets*[12], Don, how are the sheep? Are they safe and sound these days or are you still on the lookout for trouble? And how is that old dog of yours? I bet he must be a good eight years old by now. I expect he likes to toast his toes by the fire?'

'Ah, *perther mire-rats*[13]. Old Kei[14] is fine, thanks. The sheep are behind a locked gate and the ewes are in the barn tonight.'

'Why?'

---

12 *Cf fatla genes; Cornish*

13 *Cf Cornish Pur dha, meur ras: very well, thanks.*

14 *Kei: dog*

'I'm sorry to say that a few strange folk have returned to the neighbourhood.'

'And what's so strange about them?'

'They were pulling up stones but why, I don't know. There was a large mechanical digger at work on a very large stone at Carn Brea, you know it?'

'Yes, I certainly do. What happened?'

'The digger pulled a stone up and left it on its side. They covered up something inside the hole but it wasn't that itself they were interested in. I doubt whether they meant to leave it very long.'

'Is there anything else you can tell me?'

'Not really, except that the digger was from PK plant hire at Devizes.'

'How big was the digger?'

'Well, last time I used one it was for digging ditches and my digger was two tons. I reckon the one I saw was less, maybe one and a half ton.'

'Thank you Don. How are you off for cider?'

'I'll be alright if I get through this. And besides, it don't cost nothing to put the land back to rights.'

The next day, Dood picked up the telephone and spoke to the proprietor of PK Plant Hire. He said, 'I am interested in a medium sized mechanical digger for about a week. Can you please tell me what you have available?'

'Well Sir, what do you mean by medium size? We have three ton down to 1.5 ton.'

'Can I call to see the 1.5 ton machine?'

'Ordinarily you could, but I am afraid it will be out for the next two days. Chap hired it three days ago and collected it the day before yesterday.'

'That's OK. It isn't urgent and I can call back again.'

Later, he spoke to Bishop, Shilto and Oakwood by webcam, since all of them were at home. He said, 'I think our villain has surfaced and he intends to try something out again quite soon.

I think he has hired a digger and taken it onto the downs. It sounds as though he intends to do something within the next day or two.'

'I thought you said he would be washed out for a while?' said Oakwood.

'That may be, but being exhausted in astral terms need not stop him doing something else: by getting some 'honest' groundwork done instead, he would have a natural break in which to recover. At any rate, this call is to let you know that I would like to keep an eye on the place by myself for a while. There are probably no more than two or three of them and if they get difficult I will let you know.'

'Well, if you are happy with all that…'

'I am, and by the way, I will give you regular updates.'

Bishop said, 'I am just down the road and Adam is almost as near.'

Dood said, 'About the boys in blue. As we decided, I'm not going to get in touch with them just yet. I've no doubt they are keeping an eye on us anyway.'

The others said, 'OK,' and the conversation ended in a discussion about curry, beer, aches and pains and the weather.

That night, Dood collected a few bits and pieces to put in his pocket, grabbed a dark coat and hat and walked out into the cold. He traversed pathways onto the hillside and strode over hoarfrost crisp on the grass. The path, well-known to him, was a collection of bridleways and rutted chalk paths barely altered in three thousand years. Eventually he came to a particular group of standing stones and turned north to follow the ley line. Swinging his pendulum, he occasionally checked the direction of the line as he went.

He slowed down when he was within half a mile of the stone that old Regan had mentioned. He had intended to watch it until someone turned up, but there was no need to wait because it was immediately clear that torches were being used by two people nearby.

The mechanical digger had long gone, together with its driver. By now, he was able to recognise Pal and Black and both bustled round with a wooden board taken from within the trench revealed by removal of the stone. Laying it aside, they looked downwards into the trench and seemed pleased.

★

Don Regan was a thoughtful man and quiet. He had seen much of the ways of the world and believed in conserving and saving. Instinctively, he disliked the very old altar stone being removed, laid on its side and disrespected. It had always been there and should have been left in place; almost every large stone in the neighbourhood had its name in the old tongue; some were notorious and feared, but all were respected. This stone was known as Carn Brea; he had never seen below it and did not wish to be the first; he felt that it was a bad thing for it to be disturbed by outsiders and especially by those who were not *drewithion*[15].

And he could get along with those who, simply from their own misfortune, were not *drewithion*. He had always lived in equilibrium with the Church and liked Dood, just as he knew he was respected in turn. Druids and the church could happily live together; Regan made a point of attending church on its main festivals, just as Dood had failed to remove a modest stone effigy in his churchyard there. Call her what they might: Isis or Damara, names came and went, yet they both knew that she remained to offer life to those who remembered her. But these newcomers, with their mechanical digger, they were an upset to the natural order of things. They suggested that nature was dissatisfied; perhaps that the earth needed blood.

Blood! It was revered by him, but unlike Pal, it was respected by him also. It was the very essence of life; his *tas*[16]

---

15 Drewithion: druids

16 Tas: father

had taught him so, and his *tasowd*[17] before him. It could be shed under certain circumstances: only when the land required it or when annual reverence was due. Then, it could renew and give strength; the *dore*[18], the old oak: it needed to sip ox blood once per year, but the land did not ask for the blood of a man.

Regan mused; he and his friends had given enough warning. The painted face of the watcher had been refreshed; they had added the screams and howls of the big cat to the glade where the oaks still stood. Yet the outsiders had defiled the standing stones with a sheep's head and with entrails. What now, with Carn Brea open, and on its side? The time had come.

Regan sipped cider from his pewter mug and warmed himself by the fire. With his reflections at the Dog and Duck complete, he spoke to Maxton Mawr at the piano. Mawr, usually a pleasant and reserved individual, said little, but his eyes glinted behind his glasses and as he nodded, he was tight-lipped. He continued his rendition of All the Nice Girls Love a Sailor on the piano and his voice, fortified by a glass of ginger wine, was hearty. However later, he could be seen to speak quietly to Libby Long and to make a couple of telephone calls. Thereafter, the business of the public house continued until closing time, following which there were shadowy movements outside in the dark.

Regan walked home and sat in his armchair for only a short time before going out again. By then it was 11pm, but his evening was not yet over. Within an hour he had walked a further three miles, had stopped at the homes of several of his friends and they in turn had also strolled off, quite uncharacteristically for that time of night. At 1pm, Regan went to bed.

The next night was the sixth of the new moon, when she was a waxing crescent in a night associated with success, harmony and equilibrium; it was a night in which she whom

17 *Tasowd: grandfather, lit. father old*

18 *Dore: oak*

they called *lor*[19] would rise to be a ripening sickle. Regan left his sheep in the field and his sheepdog in the care of a relative. He went into a barn and ascended to its eaves, an upper storey with wooden floorboards and much straw: a store for the rest of the winter. Under some straw was a large oaken box, which he unlocked to remove an assortment of white clothing, together with a golden sickle. The sickle was in fact a very valuable item: made from solid gold and with gold wire on the handle, it had been his great grandfather's property and might yet be that of his young nephew.

Later, Regan met twenty like-minded folk from villages thereabouts. Libby Long was there, as was Maxton Mawr and other notables. Like Regan they wore white and ascended to the woods where Shilto and Dood had uncovered the ruse of the 'big cat.' Together, they led two oxen there, with symbolic horns.

Shortly, they surrounded an oak tree; it was almost as large as the well-known Big Belly oak of Savernake Forest but had no name and was unknown to the tourist. Regan ascended the oak and with his golden sickle, cut branches and sheaves of a herb for which the local names were ihelvar or sometimes allheal. Elsewhere, folk knew it mostly as mistletoe, but it had the same significance whatever called.

With strands of ihelvar Regan bound the horns of the oxen and sacrificed them with his golden sickle. Their blood drained into a dish and was offered to the God Taran[20]. He also sprinkled a little blood around the roots of the oak tree; a gift of the strength of the oxen to the soil and the maker of a vitality that would soon be that of the oak itself. Later, the bodies of the oxen were collected, correctly butchered and the meat shared by all.

---

19 *Lor: local celtic, the moon*

20 *Taran, Common Celtic for the God Taranis, cf Cornish Taran: thunder; Thunor: Old English thunder*

As Regan cut the mistletoe, they all bowed their heads since they revered it as the seed of Taranis. It was His gift to the oak which ensured that the sun would return and an assurance of the continuing life which they all revered.

Later, they drank an infusion of allheal just as their forebears had done for thousands of years. It had a special place amongst them and had long been used as a remedy for domestic ailments, but today it had a greater purpose. They drank it to purify their blood and to enhance their own fertility. They would also add allheal to the drinking water of their farm animals and they could see that they were right to do so; their ewes were in lamb and the hens were broody. Finally, sprigs of allheal were collected to hang in their homes and the white berries were taken to further oak trees nearby and placed on the larger boughs where they might grow.

When they had finished in the oak glade, the party walked to the altar stone that Pal had disturbed with his digger. Under the light of the crescent moon, they surrounded the stone, pulled away the tarpaulin and holding hands with their backs to it, danced in a circle, to-and-fro, around the deep pit that had been revealed.

Turning around, they offered a little ox blood to the soil, and casting allheal into the pit, danced to evoke what happiness they could at what they saw. There was thunder overhead, which they duly noted.

And later, with Taranis beseeched and supplicated, they returned home, leaving the stone as it was; the pit open to the elements and the heavy, ominous rumble of encroaching thunder over the downs. They had made their preparations and one night soon, would return and finally put the matter to rest so that the stone and the countryside around would be quiet again.

*

'Ah, Mr Shilto and Mr Dood, whereabouts are your friends today?'

'Oh, Peyton Oakwood is with his unit at present. He was obliged to return because he had been away for quite a while. Creighton Brakespeare is in Cambridge; he seems so busy these days. Of course, Wally and Amelia Bishop are here, and so is Emily. They are up the road if you wish to speak to them.'

Nicholby replied, 'I am glad they are well. Anyway, we all know about our good friend Johan Pal and I am pleased to have had your telephone call. How did you know he had returned to this area?'

Shilto said, 'We suspect, that is all, and so we think you should know. However, we do have one concrete piece of information.'

'Yes, please.'

'Emily Robertson said that she saw one of his henchmen, or is it henchwomen?'

'How?'

'Emily was in Devizes. I don't know why, but she mentioned that she saw Carol Black there. The two of them are quite close, that is to say, Black and Pal are, rather than Emily.'

'Is that all?'

'It's just that we think they might be working in this area again.'

'Come, now, surely this general feeling must be based on more?'

Dood broke in, 'Yes, I suppose it is. We have battled against them for quite a long time and I seem to have developed a sixth sense about them. But even without that, the mood of the locals in the village and the atmosphere in the pub in the evenings tells me a lot. They have been chatting again about unrest in the neighbourhood.'

'What kind of unrest?'

'They don't say much, but I can tell. They look serious, get into a huddle and there's a nod and a wink. The sheep get taken into the barn overnight and the locals disappear for an evening.'

'And you want the place watched?'

'That is for you to decide. We thought we owed you a call, that's all.'

'I am glad you did. In fact, the stink in the papers hasn't gone away. The Germans know that Pal came back here and the fact that we have been rather quiet suggests to everybody that we haven't been able to do much. Incidentally, although nothing came out in print, we do know there were the bodies of about ten or eleven people found in Scotland in a blaze near Loch Ness. We kept it out of the papers.'

'Why?'

'It was the burned remains of satanic regalia we found there. And our investigations disclosed that most of the deceased actually came from around here and were probably also present in Nuremberg.'

'And Johan Pal?'

'He wasn't found there.'

'Do the Germans know?'

'No! That would be very embarrassing for us. Let's just keep quiet about it, shall we? We do know you were there, by the way, because we kept an eye on you. How did you get on with the Scottish breakfast?'

'It was very good.'

'But the idea is still that we get hold of the fellow, hold a massive press conference and then everyone goes away happy. What we do not want is a headline in the *New York Times* or *Frankfurter Allgemeine Zeitung* saying 'British authorities fail to apprehend murderer with links to Nazism and devil worship after fire in Satanic crypt in Scotland.'

'We thought you wouldn't.'

⋆

Dood and Shilto put on warm clothes and actively chose black in order to remain as inconspicuous as possible. Then, walking onto the downs via familiar paths, they made towards the altar stone. It was the eighth night after the crescent moon and it was foggy in the village as they left: a fog which the wind had only partly blown away above higher ground.

For about two or three evenings beforehand, Dood had made a point of being sociable in the village. On that same evening, however, he had noticed that several regulars were conspicuous by their absence. Even Libby Long had called in sick and the place was short-staffed. Of this and all possible forthcoming nights, he thought this the most likely for surveillance to be useful. Going out therefore, and for companionship more than anything else, he had enlisted Shilto: long-since recovered from being bitten and now back to his former self.

It was cold, but they had finely woven outer garments of nylon and were sweating by the time that they reached the ley line and turned north. Within a quarter of a mile they stopped to wait and each drew his hood forward so that they were very difficult to see from as little as fifty yards.

Dood quietly rolled a cigarillo and lit it underneath a cupped hand so that there was little likelihood of being seen. His hand was also warmed and the sweet vapour gave him a pleasant reflective feeling before being dissipated in the air. By contrast Shilto, a man of different taste, drew a sip of brandy from a leathern flask but the effect on him was not dissimilar.

They settled to what might become a sentry duty of some length and as they did so, light from the crescent moon waxed and waned under swiftly-moving cloud formations which cast shadows on the low grass. Other than the sound of the wind, there was only the rustle of the occasional fox or badger or the call of a farm animal. By midnight they were still watching but the moon was higher in the night sky. It remained a sickle-shape but gave enough light for them to see when not hidden by cloud.

Soon after midnight, Shilto pointed to movement about a quarter of a mile on the opposite side of the open pit and slowly, a small party of about twenty figures approached in line. Their clothing seemed grey under cloud but in strong moonlight it soon became clear that their costume was white and their heads covered with white hoods. They moved without instruction and there was hardly a whisper from the grass as they approached, silent and unselfconscious, as though they did not expect to be seen there. With them, they carried an assortment of articles, among which were circular objects like wheels: large and small.

As they approached the pit, they took up station around it and repeatedly danced, first this way and then that; backs inward and then out; then closer to the pit and further away. Then, stopping, they held their heads downwards as if in abeyance to an entity in the middle of their circle.

A shorter figure broke away from the ring and walked inwards. Picking up one of the circular devices, he bowed low before it and threw it into the pit. As he did so, the cloud shifted so that a brighter moonlight caught it. They could see that it was a wheel with rim and spokes, but of a diminutive size. Silently, each man or woman followed suit by throwing further wheels into the pit. Some were made like cartwheels with eight wooden spokes but they varied in size and design. Many were smaller, made of clay and were flat, with carved spokes painted red or green; others were an unpainted brown. Between them, they threw twenty or thirty wheels into the pit.

They now took out staves of wood and set light to loose ends. The wood burned easily and Shilto thought that the staves must have been impregnated with a wax or oil to burn in that way. When each stave was alight, its holder raised it aloft in supplication and then threw it into the pit. There were many arcs of flame in the night and the impression was still visible in the night vision of the onlookers for a while after.

Dood said quietly, 'Druids. I have never seen them up here before although they do put on a bit of a show for the tourists down in Avebury. I think this is the real thing; a bit more serious than the Avebury crowd. They come from the surrounding villages, but we cannot guarantee that our presence will suit them. If we keep still, they won't see us.'

'What on earth are they doing?'

'They threw wheels and flaming brands into the pit. That is obviously some kind of ritual, but exactly what for, I cannot say. I will think about it when we get back.'

'Ok, but I think their ceremony is probably over anyway; look, they've started to pack up. By the way, how deep is that pit? I can't see any light or smoke from those burning brands: I would have thought that at least *some* light and smoke would be visible…at least, from a shallow pit!'

At length, the Druids bowed towards the pit and filed off. They departed the way they had come and seemed to fade into the dark about half a mile thither. Later, Dood and Shilto began to grow rather ill at ease with constant sprawling on the cold ground and after a couple of cigarillos and several sips from the leathern bottle, they decided to go home. By then it was 2.30am and Dood said, 'I doubt whether much more will happen tonight.'

'Why? '

'The place is quiet. I do not think that Johan Pal will come. If he had intended to do so, he would have started much earlier, to give enough time to get things done and cleaned up before dawn.'

'I guess you're right. But at least we have seen the place in use.'

The two men returned home for the night.

The next morning, Shilto had other things to do, but Dood spent some time researching pagan beliefs in an attempt to explain what they had seen the previous night. Later, he called round to speak to Wally and Amelia Bishop and Emily, who was also there. Shortly afterwards, Shilto, having finished, knocked on the door.

Bishop said, 'Hello, Adam, do come in. I hear that you and Callum have been doing a bit of low-key sleuthing!'

'Yes, and I wasn't especially comfortable when we are doing it. But luckily, we actually saw quite a lot last night and I think an overall picture is becoming clearer. Also, Callum promised to delve into what we saw and I can't wait to hear about his findings.'

'But in the meantime, you could all do with some refreshment?'

'Well, if there is any going…'

Later, after doughnuts and coffee, they licked their fingers appreciatively and sat down to listen.

Dood said, 'I think we saw in action the druidic circle that old Don Regan spoke about. He once said that they were keen on the area around the ley lines and altar stone and they don't seem to have been deterred by the fact that Pal seems to have pulled the stone out. I had come across occasional evidence of basic paganism in this area for many years but at long last, I have now seen them in the flesh. I think they are harmless, but this is a crazy world and I don't want two enemies, thank you.'

'Is it not an evil cult like Johan Pal's Satanism?' said Emily.

'No. Paganism can often seem cruel, but they are not celebrating evil or following evil practices for their own sake. In any case, the sacrifice of a lamb cannot be taken to be worse than foxhunting or what goes on in the slaughterhouse.'

He continued, 'The druids are worshippers of nature and renewal. They celebrate elementary forces such as sunlight, rain, lightning and thunder and appease them by sacrifice. They believe that the life of an oak tree, the flow of a river, the growing grass and the birth of a lamb are worthy of being venerated. They think that each has its own spirit, as do the seasons and the elementary forces within the earth. They believe that each has its own intrinsic wisdom and if properly celebrated, they are connected with it.'

'A sacrifice is no more than a gift of thanks for the bounty of nature, and the idea is not as alien to our own traditions as you might suppose. A coin in a church collection is actually quite similar. However to pagans, the greater the gift of nature, the larger the sacrifice required. They believe that the sacrifice of a lamb can ensure the success of a harvest or the plentiful birth of farm animals in the spring.'

'There is blood, sure, but such sacrifices are not evil and they are even mentioned in the Bible, where atonements of blood are commonplace. As a churchman, I could mention Genesis 4, in which Cain gave a gift of the fruit of the ground to God, while Abel brought an offering from his flock. Elsewhere, there are references to a burnt offering; in Genesis 8, Noah is considered to have built an altar for just that purpose. It cannot be said that sacrifices and blood invariably mean that the doer has an evil purpose.'

'Are old testament practices similar to those of our own Druids?' said Emily.

'Perhaps, but I would be much more confident in saying that Celtic worship was similar to that of other Indo-European peoples. Just as their languages came from a common origin, so too did their religion, and the names of Gods can often be translated very simply from tongue to tongue. For example, the Celtic goddess Letavia was an earth deity with direct equivalents in the ancient Greek *Plataia* and Sanskrit *Prthvi*. The root of the word in each language means *that which is spread out*, as we would expect a landscape to be. As such, the Celtic Letavia is no more than the age-old divination of the landscape, separated from Greek and Sanskrit versions only by millennia of nomadic wandering and linguistic change.'

Shilto said, 'Was not the god of thunder also connected in older languages and cultures?'

Dood replied, 'I am glad that you said that, because the answer is yes. In Old English, the thunder god was *Thunor,* with a root common to both the Thracian word *thurdos* and the Hittite *Tarhun*. Here in England, our own Celts also worshipped a thunder God they called *Taranis*. There are over two thousand years between Thunor and Tarhun, together with the distance between Wiltshire and the Anatolian peninsula.'

'Wiltshire?' said Emily.

'Yes.'

'Just a minute,' Emily continued, 'do you mean to imply that this Celtic thunder god Taranis is still worshipped today, here in Wiltshire?'

'I do, and so is Thunor. They have become one and the same. They may have had slightly different forms of veneration, but with the passage of time, Anglo Saxon and Celtic forms have become fused into a common local culture; it might be Taranis here, or Thunor in Somerset.'

'What was Taranis like?' Bishop said.

'Like all such gods, Taranis demanded votive offerings and was usually placated with votive wheels. In places where Taranis was worshipped, there have been found tens or even hundreds of clay wheels. In fact, Taranis was generally pictured with a wheel in one hand and a thunderbolt in the other. The spokes of the chariot wheel, rotating as the chariot went into battle, could also be taken to be symbolic; scythes and sickles were probably attached to the wheel of the battle chariot and the sickle was also symbolic in that culture, as was the sickle moon.'

'Votive offerings? It all sounds a bit primitive!' said Bishop.

'Well, I am sure it might to our modern ear, but such offerings to gods were a feature of many religions and frankly, can still be seen to this very day. A favourite offering was the gift of armour or weapons; elsewhere, artwork, statuettes, bronzes, precious metals and coins were left in many places of religious devotion. It was considered quite right for Taranis to receive votive wheels: they would be required for his war chariot.'

'Is Christianity the same?'

'Certainly, do not assume that Christianity is in any way different; votive offerings were common in the past and still are today. Examples are the gifts to churches and shrines of incense, candles, tablets of wax, jewellery and even flowers. Walk in Ireland and observe the many Roman Catholic shrines by the wayside; very varied votive offerings are commonplace there.'

'You spoke of the spokes of a chariot wheel. Was there any connection with the rays of the sun?' said Bishop.

'Undoubtedly, sunlight could have been symbolised by spokes of a votive wheel. Rest assured, that would not have escaped them.'

Shilto said, 'So at last I can see what the Druids were doing on the downs last night. They threw many clay and wooden wheels into the pit by the altar and after that, a number of lighted staves. I reckon the staves were thunderbolts and that we saw a ceremony to the Celtic thunder god. There were twenty people there; I wonder who they were.'

'They were ordinary people from local villages: farm-hands, milk maids, publicans, shopkeepers, probably even professionals and academics.'

'Any we know?'

'I wouldn't be surprised.'

Emily then said, 'All this begs one obvious question: does druidism really confer any advantage to them?'

Dood said, 'As a practising clergyman, with experience of all kinds of religious devotion and with half a lifetime working as both the agonist and antagonist in psychic and spiritual phenomena, I will ask you to accept that it does.'

The others looked grave, but became more so when he continued, 'I believe, as they do, that every human, cat, dog or tree has its own spirit which remains when it dies. At its passing, it will bear all the sin, truth, sacrifice, wisdom, love and hate that was extant at its passing, and that will remain for all time.'

'So do you believe in reincarnation?'

'No I do not. That is a supposition which I strongly disbelieve. There is a fundamental inequality in the fate of mankind and in all things; the gods exist to play games with us. The Arabs say, "the fate of every man is bound about his brow", and rightly so. It is absurd to suppose that a spiritual equality should be conferred by a second or third chance at life. We must accept our differences and the fundamental inequality of the world.'

'What kind of games?' said Emily.

'The whole purpose for us is to learn from whatever games the Gods apply; their game is to say that John is a rich man but stupid, while his wife Gillian is poor but clever. We shall see what their two children – rich and clever; poor and stupid – can make of life in order to amuse ourselves.'

After a long pause, Shilto said, 'What of Johan Pal?'

'Pal is playing the most dangerous game known to mankind. He seeks power from beyond to use for his own purposes, but he will never obtain it for free. He still has the Magdeburg Relic and means to use it. So far, we have confounded and hindered, but never beaten him. His abilities will have been diminished only a little by the loss of his supporters and neither we nor a few druids will be allowed to stand in his way.'

Dood continued, 'The abilities of Johan Pal are quite different from the power the druids wish to draw upon. The latter seek a continuance of nature, of prosperity and the efficacy of their seed; they wish for the birth of children and of lambs in the springtime; for clement seasons and plentiful crops in the orchard. They have a power, but I do not know whether it can harm Johan Pal.'

Finally he said, 'The pit is open, although covered in daytime. I don't know where it leads, and perhaps it would be wrong for me to try to find out. However I mean to wait on the downs once more tonight.'

Chapter Thirteen

The Wheel of Taranis

That night was the ninth of the new moon: little more than a half moon but still giving good light in a sky containing only the occasional cloud moving slowly, but without the gusts and scudding of their last visit. Dood and Shilto took up the same station at 11pm and settled to wait. They were dressed as before in black, but although the ground was dry, they felt uncomfortable both sitting and face down. They were grateful, therefore, when after as little as fifteen minutes they saw movement a quarter of a mile away.

There were two figures only on the downs and they had approached by means of an 'off-roader,' a Land Rover without lights. It made little sound and its paintwork, probably dark green, was inconspicuous against the green and grey of the winter grass. It was Johan Pal and Carol Black. Without delay, they parked, removed a number of artefacts from their vehicle and set to work.

They were dressed, entirely without any degree of concern, in the uniforms of Nazis and Pal had the manner of a man who was quietly confident. He seemed vigorous, physical even, as though rested, well-fed and fully recovered. Black also busied herself and moved around with the authority of one who has the complete trust and confidence of her Master. Perhaps, in the absence of the rest of the coven, she enjoyed the new position of 'number 2'. Perhaps also there was more; Pal touched her on the shoulder a couple of times and she seemed to respond. Warmth or love? No, that could not be.

Pal walked around the open pit and made a simple circle around it of a white powder – salt, thought Shilto – leaving a ledge of about eight feet between the ring and the edge of the pit. Then, he made a further circle within, by using the familiar strips of animal skin. Next, setting up the wooden stand and clamp, he succeeded in erecting the Magdeburg Relic and made it stable with hand outstretched, by means of rope and pegs in the ground.

The ceremony was carried out with calm competence as though with a determination to make up for previous delays. After a short while, he performed his usual ceremony of defiling the host and holy water, upended a crucifix and thrust it into the ground, and lit black candles. As before, they gave out little light and the mixture of sulfur, fat and pitch burned with a blue luminescence and could be smelled by the onlookers as they waited – and wondered what to do.

Pal turned his attention to the Magdeburg Relic and resuscitated it as a hand of glory. Its flame guttered at times, but there was insufficient wind for the blue candle to be extinguished. After adjusting the ropes that held it, he withdrew a knife, cut the throat of a small animal and collected its blood in a bowl.

Raising the bowl, he dipped his finger into it, made a mark on his own forehead and passed it over his own lips. Then, he did the same to his companion and walking around the pit, carefully sprinkled the blood so that there was a continuous ring close to the edge of the pit, and within those made earlier.

Stripping to the waist, he began to rub a liniment onto his chest, neck and face and then did the same to Black. Shortly, they began to wave in an exaggerated manner, to show a loss of general coordination and to make the familiar antic gestures. They whirled and laughed and seemed not to tire, and at one point within the innermost circle, Black made a move to peer over the edge of the pit. Sensing her danger, Pal rushed over and pulled her back onto the grass where he lay with her for a few minutes. They made strange noises and rolled about in what seemed to be lust, but the onlookers felt a sense that there was now more between them.

At length, Pal arose and began to intone guttural words towards the pit, but although quiet, the distance was too great for the words to be heard with any clarity. The onlookers knew, however, that unless some dramatic alteration should occur in his and Black's fortunes, then Pal would succeed in his great aim. The time was fast approaching when he would succeed in opening his portal to the underworld.

Both adherents of black magic were outside of the circles they had made: and these alone separated them from whatever the pit contained and from that which might soon come forth. As Pal intoned his ritual, Dood and Shilto could see a luminescence grow around the Magdeburg Relic.

Dood whispered, 'My God, the head is moving,' and as the luminescence grew, they could hear sinister words once more; half-uttered, half in the form of thoughts in the ether.

Shilto replied, 'Look, see the sides of the pit…?' As he spoke, the edges of the entrance to the pit took on a sculpted appearance, rather like marble. Visible in it, unearthly forms appeared as though newly carved out of stone, or as though they had condensed from molten lava. Shilto continued, 'The whole thing reminds me of Rodin's carving of the Gates of Hell.'

Suddenly, a human-like entity seemed to launch itself from the pit. It crouched on the edge of the grass and looked around. It had the form of a man, with short hair and glasses. It wore a black uniform with collar tabs, a diagonal leather strap and leather belt. On its arm was a red swastika armband and it wore a peaked cap with an eagle.

Dood whispered, 'My God, it's *Heinrich Himmler*. He was Reichsführer of the Schutzstaffel: the leader of the SS.'

Himmler seemed small at first, but seemed to grow as he became stronger and more confident. He straightened, looked around with a gaze both baleful and malevolent, then turned to his Fuhrer and saluted.

Behind him, other ethereal forms appeared and like Himmler before them, they paused before turning their attention towards the Magdeburg Relic. They seemed to grow in stature as they observed him there: the last earthly remains of their former leader, complete with formidable former will and purpose, and he in turn held his skeletal arm high in salute.

Meanwhile, Johan Pal crouched over a spherical crystal, which he raised aloft on a flat hand. It gave light to its surroundings: a symbolic light. In a clear analogy with the candle held by the hand of glory, he said so that all could hear: 'Behold the Golden Orb.' The two lights seemed to combine to attract many more dark figures from the pit of Hell and they began to crowd the small space within the rings of blood, salt and animal skin.

Dood said, 'If those circles are broken, they will all be free to walk the earth once more.'

Shilto replied, 'I know; they must be stopped.'

Although it was dark and they were well-hidden, Dood and Shilto felt a sudden compulsion to rise and walk towards the Satanic circle. It was an uncanny feeling and a pull like that of a magnet on steel. Although they tried to resist, they were unable to prevent themselves from standing, nor the forward movement in which their feet became like those of automata. At the same instant, the skull of the Magdeburg Relic turned to look towards them and they felt the compulsion of its will within the deep sockets of its skull-eyes, lit by a green glow from within. Then, Pal and Black also turned to look at them and despite the darkness and their black clothes, they knew they were clearly visible. Their involuntary shuffle forwards was slow at first, but their speed soon increased and with it, their desperation as they covered the ground in front of them. They knew that at last, they faced the revenge of the evil Johan Pal, a revenge long promised by him.

As his whole being was dragged forwards, Dood tried to look down upon the ground in order to detach his own thoughts; he was desperate to think clearly and knew that he had very little time to do so. What was he walking towards? The answer was death, almost certainly, but how? He guessed, or perhaps Pal made his intentions known, that he would be cast into the open portal through which the dark spirit of Himmler had emerged. By daylight, it was a pit with a dark and unseen bottom, but now, a gateway to a filthy, evil and sulfurous place with a suppurating stench and the invisible depth of the netherworld.

Similar thoughts also held Shilto, but as he glanced at the light reflected from the half moon, he felt that it was a clean light and held a kind of hope. His mind become quite clear: he was certain that the living Relic had an abundance of will, but could it physically raise the combined mass of two inert men? He now had a plan of a kind, but could it work?

Shilto leaned forward with his eyes towards the ground and although unable to prevent his own forward steps, he allowed his torso to go limp, so that when the inevitable roll came, it was in the direction of his forward motion. The overall effect was to cause a deliberate fall and he descended somewhat painfully, flat on his face. As he did so, he grasped Dood's arm as tightly as he could muster and meanwhile, managed to extend his falling leg so that it interfered with the natural gait of the other man. Both men fell together, hand to arm and somewhat intertwined. They lay winded and the physical pain seemed partly to break the spell.

Yet they had delayed the inevitable by probably no more than minutes and their fear grew again when they felt that dreadful will seek them out. They tried to hold their legs in place by wrapping their arms around their own ankles and holding tight. However like the pull of a colossal magnet, the force began to enervate their muscles and they were forced to crawl forward to where, looking up, they could see that Black held a long knife. That however, became a kind of relief; with the knife they knew there would be no conscious plunge down that dark shaft.

Shortly, they came within thirty yards of the outer circle. There, Johan Pal pulled them both onto the grass and placed a halter around their necks. With it, he half pulled and half led them towards the circle, where they fell flat before him. The full stench of the gateway was now upon them and the sinister diction of their captors was in their ears. They heard, *'mein Fuhrer, now lead us thither,'* as though all tongues could now be understood equally and *'they must die,'* as Johan Pal collected the dagger from Black and made ready for their sacrifice.

Pal grabbed Dood by his halter and with a twist of his arm forced him to lie prostrate, with his neck facing the dark sky above. Although his hands were free, Dood was strangely unable to move them and lay, awaiting his end. The dagger was raised above Pal's head and its blade glinted with foul magic and starlight from above; it must be only a matter of a few seconds before Dood would die. Yet suddenly, he heard a cry from Black, 'Master, look!' and at once the moment passed.

Freed from Pal for an instant, Dood summoned enough strength of mind to roll on his side and wriggle away. Glancing towards Black, he saw the direction of her gaze, followed it and gave vent to an exclamation of excitement and hope. About twenty yards away and closing, but far enough from Pal, Black and the Nazis to be clearly distinct from them, was a circle of twenty people dressed in white costumes. They were advancing slowly forward, holding hands and did not fear what they saw.

As was their way, round and round the circles they danced, first this way and then that, and then in and out. They bore votive wheels, which they again threw into the pit before them and lighted staves as though to make thunderbolts. Now there was cloud overhead, the sky became very dark as the intermittent moonlight was hidden more fully and very shortly came the first rumble of real thunder. Then it rained; at first a few light spots of water here and there, but soon, heavily; it became an all-pervading downfall like that of a tropical storm. Meanwhile, a few initial flashes of lightning over the downs gave way to an inexhaustible electrical discharge. They saw a constant flash of the rare sheet lightning together with diverse tongues and forks that broke the dark of the night sky and illuminated Johan Pal as he stood in wonder.

The leader of the circle of twenty, a short man and with a gait familiar to Dood and Shilto, now crossed the circles of blood, salt and skin. Closer to the pit, he retched at the stench of decay and corruption and from the smell of burning grass nearby, lighted by flashes of lightning from overhead. Once within, he pulled the halter from the neck of the two captives and waved them forcibly towards the horizon as though to emphasise that they could not be part of the struggle now ensuing. Rising to their feet, Dood and Shilto ran and did not stop until they were fifty yards away in the darkness. But it was some darkness: a deep black of pure night until lit by an overhead torrent of lightning; later the local villagers remarked on the strange electrical storm on the downs, the like of which had not been seen for perhaps a hundred years – and was it some omen? In fact they all knew that it was the final culmination of the strange struggle which had been conducted there for two years between Satanism and the Gods of Nature.

Pal and his evil followers now applied their own designs to the dreadful battle. Ethereal spirits of long-forgotten demons and pestilences approached and intimidated; giant insects appeared at the edge of the pit and presented their poisonous fangs and stings; Satanic snakes slithered in the grass; and a foul rat with yellow fangs, poisonous for sure, ran hither and would surely bite to death any white-clad human who opposed it.

But Black, Pal's loyal henchman, backed away. Retreating two feet, then five, she approached the rim of the pit and tottered; her balance was a precarious one from which shortly, it seemed she must fall. Glancing round, however, Johan Pal saw her and ran as though his life depended on it. Reaching her, he pulled her arm so that she fell onto the grass where she remained, apparently immobile for a short while. However, that action was quick and while she lay still, Pal remained at the very edge of the pit himself and was unable to control his flailing arms. Slowly, his torso followed his leading arm as he lost balance. Watching him about to fall, Shilto felt that his demise was taking place in slow motion as an illustration or object lesson.

However, Johan Pal did not immediately fall into the pit. By grasping the soft edges with his powerful hands he was able to save himself so that he hung there at arm's length on the edge of the precipice. Meanwhile, Black had recovered and saw his plight. Extending a hand, she grasped one of his and they managed by their joint effort to pull him back. Rolling onto green grass once more, they quickly recovered in time to continue to grapple with one of the hooded intruders.

In time, twenty hooded people overcame two, so that despite their strength, Pal and Black were dragged away from the middle of the circle. Very much further from the Magdeburg Relic and its sinister whispers, from the curved dagger and from the fate which they had intended for Dood and Shilto, they threw Black on the ground and tied her wrists and ankles so that she was unable to move. While they did so, four powerful men restrained Pal and he was quite unable to move until from the distance, three hooded people approached with a full-sized cartwheel. They bound Johan Pal to it with his back outwards and left Carol Black on the grass to watch. Once bound, they propped the wheel at an angle of 35 degrees from the upright by using a cleft stick inserted into the ground, so that it could neither fall nor roll.

Someone whispered, 'The wheel of Taranis.' Then, twenty white-robed and hooded people began to beat him with staves. From fifty yards away, Dood whispered 'My Lord, they are breaking him on the wheel.'

'What on earth…?'

'It is a dreadful medieval punishment used for murderers and political enemies from great antiquity. It used to be called the Catherine wheel, long before the firework was invented. A victim was tied to the wheel and then broken by beating with clubs or wooden mallets. They could turn the wheel to expose a different limb or to disorientate the victim. Death could take days and it was a terrible way to die; I have no doubt they think it suitable for Pal for the trouble he has caused them.'

'Can't we intervene?'

'What do you think?'

'I think not. We have no weapons and the two of us could never overcome twenty, even if we wished. We would be likely to be broken ourselves and anyway, there is a certain justice in their treatment of him.'

'In that case, we had better make our exit as quickly as we can.'

'But what about the Magdeburg Relic? Look at it; the blasted thing is still alight with its own motive force. See, the skull is moving from left to right, looking around and willing things to happen.'

'Yes, and all around it, see those shadowy figures. They are the awakened entities of all those who came out through the portal; see them flitting around and testing the circles. They want to get out and we have to get rid of them before some fool breaks a circle. If the circle of blood or salt were to break, then they would be released into the world. Pal would then have effectively won.'

'Well, I am sorry to say,' said, Shilto, 'that one of them appears to have been kicked away already. No look, the circles of animal skin and salt are both missing on one side. Their enclosure is weakened already. If the blood…'

Gasps came from Johan Pal as his torment on the wheel continued.

Quickly, Dood wriggled on his stomach towards the circle. Shilto, a vital reserve in case of failure, remained where he was. There was so much noise that by now, his movement went unnoticed. In the moonlight and shadows, he reached the circle at last.

Immediately, he saw that if he continued to crawl on his stomach, he was likely to break the final circle of blood, so after a minute's thought, rose to his feet and crouching low, stepped carefully over that final ring. Advancing the last few yards to the middle of the circle, he grabbed the wooden support of the Magdeburg Relic and, avoiding its gaze and whispers, threw it bodily into the pit. It fell…slowly…its spectral light finally dimmed. Immediately, the ghostly legion of the SS, flitting about, began to seethe with anger. Their baleful light started to fade until they too were gone.

In that interlude, the white-hooded men became aware of movement within the circle and turned to watch. And in an instant, Pal, exerting his particular abilities, caused the grip of the rope upon on him to weaken. He managed to free himself and ran to the circle, where in an effort to break the ring of blood before the spectre of his supporters began to fade, he slipped on the grass and fell to his end.

However, the fact of having overbalanced would not alone have caused his final demise and if left to himself, he would have been able to recover in a few seconds. Nevertheless, he was finally unable to do so; *for at the entrance to the pit was a pair of arms, with hands outstretched upwards. They grasped Pal's ankles with a primeval force and their knuckles showed white as they dragged him to his final doom.*

Johan Pal fell to his death, but whether it was to a final oblivion, none could say. All now tried to escape from the lightning which began to fall upon the pit. And the thunder also! The outburst of noise was tremendous, as though Taranis himself were overhead and free to give vent to his revenge. All remains of the hardware brought by Pal were gone; flames only were present and the walls of the pit, resembling as they did the gates of Hell sculpted by Rodin, now returned to common earth. They ran for their lives.

After an aeon, it seemed, of noise and light, all thunder and lightning was finally dissipated and the flames died. All turned to quiet and the calm world of the Wiltshire Downs returned. Twenty-two people rose from prostrate terror to observe that, approaching them in the distance, was a group of about fifteen policemen. From the leader of the druids nearby, they heard the barked instruction: *redock*![21]

All those in a white gown and hood ran in the opposite direction and they were quickly pursued. But unlike the police who followed them, they seemed to have a good knowledge of the local country. They weaved, ducked and dived into small holes in the land and behind large stones; they leapt over stiles, into thickets and always towards the dark horizon. They fanned out so that a policeman had to choose whom to follow. Then, they disappeared into the gloom where white gowns became grey or shadows only among the trees. After ten minutes, every policeman returned empty-handed, but they seemed pleased at last to arrest Dood, Shilto and Black.

Nicholby soon said, 'Mr Dood and Mr Shilto, I accept that you are not to blame for this little party, but I must ask you to report to me at the police station tomorrow morning. I am based in Swindon. Constable Smith, cut Miss Black loose and attend to her injuries if necessary.'

'Yes, Sir.'

'And Jacobs, can you get this site covered up with the tarpaulin until tomorrow? We shall need to come back in daylight and look at everything properly. Arrange for the area to be cordoned off too.'

'Yes, Sir.'

'Oh Sir,' said Smith a couple of minutes later. 'Take a look at Miss Black. I am afraid she's dead. And there's not a mark on her, not even where they tied her.'

---

21 Redock: 'run!' Cf Welsh rhedeg, Breton redek, Cornish resek.

★

Next day at 6am, Dood walked out alone on the Downs. Eventually, he reached the place at which the titanic battle had taken place and paced around for a while, carefully making sure he disturbed nothing. He ensured that he left no footprint, broke hardly a blade of grass and not a fragment of ash fell from his cigarillo in the fifteen minutes in which he examined the remains of Pal's activities.

Strangely, the police cordon was gone, as was the tarpaulin. All trace of the former rings of salt, animal skin and blood were absent. The grass seemed blackened by flame and was bare in places, but there was no trace of any votive wheel, cartwheel, cleft stick, rope or weapon. All remains of pitch candles, wax therefrom, and of religious artefacts: wafers and chalices, robes and clothing, were gone. It was as though the place had been washed clean by the storm.

The altar stone had been restored to its former position and now sat over the pit exactly at its former depth. There was now no trace of any former displacement apart from a few scuffs to the edge of the earth and a few places where turf had been replaced. However the top of the altar caught his eye; for resting there were several springs of mistletoe complete with white berries, newly-picked.

He inhaled from his cigarillo and withdrew from his pocket his pendulum of copper, together with the woollen cloth with embroidered letters. He swung the pendulum and asked, 'Is there now daylight?'

The pendulum swung towards the word 'no,' whereupon he turned the cloth and asked 'Is the gate now closed?' Immediately the pendulum swung slowly to make the word 'Ea.'

He walked slowly home. He was obliged to relight his cigarillo after one hundred yards, but the smoke of myrrh: perfume, incense and medicine, was aromatic in the morning air.

*

'You can rest assured,' said Nicholby in an office in Swindon, 'we had no intention of letting you loose by yourselves, not when there was so much at stake. We had the downs under surveillance and we knew exactly when Mr Pal would move in. His was the only vehicle in the neighbourhood; that is to say, the only one which came up by those paths. It was hired, by the way. All the other stuff there was regular farm vehicles, tractors and the like, and we knew them quite well by then.

'What of Miss Black?'

'I can see that you speak with some regret, Mr Shilto. We had her looked at, obviously. She had applied some kind of tincture to her body, a mixture of alkaloids, which if absorbed, would have given her considerable excitement and euphoria, but at the expense of judgement, coordination and balance. Such a chemical cocktail has been known to cause a heart attack, rather like the Jägerbombs which people drink here in Swindon on a Saturday night. Anyway, we think it was that, but there may have been more.'

'So what now?'

'We have spent rather a long time chasing after you and were not naïve enough to suppose you would actively consort with the police, except by making token contact as you did. Nevertheless the help you gave us enabled the police to break an important Satanic circle; one which probably contained a murderer as its leader. There were no survivors and the means by which they carried out their business has been removed.'

'And the press?'

'This is exactly what we want to talk to you about. You will appreciate how embarrassing the present investigation could have been…' He paused.

'…So we would like to take complete control over the facts as they are released to the press. It is imperative that, should a journalist approach you, you will know nothing about the investigation. This, too, must also apply to your friends and we shall interview them in due course. By the way, would you please sign this document while you are here?'

'What is it?' said Shilto.

'Oh, just a formality; we would like a signed account of events last night as a statement regarding your own involvement.'

'Do we have a choice?'

'Come now. You are free to make changes as long as they do not disagree substantively.'

'By the way,' said Dood, 'what did you find at the place these events occurred? Is there anything useful that we should hear about now?'

'Yes there is. The stone was replaced and the site completely cleared. We've no idea who the so-called 'druids' actually were, and in fact, we don't really think they can actually be charged with anything apart from beating Pal with sticks. Trouble is, to charge anyone we would have to catch them first. We think it may be better to let sleeping dogs lie.'

'Are you going to pull the stone out again?'

'We have already done so, in search of bodies, and there were none. In fact, there was nothing except a pit about two feet across. You saw it open; how deep would you describe it?'

Dood said, 'It was bottomless and it stank. I didn't like to go anywhere near the edge. I do remember that it was warm, as though some great heat lay below.'

Nicholby shifted in his chair. 'Well, when we looked at it, the base of the stone was on cold brown earth. There was a pit in the middle, but it was only a yard deep. We took off some chalk with the digger but there was nothing at all. We couldn't see the point of going deeper, so we replaced the stone.'

'Perhaps there was no body?'

'Come on, we all saw him fall in!'

'Or maybe somebody removed it?'

'Yes, but if so, where is it now? We cannot afford any loose ends, you see.'

'Quite. Can we go now, please?'

'Certainly, but we may be in touch.'

On the way home, Dood bought a copy of the local paper and read the leading article.

'Police are investigating a disturbance which took place on the Wiltshire Downs last night, where it is alleged that Satanic rites were carried out by members of the same sect connected with recent disturbances at the former Nazi Party Parade grounds at Nuremberg. A contact at the German Embassy stated that the German authorities are still interested in the case and await confirmation that members of the sect have finally been caught.'

There was little else in terms of hard news; only supposition and the repeat of vague allegations. Dood turned to the advertisements and with a pencil circled the name of a curry house.

*

Bishop telephoned Oakwood, Brakespeare, Shilto, Dood, Freya Sampson and Kayla Raddle. To them all, he said, 'Amelia, Emily and I would like to invite you round to our place for a small party this weekend.' To Oakwood, Brakespeare and their wives he also extended an invitation to stay. Later, he checked with Harry Devine, his contact in the antiques business and they spent about twenty minutes on the telephone.

'Hello Harry, what have you got for me from Poland, then?'

'A few pictures, religious and devotional stuff, you know. Most of it originally came out of Russia.'

'Please don't say that, Harry. That's where your Magdeburg Relic came from!'

'Has it caused you very much trouble then?'

'Just a little. It was stolen by a sect of black magicians and used in their ghastly rites.'

'Never! Where is it now?'

'Unfortunately, it was destroyed in the fun and games which followed. I say unfortunately, but it was perhaps for the best. The police were involved; I wanted to know how much I owe you for it.'

'Nothing, Wally. In fact, I will guarantee you lunch next time we meet for taking it off my hands.'

'Thanks, Harry.'

Later that day, Wally and Amelia Bishop and Emily began to prepare for their visitors that weekend.

Amelia said, 'Indian, Chinese, Thai, French, Italian or Spanish?'

'What about Indian on Saturday night and a traditional roast dinner on Sunday?'

'That's a great idea. Let's do the curry on Saturday and then I can book the Dog and Duck on Sunday. I want to do the cooking with Emily – she's brilliant – but can you arrange to get the beers in please?'

Emily said, 'How hot?'

Bishop said, 'Let's do the whole range, from the mildest right up to that stuff which Callum eats!'

*

The following weekend, Wally and Amelia Bishop entertained everyone else and they all lounged around in chairs, plates in hand. The food was truly excellent and the spread so impressive that, when he saw it, Callum Dood said, 'This would do justice to any black mass!'

Strangely, he had brought his car only 500 yards, and this caused some amusement until it emerged that he had used it to carry three crates of his favourite lager, especially chilled and obtained direct from his supplier in Calne. Enlisting some help to carry it in, he had with it a polypropylene chest of deep-frozen ice.

In fact, he was in fine form, having smoked two cigarillos, each containing different fragrant herbs from his garden. Inevitably, he was eventually quizzed about them by Kayla: 'Callum, is that marjoram in your cigarillo? It's certainly pretty fragrant.'

'Very close,' said Dood, 'and as you can see, it makes the hair go curly.'

'Well if you want dreadlocks, you can get it permed for £25 instead.'

Lounging around, they started with popadums and Masala Idli, a steamed, spiced dumpling made from foaming semolina batter that had been fried in mustard seed, cumin and lemon juice. They ate several of each and complemented Emily on their manufacture.

With a special gesture, Wally Bishop appeared with a further starter, a large dish of Mysore Bondas: fried pastries of flour, yogurt and spices; they were crisp outside and fluffy within, and were served with coconut chutney.

Since they were quite obviously still hungry, they chose main dishes from an aloo and tamarind salad, a vegetable Madras or a Goan prawn and coconut curry, each with the option of ginger rice. As with the best Indian food, they felt a deceptive first mildness, but heat grew in the mouth to give a lasting finish which necessitated a visit to the polypropylene store of beer on ice. Later, they were all able to do justice to a desert and so ended with Kheer, an Indian rice pudding flavoured with cardamom and rose water.

Shilto and Emily discussed the merits of having separate 'dustbins' inside for savoury and desert. 'I can fill myself up with curry and still have an empty pudding dustbin,' said Emily.

'That's fine,' said Shilto, 'but I only have one dustbin for food; the other one is for beer!'

After a while, Shilto said, 'Amelia and Emily, I must congratulate you. I have not eaten so well for ages.' The others concurred.

Wally Bishop said, 'Perhaps we should have invited Nicholby?'

'I don't think he would have come,' said Shilto. 'I am sure everyone would have been very pleasant, but that kind of fraternisation would have placed him in a difficult position if it turned out we had done something. We haven't, by the way, have we?'

He continued, 'Ah, the silence tells all.'

Bishop said, 'From your tale, do you think that Pal's lot actually lost? By that, I mean did his power simply desert him? From what I could gather, you always implied he had enough personal influence to beat a few druids in the power stakes.'

Dood replied, 'What a question! I really have no idea. He was certainly weakened without his supporters, but was still able to carry out a successful ritual using the Magdeburg Relic. His magical power could never have extended to overcoming a direct assault by twenty people anyway, but given time, he could certainly have imposed upon any individual there the imperative to kill or maim; or he could have done it himself at a distance.'

He continued, 'But whether his powers were stronger, I cannot say. We saw how the druids managed to elicit the help of their thunder god. They seemed able to draw down thunder and lightning, so their powers could be said to be of nature. Those of Johan Pal were from somewhere else altogether.'

'So were the druids and devil worshippers actually opposed?' said Amelia.

'Well yes, I think they were. Pal wanted to gain personal power. Just like other devil worshippers, he would have obtained power in reward. By contrast, the druids sought natural power to conjugate, create and perpetuate. Since it was for a constructive purpose, one could call it white magic. But again, they would need to pay dues to their Gods and I was interested to observe there is still a local cult dedicated to the worship of Taranis. I am sure that they also worship other Celtic gods hereabouts.'

'Such as?' said Freya.

'I believe they also worship Apollo. Around here, the Apollo of the Romans was known as Belenus; see how similar the Celtic and Latin names are. Like Apollo, Belenus was a god of the sun. If they still celebrate Beltane on the first of May, as I know they do, then they are celebrating Belenus. In fact, it may interest you to know that the herb henbane, which contains the name Belenus, was known as the herb of Apollo by the Romans.'

'You know for sure that they still celebrate Beltane?'

'Yes, I am quite sure of that. I have even seen the local folk return afterwards, quite the worse for wear!'

'I also know they worship the goddess Damara. She is by far the best-known of the old gods and goddesses and is still revered throughout England as the Queen of the May. We have probably all worshipped her ourselves on garland day, when garlands of flowers are blessed in church and used to decorate homes and villages; or on fishing boats, where garlands are thrown onto the sea to improve the catch and keep the waters calm. For the favours of the lovely Damara, the flower queen, the goddess of greenness and beauty, the Queen of the Fairies, we still bring in May blossom, leave it at the door of a friend or make a May garland. There is by now a complete fusion of the beliefs of Anglo-Saxon England with those of the Celtic people with whom they mixed. Around here, Celtic gods and the Anglo-Saxon Wicca go hand in hand.'

Shilto now said, 'If these old gods are still worshipped, why do local people do it? Does the magic of all natural things: rocks and stones and thunder offer a power to influence events, as we believe of the Christian God and the Devil?'

All looked toward Dood as he thought for a minute. Then he said, 'Yes, I believe they do. We can all draw upon our own personal source of spiritual power. We believe that humans have an innate spirit and many believe their pet animals do also. It is not so much of a leap of faith to extend that to all animals, trees, and even inanimate objects also such as rivers, hills, rocks and even sunlight. If they have a spirit too, as druids believe, then the answer must be yes.'

'Why are you so convinced of this?' said Creighton.

'Humans are wonderfully sensitive. One day I was out walking and saw sunlight on a field, but by the following month, it had been reduced to a patch of concrete. I felt its sadness as I walked by, a feeling that was quite clear to me. It would be in darkness now, perhaps for a long time.'

'And what of Johan Pal? Was he totally evil?'

'How can one say? Had he been so, he might have tried to poison Creighton when he had lunch with him or enacted some strange revenge on his own supporters. I would also point out that he tried to rescue Carol Black from falling into the pit at the very end, so perhaps he finally knew love. I would say that all humans have some good and bad in them, but in differing proportions, and very few are ruined completely.'

'Anyway, here's another beer, we've beaten Johan Pal, haven't we!'

Later, Shilto and Dood were strolling in the garden, when Shilto said, 'Did you see those white hands grab Johan Pal's ankles and drag him down into the pit?'

'Yes.'

'Do I take it that they were some nasty demon conjured up from down below?'

'Local lore speaks of Carn Brea as a gateway to the underworld. And it was to the underworld that Pal was dragged, as a revenge for desecrating the altar of Taranis.'

'So how did Pal manage to arrange for the Fuhrer's supporters to leap out of it?'

'They came from the underworld too. Pal used a black magic invocation to open it. But Taranis controlled that gateway, and it was for that reason he is still revered. Pal paid the price for failure.'

'More beer?'

'No, make it brandy.'

Chapter Fourteen

Easter, Beltane and May Day

In that year, Easter Sunday was early, on 27th March. Callum Dood dressed at 6am and over a breakfast of toast and coffee, read through his sermon and arrangements for that morning, the most important in the Christian calendar.

In Church, at 8am and in a thurible he lighted a sample of the resin from the Boswellia tree – the erstwhile frankincense – and paused for a while to watch it as it sweetened the air within. It was a comforting smell, and familiar, and he knew his congregation would enjoy it. Although costly, that day was one on which he could fully justify its use.

Shilto was there before long and they each breathed deeply the fragrant air within church.

Shilto said, 'Is this stuff really alright?'

'Sure it is. Frankincense has been known for years to be an anxiolytic drug. It promotes a feeling of well-being in those who come to Church. I often put a bit of frankincense in a cigarillo; and some say it can even be eaten.'

'Yes, I must say I feel quite calm.'

At ten-thirty the choirboys arrived at church and changed into their surplices, broad-sleeved white garments of linen. They were in a jovial mood and that augured well, for the singing would be lusty. By eleven o' clock, the church was full for the Easter Eucharist. All of the vibrant resources of the church were in evidence; music, flowers, bells and colours. The 'Alleluia' that had been silent through Lent was back in fashion! The choirboys sang,

Now the queen of seasons, bright
With the day of splendour,
With the royal feast of feasts,
Comes its joy to render!

and the hymns were a wonder; Dood surprised himself with his own lusty voice and he noted that the congregation excelled themselves with the strength and gusto of theirs. The singing was indeed wonderful and the church held at least two-hundred local people.

The lovely Libby Long sang with her sweet tones and Don Regan with his deep bass. Freya Sampson, Emily Robertson and Kayla Raddle sang in their clear voices and Maxton Mawr was the absolute master of the organ. Farmers and local tradesmen from far and wide made a point of singing with an expanse and range that would have done full justice to any Welsh male voice choir.

Christ the Lord is risen again;
Christ hath broken every chain;
Hark! Angelic voices cry,
Singing evermore on high,
Alleluia!

Eventually, Dood started his sermon:

'Dear friends, it is essential that we understand the origins of Easter. This great day, Easter Sunday, is perhaps the most important of all in our calendar. It is the day when Christians celebrate the resurrection of Jesus Christ and it marks the end of Lent, a 40-day period of prayer, penance and fasting. During this

last week we have followed our Holy Week, in which Christians observe Palm Sunday, which marks Jesus' return to Jerusalem; Maundy Thursday, upon which Jesus held his last supper with his disciples; and Good Friday, which is when Jesus was crucified. Easter Sunday is only the beginning of the season of renewal, which ends on Pentecost, fifty days later. Easter Sunday is therefore a new start; a new liturgical season, at the end of which Christians celebrate the gift of the Holy Spirit. Today, however, the joy of Easter is the joy of the resurrection of Jesus Christ, and Christians view Easter Sunday as a day of new birth. In these days, however, it is essential that we recognize the background of Easter. The word Easter has its roots in the older word "Eastre," and it is important that we remember our former traditions in order to understand our present ones the better.

Easter was the festival of Eostre, *the Old English goddess of spring, connected with the Greek Eos, of the dawn. We think, and we may be right or wrong, that Eostre had the consort of a hare, and so we talk about the Easter bunny having visited us. So too, the Easter egg is a symbol of renewal and fertility: we paint Easter eggs, hide and find them in the manner of those seeking renewal and the gift of fertility'* – members of the congregation nodded – *'thus we have taken purely local traditions to enhance our understanding of Easter and to help us celebrate spiritual renewal within our own Church…'*

Later, the church collection was full and the congregation filed out into the spring sunshine where lovely primroses were yellow in the sunlight, while a few early cowslips had started in clumps around the churchyard. The early purple orchis was not quite in flower but many thick stems had arisen from spotted leaves and their buds pressed to unfurl. There was greenery everywhere and the ground was lush, damp and full of promise. A few of the congregation picked small sprigs of yew to place in their button-holes and Libby Long was kind enough to affix one to Callum Dood as he stood, shaking hands with those of the congregation who had stayed to chat. All were full of benevolent feelings and smiled at the white, flitting clouds in the distance and their portent of gentle, spring rain to come. Meanwhile, beneath the church, rainwater from the chalk hills continued on its way in an underground sap towards the sea.

The small village continued its routines; quiet routines, devoted to the culture of gardens, the schooling of children, life around the village shops and the local public house in which by now, the modern preference for craft beers and ciders, together with gourmet cooking, had taken precedence over the keg, cooler and deep fat fryer. Farms were prosperous too, and there was talk about the planting of new vineyards to produce wine by the *Méthode Champenoise*; its labour-intensive and costly process, whereby wine undergoes a secondary fermentation inside the bottle to make bubbles, was considered to be good for the economy of the area, despite the fact that the bubbles made one sneeze.

By the evening of 30th April, a Saturday, Dood had made it clear that he would be absent for 48 hours on important family business and a locum was brought in to provide for Church services the next day, which was a Sunday.

Later that evening, and after a few drinks at the Dog and Duck, he rolled a few cigarillos using a wide variety of newly-dried herbs from his garden, lit one and inhaled deeply. Then following the other villagers who were leaving the village in dribs and drabs, he walked along village pathways, past allotment fields, upwards to where the gardens finally gave out, and via old bridleways and parish boundaries, up onto the downs. It was the time of Beltane.

Following local tradition, all fires in the village were extinguished that day and homes were by now rather cold; nevertheless the people were warm, for most walked the same path in front of him. Among them were those who could never quite celebrate the political holiday of Mayday yet like the others, they were quite at ease with the principles with which they now walked towards a distant farm, well away from prying eyes, that stood in a slight depression amongst the standing stones and Neolithic barrows and behind a copse of oak trees; yet slightly incongruous on the windy, open expanse.

Old Don Regan welcomed them and gave an especially warm welcome to Callum Dood, Libby Long, Maxton Mawr and some others, shaking their hands in turn.

Later, he lit two large bonfires and enlisted the help of his friends in leading a procession between them of all the livestock on his farm. Animals belonging to other owners followed behind and eventually, all had walked a ceremonial path between the two fires.

All felt the importance of this ceremony of rebirth; there was dancing around the fires, and some older children were allowed to accompany their parents in leaping over smaller flames or over the embers of those allowed to die down; while nearby, horses and cows had been decorated with yellow and red ribbons and with green; and on Regan's barn, the face of the Green Man, rather grubby after the summer dust and winter rain, had been cleaned off once more and decorated with yew, holly and ivy.

All around the premises, decoration and celebration was evident everywhere. There was a trestle table in the barn, and a sheep had been killed for the purpose of providing food for the gathering. The barn itself, and trees and shrubs were decorated with spring flowers. So too was the hawthorn tree; the lovely May Tree with her white blossom, flowering in that month alone; Regan was proud of his, and had decorated with ribbons the beautiful specimen in his farmyard.

Ah, the May Tree! Others had admired it and Regan had given cuttings to them; in particular Dood, always keen to lower his blood pressure and levels of stress and to improve his digestion, had decided to observe its effects himself. He now remarked on its chemistry to Regan, who listened patiently:

To Dood it seemed that the colour of the haw berries arose from the bright-hued chemicals found within. These, the antioxidants, were admired by scientists and were comparable to those of notable medicines such as red wine, cranberries, purple grapes and green tea. He had a positive view of their efficacy and was actively in favour of the juice of most berries, whether fermented or not. Now, he proclaimed that his heart had positively skipped a beat at the thought of the antioxidants in red wine and the sweet waters the haw berries contained. Regan lifted his glass to that and said '*clech en*'[22] and drank his cider down in one.

Later, and after the feast and ceremony of the bonfires, there was dancing and singing. Some husbands and wives, and a few lovers and sweethearts donned ceremonial horns and enacted the celebration of the union of the May Lord and Lady. Discreetly, a few left in order to visit the Cherhill White horse, a place that was considered to have a profound effect on the natural order of things.

As the night wore on, so the flames died down and ashes were collected to apply to flower beds and fields. Later, it grew cold, so the morning dew condensed on the grass and was collected by young women and not a few older, who cleansed their faces and hands in order to promote health and beauty.

By dawn, the air was clear and bright; all nature was celebrated and the villagers were content to help Regan store tables in the barn and to clear away the remains of the feast. They returned home early that morning and as they did so, they followed the bearer of a burning brand kindled from the fire of the previous night. Once back in the village, they relit their hearths with flames from the brand, symbolising a rekindled flame in their own homes.

That day was Maytime, when the children danced around the Maypole and homes were decorated with ribbons and May blossom, and garlands of all flowers were brought into homes. It was a day when creamy-white May blossom, known locally

---

22 *Clech en: it's got bells on*

as bread and butter, was ceremoniously nibbled by all as the provender of the sacred tree.

And it was a day when Dood went to the churchyard and once again left a coin in the bowl of Isis to join rose petals, spells and good wishes written on scraps of paper. It was a day of renewal, when nature was celebrated and all was in complete harmony.